Select praise for Viola Shipman

THE SUMMER COTTAGE

"Every now and then a new voice in fiction arrives to completely charm, entertain and remind us what matters. Viola Shipman is that voice and *The Summer Cottage* is that absolutely irresistible and necessary novel."

— Dorothea Benton Frank, *New York Times* bestselling author

"Sometimes funny, sometimes bittersweet…*The Summer Cottage* is a keeper and goes to the top of my most cherished reads. I loved, loved, loved it!"

—*Fresh Fiction*

"*The Summer Cottage* is not only a lighthearted read about a woman discovering her authentic self, but it also offers a glimpse into coastal Michigan's history with its charming depiction of the locale sure to make every reader want to visit."

—*New York Journal of Books*

THE CHARM BRACELET

"*The Charm Bracelet* is a keeper, a novel that will be passed from one book club member to the next until everyone has read this heartfelt, intergenerational story of love and forgiveness."

—Adriana Trigiani, *New York Times* bestselling author

"Rich in character and story, *The Charm Bracelet* is utterly charming!"

—Debbie Macomber, *New York Times* bestselling author

THE HOPE CHEST

"Viola Shipman has written a graceful, touching novel that explores the temporal nature of life… A moving, emotionally impactful read."

—Garth Stein, *New York Times* bestselling author of *The Art of Racing in the Rain*

"Saugatuck, MI, springs to life in this nostalgic, gentle story of lifelong love along with the emotional support and care that families and friends can provide."

—*Library Journal*

Also by Viola Shipman

THE SUMMER COTTAGE

THE HEIRLOOM GARDEN

VIOLA SHIPMAN

GRAYDON HOUSE

GRAYDON HOUSE®

ISBN-13: 978-1-525-80461-8

The Heirloom Garden

This edition published by arrangement with Harlequin Books S.A.

Graydon House
22 Adelaide St. West, 40th Floor
Toronto, Ontario M5H 4E3, Canada
www.GraydonHouseBooks.com
www.BookClubbish.com

Printed in U.S.A.

To gardeners everywhere.
This book is for you. You understand, better than most, the grace and gifts of this world.

And for Dottie Benton Frank: there was no greater author, spirit, light, soul, force of nature or character. Your work, kindness and generosity changed me greatly, and I will never forget you. The world and I will miss you, but we will have your novels forever.

THE HEIRLOOM GARDEN

*"If I had a flower for every time I thought of you,
I could walk in my garden forever."*

—Alfred, Lord Tennyson

PROLOGUE

THE ROSE

"You may break, you may shatter the vase, if you will,
But the scent of the roses will hang round it still."

—Thomas Moore

IRIS

LATE SUMMER 1944

We are an army, too.

I stop, lean against my hoe and watch the other women working the earth. We are all dressed in the same outfits—overalls and sunhats—all in uniforms just like our husbands and sons overseas.

Fighting for the same cause, just in different ways.

A soft summer breeze wafts down Lake Avenue in Grand Haven, Michigan, gently rustling rows of tomatoes, carrots, lettuce, beets and peas. I analyze my tiny plot of earth at the end of my boots in our neighborhood's little Victory Garden, admiring the simple beauty of the red arteries running through the Swiss chard's bright green leaves and the kale-like leaves sprouting from the bulbs of kohlrabi. I smile with satisfaction at their bounty and my own ingenuity. I had suggested our little Victory Garden utilize these vegetables, since they are easy-to-grow staples.

"Easier to grow without weeds."

I look up, and Betty Wiggins is standing before me.

If you put a gray wig on Winston Churchill, I think, *you'd have Betty Wiggins, the self-appointed commander of our Victory Garden.*

"Just thinking," I say.

"You can do that at home," she says with a frown.

I pick up my hoe and dig at a weed. "Yes, Betty."

She stares at me, before eyeing the front of my overalls. "Nice rose," Betty says, her frown drooping even farther. "Do we think we're Vivien Leigh today?"

"No, ma'am," I say. "Just wanted to lift my spirits."

"Lift them at home," she says, a glower on her face. Her eyes stop on the hyacinth brooch I have pinned on my overalls and then move ever so slowly to the Bakelite daisy earrings on my earlobes.

I look at Betty, hoping she might understand I need to be enveloped by things that make me feel safe, happy and warm, but she walks away with a *"Hrumph!"*

I hear stifled laughter. I look over to see my friend Shirley mimicking Betty's ample behind and lumbering gait. The women around her titter.

"Do *we* think we're Vivien Leigh today?" Shirley mimics in Betty's baritone. "She wishes."

"Stop it," I say.

"It's true, Iris," Shirley continues in a Shakespearian whisper. "The back ends of the horses in *Gone with the Wind* are prettier than Betty."

"She's right," I say. "I'm not paying enough attention today."

I suddenly grab the rose I had plucked from my garden this morning and tucked into the front pocket of my overalls, and

I toss it into the air. Shirley leaps, stomping a tomato plant in front of her, and grabs the rose midair.

"Stop it," she says. "Don't you listen to her."

She sniffs the rose before tucking the peach-colored petals into my pocket again.

"Nice catch," I say.

"Remember?" Shirley asks with a wink.

The sunlight glints through leaves and limbs of the thick oaks and pretty sugar maples that line the small plot that once served as our cottage association's baseball diamond in our beachfront park. I am standing roughly where third base used to be, the place I first locked eyes with my husband, Jonathan. He had caught a towering pop fly right in front of the makeshift bleachers and tossed it to me after making the catch.

"Wasn't the sunlight that blinded me," he had said with a wink. "It was your beauty."

I thought he was full of beans, but Shirley gave him my number. I was home from college at Michigan State for the summer, he was still in high school, and the last thing I needed was a boyfriend, much less one younger than I was. But I can still remember his face in the sunlight, his perfect skin and a light fuzz on his cheeks that were the color of a summer peach.

In the light, soft white floaties dance in the air like miniature clouds. I follow their flight. My daughter, Mary, is holding a handful of dandelions and blowing their seeds into the air.

For one brief moment, my mind is as clear as the sky. There is no war, only summer, and a little girl playing.

"You know more about plants than anybody here," Shirley continues, knocking me from my thoughts. "You should be in charge here, not Betty. You're the one that had us grow all these strange plants."

"Flowers," I say. "Not plants. My specialty is really flowers."

"Oh, don't be such a fuddy-duddy, Iris," Shirley says. "You're the only woman I know who went to college. You should be using that flower degree."

"It's botany. Actually, plant biology with a specialty in botanical gardens and nurseries," I say. I stop, feeling guilty. "I need to be at home," I say, changing course. "I need to be here."

Shirley stops hoeing and looks at me, her eyes blazing. She glances around to ensure the coast is clear and then whispers, "Snap your cap, Iris. I know you think that's what you *should* be saying and doing, but we all know better." She stares at me for a long time. "The war will be over soon. These war gardens will go away, too. What are you going to do with the rest of your life? Use your brain. That's why God gave it to you." She grins. "I mean, your own garden looks like a lab experiment." She stops and laughs. "You're not only wearing one of your own flowers, you're even named after one! It's in your genes."

I smile. Shirley is right. I have been obsessed with flowers for as long as I can remember. My Grandma Myrtle was a gifted gardener as was my mom, Violet. I had wanted to name my own daughter after a flower to keep that legacy, but that seemed downright crazy to most folks. We lived next door to Grandma in cottages with adjoining gardens for years, houses my grandfather and father worked themselves to an early grave to pay off, and now they were all gone, and I rented my grandma's house to a family whose son was in the coast guard.

But my garden was now filled with their legacy. Nearly every perennial I possessed originally began in my mom and grandma's gardens. My grandma taught me to garden on her little piece of heaven in Highland Park overlooking Lake Michigan. And much of my childhood was spent with my mom and grandma in their cottage gardens, the daylilies and bee balm towering over my head. When it got would lie on the cool ground in the middle of my woodland hydrangeas, my back pressed against her old black mutt, Midnight, and we'd listen to the bees and hummingbirds buzzing overhead. My grandma would grab my leg when I was fast asleep and pretend that I was a weed she was plucking. "That's why you have to weed," she'd say with a laugh, tugging on my ankle as I giggled. "They'll pop up anywhere."

My mom and I would walk her gardens, and she'd always say the same thing as she watered and weeded, deadheaded and cut flowers for arrangements. "The world is filled with too much ugliness—death, war, poverty, people just being plain mean to one another. But these flowers remind us there's beauty all around us, if we just slow down to nurture and appreciate it."

Grandma Myrtle would take her pruners and point around her gardens. "Just look around, Iris. The daisies remind you to be happy. The hydrangeas inspire us to be colorful. The lilacs urge us to breathe deeply. The pansies reflect our own images back at us. The hollyhocks show us how to stand tall in this world. And the roses—oh, the roses!—they prove that beauty is always present even amongst the thorns."

The perfumed scent of the rose in my pocket lingers in front of my nose, and I pluck it free and raise it to my eyes.

My beautiful Jonathan rose.

I'd been unable to sleep the past few years or so, and—to keep my mind occupied—I'd been hybridizing roses and daylilies, cross-pollinating different varieties, experimenting to get new colors or lusher foliage. I had read about a peace rose that was to be introduced in America—a rose to celebrate the Nazis leaving France, which was just occurring—and I sought to re-create my own version to celebrate my husband's return home. It was a beautiful mix of white, pink, yellow and red roses, which had resulted in a perfect peach.

I remember Jon again, as a young man, before war, and I try to refocus my mind on the little patch of Victory Garden before me, willing myself not to cry. My mind wanders yet again to my own.

My home garden is marked by stakes of my experiments, flags denoting what flowers I have mixed with others. And Shirley says my dining room looks like the hosiery aisle at Woolworths. Since the war, no one throws anything away, so I use my old nylons to capture my flowers' seeds. I tie them around my daylily stalks and after they bloom, I break off the stem, capture and count the seeds, which I plant in my little greenhouse. I track how many grow. If I'm pleased with a result, I continue. If I'm not, I give them away to my neighbors.

I fill my Big Chief tablets like a banker fills his ledger:

1943—Yellow Crosses
Little Bo Beep = June Bug x Beautiful Morning
(12 seeds/5 planted)
Purple Plum = Magnifique x Moon over Zanadu
(8 seeds/4 planted)

I shut my eyes and can see my daylilies and roses in bloom. Shirley once asked me how I had the patience to wait three years to see how many of my lilies actually bloomed. I looked at her and said, "Hope."

And it's true: we have no idea how things are going to turn out. All we can do is hope that something beautiful will spring to life at any time.

I open my eyes and look at Shirley. She is right about the war. She is right about my life. But that life seems like a world away, just like my husband.

"Mommy! Mommy!"

Mary races up, holding her handful of dandelions with white tops.

"What do you have?" I ask.

"Just a bunch of weeds."

I stop, lean against my hoe and look at my daughter. In the summer sunlight, her eyes are the same violet color as Elizabeth Taylor's in *National Velvet*.

"Those aren't weeds," I say.

"Yes, they are!" Mary says. She puts her hands on her hips. With her father gone, she has become a different person. She is openly defiant and much too independent for a girl of six. "Teacher said so."

I lean down until I'm in front of her face. "Technically, yes, but we can't just label something that easily." I take a dandelion from her hand. "What color are these when they bloom?"

"Yellow," she says.

"And what do you do with them?" I ask.

"I make chains out of them, I put them in my hair, I tuck them behind my ears…" she says, her excitement making her sound out of breath.

"Exactly," I say. "And what do we do with them now, after they've bloomed?"

"Make wishes," she says. Mary holds up her bouquet of dandelions and blows as hard as she can, sending white floaties into the air.

"What did you wish for?" I ask.

"That Daddy would come home today," she says.

"Good wish," I say. "Want to help me garden?"

"I don't want to get my hands dirty!"

"But you were just on the ground playing with your friends," I say. "Ring-around-the-rosy."

Mary puts her hands on her hips.

"Mrs. Roosevelt has a Victory Garden," I say.

She looks at me and stands even taller, hooking her thumbs behind the straps of her overalls, which are just like mine.

"I don't want to get dirty," she says again.

"Don't you want to do it for your father?" I ask. "He's at war, keeping us safe. This Victory Garden is helping to feed our neighbors."

Mary leans toward me, her eyes blazing. "War is dumb." She stops. "Gardens are dumb." She stops. I know she wants to say something she will regret, but she is considering her options. Then she glares at me and yells, "Fathead!"

Before I can react, Mary takes off, sprinting across the lot, jumping over plants as if she's a hurdler. "Mary!" I yell. "Come back here!"

"She's a handful," Shirley clucks. "Reminds me of someone."

"Gee, thanks," I say.

Mary rejoins her friends, jumping back into the circle to play ring-around-the-rosy, turning around to look at me on occasion, her violet eyes already filled with remorse.

Ring-around-the-rosy,
A pocket full of posies,
Ashes! Ashes!
We all fall down.

"I hate that game," I say to Shirley. "It's about the plague."

I return to hoeing, lost in the dirt, moving in sync with my army of gardeners, when I hear, "I'm sorry, Mommy."

I look up, and Mary is before me, her chin quivering, lashes wet, fat tears vibrating in the rims of her eyes. "I didn't mean to call you a fathead. I didn't mean to get into a rhubarb with you."

Fathead. Rhubarb. Where is she picking up this language already?

From behind her back, she produces another bouquet of dandelions that have gone to seed.

"I accept your apology," I say. "Thank you."

"Make a wish," she says.

I shut my eyes and blow. As I inhale, the scent of my Jonathan rose fills my senses. The rumble of a car engine shatters the silence. A door slams, followed by another, and I open my eyes. The silhouettes of two men appear on the perimeter of the field, as foreboding as the old oaks. I notice the wind suddenly calm and the plants stop rustling at the exact same moment all of the women stop working. A curious hum begins to build as the men walk with a purpose between the rows of plants. The women lean away from the men as they approach, almost as if the wind had regained momentum. Row by row, each woman drops her hoe and shuts her eyes, mouthing a silent prayer.

Please not me. Please not me.

The footsteps grow closer. I shut my eyes.

Please not me. Please not me.

When I open them, our minister is standing before me, a man beside him, both of their faces solemn.

"Iris," Rev. Doolan says softly.

"Ma'am," the other man says, holding out a Western Union telegram.

The world begins to spin. Shirley appears at my side, and she wraps her arms around me.

Mrs. Maynard,

The Secretary of War desires me to express his deepest regrets that your husband, First Lieutenant Jonathan Maynard, has been killed…

"No!" Shirley shouts. "Iris! Somebody help!"

The last thing I see before I fall to the ground are a million white puffs of dandelion floating in the air, the wind carrying them toward heaven.

ABBY

MAY 2003

"This is the house I was telling you about."

I twist to look out the open car window. A smile overtakes my face as soon as I see a rambling bungalow with a wide front porch. A warm summer breeze shakes the porch swing before making the American flag on a corner pillar flap.

Our Realtor, Pam, parks her Audi on the narrow street, barely wide enough for one car to pass at a time, which sits at the top of a very steep hill. The street—and whole neighborhood—reminds me of the time I visited San Francisco, only in miniature. Pam rushes around to open our doors.

"Did Daddy put the flag there?"

"Yes," Pam lies to my daughter, Lily. "He's a war hero!"

I can feel my heart split, as if it's been cleaved in two by a butcher.

Pam and I are roughly the same age, early thirties, but Pam is somehow still filled with the same unbridled enthusiasm as Chance, the Irish setter we had growing up. I am filled only with a dull ache brought on by silent rage due to a confusing war that has stolen the husband I once knew.

Pam salutes Lily, who mimics the patriotic gesture. Pam turns to me and salutes.

"Don't," I say.

"I'm so sorry, Mrs. Peterson," she says, quickly lowering her arm. Her blond bob trembles in the breeze, just like her lips, which are slathered in pink gloss.

"Abby," I say.

"I understand, Mrs.... Abby. It's okay. You must be so nervous about your husband all the time."

I force a smile. "I am," I say. "Didn't mean to be so short."

She turns toward the house, and her Chance-like enthusiasm returns as she reenters agent mode. "This is a Sears kit home," Pam says as my daughter sprints for the front porch and jumps into the swing.

"A what?" I ask.

"A Sears kit home," she continues. "Oh, my goodness, Abby. They're historic now. Sears homes were shipped via boxcar and came with a seventy-five-page instruction manual. Most homes were sent via the railroad, and each kit contained thousands of pieces of the house, which were marked for construction. You can still find lumber that is numbered throughout the house. They did lots of different styles, from bungalows to Colonials.

"This house and the one next door were both Sears homes," she says, before nervously beginning to babble, "but...um... but...the two homes are nothing alike."

I look at Pam, whose face is registering absolute panic, and then turn to look for the first time at the neighboring house.

"That's an understatement," I say. "It looks like a prison."

An imposing wooden fence, which is—no exaggeration—at least ten feet tall, surrounds the property. The second story of the home, which looks to be identical to this one, despite what Pam has just said, is all peeling paint. Moss is growing on the roof's shingles on a shady section under a towering tree whose first leaves are blush red.

"What's the story?" I ask.

Pam's face turns the color of the tree. She takes a deep breath.

"A very old woman lives next door," Pam says. "Rumors in town are that she lost her husband in World War II and then her young daughter died, too." Pam glances back at the house and then whispers, "Went crazy and has lived alone for years." She stops and resumes speaking in a normal tone and nods at the house for rent. "This is her house, too. Used to be her mom's...or her grandma's...no one really knows anymore. I heard she has to rent it now for money."

"Why would she need more money at her age?" I ask. "These surely have to be paid off by now. Is she sick?"

Pam again whispers, "I don't think so. Who knows? There're lots of rumors about her and that house. They say she has a virtual Garden of Eden behind that fence. She breeds plants, or something like that. She's like a flower scientist. Used to call her the First Lady of Flowers around town. Anyway, I hear she spends all of her money to buy different varieties of flowers. Specimens. In fact, this house used to have a beautiful garden in the backyard. The two gardens were combined at one time. This one has fallen into a bit of disarray, but I think it could be brought back to life with a little love.

"But don't focus on all that," Pam says. "Focus on that."

Pam sweeps her well-manicured hands in front of her like a *Price Is Right* model and a flash of blue catches my eye. For the first time, I realize that we're not on a hill, we're tucked atop a dune overlooking Lake Michigan.

"There's only a peek of the water from the front yard, but the house overlooks the entire lake," she says. "You can even see the pier from your deck if you stand on your tippy toes. This cottage is part of what's known as Highland Park. It's an association of cottages built atop these dunes and dates back to the late 1800s. Isn't it quaint?"

"You buried the lede, Pam," I say. "But I'm sure we can't afford anything on the water. What's the monthly rent?"

She looks at me and tries not to look next door, but her eyes betray her. "I'm sure we can work out a deal if you're interested."

I turn and stare at the imposing fence. *Why would she want someone living next to her when she's trying so hard to keep everyone out?*

Pam leans toward me. "I can read your mind. Want to know what I think? I think she's just lonely. Wants someone next door in her final years. This association is filled with families. They just pass along the houses from one generation to the next. There's no one left after her." Pam waves for me to come closer, and I lean in even farther. "She has final approval on who rents this house," Pam whispers, even more softly.

"You've met her, then?" I ask. "What's she like?"

"Not exactly," Pam says. "We communicate only via email." She stops. "Sometimes, she'll just leave a note in the wreath on the door of her fence. It's written in longhand on a yellow sheet of paper, like they used back in the olden days." Pam stops again. "She's turned down a half dozen other applicants. She'll just write, 'No!' on a piece of paper after I've shown the listing. I don't know how she knows since she never leaves her property. She's like an agoraphobic spy. Personally, I think she's holding out for a young family. I think it's pretty black-and-white."

Her words ring in my ears.

I've always thought it must be a blessing to see life in black or white. It must be easier if things are cut-and-dried. If emotion is removed, decisions are clear-cut. Me? I've always seen a thousand shades of gray. And that has made for a more difficult existence.

"What brings you to Grand Haven, by the way?" Pam asks. "Did you grow up here? Do you have family here? Are you just wanting to spend a summer with your family near the water?" She stops and looks at me with great concern, before lowering her voice. "I could certainly understand if that were the case."

"No, no, no," I stammer. "I grew up in Detroit."

How do I explain? I think. *Why do I have to explain? I'm too tired to explain any more.*

A buzzing sound grows in my ears, as if cicadas have nested inside my head. The world tilts—like an old *Batman* episode—and all its color—the American flag, the brown bungalow, the blue sky, the red tree, Pam's pink lip gloss—turns black-and-white.

"I got a job offer," I continue.

"But," Pam starts, "your husband…"

"Oh," I stammer again. "He…uh…he's back from the war."

"What a blessing!" Pam cries. "I didn't realize that. I thought he was…"

She stops short.

Dead? I want to ask. *He is. Just not literally.*

"Goodness," Pam says in a too chipper tone. "Why didn't you say so?"

Say what? I want to ask. Say that my husband was returned to me as a shell of his former self? Say that our lives were upended because of a war I never believed in? Say that I'm always worried about my husband because I have no idea where he is or what he's doing half the time when he's not drinking or depressed? Say that I'm an awful person for thinking all of this?

A thousand shades of gray.

"Yes, it is a blessing," I reply. "It's just hard to talk about."

"I understand," Pam says. She reaches out and touches my arm. "You're doing what you can for your family."

"Yes," I say, forcing a smile.

"Are you a teacher?" she asks. "Or a secretary?"

I bite the inside of my cheek. "I'm a chemical engineer," I say.

"Oh!"

"I work for a boat and yacht paint manufacturer here," I continue. "I'm developing a new marine paint—in interesting colors—to prevent rust and barnacles on ships and docks."

"That's amazing," Pam says. I don't know if she's referring to the job or the fact I'm a chemical engineer. She looks at me closely, as if for the first time, and I can see myself reflected in the slippery gloss coating her lips: my brown shaggy hair, little makeup, big black eyeglass frames. I think of the neighbor's fence: *perhaps I'm trying to keep the world at bay, too.* "I never think of engineers as being, well, creative."

I nod. "People always say engineers aren't creative, but we are. In fact, my work is a sort of art, scientific painting if you will." I raise my hands and wave them around. "Our world is made of scientific paint mixing. I mean, just look at the air we breathe. It's made up of lots of other things besides oxygen, which is only about 21 percent of air. About 78 percent of the air we breathe is made up of nitrogen. There are also tiny amounts of other gases like argon, carbon dioxide and methane." I stop and gesture at the lake. "And what is water made of?"

Pam is staring at me.

"Fascinating," she says as she reapplies her gloss. "Well, this is a perfect place for your family, then. Grand Haven is a water and boating haven. You know this is the Coast Guard City of the US, right? And we hold the annual Coast Guard Festival, which honors and respects the men and women of the US Coast Guard. Your husband should be right at home here. And you, too." She smiles. "Now, let me show you the house, okay? And that view!"

Before we can move, Lily races down the stairs and over to the fence separating this yard from the one next door. She clambers atop a large river rock and jumps up to grab a big shepherd's hook jutting off the side of the wooden fence where it looks like a hanging plant once was located. She tries to climb up the fence like a squirrel, her sneakers raking against the wood.

"Lily!" I yell. "You're going to hurt yourself."

She jumps down.

"Mom," she whines.

"She's a bit of a tomboy," I say to Pam, who cannot hide her disappointment.

Lily presses her face between the tiny slats in the fence. "Whoa!" she says. "You have to see this!"

I walk over to where Lily is standing and position my right eye against a minuscule opening and squint. Beyond the fence is a garden that resembles one of my own chemical experiments: there are dozens of stakes everywhere with small flags attached, and they're fluttering in the breeze. Daylily stalks are everywhere, and there is something odd attached to them that I can't quite figure out.

Little is in bloom this early in the season, but I can only imagine what is to come.

I reposition myself and try to peer farther into the yard, but it's too narrow and strains my eye. The one thing I can make out right in front of me, however, is a beautiful arbor with a trellis that looks as if it not only might grow roses but might also have been a pathway between these two houses.

I feel the fence shaking. I look up to see Lily trying to scramble up it again.

"Lily!" I call again.

She hops back to the ground and sprints toward the porch.

"Why don't I show you the house?" Pam asks again. "You just have to see that view."

"Of course," I say.

I turn and start toward the little flagstone pathway leading to the house. Before I head up the stairs, I look back at the neighboring house.

A curtain moves, nearly imperceptibly, upstairs. I take one step, stop and look again. The window is not open, but the curtain is still swaying slightly.

I take another step, turn on a dime and narrow my eyes behind my glasses.

A shadow flutters and then disappears.

PART ONE

LILACS

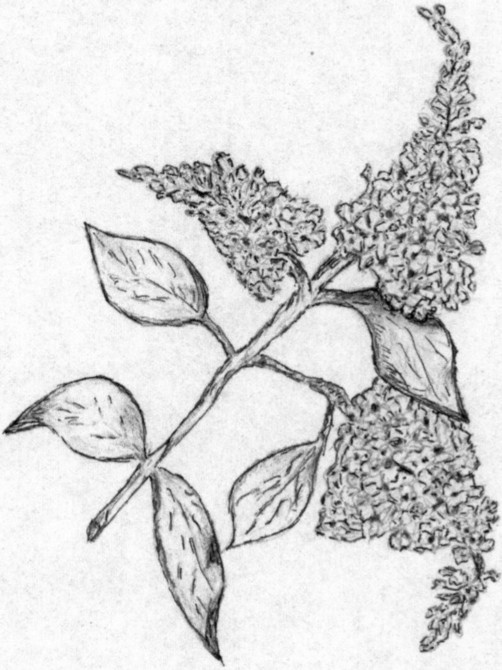

"The smell of moist earth and lilacs hung in the air like wisps of the past and hints of the future."

—Margaret Millar

ABBY

MAY 2003

Snip, snip, snip…

I am lining the kitchen cupboards, pantry and drawers with contact paper. I am not what you would call innately domestic, but my mother—the master of focusing on the innocuous—has ingrained in me an orderliness and tidiness that borders on OCD.

Perhaps that's why I became an engineer.

I don't deep clean—I'd prefer to have someone come in and do the windows, wipe down baseboards and stand on stepstools to dust ceiling fans—but I do, what I term, "tidy house." The bed must be made, dishes cannot be left in the sink, Lily's toys must be returned to her room.

Things must be in their place.

I put the scissors aside and look around the surprisingly spacious kitchen of our new rental home. It was obviously renoed since it was built in the—*when did Pam say?*—1920s, but not updated again since Truman was president. The reno is more *Happy Days* than today. The cabinets are bright yellow, and I mean *bright* yellow. Pam pitched this as a "sunny kitchen," but it borders more on blinding. The cabinets have flat fronts and vintage hardware, and the countertops are sparkly pink Formica. A matching retro pink dinette set remains in the corner by a big window, as does a pink rotary phone in a little nook that has a pulldown drawer. I've already staked this out as my home office, my Mac as out of place in this time capsule of a kitchen as the newer stainless appliances.

I'm not quite sure if the kitchen is retro or tacky, but I love it. It reminds me of my grandparents, and the space feels like a warm hug.

I found rolls of contact paper in the basement. The paper is what the HGTV designers call "atomic," and it's dotted with aqua and lime green jacks, like I played with as a little girl. When I initially unrolled the paper, the edges were wavy from moisture and humidity, but I ironed them flat, another trick I learned from my mom.

I line another shelf, walk over to an open box sitting on the counter and begin to unwrap glasses and coffee mugs, tossing the newspaper on the floor as I go.

We are starting over, I think, *in so many ways.*

I think of our house in Detroit with its open concept and tidy gardens. It was supposed to be our forever home but it ended up a house of horrors. We sold the updated home we had a mortgage on in the city to rent an old house in a resort town neither one of us knows a thing about.

I look around the colorful kitchen. *Not so black-and-white, Pam,* I think.

"No! No! No!"

I sprint into the living room holding a glass. My husband, Cory, is screaming in his sleep.

"Honey," I say, taking a seat on the edge of the couch, modulating my voice so as not to frighten him any more. "It's okay. It's okay. You're all right. You're all right."

Cory wakens with a start, jolting upright. He knocks the glass from my hand, and it flies into the air, crashing on the wood floor. The sudden explosion causes Cory to cover his ears and sink into the couch.

"Ssshhh," I whisper to my once-invincible two-hundred-pound husband, who is shaking.

"Where am I?"

"Home," I say, smoothing the golden hair over his forehead. "Our new home. Grand Haven. Remember? It's okay. I'm right here."

He nods, his eyes glassy, and reaches for the beer he'd left on the side table.

"Are you sure you need that?" I ask.

Cory narrows his ice-blue eyes, which match the logo on the can, and glares at me.

"Yeah," he says. "I'm sure."

He drains his beer and hands the bottle to me. "Bring me another one," he says.

I grab the remote and begin to turn off the TV, which is always turned to a news station, CNN, Fox, MSNBC, it doesn't matter. Cory is obsessed with watching reports of the war, stunned to return home to find that so many people in the country he was defending don't support the war, but also to see growing reports that there were never likely any weapons of mass destruction to begin with.

"Don't," he says.

"Honey, this just makes you more anxious. Why don't you watch something a little lighter?"

Cory shakes his head like he does when he's watching the news.

You're a traitor, too, his eyes seem to say.

"Let me get you a beer," I say to appease him.

I walk toward the kitchen and stop cold in the dining room. Though we've just moved in, Cory's military paperwork—for insurance, benefits, counseling—covers our dining room table. Although we're supposed to be a more online society now, paper rules: there is paperwork in boxes, paperwork in files, paperwork in manila folders and binders, paperwork teetering in piles.

Clutter that never goes away.

I move into the kitchen and stand inside the door. I watch Cory's head bob—once, twice—and hold my breath until I know he has passed out again. I push my forehead against the door frame as if I'm pushing all of my festering emotion back inside. I tiptoe back into the living room—the old wood floor, whose squeaky boards I have yet to learn, doing their best to give me away—grab the remote and turn off the TV.

Blessed silence.

I watch my husband sleep. For a few seconds he looks at peace. His face is relaxed, his breathing rhythmic.

"No!" he suddenly yells, his legs twitching, his face in agony. I hold my breath.

And then he is at rest again.

Cory has shared little with me about what happened during his deployment in Iraq, but I know a homemade land mine hidden in the desert sand was tripped and killed two of his platoon, including his best friend. Cory's body is dotted with scars, his mind blotted with that scene, and although he says he prefers to spare me and Lily from the horror, his nightmares, his drinking and his growing isolation speak volumes.

The irony that the US has the latest weapons and technology at its disposal but a jimmy-rigged mine killed his friends haunts my husband.

War is war. No shades of gray there.

I take a deep breath to steady myself. I am exhausted, but I must soldier on: the house has to be in order before I start my new job in a week. And Lily must meet new friends in a new city this summer. I look at Cory: I've yet to tell him I have signed Lily up for nearly every camp and class I could find, from swimming to sailing. I don't want him to think that I don't trust him, but the truth is, I don't. He loves Lily more than his own life, but that would not keep him from drinking too much, or passing out, or simply forgetting she was in the yard playing.

My husband is but a ghost of who he was.

I inhale again.

The living room smells of floor polish and beer, just like The Twilight Inn, the dive college bar where I used to work. On Mondays I'd mop the floor and throw away all the bottles and plastic cups, attempting to eradicate the history of the weekend. But it still always smelled like floor cleaner and beer.

Cory moans.

The ghosts always remain, I think.

I eye a window on the front of the house.

I need to air out this room, I think. *Give the ghosts a chance to escape.*

I tiptoe toward the beautiful antique double hung window. There are two such antique windows in the living room and two in the dining room, the original windows encased in beautiful molding thick with white paint. I run my hand over the wavy glass and the pretty panes.

The stories you could tell.

I pull up on the frame, but it refuses to budge. I squat and put my back into it, the window moving—oh, an inch, perhaps—

my vertebrae cracking so loudly that I actually shush them. I stop and study the windows.

You may be pretty, I think, *but you're old and cantankerous.*

The windows have the old sash cords. The frames are swollen from the water and humidity from the lake. I lower my glasses onto the end of my nose and peer down where the rope enters the side of the window frame. These work by using old-school counterbalance weights, which sit in the cavities beyond the window jambs. When you raise or lower the window, the weights—attached to the cording—move up or down and keep the windows open without a need for a stay.

Fascinating, these old inventions, I think, before chuckling at myself. *Aren't engineers fun?*

The sash cords are frayed, and I'll need to work on them. I take a deep breath, position my hands under the frame one more time and push upward like a strongman at a carnival. The window suddenly flies open as if we're on the moon and there is no gravity.

I can hear Cory stir. I turn around, holding my breath again. He rolls into the couch and snores.

I exhale and take a deep breath. I pivot in my running socks to return to the kitchen and grab a broom and dustpan to clean up the broken glass in the living room but stop midmotion and swivel back toward the window, my nose in the screen, sniffing like an old dog. In just a few days the lake has already become a familiar smell. The woody, watery scent has a powerful effect on me as if I was always meant to be by the water and have finally come home. The smell of fresh water mixed with pine carried on the breeze calms me, even more than the antianxiety meds Cody's doctor administered to both of us and which we both refuse to take.

But there is something else in the air tonight, a perfumed

scent that is so sweet and familiar, so overwhelming that I can't help but close my eyes and inhale again.

Lilacs!

I am immediately transported back to my grandmother's house in suburban Detroit. Every wall in Grandma Midge's home was painted a shade of pink or purple.

"It's like a bottle of Pepto-Bismol blew up in here, Miriam," my dad used to say to my grandma.

"Your entire world is beige," Grandma Midge would reply. "Beige is not even a color."

And she loved her favorite colors: her bathroom was painted dusty rose and her kitchen hot-pink. Pink depression glass and desert-rose dishes filled cupboards, and Hummel figurines and glass birds graced corner cabinets. But walking into her bedroom was like walking into a room filled with her favorite flowers: soft purple walls with a slightly pinkish hue, a white headboard painted with lilacs, floral drapes and purple shag.

When we would visit her for Mother's Day, her lilacs were usually in full bloom. She would wait for me to come before cutting the fragrant flowers.

"Wouldn't it be amazing if our arms were lilac branches?" my grandma would ask. "How beautiful would life be?"

My grandma lived in an old neighborhood filled with families whose husbands were lifers in the auto industry. Over time, however, the rows of tiny homes perched just an arm's length away from one another became occupied by widows, all of whom it seemed had a penchant for growing lilacs and playing bridge.

"Lilacs require a pretty vase," my grandma would instruct me. "*Life* requires a pretty vase."

She would lead me to one of her many corner cabinets and give it a soft kick with her slipper to pop open the sticky door. We would pick out her most beautiful McCoy vases, ones in the shape of hyacinths or towering vases of aqua designed with birds and branches.

We would smell nearly every lilac before cutting armfuls of blooms and carrying them into the house. We'd fill countless vases, placing them in every room, until her house smelled as if it had been soaked in heavenly perfume.

And when I'd go to bed, she would lift the vase from the nightstand and hold it to my nose.

"Dream of flowers, my angel," she would whisper. "Dream of lilacs."

Cory rustles on the couch, and I sneak away from the window. I tiptoe through the kitchen, grab a flashlight and quietly open the door that leads into the large porch overlooking the lake. There is a bright moon, which shimmers on the lake, making me feel as if I'm in an old movie awaiting my husband to return from sea. The moon is not quite full, but getting more illuminated every night. I've learned already from local meteorologists, who seem to be obsessed with moon phases on the western side of the state, that we're in a Waxing Gibbous phase, the one that precedes a full moon.

Lilacs catch my attention again, and I follow my nose, which leads me onto the deck and then down the stairs into the ramshackle yard. It is a relatively warm May night by Michigan standards, meaning I am not shivering without a jacket, nor can I see my breath. I thought I'd be colder by the lake than I was in Detroit, but the lake water has warmed more quickly than usual and that serves to keep the surrounding lakeshore a touch more temperate.

At least until the lake water turns over again, the local meteorologists said on TV.

Our new backyard is fairly large, but consists mostly of dirt, sand and weeds. There are lake-stone borders where it looks as if gardens once stood, and random concrete birdbaths and decorative garden globes that are crumbling along with rusting metal stakes, all of which are unable to survive the harsh Michigan winters forever.

This will be a project, if I ever have the time. Cory used to love to garden. Before…

I turn, and the moon illuminates the foreboding fence. It is, truly, like being on the outside of a prison.

Or a castle, I think. *Either the old woman in the house is trying to keep everyone out, or keep herself in. I'm not sure which.*

I walk to the fence and flip on the flashlight, shining it along the fence. I search left and right, up and down, and there—on one of the thick fence slats, about three quarters the way up—is a small hole. It looks as if a woodpecker took out all of his frustrations on this single board.

I turn and scan the yard. An old rusting chair, like the vintage ones my grandma used to have on her front porch that have become popular again, sits abandoned across the yard. I walk over and drag it toward the fence. I test it with my foot to ensure the seat is intact, and step onto it, the flashlight strobing across the yard. I find the hole and lift my nose to it.

The scent of lilacs fills my nostrils.

I point my flashlight through the hole. Through the narrow opening, I can see a thick row of lilacs in full bloom, their purple arms illuminated in the moonlight, bobbing in the soft breeze, waving at me as if to say, "Hi, Abby, it's so nice to meet you."

I try to scan my neighbor's yard, but the hole is too narrow. I can only see what's straight in front of me. I turn off the flashlight, shut my eyes, praying the chair underneath me won't collapse, and, for one brief moment, I am a little girl again, in bed at my grandma's house. I am safe, warm and completely unaware of the horrors of the world.

And I am dreaming of flowers, dreaming of lilacs.

IRIS

MAY 2003

I like to work by moonlight in May.

The evenings are crisp and quiet, the lake humidity yet to arrive, like the tourists who will descend upon the surrounding cottages and beach like locusts.

I look around my garden, which is illuminated by solar lights tucked here and there.

No locusts here, I think. *I can control those.*

I look at my fence.

I can control any outsider who dare invade my home.

And then I see purple arms waving at me in the moonlight. I wave back.

But the best part to me about May is the scent of lilacs. They fill the air like an ancient perfume, something Aphrodite might have worn. The smell makes me feel safe, like a little girl. I think of my grandmother and close my eyes.

"Heaven will smell like lilacs, Iris," I mouth silently, remembering what my grandma used to say when she'd tuck me into bed. I stop the thought.

There is no heaven, Iris.

Even six decades later, nights remain the hardest part of each day for me. They are a constant reminder I am not safe, I have never been safe, none of us are ever safe. Sleep refuses to come, and when it does, it's riddled with nightmares of my husband and daughter, both screaming to be saved, me unable to do so.

The sweet scent wafts past me again, and I finally open my eyes. The lilacs continue to wave in the soft breeze.

Only these I can save. My flowers.

I look out and up at my fence. *Only myself I can protect.*

I set down the seeds I am counting and pick up the desert-rose teacup. I sip my chamomile tea and look around my screened porch.

Everything around me is old.

I sit the delicate cup back into its dainty saucer, which rattles under my unsteady hand.

I am old.

My screened porch has become my office and my sanctuary, especially in Michigan's mellowest months, May through October. The most optimistic and literal of Michiganders might call November autumn and April spring, but in the Mitten State, they both still officially count as winter. You can't even safely plant your annuals until Mother's Day in Michigan. My window boxes remain on standby.

I had my screened porch built decades ago, when I put up my first fence, along with an expanded greenhouse.

"Are you sure, ma'am?" the builders asked when I told them how high I wanted my fence. "What about your neighbors?"

"I own the house to the south, and the one to the north was bought by strangers. Highland Park is all strangers now. Don't they teach children not to talk to strangers?"

Up went the fence, lickety-split, no more questions.

But the real reason I first put up that fence was that I couldn't stand the stares and the looks people gave the woman who lost her family, as if I were some sort of circus oddity. I couldn't take the way husbands grabbed their wives and the way that mothers wrapped arms around their children—neighbors and friends, no less—gestures that said, *Don't get too close. Her bad luck just might rub off.*

Yes, the first fence was to keep people from looking in, but the second fence was to keep people out.

Forever.

Ironically, I no longer see it as a fence anymore. It is a canvas. Clematis, roses, trumpet vine and sweet pea climb and trail over the wood, while hearty hibiscus and rose of Sharon in pink and white cover it in wide swaths of color.

The screened porch is elevated and features a vaulted, gabled ceiling that offers panoramic views of Lake Michigan in all her glory as well as my backyard. It's a soaring room, screened on two sides and walled on one. The northern side is walled, save for an old, paned window graced by a vintage bentwood lamp and lampshade my grandfather won during a fishing bet in northern Michigan. My grampa used to take us to an old cabin on Lake Superior, where the water was colder than an ice bath even in the height of summer. He went there for one reason and one reason only: to fish for muskie. At the lodge where we used to stay, he bet the bar owner, after a few beers and shots of whiskey, that he could pull a muskie from the lake that was bigger than any the barkeep had ever mounted on his wall. I was with him when the monster hit, the fish following the bait for hours. The muskie's size and dinosaur teeth scared the life out of me, but my grampa eventually hauled it in.

"What do you want, Grampa?" I asked. "He said he'd give you anything."

My grampa walked out with that lamp, which he read the Sunday paper under for years, despite the fact that lamp smelled like cigarette smoke and cheap beer until it had a chance to air out on this porch for a few decades.

Now my two favorite sources of light—that lamp and the moonlight—softly illuminate the yellow tablet of paper on which I record the seeds and results of the daylilies and roses I propagate. It now takes multiple light sources and two—yes, two!—sets of glasses for me to do all this at my age. I prop a set of readers on the end of my nose just beyond a set of bejeweled cat-eye glasses with lenses as thick as the bottom of a soda bottle.

I take a sip of tea and inhale the lilacs.

My body stiffens at a creaking sound, and I tilt my head toward the part of the porch that is screened but hidden, hugged by a line of small pines and rows of wild hydrangea—"volunteers" I dug up in the woods near the dunes when I used to hike the state park around the beach. They have grown to be nearly eight feet tall and will bloom with massive, lacey white blossoms as big as baseballs. I listen.

Must be a tree limb, I think. *Or my body.*

I chuckle to myself and take another sip of tea.

The porch now feels as if it's been around as long as I have, largely because it's decorated with all my mom's and grandma's favorite things.

A floor-to-ceiling fireplace, comprised of round, colorful stones that I hauled up from Lake Michigan after they washed in following powerful thunderstorms, towers in the corner with a mantel—still sporting a horse hitch—that was salvaged from an 1800s barn that was demolished just down the street to make room for a cookie-cutter mini-mansion.

A mini-mansion! In Highland Park? Can you imagine?

I turned my grandfather's old glass minnow catcher into a light, and around the window I hung vintage curtains—featuring deer romping in the woods on a crisp autumn day—that my grandma made when my mom was just a girl. The canoe that my dad and I rowed onto Lake Michigan every weekend morning hangs from the tippy top of the vaulted ceiling, the red-and-green paint peeling. Two barn lights hang from its bench seats. Every tabletop and corner is filled with artwork and mementos collected by my family, and tiny watercolors of my favorite flowers hang from posts and cover every square inch of wall space.

My heart—*no, my family's heart!*—beats in this porch.

Even the massive table on which I work was crafted by my grandfather, a woodworker who built it from a walnut tree that was struck by lightning in our backyard. Its legs are made from turned logs and tree stumps. It is sturdy and worn like me. Its wood has absorbed countless tears and only grown stronger, it seems. It is so heavy, I can no longer move it inside in the winter, or scooch it in a torrential downpour when the winds blow the rain in sideways through the uncovered screens. It remains rooted in the center of this porch.

I finish my tea and look around, the moonlight and lamp draping the porch in an ethereal light.

Even as a little girl, I loved heirlooms. I snuggled under my grandma's quilts, I wore her aprons, even though they dragged on the floor, and I used her rolling pin to make the crusts for her blueberry pies. I kissed every antique Christmas ornament as I hung it on the sturdy blue-green limbs of the Fraser fir, and I listened to my mom's music box as I brushed my hair.

But it was my family's flowers that captured my heart. To hear the stories of how each flower was passed along—mother to daughter, friend to friend, garden to garden—and what they meant to each gardener was a tribute to patience, care, time and love.

But most of all, it was a tribute to hope. Hope that something beautiful would grow despite the harsh winter, the frozen earth and a world that was constantly at war.

Everything must hibernate in order to grow anew, my grandma said.

I lift my yellow lined tablet and review what is growing in my tiny greenhouse, which sits in the back corner of my yard, and what will need to be planted. I begin to write with a pencil, my penmanship like chicken scratches, barely legible even to me. In this technological age, I still do this all by hand. Even write in cursive, which I understand is disappearing from the world. I glance down at the cut-up stockings that hold my seeds.

The world would laugh at me if they saw how I still lived.

I'm Wilma Flintstone in a Judy Jetson world, I think.

But then I see my Blackberry and my Apple Powerbook sitting just beyond my tablet of paper, and I sigh.

Maybe I'm a little Judy Jetson, I consider, staring at the shiny devices that have begun to change the world. *They are now my conduits to the outside world. I can call and have groceries, potting soil, light bulbs delivered without leaving the house. I can even email and have things delivered locally without speaking to another human. I'm beginning to like technology, in fact*, I think with a laugh.

I begin to write when the smell of lilacs drifts onto the porch again. Their scent is so strong, so intoxicating, so magical, I cannot help myself. I set my readers down and push myself up with the help of the table and slowly make my way over to the steps leading to the yard. I pause briefly as I open the door. A small bell tinkles lightly. It's the bell my grandma used to ring in order to call us to dinner when we were on the beach playing. Before I walk out, I stop: a shadow box filled with three mementos—a medal of honor, a dried dandelion that is nothing more than a wilted stem and a dried rose whose peach color has long faded—sits askew on a nail. I straighten it just so with my trembling hand and then make my way out, the bell tinkling. Slowly, one step at a time, my body at a forty-five-degree angle against the handrail, I follow the scent of the lilacs.

When I reach them, I stoop over and hold the blooms to my nose. I am transported in time, back to my grandmother's house, which smelled of lilacs in May. I analyze the pretty purple bloom and the intricate flowers that comprise it. I've always loved lilacs in Michigan: they are reliable bloomers if cared for properly.

I have a series of shrubs, each with about ten canes. Neighbors used to come to me every May and say, "My lilac isn't blooming, Iris. What do I do?"

I'd head to their yards and sneak a peek. Most times, they had pruned their lilacs incorrectly and at the wrong time. Lilacs bloom on old wood. The flower's buds for next spring's blooming are set on growth produced the prior year. Many inexperienced gardeners prune the dormant flowers, or do major cutting in early spring.

I sniff the blooms again and smile to myself at the irony, thinking of my lilacs, my porch and my body.

Beauty can bloom from old wood, I think.

I try to remind myself of that every day, as my body surprises me in new and unflattering ways. I am not pretty like a lilac, but I am hardy. The old wood is strong, the canes intact. I look down at my sweater.

And I do love purple, I realize.

I break off a bloom and hold it to my nose.

Creak!

This time the noise is close, very close. I stop cold and tilt my head.

Another creak. It is not my body nor a tree limb.

I tiptoe toward the fence where the new renters have just moved into my grandmother's home. I have not met them. The only thing my overly ambitious Realtor emailed to me was that it was a young family. A woman engineer. A daughter named Lily. A husband home from the war.

All of that had sealed the deal for me, although I acted as if I didn't care.

A husband who'd actually made it home from the war. A daughter who had both parents and needed a stable home. An educated working mother with a career.

As quietly as I can, I lean against my towering fence. Above me, I swear I can hear someone breathing. Not just breathing, but inhaling. I tiptoe back to the steps and up the porch, grabbing the bell to silence its tinkling. I set down the lilac and grab my readers as well as a pair of binoculars that I always keep on hand to look out at the water. I adjust both sets of glasses and refocus the lenses until the scene becomes clear from my elevated vantage point.

A woman is standing on a chair, her nose pressed against my fence.

What in the hell is that crazy woman doing?

Suddenly, the scent of the lilac I broke off and brought back to the porch fills the air, and I feel as if I'm floating. I lift the binoculars again. I can see the woman, her nose in the air.

It couldn't be, I think. *She wouldn't be.*

I look again.

She is!

The new renter is trying to smell my lilacs.

PART TWO

BLEEDING HEART

"What the heart has owned and had, it shall never lose."

—Henry Ward Beecher

ABBY

MAY 2003

Lily is looking at me like the proverbial cat who ate the canary. Her thick, blond hair—that she got from her father, thank goodness, and not my thin mousy brown hair, which I used to drench with Sun In to try and get that sun-kissed color but only turned it orange—is simultaneously tangled and filled with static electricity. It resembles knotted boat ropes flying in the wind.

Lily's lips are smeared with blueberries, and her mouth is filled with Kashi Toasted Berry Crumble cereal. It's taken me nearly a year to move her from sugary cereals and empty calories to a healthier breakfast. While Cory was at war, I bribed a frightened Lily to eat in any way possible: donuts, waffles, cereals in unicorn colors. I grew up a girl who gorged on

Count Chocula and Pop-Tarts, and I swear the ten pounds I gained back then has stayed with me forever, a giant Sugar Smack attached to my stomach and hips.

Lily bounces in her seat. She is obviously excited about something.

"What's going on?" I finally ask. "Be careful."

Like a bad magician, she winds a hand up her pajama top and produces a piece of folded paper.

"Happy first day of work, Mommy!"

She jumps up and runs to me, holding out the paper, her animated face and padded footsteps filling my soul with happiness.

"I made something for you!"

I open it up and, as I take it in, tears fill my eyes.

Lily has drawn a giant heart, which she's filled in with red glitter that immediately begins to drift to the floor like magical rain. Underneath the heart, she's written, I Love You! Below that, she's drawn her family. For a young girl, Lily's rendering is remarkably accurate: I am holding her hand in front of our new home, while her father stands at a window inside, watching us, holding a can, a TV set on in the background.

"Oh, honey. It's so beautiful. Thank you."

I lean down and hug her with all my might.

"It's like your first day of school," Lily says, her voice serious. "You've gotta be nervous. And your new office is probably empty. I thought you needed something to make you smile."

A lone tear quivers in my eye. I cover my face with my hands, wiping away the tear without Lily's knowledge. When I uncover it, a huge smile is plastered across my face.

"It worked!" I say. "Thank you."

"You're welcome!"

"It's a big day for you, too," I say. "Are you ready?"

"I'm ready!" Lily says.

"But you're not ready," I say, grabbing her pj's and giving them a soft tug. "Now, go get changed. T-minus thirty!"

Lily giggles and races upstairs. I quickly clean the sunny kitchen and then head upstairs to check on Cory. He is still sound asleep.

Not asleep, I surmise instead. *Unconscious.*

Suddenly, his utter lack of concern for my first day of work and Lily's first day of camp infuriates me, and I make as much noise as possible to try and wake him, tapping my toothbrush on the sink, rattling my makeup on the counter, flushing the toilet over and over. I walk to our bed and sit on it as heavily as I can, humming as I put on my shoes, which I thump as I walk around the room.

Cory snorts, rolls onto his side and covers his head with a pillow.

I stomp down the stairs and gather my and Lily's things: Powerbook, briefcase, purse, backpack, juice box, travel mug of coffee. Lily comes down the stairs a few minutes later looking like the tomboy she is: hair still a mess, but in a semblance of a ponytail, little overalls, tennis shoes and a black T-shirt with gold lettering, which is covered by her overalls but that I know reads I'm a Girl. What's Your Superpower? A Detroit Tigers ball cap is tucked into the front pocket of her overalls.

"Ready?" I ask.

"Are you ready?" she counters.

She sounds like my *mother*, I think.

"I am," I say.

We head out the door and down the steps, across the yard and down the long gravel driveway. There is no garage, but I've still been parking my car toward the back. It's easier to take the groceries through the porch and into the kitchen than risk waking up Cory on the couch.

"What's that smell?" Lily asks, her nose twitching.

I inhale. "Lilacs," I say, smiling to myself, thinking of a few nights ago.

"Why don't we grow lilacs?" Lily asks.

I look around the moribund yard. "Maybe one day," I say. "We have a lot on our plates right now."

I unlock the SUV and begin to put my things in the trunk. "Backpack, please," I say. "Lily? Lily?"

I look up, and Lily is at the fence, sniffing. "We need that smell in our yard," she says.

"One day," I say, before gesturing at the SUV. "C'mon. We're already behind schedule."

"What's this?"

I look up again, and Lily is squatting at the fence.

"Don't touch a thing," I say, rushing over. Lily is one of the most inquisitive creatures on the planet, and one of its least fearful, although I now prefer to say most trusting. She's been known to grab a spider, turtle, bee, tadpole, pretty much anything that would reduce other little girls to tears. "Oh," I say, when I reach her. "It's a flower."

"It is?" she asks. "It looks fake. It's sooo pretty. We need these in our yard, too!"

An arcing stem has somehow wound its way through a small gap in the bottom of the fence. A row of pink, heart-shaped flowers dangle dramatically from the delicate stem, like earrings off a lobe. The little hearts are full and round, like tiny balloons, nearly three-dimensional, and in the morning sun, they are incandescent.

I kneel and take the tender hearts in the palm of my hand. I am mesmerized by their beauty. In fact, they are about the most wondrous, magical flowers I have ever seen.

"What are they?" Lily asks.

"I don't know," I say, feeling foolish. "I should."

"Look," Lily says, pointing at the blooms. "They look like they have a little drop of blood dangling at the bottom. Are they hurt?"

I nudge my glasses down onto the bridge of my nose with my free hand and analyze a bloom. A tiny appendage that, as Lily just said, looks like a drop of blood hangs off the bottom of the heart. An elongated drip of white trails down that droplet.

For a brief moment, I feel like a trespasser, an interloper on my reclusive neighbor and her secret garden. I look again at the flower, which seems to have grown this way solely for the purpose of reaching me.

The flowers are simultaneously beautiful and sad, life-affirming and heartbreaking.

"They're not hurt," I say. "They're just showing the world the depth of their soul." I smile at Lily. "They'll be here when we get home. We gotta hit the road."

And it's a road I'm none too familiar with. I actually have a map—an old-fashioned map—spread out on the seat beside me. I am halfway between my parents and my daughter, embracing technology while holding on to my past. I make my way down the steep, winding hill leading from Highland Park and along Harbor Drive, the little beachside road that meanders alongside Lake Michigan. Grand Haven is a resort community, and all the signs of summer are returning to life.

"Look!" Lily says, pointing. "Cute!"

Pronto Pup, the famed, cash-only corndog stand that everyone in town talks about whether in line at the grocery or at the gas pump, has popped up on the boardwalk. Umbrellas are also popping up on restaurant patios, and even the beach is filling with umbrellas. It's a pretty day, a gift since locals say that it can still spit snow here in early May.

Tiny cottages fill the neighborhoods, and the town feels like I might be on the set of *Dirty Dancing*. I drive past Grand

Haven State Park and the pier, mesmerized by the beauty and grandeur of the lake.

I glance at the map and realize I haven't been paying attention. Without warning, I do a U-turn, which causes Lily to squeal in childish delight. I follow the streets on the map for the next few minutes and arrive at the Loutit District Library. Lily's first camp of the summer is at the local library, a pretty brick building that has married the old with the new. It's a reading-and-writing adventure camp. Kids read in the morning—about shipwrecks on Lake Michigan, or the different rocks found in the lake—and then they set out to learn more in person, which they write about at the end of every day.

I pull up, and a group of volunteers is waiting out front in matching T-shirts that exclaim, Let's Read! Let's Explore!

"Hi," I say, getting out of the SUV. "I'm Mrs. Peterson." I unlock the back door and undo Lily's seat belt. "And this is Lily!"

I pop open the trunk as the volunteers take Lily by the hand. I grab her backpack. "Call me if you need anything," I say, more to Lily than the volunteers. I lean down and hug her, kissing her over and over. When I look at her, my lips are quivering.

"Mom," Lily says in embarrassment.

"It's not you I'm worried about, it's me," I say. She nods, knowing it's the truth. The two of us are inseparable, our bond made even tighter by her father's absence and troubled return. I actually don't worry about Lily; she's more social than I am. She's never met a stranger, and kids take to her strong personality. She was popular at her school in Detroit, and I know she'll make fast friends here. "Her father will pick her up at three," I say to the volunteers.

They nod, and I walk to the car. "Have fun!" I yell before I get in the front seat. But it's too late. The front doors have already closed, and I can see Lily skipping as she holds the volunteers' hands.

My company, Whitmore Paints, is actually located in Spring Lake, a neighboring community just over the drawbridge from Grand Haven. It's in a manufacturing plant that sits on a small lake fed by Lake Michigan. It's the perfect location to test paints on boats in the water as well as to test paints in all kinds of weather.

I merge onto the small two-lane road that actually serves as the highway. On the western side of Michigan, the highway meanders through the resort towns, and I've heard the traffic can be as monstrous as any city's. This morning traffic is barely moving. I crane my neck and can see that the drawbridge is open.

"Of course," I say to myself, checking the clock. "Good impression to be late my first day."

The longer I sit, the more I stew, thinking of Cory.

If he'd gotten up and helped me with breakfast and Lily, I'd be on time, I think. *Lily should be home with her dad right now anyway. What kind of mother doesn't trust her husband enough to leave her daughter alone with him for the day?*

I can see the arc of the bridge slowly lower, and traffic begins to move. I make it to work with a few minutes to spare, sweating and nervous from panic and caffeine.

"Morning!" I say with way too much enthusiasm to the receptionist sitting in the lobby.

I beeline to my office, weighted down by my laptop, bag and briefcase. I have just put my things down and turned on the lights when I hear, "Good morning."

I turn, and my assistant, Traci, is in my door. She looks as fresh as the morning dew.

"Morning," I say. I push my glasses up on my nose and sigh. "A bit of rush my first day."

"It always is, isn't it?" she says with a smile. "And I hate to keep the rush going. But your first meeting is about to start."

"Okay," I say. "Let me grab my things."

Traci takes a step into my office and leans forward. She puts a hand around her mouth and whispers conspiratorially, "I hear Mr. Whitmore already loves the concepts of your new metal flake paints."

My heart lifts. "Really?" I ask.

"Really," she says. "I'll say you're on your way, okay?"

"Thanks, Traci."

I grab my laptop and power it on. It brings up all the new paints I've developed, the ones that I was developing to launch my own company before...

I think of Cory again.

...but these paints are the ones I promised to Mr. Whitmore to get this job. I smile at my work. They are vintage paint colors with a luminescent glitter shimmering underneath. The colors are inspired by my favorite Michigan summer flowers, and the names are nostalgic in order to appeal to women who are quickly becoming the main buyers and influencers for boats and yachts: Hydrangea Blue, Summer Iris, Pink Peony, Climbing Rose, Purple Phlox.

I'm part engineer, part marketing guru, I muse. *Now we just have to test them to ensure the colors can withstand the cold lake waters as well as the salty ocean waves.*

I suddenly think of Pam, our Realtor.

There are a million shades of gray, I think. *A million colors in this world.*

And, just as quickly, my mind turns to Lily and the drawing she made for me. I dig it out of my bag, unfold it, and a smile covers my face. It's as if she was channeling not only my work but also my love for her: a brilliant red heart filled with glitter.

I pull off a piece of tape and stick it to my wall. I grab my laptop and begin to walk out of my office, before remembering I need my notes. I turn to grab them and notice Lily's artwork again. Drops of glue trail underneath the heart, and red glitter has stuck to them.

Ironically, I now realize Lily's heart looks as if it's bleeding, just like the flowers we saw this morning.

IRIS

"Shut up!" I scream at the TV.

I throw the remote across the room, and it doesn't stop until it hits the wall. The back flies off the remote, batteries rolling across the wood floor.

The TV continues to blare, oblivious to my reaction, just like the pundits who have spent the past ten minutes debating the Iraq War.

"What is there to debate?" I ask the TV. "It's war. People will die."

The talking heads wear colorful ties, graphics flash in bright colors, and a red scroll screaming *Breaking News* trails along the bottom of the screen. And yet everything to these people—especially war—is black-and-white.

When we really all know it's about the green, I determine.

I gather the batteries, put them back into the remote and click off the TV, my hands shaking, my heart feeling as if it is going to explode.

"Why do you do this to yourself, Iris?" I ask myself. "Why?"

I place the remote on the TV cabinet, and my eyes catch a glimpse of an old photo that has been pushed into the far reaches of one of the cabinet's shelves. It totters atop a stack of books. I pull the photo from the shelf, and the backing nearly falls off the rickety old frame.

"We were just babies," I whisper to a black-and-white photo of me and Jonathan.

I am very pregnant with Mary, and we are standing in front of my mother's gardens, hydrangeas hugging our bodies. Jonathan's hands are on my stomach, and he is acting as if he's listening to my pregnant belly. I am laughing, my eyes shut, holding a peony to my nose.

SEPTEMBER 1945

All of Highland Park's cottages are lit up like fireflies. I sneak along the top of the dune, trampling dune grass as I go. It's a familiar path to me, and one that is starting to become worn from my footsteps.

It's a perfect Labor Day Sunday, and everyone has come to their cottages to celebrate not only the end of summer but also the official end of the war.

Earlier today, General MacArthur signed documents on the deck of the Battleship Missouri to end the deadliest war in human history.

"Today the guns are silent," General MacArthur said. "A great tragedy has ended."

Mine is just beginning, sir.

I am a young widow with a young daughter. I am a wife without a husband. I am now a woman without a heart. How many millions died we still don't know, but for me, I focus on the one I lost and can never get back. Jonathan's body has yet to be located or identified—his body declared "nonrecoverable"—but I continue to press the military to not stop searching.

The case cannot be closed, or there will never be closure for me.

I dream he is still alive out there, somewhere, cold and shivering, fighting to get back to us.

Music is spilling out through the open windows, and I watch families dance and drink. I sent Mary off with her summer friend, Nellie Flanagan, to play on the beach and to celebrate with neighbors.

I'll be just fine, I told Mrs. Flanagan, whose cheeks are always as red and happy as her hair. *But Mary deserves to be a child, even for a night. She's not one anymore, you know.* Mrs. Flanagan nodded and scooped Mary into the crook of her ample body, and off they went to be happy.

Happy, I think. *What is that?*

I hear a woman's excited yelp. I look up, and a man in uniform is kneeling on a patio, a ring box open in his palm.

"Yes!" she screams. "Yes!" She kisses the man, who picks her up and twirls her around and around. "Mother, hurry! Look!" the woman yells when he sets her down.

"I am off to see my husband, too," I whisper into the wind.

When I arrive, my heart sinks.

The Victory Garden is in total disarray.

Rabbits are lined up along the rows of vegetables as if they're eating directly off a buffet table. A few deer look up at me, freezing in midmotion. When they see it's me, they twitch their tails and begin to feast again.

I have left my tools here: a shovel, rake, hoe, wheelbarrow, spade. My hosiery dangles from nails on the fence as if they've been hung out to dry. They are filled with my seeds, my experiments, my hope, my memories of Jonathan.

People have already forgotten about this Victory Garden. It's now been a year since we all were here; it's served its purpose. Now the women who worked here view it as a bad memory, an anchor to the past. I view it as a memorial to my heart, a tribute to all those who sacrificed so these families can celebrate tonight.

I want this garden to be as beautiful as my Jonathan was.

I pick up a hoe and begin to turn the earth. Rabbits hop away but then return to the garden's edges to nibble. I dig up tomatoes and beans, and return with my hose.

1943—Yellow Crosses

Come Home, Jonathan = Yellow Fellow x Peach Perfection

I turn the hose inside out, dropping the seeds into the earth. I've placed old tin cans that used to contain beans and soup around the fence to collect rainwater. Although the war is over, I still cannot bear to waste a thing.

Even this garden.

I gather a few of the cans and water my seeds. Suddenly, my legs feel as if they are going to give out, and I take a seat on the ground. I stare at the wet seeds and, without warning, begin to weep, my tears watering them.

When these daylilies bloomed in my greenhouse this summer, after three years of waiting, I felt as if my Jonathan were with me once again. The color of their petals matched the color of his cheeks to perfection, and—for one fleeting moment—I could feel him again with me. When I lay next to Jonathan, I used to joke he was like a woodstove because he put off so much heat. That day I shut my eyes in the greenhouse, and its warmth made me feel as if he were holding me again on a Sunday morning.

"I thought I'd find you here."

I start. Shirley is standing at the fence.

"What's buzzin', cousin?" she asks.

I turn the dirt over the seeds with my bare hands and then pat down the earth. I pour another can of water over the soil.

"Saw Mary with the Flanagans," Shirley continues. "Knew this is where you'd be."

I continue to pat the soil.

"Did you see the church planted red geraniums in a V for Victory?" Shirley says. I hear the gate squeak open. Suddenly, I can see Shirley's shiny shoes in front of me. "Look at me, Iris."

I look up.

"Talk to me, Iris."

I grab my hoe and lift myself until I'm looking into Shirley's eyes. Her face is sad and stern, so un-Shirley-like.

"I can't stop thinking about the irony of time, the what-ifs," I say.

"What do you mean?"

"What if Jonathan's troop had been delayed a day? What if the war had ended earlier? What if he had enlisted six months earlier, or six months later? What if..."

"If ifs and buts were candy and nuts, we'd all have a Merry Christmas," Shirley says.

"What does that mean?"

"My grandma used to say it," Shirley says. "It just means you can second-guess things your whole life, wish it all away, hope for a different outcome, but it doesn't mean anything is going to change." Shirley shrugs, her typically rambunctious tone soft and gentle. "You have to live in the moment, Iris. You have a daughter."

"That's easy for you to say. You have a husband who's alive!"

I suddenly scream. "He came home. Mine didn't. I love that everyone whose life didn't change is such an eager beaver to give advice."

"My life did change!" Shirley yells.

My eyes widen at her tone.

"Sometimes, I think you're better off that your husband died," Shirley says.

Tears fill my eyes. "Shirley!" I whisper. "Take that back!"

I begin to cry.

"I'm so sorry," she says, "but I'm going to tell you something I haven't told anyone, not even the priest. Promise me you won't tell a soul, Iris. Promise!"

"I promise."

"Jack is not the same man who went to war," Shirley says, her eyes big, her chin quivering, her voice cracking. "He can't cope with the children, he can't cope with work and doesn't like that I work, he drinks too much…he keeps saying it's a different world than when he left," she continues. "I tell him, 'You helped save and change this world.' But he just can't wrap his head around the fact that life is normal again." Shirley stops. "Iris, it's like I'm married to a ghost. It's like Jack's already dead."

Shirley begins to cry, and I pull her into my arms.

"People would think I'm a monster for saying that," she sobs.

"Ssshhh," I whisper. "Ssshhh."

I whisper the same sounds Shirley whispered to me for weeks after Jonathan died. She stayed with me, never leaving my side, my bed, until I was able to stand again. She fed Mary and me, got my daughter to school, helped her with her homework—*saved me*—and yet I felt only anger and jealousy when her husband returned, never bothering to check in on how my friend may be doing.

"We're both haunted," I say as my friend weeps on my shoulder. "But your husband is alive. Never forget that. Fight for that."

Shirley steps back, wipes her eyes and nods. "And your daughter is, too. Fight for that."

Shirley grabs my hoe, which I still have gripped in my right hand. She pulls it from me and tosses it onto the ground.

"You have to go on, Iris," Shirley says. "This is a monument to the past. Let this go. Go back to work. Find your passion again."

I look around the garden. "If this dies, he dies, too," I say in a shaky voice.

"Jonathan will never die, Iris," Shirley says. "He's alive in your heart. He's alive in your daughter. He's alive in your flowers and in every sunrise and sunset. Fight like he fought… for Mary, for women, for yourself."

Shirley looks down. We are standing on the daylily seeds I just planted.

"This earth connects us all," Shirley says. "And from this earth, great beauty is eternally reborn." She stops. "Make your home and garden a testament to your talent and the love of family. That way you can appreciate it every day."

Shirley takes my hand and leads me from the park.

Sometimes, a friend is your lifeline, your counselor, your sounding board. And sometimes your friend is a bridge to the other side, a bridge back to the world of the living. I hug her when the gate slams behind us.

"Thank you," I say. "For everything. But mostly for being my friend."

"I think we might need to find a little hooch," she says, before slapping me on the rear.

2003

I stare at the photo I'm still holding. It is hauntingly beautiful and also simply haunting. I don't remember it being taken, and the fact that I don't remember things as vividly as I used to shakes me to my core. Some of my memories are becoming faded, just like this photo. It seems, more and more, that some days I can't remember a thing.

"We were just babies," I whisper again, but this time my words are choked with sadness. "We didn't know. We didn't know."

I give the photo a little kiss and place it back on the shelf, my eyes stopping on my reflection in the TV. Six decades have passed, and nothing has changed but my appearance. We are a world enraptured by war, cloaked in greed and choked with fear.

The country is two years removed from 9/11, months removed from the invasion of Iraq. We were told by our government after the horrific attack on America that Iraq possessed weapons of mass destruction and that the Iraqi government posed an immediate threat to the US and our allies. We were told Saddam Hussein harbored and supported al-Qaeda, but we found no evidence of WMDs nor of Iraqi collaboration. In other words, our government lied to its people. As an old woman, I remember our history—Vietnam and the Pentagon Papers—and I know it's not the first time this has happened nor will it be the last. America no longer remembers its history: we have the collective memory of a flea. We are distracted by news headlines in blaring red, MySpace, emails. We think old is yesterday. We think we know everything because we know nothing.

What I know is that war, sadly, is sometimes necessary not simply to protect a people but to save the world from evil. But too often war is used as a way to keep people in fear and, thus, in line. It is a false symbol of safety.

I walk over to the large window overlooking my grandma's former house. I keep my curtains closed, day and night, often unable to tell if it's noon or midnight. My curtains are thick burlap, brown, too, with liners no less, to keep out all the light. I can spend endless time at the many windows, not looking out, but ensuring that my curtains are interlaced, wound, overlapping so that they remain an impenetrable barrier. I pull back a curtain and wince in the bright light. Slowly, my world—a giant fence—comes into view.

"You old fool," I say to myself. "You know better. Why are you still at war?"

What I know is this: walling out the world doesn't protect

me. It simply isolates me. Anyone could jump that fence at any time. Anyone could fly over my home and inflict harm. Anyone could break a window and rip open my curtains. This is all an act, a show of bravery. But I am not brave. I am filled with fear. And only the fearful isolate themselves. I was brave—I was fully alive—when I was out *there* experiencing the world and all its beauty and horror. No, you're brave only when you're willing to love, lose, get hurt.

Now I am but an illusion of the living just like these curtains are an illusion of protection and that fence is an illusion of safety.

A shaft of sunlight shifts across my body and warms me, calms me, thaws me from inside out. It is getting warmer. It is nearly summer. I think of the photo and my grandmother's gardens.

"You have work to do, Iris," I say.

I head into my kitchen, a glorious tribute to the 1950s, to make some tea. I put on the kettle and look around.

"Hello, Pepto!" I say. The kitchen instantly brightens my dark mood.

The kitchen is pink, pink and even more pink, from the Formica countertops to the refrigerator. When my Realtor Pam visited me the one time I let her into my home to discuss renting the house next door, she called this "vintage."

"I guess I'm vintage then," I said to her.

She laughed in a polite way that simply said, "No, you're *old*."

Pam had told me I needed to update the kitchen next door if I wanted to rent it for "top dollar." She casually suggested I do the same here in case I ever wanted to sell it "when the time came."

"I plan to die here, Pam," I said.

She excused herself.

I'm also old enough to realize that what goes around comes around. The fashion, hairstyles, musical influences and home design all return. We're not as clever as we think. We rarely invent; we constantly reinvent because we can't remember squat.

But once we rid ourselves of something, we can no longer get it back.

My kettle screeches.

I can't, for instance, go into a home-goods store and buy this kettle. It might be made to look old, but it won't have the history. It wasn't used by my mom and grandma. We think we can re-create everything, but we can't.

Like my flowers, I think.

I make my tea, head onto the porch and then out into my yard.

I could easily buy annuals every single spring at any nursery or home improvement store, but they wouldn't have the history of my beloved perennials: my roses, Shasta daisies, peonies, hollyhocks, gladiolas, hydrangeas, trillium, surprise lilies, tulips, daylilies, Lady's Mantle, monarda, clematis, snapdragons, balloon flower, hearty hibiscus, ferns, salvia, dahlias, lavender, Russian sage, coreopsis and pincushion.

These all have a story. These all have a history. These are my family.

And to lose one would be to lose a piece of my own history, a chunk of my own soul.

I cannot lose anything else in this world. I have lost too much already.

Especially these: my bleeding heart.

Bleeding heart.

I smile at the irony. The debate I just watched on TV was waged between "an old-school conservative" and "a bleeding-heart liberal."

But what does that mean? Why do we define ourselves in such unforgiving terms?

Bleeding hearts were one of my grandma's favorite flowers, and—considering Michigan is a wetter, cooler zone—she grew them in various sunny spots around her gardens, but they took center stage at the entrance of her old potting shed whose shingles were green and mossy. Bleeding hearts framed the flagstone steps that led to the old screened door to her shed.

"They're so whimsical, so fragile and so beautiful," she said. "I can admire them every time I retrieve something from my shed."

Her potting shed is now mine, I realize, walking over to the little building.

Over the years I've had to rehab her potting shed, sometimes out of necessity, sometimes out of reinvention. I've reshingled it many times, as Michigan winters constantly wreak havoc on the fragile wood. It splinters and turns gray, just like my body.

But, I think, *I can renew that old structure.*

I also expanded it a couple of decades ago, making it wide enough to hold not only all my gardening tools, pots, soil, statues, flags and gazing balls, but also a comfy chair and little table. I like to have my tea in there on pretty days, or read a book on cloudy ones. Men have man caves now, and women have—*what do they call them?*—she-sheds. My grandma simply called it her place of peace.

The screened door remains—now sporting a vintage curtain featuring deer and rabbits frolicking in a field of ferns and trillium—flanked by two small windows. I moved the shed next to the fence near my grandma's house because it just seemed like it should be as close to its original home as possible.

I take a seat on the flagstone step leading to the shed. I set my tea down and shuck my sweatshirt, placing it under my behind, which is as rocky as the flagstone step. I reach over and take the beautifully shaped flowers of the bleeding heart in the palm of my hand, admiring them as I might the charms on an old bracelet.

The Latin name of bleeding heart is *dicentra spectabilis*, which translates to *two spurs*, a distinction that is easy to spot on the flowers. The flower grew wild throughout Asia for thousands of years but didn't get established in Western gardens until the mid-1800s.

A feeling of elation infuses my soul.

My memory hasn't faded entirely yet, I imagine, recalling things I learned in college and at work a lifetime ago.

I suddenly recall the story from Japanese folklore my grandma used to tell me about bleeding heart. I shut my eyes, and I can hear her voice speak to me in the breeze through the pines.

I grab my tea and stand, slowly, my body making its way northward like an old jack-in-the-box. I head into the shed and look around.

What to do first, I wonder. Head to the greenhouse or start here?

A white garden flag dotted with daffodils reading, Happy Spring! sits in a corner, while a garden gnome waves at me from a long table. I may be a master gardener, but I am also a child at heart, and that means my flowers—and I—need company: friendly flags and happy gnomes, gorgeous gazing balls, sculptures made of lake stones and of swimming fish in copper. I have made dozens of garden stakes that feature my family's old dishes and teacups.

I may be alone, but every day is like a garden party when I'm surrounded by the things I love.

"Okay, lazy, get a move on," I tell myself. "It's midafternoon, and you've got so much to do."

I grab my little gardening gnome and his tiny home and

walk it to the gnarled redbud tree on the other side of my big yard, placing it in a hole at the base of the trunk where he has lived for years.

"You're home for the summer, little man," I say.

I return to the shed and find the "face" for my old oak: two big eyes, a bulbous nose and an expressive mouth in the shape of an *O*. I hang them on the nails that have been on the massive tree forever, and the giant trunk suddenly comes to life.

"Oh, my!" I say with a laugh.

I head back to the shed and stop to catch my breath, sipping my tea. I am starting out the door of the shed again when I see a stem of my bleeding heart moving.

What in the world?

I tiptoe out of the shed, being careful not to slam the screened door. The flower moves again. I look at the trees, but the branches are fairly still, the breeze light. I head down the steps and toward the fence.

Due to their toxicity, bleeding heart are deer and rabbit resistant, so I can't imagine anything nibbling on it. I look around. No animals are hiding behind the shed or near the fence.

I suddenly see two tiny fingers jut through a narrow gap in the fence. One long stem of my bleeding heart snaps off and disappears through a slat.

I bend down and peer through the fence. A little girl is sitting on the ground. She is tying my flowers around her wrist as if she's putting on a little bracelet.

My heart is pounding so loudly it's nearly deafening. I feel dizzy and nauseated. *Do I confront her? Or stay quiet?* I attempt at all costs to avoid confrontation. Despite my outward demonstration of fight, I prefer flight. Even my conversations with strangers, be it a Realtor, a plumber, a clerk, only occur now when required.

"Hi!"

I nearly jump out of my skin before falling to my knees.

"Ow!" I say.

"Are you okay?"

I see a little blue eye.

"You stole my flowers," I say, the words coming out ragged and rushed.

"I'm sorry," the little voice says. "I thought these were ours. They were sticking through the fence."

Silence.

"Do you want them back?" she asks. "I'm really sorry."

Silence.

"I'm Lily," the little voice adds.

Lily. Lily. Lily. My head grows dizzier when she says her name. *Daylilies. My beloved flower.*

And now I remember: I heard her mother say her name when they were first looking at the house. I love that name. *Lily.* The irony is literally too much for me to bear.

"Hello?" a little voice asks again.

Suddenly, my anger overwhelms me, like it did earlier when I was watching the news: *Do these people have no boundaries*? Her mother was just hovering at the fence the other night smelling my lilacs. *Have they not read the rider to the rental contract*? Any contact with me, or infringement upon my yard or gardens, means their contract is null and void. Eviction immediate. Loss of first and last month's payments.

"What's your name?" the tiny voice asks through the fence.

Her voice is so innocent, so pure, just like Mary's.

Before…

"I'm Iris," I say without thinking.

Lily giggles. "We're both named after flowers." Lily holds her tiny wrist draped in flowers up to the fence. Suddenly, my initial shock and anger subside. I can feel the little girl's innocence shimmer like the sun on this spring day. "So pretty," Lily continues. "What is this flower called? My mom didn't know. And she knows everything."

"It's called bleeding heart," I say.

"Ooooh," Lily says. "Sounds bad."

"No, no," I say. "It's a beautiful name for a magical flower." I look at the bleeding heart and memories crowd my mind, my own heart seeming to burst with love and break all at the same time. I want to leave, get as far away from this little girl as possible, but something—or someone—stops me, forces me to remain still. After a long pause I ask, "Want to hear a story about it?"

"Sure," Lily says. I can hear her rear scoot closer to the fence.

I inhale to steady myself because I am now surrounded by ghosts.

Mommy, I can hear my Mary say. *Tell me that story again about the heart flowers. Pleeease.*

"There once was a young Japanese boy who fell dearly in love with a beautiful and wealthy maiden. In order to win her love, he made her lavish gifts. The first gift he gave her was a pair of beautiful rabbits to keep as pets." I stop. "Hand me one of the little hearts."

A pair of fingers appears along the fence. I pull the heart-shaped flower in two halves and place them in my palm. "Look," I say. "Two rabbits."

"What?" Lily says, before exclaiming, "I see it now! I can see them!"

I continue. "The maiden took the gifts but not his love, so he tried again, making her slippers of the finest silk." I take the bottom of the flower—the elongated drop of blood—and halve it. Two slippers of white and gold appear.

"Wow!" Lily says. "What happens next?"

"She accepted these gifts, too, but—again—not his love. Now desperate, the young man took all of his modest savings and bought her the most beautiful and expensive pair of earrings possible." I take the outer portion of the rabbit and fashion into earrings, with delicate gold at the ends. "The maiden accepted the jewelry but still refused to marry the young man."

"That mean, ol' maiden," Lily says. "She's just awful!"

"The young man grew depressed, and knowing he was out of money and gifts, took a knife and pierced himself through the heart." I reposition the earrings into the shape of a heart and take the stem of the plant from which the bleeding heart dangled to make a sword. I place it through the heart.

Lily's eye is darting back and forth through the slat in the fence.

"The flower, which represents all of the young man's gifts as well as all of his love for the maiden, sprang from the place he died."

There is silence for a second. Finally, I hear Lily sniffle.

"I'm sorry," I say. "I didn't mean to make you sad."

"You didn't," Lily finally says. "It just reminds me of my mom and dad. He doesn't—what's the word?—appreciate my mom's gifts."

I sit up at her admission and insight.

"Where are your parents?" I ask.

"My mom is at work, and my dad forgot to pick me up from camp at the library."

I again feel dizzy. "Forgot?" I ask. "How did you get back home?"

"I walked," she said. "I told my camp counselors my dad was meeting me in the parking garage."

"But you could've..." I stop, not wanting to frighten her.

"Is this your house?" Lily asks out of the blue.

"What do you mean?"

"The one we're living in. Is it yours?"

"It was my grandma's," I say. "I live in my mom's house."

"That's nice," she says. "You must like that."

I catch my breath. "I do."

"I do, too," Lily says. "I like living here. It feels like…" She stops. "Home."

Tears fill my eyes. I blink them away.

"Who are you talking to?"

"Daddy!" Lily yells. I can hear the shuffle of her standing up and running across the yard. "Where have you been?"

"Out," he says in a gruff tone. "Who were you talking to?"

I stick my eye to the fence. I can see Lily look back. Her father's voice is slow and slurry as if he's been drinking.

"Myself," she says. "Playing a game until you got home." She stops and when she speaks again, her voice is sad. "You forgot to pick me up at camp this afternoon."

"Don't tell your mother," he says.

What? I want to scream. *Your little daughter walked home by herself. Anything could have happened to her.* I stop and have to shut my eyes to keep the memories from crowding in again. Too late. Like my Mary. If we can't protect our children, what good are we?

"Okay," Lily says. "Look at my pretty bracelet."

The father doesn't react. I can hear the back door slam.

"Don't say anything to my parents about today," Lily asks, her face against the fence again. When I don't immediately respond, she says, "Promise?"

A bent stem of bleeding heart appears through the fence.

"Cross your heart and hope to die," Lily presses.

I take the flowers. "Cross my heart," I say.

"I better go make my dad something to eat," she says. "Maybe we can talk again tomorrow. Same place," she giggles. Footsteps echo across the yard, and then I hear a back door slam.

I press my head against the fence, my mind whirring. And then I take the flowers and tie them around my wrist, making a bracelet just like Lily.

Just like my Mary did, too.

I've crossed a lot of flowers in my lifetime, and there is a proven method and science to doing so. But there is nothing proven nor scientific about matters of the heart and soul.

"Cross my heart," I whisper to myself again, my voice tinged with regret. I do not bother to finish the rest of the sentiment.

PART THREE

TRILLIUM

"There is a music of immaculate love,
That breathes within the virginal veins of Spring:
And trillium blossoms, like the stars that cling
To fairies' wands."

—Madison Julius Cawein

ABBY

MAY 2003

I feel as if the world is being eaten alive.

A thick fog, which started over the lake, is creeping inland and gobbling up everything in its path. What began as a quiet, sunny morning has turned dark and ominous.

It's just like a Stephen King movie, I think, before amending my thought. *No, it's a bit too close to my reality right now.*

The wind has turned to the north, and it is noticeably cooler. I pull on the hoodie I had shucked earlier and draw my arms around my body. I had been sitting on the back porch enjoying a cup of coffee in the quiet of an early Saturday morning. I was unable to sleep, still fueled by the adrenaline of my first week at a new job, the tasks I need to finish before Monday and the overwhelming amount of work I have to do at home. There is a proposal, laundry, dishes, bills, a run to the grocery store and the ever-growing stack of paperwork for Cory.

I had been pondering what to do with my moribund yard, missing my gardens that would now be starting to bloom in my former home in Detroit.

I look into the sad backyard.

Missing my husband most of all. Before…

Before he was deployed, Cory was my counterbalance: spontaneous, funny, sexy, impulsive. He was happy, like a kid, with the simplest of things: an ice-cream cone, a sunny day, time with me. I always believed I would have a relationship the exact opposite of my parents, one in which my partner not only supported me and believed in me and my dreams but also made me a better person. Every day.

I think of the time before when Cory and I would garden. We were a team. My mind turns to Lily's sudden fascination with flowers.

Growing up, Saturdays were gardening days. But my mom and dad approached their tasks—like their lives—independently. My father tended his vegetable gardens and my mom her pots and window boxes. I was the assistant who unkinked hoses and stuffed clippings into garbage cans. I was the conduit.

I had also been sitting here watching sailboats on the horizon, mesmerized by their quiet beauty. From a distance and with their white masts, the sailboats had resembled gulls sailing above the sparkling water. That old song, "Brandy," which my father loved, had popped into my head, and I'd been singing the lyrics about a barmaid who lost her heart to a sailor who fell in love with the sea more than her.

How can I remember the lyrics to a song I haven't heard in decades but forget to put gas in the car?

But slowly the fog began to appear and thicken, seemingly

out of nowhere. The sailboats looked as if they were being erased on the horizon. And then the fog seemed to set its sights on me, the fine mist creeping across the water, the beach, the dune, my yard and, finally, through the screens on the porch. I am paralyzed as it settles atop me and drapes me in its dampness. I can barely see my hand in front of my face.

I pull an old camp blanket I purchased just for this porch and very occasion off the back of the couch and drape it over my lap. I sip my coffee and inhale its familiar scent. The fog settles into my bones and then into my soul, reminding me how tired I really am. I am exhausted from the move, the new job, the new city, the new Cory, our foggy past and our even foggier future.

March 2003

"I'm sorry. I think I have the wrong house."

I hear a door slam, and I rush from the kitchen into the foyer.

"Who was that?" I ask Lily.

"A man," she says. "He looked like a soldier."

I throw open the door; a tall, broad man in camouflage is standing with his back to the house, a duffel bag slung over his shoulder, hands on hips.

"Cory?"

He turns, takes off his sunglasses, and my heart leaps into my throat. "Abby?"

Cory drops his bag and sprints up the sidewalk to our house. He grabs me and kisses me deeply.

"Daddy?"

"Lily!" Cory says, picking her up, kissing her face and spinning her around in his arms.

"Daddy!" Lily yells, her voice a happy shriek. "You're home!"

"I'm home," he says.

"For good?" she asks.

"For good," Cory says.

Without warning, he begins to sob. Cory pulls me into his arms along with Lily and hugs us so tightly we gasp for air.

"Oh, honey," I say. "It's okay. It's okay. We're here. We love you. It's all going to be okay now."

"I wanted to surprise you, but I didn't recognize Lily," he whispers into my ear. "I didn't recognize my own daughter at first. She's grown so much. I thought I had the wrong house. I can't remember. I can't remember this life. What's wrong with me?"

Cory sets Lily on the ground and looks at her.

"How come I didn't know you?" Lily asks. "You don't look the same, either."

My heart shatters.

Cory looks at me, for the longest time, and—for the first time—I see my husband as he is now.

I don't recognize you, either, I think, my heart dropping, fighting to hold back tears.

The young man that went off to war has returned a shadow of his former self: his cheeks are sunken, his face ashen and pitted, much thinner than the hulk who set off to avenge 9/11. Only his eyes are the same: blue as the sky the day the towers came down. Blue as the day he left.

As blue as the sky the day he returned.

"Daddy's home! Daddy's home!"

Lily sings and dances around her father.

"I am, baby," he says. "I am home."

I awake with a start.

Little did I realize my own war was about to begin.

How was it before he left? I try to remember. What was life like?

Before...

My dad once said youth made him oblivious to life in his 20s. His 30s and 40s were a blur of work and raising a family, his 50s were about saving money for retirement, and his 60s were already flying by so quickly he was constantly panicked about how little time he had left. My mother, of course, ignores all of that. If we do not speak of unhappiness, my mother believes, no one is unhappy.

We all seem to be going our separate ways. Cory remains isolated, content to drink beer, watch TV and sleep on the sofa. Lily is at camp. I am at work. A family, divided.

I think of growing up, my father's big weekend breakfasts.

No, I think, *we don't have to be.*

I must be the conduit again.

I stand, fold the blanket, shake my head to wake myself up and then stretch to revive my body. I head into the kitchen and begin to make pancakes and bacon. The smells of a weekend breakfast rouse Cory and Lily before I even have to wake them.

"What's all this?" Cory asks, wiping his eyes and grabbing a mug for coffee.

"Family breakfast," I say. "Time for new routines."

"What's going on, Mommy?" Lily asks, shuffling in her footed pajamas, rubbing her eyes, her hair standing on end.

"Fuel for a busy day," I say, plopping two pancakes and a slice of bacon on her plate. "We're going for a hike today. And then a garden center."

"What?" they both ask at the same time.

"Family time," I say, not giving them time to whine or complain. "Syrup and butter are on the table."

"Tigers are on this afternoon," Cory says.

I turn, spatula in midair, and glare at him. "Family time," I say, stretching each word for emphasis. "We all need some fresh air and time together."

Cory nods and stuffs a forkful of pancake into his mouth.

After breakfast I hurriedly rinse the dishes but, against my better nature, leave them in the sink. If I let too much time pass, Cory and Lily will be doing something else.

I throw on jeans, sneakers and a sweatshirt that reads Lake Michigan: No Salt, No Sharks! I grab a hiking backpack and fill its reservoir with cold water and toss some trail mix and energy bars into the pack, along with bug spray and suntan lotion.

Always both the realist and the optimist, Abby, I think.

"Where are we going, Mommy?" Lily asks once we're in the car.

Good question, I think to myself. *I hadn't thought that far ahead.*

As I'm driving, I suddenly have a visceral memory of childhood. On pretty summer weekends, my father would suddenly load the family into the wagon and take off with no explanation, yelling only, "Grab your swimsuit!" And then he would drive, usually north or west, to the myriad unique resort towns that dotted Michigan's coastline.

"The beauty of living in Michigan," he would say, windows down, the wind barely ruffling his slicked-back hair, "is that you never have to go on vacation. Vacation surrounds you."

One weekend we went to a town called Saugatuck, a quaint artists' colony nestled in the dunes of Lake Michigan. We played on the beach, hiked and went on the Dunes Ride, a hair-raising buggy ride through the towering sand dunes.

"We'll know when we get there," I say, finally answering Lily's question. "You know, the beauty of living in Michigan is that you never have to go on vacation. Vacation surrounds you."

Lily claps and Cory turns the radio up on a report about the ground fighting that continues.

"Let yourself have one day," I say softly to him. "One day where the only thing in the world that matters is us."

Cory nods and turns down the radio, but does not turn it off.

I head south, through the mist, and follow the signs until I pull down a heavily wooded road. There is a gravel parking area that is largely empty, and I park.

"Where are we?" Lily asks.

"Saugatuck Dunes State Park," I say. "Dunes to hike. All paths lead to the lake."

"Yeah!" Lily yells.

We jump out, grab our stuff and head onto a dirt path that quickly turns to sand. Less than two minutes into our hike, we are already deep into the woods, the path now soft and covered in pine needles. The fog thickens.

"Look!" Lily says. She exhales, and her breath hangs in the air, a puff that slowly becomes one with the fog.

There is no one on the trails, and it feels as if we are in an adventure movie, lost and trying to find our way back to civilization. The three of us walk in silence as the path meanders deeper into the state park, Lily scampering ahead of us every so often, me calling her back as soon as her tiny body disappears in the fog. Cory is eerily silent. In the past he would have been chattering nonstop, like the squirrels. After about twenty minutes, we begin to climb straight up a wooded dune. Cory and I finally look at each other, our faces red, our eyes wide in disbelief that our bodies could betray us this early in our lives.

"I was in such good shape in the military," Cory says. "Before..."

Images of his sculpted body—hard and muscular like a Greek sculpture—invade my mind.

"I used to run 10ks when we first met," I say.

Cory shakes his head as if to say, "What happened?" I want to say, "Life happened," but I hear Lily yell, "Mommy! Look!"

I jog up to find Lily standing in the midst of a massive dune.

A small sign reads The Bowl, and I remember standing here with my parents as a kid.

"I'd forgotten this was here," I say.

The Bowl is, quite literally, a giant bowl made of sand, most likely carved by glaciers and once existing as a small lake. It is spectacularly beautiful to be standing in the middle of a massive, real-life terrarium. It is also spiritually and physically overwhelming to be reduced to a tiny fragment of the world and reminded of just how small each of us really is. I shut my eyes.

"Ssshhh," I say to Cory and Lily. "Listen."

The wind whistles across the dune, making the sand sing. I feel as if I'm standing in the middle of a sound bath and someone is playing a crystal bowl. The sound is both comforting and magical. I open my eyes, and Lily is scampering up the towering dune, her feet churning through the deep sand, her body making little progress. Cory and I trudge up to Lily, take her hands and begin our ascent, taking breaks every thirty seconds or so to catch our breath. Though it is cool, we are drenched in sweat and covered in sand by the time we reach the top.

"Mommy! Daddy! Look!" Lily says.

I finally look up. Lake Michigan spans before us. There is a glint of sun on the horizon, and as we stand atop the world, we watch the fog dissipate, the warmth of the sun gulping up the mist as if it were dying of thirst. I smile, taking Mother Nature's demonstration as a hint. I pull the tube from the backpack and hand it to Lily, who takes a long drink. She hands it to Cory, who drinks before handing it to me.

Without warning, Cory yells, "C'mon!" He grabs Lily's hand and runs down the dune toward the lake, both of them screaming in glee. I watch, stunned by Cory's sudden burst of spontaneity. I follow, a bit more slowly, and we walk along the lakeshore, picking up lucky stones and pretty rocks as we go. Lily chases seagulls, her arms out as if in flight. Slowly, the sun warms the shoreline, and we stop to have lunch. On our hike back, we take a different route through a more deeply wooded area of the state park. In the middle, the trees are so dense, they choke out the sunlight. Gigantic, two-foot-tall ferns—thick and green—fill the woods along the path.

"It's like we're in Jurassic Park!" Lily says. "I can't wait to see it next month!"

Ferns turn into fields of blooming May apples.

"Do dinosaurs live here?" Lily asks in complete seriousness. "Or gnomes?"

It does look like a perfect place for either: foot-and-a-half-tall waxy green plants that look like miniature tropical trees stand guard. Two broad leaves swoop from each May apple's stalk, and a single, pretty, small white flower blooms in the fork of each plant.

"I have to take a picture," I say, nabbing my little camera from the backpack. "It's so magical."

While I snap photos, Lily and Cory walk ahead.

"Mommy, look!" Lily says yet again, repeating her favorite phrase to capture my attention.

I walk quickly along the path and stop cold. A thicket of white flowers covers wide sections of the forest floor.

No, not really a thicket, I realize, *but a carpet of white and green.*

"What are they, Mommy?" Lily asks.

"Notice how she doesn't ask me?" Cory asks with a big smile. I laugh at his joke: his sense of humor has disappeared along with most of the other traits with which I fell in love. It's nice to see even a glimpse of it again.

I know this one, I think, *remembering the beautiful heart flowers I couldn't name the other morning. Every Michigander should know this one.*

um," I say.

...y name," Lily says.

I kneel down and look at the trillium: elegant three-petal white blossoms seem to float from three dense green leaves that resemble tiny hostas.

Lily reaches out to touch one of the flowers.

"Don't pick any!" I say, my tone startling her. "Sorry, sweetie. But I think these are protected in Michigan. They're very fragile."

Trillium bloom, depending on the weather, from late April to early June, emerging in Michigan's forests or heavily wooded areas. Michiganders consider them a harbinger of spring, but I always considered them a harbinger of hope, the first sign that winter was over and beauty was about to be reborn across the state.

"Family photo time," I say, motioning Cory and Lily over to me. We pose in front of the trillium, and I hand the camera to Cory. "You got the wingspan," I say. He extends his long arm to encompass the carpet of trillium behind us.

Lily takes pictures of flowers and trees the remainder of the hike to show her fellow summer campers and makes up songs about them—"Trillium Are Sillium" and "Sweet, Sweet, Sugar Maples"—which elicit lots of laughter and head-scratching from me and Cory. As soon as we get Lily buckled up in the back seat, Cory says, "I'll drive."

My heart stops for a split second. He has rarely driven a car with me and Lily as passengers since his return from Iraq. I always drive. He only drives if he's in the car by himself. I nod and hand him the keys. I watch him closely. He notices immediately and gives me a confident shake of his head. I act not only as if I wasn't just staring but also as if nothing has happened, and I click on my Blackberry.

The SUV bumps over the rocky drive out of the park.

There is a text from my mother, the *Queen of Ignore the Elephant in the Room* and *Princess of Pretend Everything is Okay Even When Your World is Falling Apart.*

Is Cory enjoying the game? Tigers up big!

My mother once thought smartphones were the downfall of civilization. Now she texts more than a teenage girl.

Went on a family hike. Wonderful day together.

I wait, knowing my mom is furiously typing something with her thumbs. This could take hours, I think, knowing how slowly my mom types. My heart booms in my chest, and I take a deep breath to steady myself.

Why would you take that man's Saturday from him? He loves the Tigers. Just needs a normal weekend.

Normal weekend?

I shake my head and steady my thumb. I type So do we! Then I take another breath and erase it. Talk later, Mom. Driving.

I stare out the window. A small billboard for a local furniture store shows a happy family snuggled on a new sofa watching TV, the mom holding a tray of cookies.

That's how my mom views the world, I imagine. *Fake advertising.*

Irony of ironies, my mom's name is June. Just like June Cleaver. The quintessential mom from *Leave it to Beaver*, which I watched in reruns after school for years, along with *Happy Days* and *The Brady Bunch.*

And my mom was the quintessential mom.

When I was a child, I add.

June made me three-tier birthday cakes with moving carousels on top. She was my classroom mother *every single year.* She taught me to bake and sew and do all the things little girls are supposed to do when they want to be just like their mothers. The only problem was I didn't want to be just like my mom. I loved her, but I wanted more. Out of everything. I think of my dad, who cheated on my mother for years. She knew and still stayed with him.

"How would it reflect on the family?" she always asked me.

No, Mom, how would it reflect on you? Even though you did nothing wrong. The ultimate secret keeper.

When I took AP science, she suggested I take home ec. When I took calculus, she asked how I would ever meet a nice boy if I *acted* smarter than they were. And when I got into college, she said, "At least we're investing in finding you a husband."

She was thrilled when I met Cory. He was a stereotypical Michigan man: strong, tall and blond. He was majoring in business. I didn't know he was in the ROTC until I'd been dating him a few months.

Secrets, I think. *Cory was as good at secrets as my mom.*

And my mom was actually thrilled when Cory went to Iraq. He was a man's man. I was now a military wife. I would put my silliness aside for the sake of my husband.

The car jolts to a stop. Cory has pulled off to the side of the road just before we are about to merge onto the highway.

"I can't," he says.

I reach out and grab his hand.

I take another deep breath for what I'm about to do. I am not my mother. I cannot be my mother. I cannot be a secret keeper, nor can my husband.

"I'm so, so sorry," I say. I inhale. "But I can't, either." I stop. "What happened?"

"I don't want to talk about it," he says.

"You have to, Cory," I say. "You're not well. If you don't want to talk about it with me, you have to talk about it with a counselor."

Cory looks at me and shakes his head.

"Please," I beg.

"I was driving," he finally says, his hands gripping the steering wheel so tightly his knuckles are turning white. "We were in the middle of a sandstorm. Couldn't see more than a few feet in front of me. The tank in front of us hit a land mine. I swerved but caught part of a mine, too."

Cory drops his hands from the steering wheel. I can see they're shaking. He looks at me, his mouth a maw of grief. I reach out and grab his arm. "I'm so, so sorry," I say. "Why didn't you ever tell me?"

"No one else needs to experience it," he says.

"I'm your wife," I say. "Your heart and soul." I stop. "I am. I am experiencing it."

"I know," he says. Then, without warning, he is bawling, big tears plopping off the steering wheel. "I can't do it alone. I've been trying to do it all alone."

"I know," I say, reaching over and wiping his tears. "Me, too."

"Help me," he says.

"I will. But you're right, we can't do it alone. You have to talk with someone, Cory. A professional. I'll go with you."

Cory shakes his head. "No," he says. "I can't. No matter how many times the military requests it." He stops and looks at me. "No matter how many times you ask. It's just not in my DNA."

I look at him. I begin to nod, to appease my husband, but I am not a secret keeper, I think again. It's not in *my* DNA.

"I'm not asking anymore, Cory," I say. "I'm telling you.

You have to go talk to someone. I love you, but that's not enough to help you through this. It's not enough to help any of us through this." I stop and motion to the back seat. Lily is, thankfully, fast asleep. I lower my voice. "We're all suffering from PTSD. I'm anxious all the time. Lily is nervous around you. We're all waiting around for something bad to happen. Something has to change. Or we're not going to make it."

Cory exhales with all his might, and his shoulders sag as if all the weight in the world has been removed. "Okay," he says. "Okay."

This time I cry without warning, and he reaches over to hold me.

We quietly switch seats, and I drive home. On the highway, Cory grabs my hand and holds it until we pull in the driveway, me thinking of trillium the entire way, of how we are all just like them, so fragile, so in need of protection, but also, always, a harbinger of hope.

IRIS

MAY 2003

I run my finger along the inside of the mixing bowl. I lift my finger to my mouth and taste.

Perfect!

I stop the old pink mixer I still own—the one that sounds as loud as a trash truck—and lift the top. I remove the beaters and stand over the sink, licking the buttercream frosting from each one until they are clean.

Just like you used to do, my beautiful girl.

The frosting is rich, dense and intensely sweet, and its taste catapults me back in time. *I remember all of the birthday cakes I made for you, and how much you loved this particular cake: homemade funfetti with vanilla buttercream frosting.* It wasn't called funfetti back then, of course. I called it Mary's Magical May Birthday Cake, and I used special sprinkles to brighten the white cake.

But that wasn't all that made it magical, was it, my sweet?

I remove some of the frosting and place it into two separate bowls. I add some green food coloring to one and yellow to another. I frost the cake with the rich icing and then fill three piping bags with green, yellow and white icing, before adding my tips.

The sun has yet to rise, and I look out my kitchen window over the lake. A small line of light rims the horizon.

"You better hurry up, Iris," I tell myself.

I turn on every lamp and light in the kitchen to help my eyes, adjust my two pairs of glasses as if I'm about to perform surgery, and then I stop and take a deep breath to steady my growingly unsteady hands. My hands now have a mind and spirit of their own, tremoring even when I fully concentrate on making them cease. I mouth a small prayer and lower a bag with green icing over the cake.

I do not stop. I know if I lift the bag, or analyze my work too closely, I will be doomed. I work without a guide, utilizing only my years of painting, and, thankfully, my muscles seem to follow along by rote memory.

I switch the bag of green icing for the bag of white, before finishing with the yellow.

When I finally lift my hand and step back, I smile.

You still got it, old girl!

A carpet of trillium is spread out atop the cake.

I lay down the bag of icing and lift a wavering palm to my mouth, but it's too late: a mournful wail sadder than that of any lonely loon escapes from the very pit of my soul, and I lower myself over the sink and sob. When I finally lift my head, I can see the rim of light on the horizon expanding. It's now a roll of yellow ribbon. I take a deep breath to steady myself and then cut two slices of cake, wrapping them tightly in foil with two plastic forks. I wash the knife, open my grandmother's old bread box that now holds—*No! Hides, rather*—my endless array of vitamins, essential oils and medications. I do not like to take medication. I do not trust doctors, who give pills to mask a problem rather than getting to the root of it.

I look over at the cake and think of Mary.

I prefer to focus on the root—the actual roots—and rely on plant-based vitamins, minerals and oils to address my aging body. I fish a hand into the old bread box, which used to hold fresh, doughy slices of Bunny Bread and an assortment of Little Debbie snack cakes.

Just not today, I think. *I need my medication.*

I pull out a bottle of anxiety medication and spend nearly two minutes trying to open the childproof cap. That's the thing about aging: every cap and lid and tab is a cruel joke. Their name is a lie: they're not childproof. Children and their nimble, limber fingers could open these in a flash. No, they're old-age proof.

Everything betrays you as you age: your fingers, your eyes, your mind, your skin, your memory, your legs, your back.

But the cruelest betrayer is time, which keeps on soldiering forward no matter how much you wish you could slide it in reverse. I hear the kitty-cat clock tick-tock in the background, eyes moving left, tail right, eyes right, tail left.

I reach for a big, old rubber band I keep in a drawer for occasions like this. I wrap it around the lid and—*Voila!*—it pops right off.

I grab the cake knife and chop the pill in two.

Just enough to get me there, I think.

I down it with no water, and then dash into the bedroom, pulling on some thick corduroys and a green-and-white Michigan State sweatshirt.

Spring green! Go, Green!

I pull on my sneakers, grab the cake and head for the screened porch. Just as I am about to leave, I stop and retreat, grabbing what I'd forgotten.

What was it I'd just said about the memory?

I head in the still-dark morning into my backyard and toward the gate that heads to the beach. When I reach it, I stop, my heart in my throat.

You can do this, I determine. *You must do this. Once a year, that's it.*

I open the gate, and the world in front of me—the beach, the lake, the sky—kaleidoscope. I grab the fence, nearly dropping the cake, and steady myself.

This is my annual pilgrimage. The one trip I intentionally take outside my gardens.

I take a step, stop, shut the gate and take another. I stop again, waiting for the world to stop spinning and for the pill to take effect. I shut my eyes, breathe and run my hand along the familiar feel of my fence, counting the slats until I'm at the end. I open my eyes and remove my hand from my fence. I feel akin to John Glenn and, for a few seconds I am free, floating, my feet not seeming to touch the earth.

There is a mulched pathway, a common trail, for the community that runs along the top of the dune and behind Highland Park's historic cottages. I helped create this same path decades ago for my neighbors and friends, hacking through tree roots and whacking dune grass until my hands were raw and my arms bloody. I have few allergies, but my skin turns raw and welted when I come in contact with any ornamental grasses. I hear a loud crunch, and I stop in my tracks. I look down: a broken branch lies under my foot. I shake my head and chuckle to slow my heart.

Now the only things I'm allergic to are people, I muse.

This path was sort of a Yellow Brick Road for my neighbors: if we needed anything—sugar, butter, eggs, a hug—this little path served as an extended welcome mat.

I look up and see the path swerve unevenly atop the dune in the first light.

This little path served as an entryway to the baseball field and a runway to our Victory Garden.

I make my way along the path, still wet and spongy from the winter snow and spring rain. I like the way the Norway maple saplings I planted so long ago have created a canopy over the pathway, something I envisioned but never dreamed I'd live to see realized. Moreover, their first spring leaves emerge in blazing red, basking the path in an ethereal light, making every spring walk on the path like walking at sunrise or sunset.

These days few Highland Park residents see these leaves of red. They are true summer resorters who show up on Memorial Day—when these maples are deep green and the temperatures have warmed—to open their cottages. They return again on the Fourth of July with family and friends to barbecue and drink wine and then again in August for a week of vacation. The curtains on these cottages often close again for good on Labor Day, before these maples' leaves have even turned golden.

This is a world of transients now. We can come and go, travel at will these days. I stop and run a hand over the trunk of a maple.

Unlike you, I think. *Unlike me. There is something about planting our roots somewhere. Forever. No matter how difficult the seasons.*

The path takes a severe right at the last cottage, and I follow it to a fenced plot of land. I open the gate, shushing the handle as it squeaks, and shut it behind me.

Now it's just you and me, my dear.

The rows of tomatoes, carrots, lettuce, beets and peas are

long gone. Sad grass grows in the sparse light the towering oaks and sugar maples allow to filter through. This is officially an association park now, but one that no one uses. There is no sign marking its history, either as a baseball field or Victory Garden, no sign marking it as a park.

There is no sign of life here anymore.

Until I shut my eyes.

The wind whispers through the emerging leaves, and I can hear Shirley laughing, Mary playing, the crack of Jonathan's bat, whistle of the baseball and the excited screams of the crowd as he rounds the bases.

I open my eyes, and there is nothing.

Ghosts, Iris. Only ghosts.

I head toward the only occupant of the park: a bowed, wooden bench with a metal back featuring rusting hummingbirds. I dragged it here years ago. I set down the cake on the bench and head into the corner of the park where the maple and oaks are the thickest. The wind has blown all of the leaves into this corner, and they sit—caught—in a wet clump. I begin to kick at the top of the leaves with both of my feet and then lean down and claw at them with my hands, like a dog trying to bury a bone. I gasp out loud when I see them, my cry cutting the silence of the morning quiet.

You're still here, I think. *Still alive.*

I lean down and clear all the leaves, broken branches and clumps of dirt away until they are free.

My trillium! I think. *Our trillium!*

I run a trembling hand over the beautiful blossoms and smile.

Trillium were Mary's favorite flower, a symbol of her birthday. To me they represented a symbol of her purity and—at one time, long ago—a symbol of hope.

"You came to me after a long winter of hibernation," I used

to tell Mary when we would hike in April and admire the trillium, which were among the first signs of spring in Michigan. "You're just like the trillium. You represent eternal hope."

After Jonathan died, Mary and I found some "volunteers" from the state park. That's what my mother used to call plants and flowers she'd transplant without someone's permission: volunteers. Trillium are a protected wildflower in Michigan, as they are very fragile. All variety of trillium were once protected by an old law called the Christmas Greens Act, passed to keep people from overcollecting them. Most people only know of the white trillium, but there are many varieties, a few of which are still protected under the State Endangered Species Act.

Should I have moved those trillium? No. Would I do it again? Yes. Because they are the only living symbol I have of Mary and Jonathan, my family, in this sacred spot now.

Without thinking, I take a seat on the damp ground. I can feel the wet earth seep through my pants, but I don't care. Trillium are often called the trinity flower because of their perfect symmetry: three leaves, three sepals, three petals. Nature's perfection.

I again think of Mary. Her face was perfectly symmetrical, too, almost like a doll: strong nose and chin, soft, round cheeks and two violet eyes set equidistant apart.

I stop and shut my eyes, my heart racing.

Was it? Is that what she looked like?

I gasp, which causes squirrels to scamper over the fence and up the trees.

Sometimes I can picture Mary as if she never left me, and sometimes I struggle to remember her features.

I open my eyes. Ironically, I, too, am like the trillium, but in the most different ways: I am so, so fragile. I do not do well when I am moved. And, come July, when the weather turns dry and the forests' trees begin to use all of the soil's moisture, trillium take the easy way out and go dormant.

Just like I did.

I shut my eyes even tighter and try to picture my daughter, imagine her with me here right now.

MAY 1947

"You be my lookout, okay? Just let me know if someone is coming?"

"How? What do I do?"

"I don't know," I say. "Make a bird call. Like a whip-poor-will."

Mary looks at me. "I can barely whistle."

I put my lips together and call. *Whip-poor-willllll! Whip-poor-willlll!*

Mary looks around nervously, her violet eyes wide, and giggles. "I feel just like Nancy Drew!"

It is a beautiful morning, filled with the sounds of summer on the lake: waves crash, birds sing and a soft breeze carries the screams of children jumping into a still-brisk Lake Michigan. It is nearing Mary's birthday, her third since her father left us.

I eye the trillium in the middle of the woods.

Time marches on.

I look at Mary, her eyes growing even wider, and smile. There is a beautiful wildflower, beach pea, that grows along the Michigan shorelines. They grow right out of the sand, delicate purple flowers that resemble violets blooming off dense green, trailing bushes. The blooms are the color of Mary's eyes. She *is* a Michigan girl.

I put my finger over my mouth and head toward the trillium. I lift the tail of my shirt and produce a spade and some wet paper towels from the back pockets of my trousers. I begin to dig up the trillium, going as slowly and carefully as I can so as not to disturb the plant or the ones around it. I wrap them in paper towels and then place them in the back of my trousers again, my skin jumping at the cool dampness.

Whip-poor-willlll!

My heart leaps, and I drop my spade. I look up, and Mary is bent over laughing.

"Gotcha!" she laughs.

"You little minx," I say, picking up the spade and rushing over to softly swat her on the rear with it. "Why'd you do that?"

"To see you smile," she says. "You need to smile more."

My heart melts, and I wrap her in my arms and kiss the top of her head. She smells like sunshine and little girl, sugar and spice. My mind turns, suddenly thinking of the birthday cake we need to make.

"You ready to hike back? We need to make your birthday cake."

Mary nods and rushes ahead, jumping over fallen branches

that litter the hiking path. We walk for a few moments when Mary comes racing back to show me a pinecone she found.

"Pretty," I say. "Are you going to keep it?"

She turns and walks backward in front of me for a few seconds, before stopping. I stop walking. "Are you okay?" I ask.

She looks up at me, her eyes filled with tears.

"Oh, sweetheart," I say. "What is it? What's wrong?"

"I used to collect pinecones with Daddy, remember?"

I had forgotten until now.

"You used to flock them and put them on the Christmas tree," I say, memories flooding back.

"I'm having trouble remembering him anymore," Mary says, her voice soft and vulnerable. "What he looked like, what he sounded like…" Her voice trails off and her eyes fill with tears that plunk onto the ground like raindrops.

"I know," I say. I kneel down until I'm face-to-face with her. "The only thing that matters is that you remember how much he loved you. And that memory will never fade. It will live right in here forever." I put my hand on Mary's heart.

She looks into my eyes and says, "I think I'll keep this pinecone. For this year's tree."

I nod. "I think that's a grand idea."

When we get home I race to the park and plant the trillium before making Mary's birthday cake. Though wartime rationing has ended, I still have difficulty wasting a thing, so I make the cake I always made for Mary and Jonathan on their birthdays: a One-Egg Victory Cake. I got it out of a cookbook the church handed out when rationing and scarcity ruled our country, and the American homemaker had to be smart on how to feed a family without using up too many staples. The cake requires only the smallest amounts of shortening, sugar, vanilla extract, corn syrup, milk, cake flour, baking powder, salt and—of course—a single egg. I add sprinkles to make it pretty and "fun." Mary helps me with the cake and when we slide it into the oven, I take her hand and lead her to my bedroom. I pat the mattress, and Mary jumps on the bed. I join her, her smaller body sliding toward mine until our bodies are touching.

"I can still feel your father beside me in this bed," I say, my voice barely audible. "But I can't smell him on the pillows anymore and…" I stop and breathe deeply. "There are some times where I nearly go all day without thinking of him." I reach over and grab two photos from the nightstand. "I've lost too many too early in my life," I continue. "My parents and grandmother. My husband. I never thought the world would change so much in so little time." I hand Mary the photo of me and Jonathan in front of my mother's hydrangeas. "I was so pregnant with you in this picture. Do you see how much he loved you, even then?"

Mary traces her finger over her father. "I do," she says.

"I live for you now," I say. "The fact that you will have children of your own and that you will continue our family gives me hope and strength. I can see my future in you."

Mary looks at me and then the photo. She places her finger on the hydrangea and then points at the peony in the picture. "What about your flowers?" she asks.

"They give me hope, too. I can see the future in them, as well."

"Is that why you dug them all up from Grandma's house next door? So you can see them all the time?"

I nod.

"Is that why you rent out the house next door?" she continues. "So you won't feel so all alone?"

I nod again.

"Everyone is gone. It's just us."

Mary looks at the photo one more time and hands it back

to me. "No, it's not," she says with a definitive nod of her head. She gestures at the photos in my hands and then to the ones on the bedroom walls. "They're still here." She puts her little hand on my heart. "And here."

"You're right," I say. "Now, let's go decorate your cake."

Mary jumps off the bed in one bound and puts a hand to her head as if she's in deep thought. "I got it!" she says.

"Got what?" I ask, returning the photos to the nightstand.

"You know how you always decorate my cake in trillium? Well, next time we make Daddy's birthday cake it should be decorated in peach roses. I mean, you invented them for him. And they will live forever, right?"

She extends a hand and helps me off the bed. "Right!" I say.

The light grows on the trillium, turning their showy white blooms into spring's wedding dress, and I know I must hurry. I stand and wipe my backside, grab the cake off the bench and unwrap it.

I pull my nearly forgotten bounty from my pocket.

I place a birthday candle in the middle of the cake and light it with a match. *I shut my eyes and can hear your happy giggles.* I make a wish—one I know will never come true—and blow. I set the cake in the midst of the trillium, barely able to distinguish it from the flowers.

"Happy birthday, my angel," I say. "Give your daddy a kiss for me. I love you."

PART FOUR

IRIS

"Thou art the Iris, fair among the fairest."

—Henry Wadsworth Longfellow

ABBY

MAY 2003

The conference room is dappled with light.

Whitmore Paints sits in a 1970s office building between a secondary road just off the highway and a small interior lake that is fed by a river from Lake Michigan. However, there is nothing retro or cool about this '70s design: it has none of the midcentury charm that has become so hip of late nor any of that funky *Brady Bunch* vibe. It's more like my old grade school: linoleum tile, harvest-gold carpet, claustrophobic drop ceiling tiles, fluorescent lighting and windows hung with thick brown curtains and dusty, dented blinds.

"Good morning!" I say. "Morning, Phil. Good morning, Mr. Whitmore."

When I enter, the men are clustered in a corner with their

company coffee cups laughing and talking about their golf games. Two women—one older, one younger—are seated at opposite ends of the table, laptops open in front of them.

"Good morning, Abby," Mr. Whitmore says.

I wait for a question to be directed toward me: *How was your weekend, Abby? Are you getting settled? How's your daughter doing? Let me give you some ideas on what to do in Grand Haven, okay?*

None come.

In many ways this feels like my grade- and high-school days. The boisterous boys clustered in a corner fluffing their feathers while the girls sit meekly at their desks ready to get to work. I take a seat and nod at the two assistants.

"Would you like a cup of coffee?" Tammy asks.

"No, thank you," I say. "One more cup, and I'll be as jittery as a June bug." Tammy smiles. "My grandma used to say that. Always stuck with me." I stop. "And, by the way, I can get my own coffee. You never need to do that."

Tammy's face flushes. "Thank you," she whispers.

I look back at my coworkers.

No, this reminds me of college and graduate school.

I was often the only woman in some of my engineering classes. "Are you in the right class?" I was often asked by the men. "Education building is just down from here."

I open my laptop, and my reflection returns a dumbfounded gaze.

I am not most men's fantasy, the stereotypical American beauty. I am what many might call "handsome," or even "patrician." My features are strong, regal, like my grandmother and grandfather, but I've intentionally hardened my look over the years in order to be taken seriously. The glasses, the haircut, the pantsuits.

I look around as the men gather at the conference table.

And yet, I'm still a unicorn. I'm still the only female engineer at the table.

"Let's get this meeting started," Mr. Whitmore begins in a deep voice similar to Donald Sutherland's.

The meeting always starts with the business director, a red-faced man with a buzz cut and zero personality. In my first few weeks he has yet to look at me, much less address me.

As he drones on, my eyes return to the dappled light in the room.

Lily used to have one of those night-lights in her bedroom that spun stars on the ceiling and around all the walls. I would lie in bed with her, and we would both watch the show wide-eyed as if we were front and center for the northern lights. I pulled it back out when Cory was overseas. Neither of us could sleep, and Lily would constantly ask, "Where's Daddy?" I would point up at the stars and tell her, "He's looking at the same stars we are," and she would finally fall asleep.

The conference room is glass on three sides, and the sunlight's reflection off the water as well as the windshields of passing cars gives the dull room a magical air.

"Abby?"

My heart leaps. *Busted.*

"Here!" I say, raising my hand as if I was in school, trying to cover with a joke. No one laughs.

"Your paints are holding up well in our tests so far," Mr. Whitmore says, shuffling through a pile of papers. "And marketing is reporting that consumers are reacting very positively to your new color line. But we have a few questions regarding that. Pete?"

I take a breath to steel myself.

Pete is head of marketing. He's a former Caltech whiz kid whose family, I hear, owns a few hundred acres of prime beachfront property that they want to develop although they've been thwarted numerous times so far by conservancy groups and the state. Pete is all slick hair and vacation tan, booming voice and capped teeth. He oozes confidence. He literally swaggers in his chair. He asked me in my interview if I planned to have more children. The room spun when he asked me that, but I kept my mouth shut and shook my head.

Why didn't I report him? I think. *Oh, yeah. I needed this job. I needed a stable home. These are the decisions women face every day. Ethics vs. career. And when we fight back, we are called liars.*

"I'm just not jibing with some of your proposed colors and names," Pete says. "What is this...this—" Pete stops and shuffles through his papers. He looks up, a virtual sneer planted on his face "—this *Iris* color. Does anyone know what color a Summer Iris is? I mean, men own boats. They won't paint it Iris, Abby." He looks through his papers again and laughs. "Or Pink Peony?" He looks around the table. "I mean, c'mon. Bob, would you buy Pink Peony? Frank, I can't really see you taking your Purple Phlox boat out for a ride with the boys and a few beers, can you?"

The men chuckle and nod.

I nod at Pete as if he's just made the most valid point in the world. "I understand your concerns," I start. "But the National Women Boaters Association reports that nearly a quarter of all boat owners are now women. Moreover, 85 percent of women make the purchasing decisions for their families."

"Not mine," Pete says with a laugh.

I wait for the group to self-correct Pete, but none of the men do. They nod and chuckle and shuffle their papers. I narrow my eyes and smile. If I don't smile, the men will think I'm a bitch, and I'll get nowhere here.

"Must explain the way you dress then, Pete," I say.

Every man's head shoots up, and then Mr. Whitmore bursts out in laughter.

"I was wondering about that tie myself," he says.

Pete's face turns as red as the convertibles on his cheap, midlife crisis of a tie, and I can literally see steam shooting forth from his ears like in a cartoon.

"Let's look at the way Benjamin Moore or Sherwin-Williams markets their paints today," I continue. "Even car companies. Or the influence that HGTV has had on the way consumers consider color. Nothing is red or white or yellow anymore. White is Chantilly Lace or Swiss Coffee. Red is Caliente. It sets a mood, a feeling, and that's what I'm trying to do with these colors. That's what we need to do with these colors. I guarantee you, men's names may be on the title for the majority of pleasure boats but it's the women who put their signatures all over the boat's interior and exterior. And we're not just marketing a new color line. We're inventing a new market."

A few of the men nod. "But you still haven't answered my question. What color is an iris?"

"What color is a rainbow, Pete?"

"What does that mean?"

I look at the light and then at Pete. "Well, let me explain it like I do to my daughter, Pete."

A few of the men catcall and rib Pete, but I stop them. "I mean that in a complimentary way, actually, because my daughter is one of the brightest humans on this planet." I stop. "I'm probably one of the few engineers to study Greek mythology in college, but I did because it fascinated me. The flower gets its name from the ancient Greek goddess, Iris, the Messenger of Love. Greeks believed she used the rainbow as a bridge between heaven and earth and that the rainbow was actually her flowing, multicolored robes and the many-colored iris were the flowing veil. Greek men often planted an iris on the graves of women as a tribute to Iris and to mark where she could find the women in order to take their souls to heaven. The flower was named in honor of her and to bring favor on the earth." I stop. Pete's eyes are wide.

"And?" Pete asks in a bluster.

"I think if we put a beautiful narrative with the paints, it will entice buyers," I say. "Iris would be a paint color that symbolizes love. Iris bloom in many colors—purple, blue, yellow, white, pink, red, chartreuse, brown and black. For instance, purple iris symbolize royalty. Blue is symbolic of hope and faith. Yellow symbolizes passion. White expresses purity. This could be part of a summer line of flower-inspired colors. I think women would eat this up." I stop. "And I think men would, too."

Pete opens his mouth to say something, by his expression I assume something demeaning or derogatory, but Mr. Whitmore cuts him off. "Outstanding work, Abby. You are truly an engineer in the brain but an artist at heart." He smiles. "And likely a darn good gardener, too, I'm guessing."

"Thank you," I say.

After the meeting wraps up, Tammy sidles up next to me after the room has cleared and says, "You were amazing. You handled Pete really well."

"Thanks," I say, before lowering my voice. "I was about to tell him he should paint his boat Iris Yellow because I'm sure his wife could use all the help she can get."

Tammy lets out a huge laugh that echoes through the now-empty conference room, before clamping a hand over it. "It's nice to have you on board," she says.

"I appreciate that," I say. "And good reference for here—on board."

Tammy smiles and leaves me alone in the room. I gather my laptop, calendar and papers. The light plays across the room, and I stop and watch it for a second.

Always claim your light, Abby, I say to myself.

"Abby, Iris on line two."

Tammy's voice booms through the intercom, filling the room.

Ha-ha, I think. *Good joke, Tammy.*

"Abby, Iris on line two."

I walk over and pick up the conference room phone.

"Good one, Tammy," I say. "Very clever."

"What?" she asks. "No. No. There's really a woman named Iris calling for you on line two."

"Iris?" I ask. "I don't know an Iris. Are you sure it's for me?"

"I'm sure," Tammy says.

I click off and pick up the call.

"This is Abby Peterson," I say.

"This is Iris… Iris Maynard." It's a quavering voice that sounds as if it belongs to an older woman.

"Yes?" I prompt.

"It's your neighbor," she says. "You're renting your house from me."

"Oh," I stumble. "I'm so sorry. Is something wrong? Did you not receive our first and last month's payment?"

I can hear her breathing.

"No," she says. "Your husband and daughter were just with me."

"Is something wrong?" I ask again, hearing my voice escalate in panic.

"No," she says. "They're okay." She stops. "I mean, physically." She stops again. She is breathing heavily on the other end. "Well, they're not okay. I think we should talk. Do you have a few moments?"

"I'm about to head into another meeting," I say. "Why don't I come over after work? I can call you when I'm on the way."

"I don't really… I don't really have people in my house,"

Iris says. "Until today." There is a long, uncomfortable silence. "Fine," Iris finally says. "Call me on your way home. Here's my number." Silence again. "I'd prefer if you didn't stay too long, though."

"All right," I say, writing down her number. Iris hangs up without warning, and I immediately call Cory.

"Is everything okay?" I ask.

"I have something to tell you," he says. "Promise you won't get mad."

My head grows dizzy as I listen to Cory.

"You lied to me, Cory! You lied!"

My voice is echoing through the conference room. Two coworkers stop at the door, their bodies still, their coffee cups frozen in midair, mouths open, watching me. I rush over and shut the door.

"You promised me you would go to therapy! You promised me! You're putting Lily in danger. I can't do this anymore, Cory. You need help. I can't even go to work without worrying what might happen." I stop. "If you don't call to see someone by the time I get home tonight, then—" I stop again "—then we're going to have to make some hard decisions."

Cory is heaving on the end of the phone. "I know, I know," he says. "I will. I will."

When I hang up, I take a seat and watch the light dance across the room.

I look out the window, and a boat is being launched from our dock. As it motors into the lake, mini-rainbows are formed in the spray from the boat's mist.

"Take care of my little girl, Iris," I say to the rainbow, unsure if I'm referring to the old woman or the Greek goddess.

IRIS

MAY 2003

"Hello, ladies. My namesakes sure look lovely this morning."

I am kneeling on my cushy gardener's pad, making small talk with my flowers. One end of the garden that runs the entire length of my front yard is filled with iris of every color and variety. I grab a beautiful bearded iris.

This particular iris is called "Stairway to Heaven," and it seems perfectly named. Its flower is white and its beard a showy violet blue. In the sunlight the flower's petals do resemble a heavenly staircase leading through the sky and clouds to heaven. I stare at the flower and then look into the spring sky.

"Is there such a staircase?" I ask the flower. "Is there a heaven? Is my family waiting?"

The flower's petals shimmer in the wind, softly floating up, down and sideways.

"That's rather noncommittal," I say to the iris.

There are two types of iris: bearded and beardless. Bearded iris look, of course, as if they have a tiny beard. The "falls," the flower's drooping lower petals, are actually fuzzy. I stop and feel my chin.

"No wonder I'm named after you," I say with a laugh, giving the stem a shake.

This time of year in Michigan, there is always a gardener's battle between their favorite flower: tulip versus iris. In western Michigan, especially, tulips typically prevail due to the overwhelming Dutch ancestry present here. Holland, a resort town just south of Grand Haven, is famed for its Dutch history, its windmills and its spring Tulip Festival when thousands of tulips are in bloom. It's quite spectacular, and a Technicolor reminder that winter is over and spring has finally arrived. I adore tulips, and I have them circling the base of many of my trees, just like my mom and grandma used to do. They remind me of little, jewel-toned lollipops.

But to me, there is just something regal about an iris. They are not only colorful and beautiful but also strong and powerful. Most of my iris are tall, many towering a few feet into the air, and their size and colorful personalities literally force one to take notice.

Like children, I think.

My Mary had fanciful names for the iris just as she did her dolls. The white ones were Cinderella, the purple were named Violet, the yellow were called Tweety after the cartoon bird she so loved.

I remove my glove and dig my hand right into the wet earth. It's still cold below the surface. My hand hits a root and I admire its unique beauty, too. Iris reproduce via swollen roots, with bearded iris producing a rhizome that looks like a long potato.

I consider my iris garden to be a microcosm of the world. It is filled with every color, each more beautiful and more perfect than the other. I've always been most taken by the chocolate and black iris, moodier colors that seem to capture the flower's soul and spirit. My double chocolate bearded iris are the color of burnished leather, almost cordovan, with deeper chocolate falls and copper highlights. It's a stunner. And my deep black bearded iris is simply breathtaking.

"You know you're gorgeous, don't you, girl?" I ask it.

The flower looks like onyx in the sunlight. Its flowers and falls are ruffled like a wedding dress, and it is undeniably sexy, a Georgia O'Keeffe painting come to life.

I stand with some effort, my knees popping and my lower back trying to go AWOL on the rest of my body, and stop midstoop. I look over my iris. My heart races in excitement and then falls in sadness.

"Which of you ladies wants to come inside and brighten my home?" I ask.

My grandma's gardens were all designated as cutting gardens. Her flowers were meant to beautify not only her garden but also her home. She filled her rooms with flowers every week, every month, every season, from the first daffodils to the final mums. Even in winter my grandma's home was filled with greenery: pine and holly branches tucked on the mantel and into window boxes. I have her Christmas cactus, which I have babied for decades and which still blooms every holiday season. I would estimate that cactus to be nearly fifty years old now. Gardeners would laugh in my face if I told them that, but it's true.

I remember the exact day it came into my life, I reflect.

"Your home should bloom in every season just like your garden," my grandma used to say.

I reach into my "kangaroo pouch," retrieving a pair of clippers from my gardening belt. I snip a few purple and yellow, which I always think look so pretty and happy together and which will be perfect in the kitchen. Then I cut two chocolate, two black and two white, which will make a dramatic arrangement for my worktable on the screened porch. I walk them inside, lay them on the drain board of my old farmhouse sink and head to the corner cabinet in the dining room.

"Darn humidity!" I say, hitting the edge of the cabinet just so with the palm of my hand to pop it open. "Voila!"

An array of vintage McCoy pottery sits before me. I grab two tall vases—one white, one aqua—to hold the towering iris, retreat to the kitchen and fill them with water. I snip the ends of the iris at an angle and arrange them in the vases.

"Thank you for blessing my home," I say to each arrangement as I place them in the kitchen and on the screened porch before heading back outside.

I return to the ground, digging my bare hands into the soil. I love the earth in my hands, the feel and smell of it. If I meet a gardener who tells me they don't, or who says they hate to weed, mulch or deadhead, I will know they are not a true gardener. There is something about those acts that not only ground me to the earth but also prepare it for what is to come. It's like cleaning your house for a party: it allows it to show off its best side. Moreover, it keeps the garden in its best shape.

We all have to shake off that extra winter snow, I think.

I pull out clumps of leaves still trapped from the winter's wind and toss them into the yard. I grab my wheelbarrow, walk it to the backyard and fill it with the endless yards of wood mulch I had delivered a few weeks back. I kneel again, gingerly tossing the mulch into my beds and around my flowers. I step back and smile: mulching reminds me of putting on makeup. It helps to accentuate the existing beauty.

It is one of those coastal Michigan spring days where the weather is a bit bipolar. The sun screams spring, while the wind yells winter. In the sun, protected by the fence, I am warm, nearly sweating. When I stand and the wind hits me, my body explodes in goose bumps. Just a few miles inland it is likely ten degrees warmer. Here by the lake the wind whisks across the still-cold water and sobers you instantly.

I stop and grab my flask of water leaning against the fence. I take a long drink and listen to the world beyond the fence: cars driving by, people walking and talking, radios and TVs.

The world continues, I think. *With or without us. It doesn't miss me. And I don't miss it.*

Soon, the bumblebees and butterflies will come, and they are the only living companions I need alongside me.

Before I had this fence, before my soul was walled off from the world, people would stop and admire my gardens, especially my iris, which stood tall and proud.

"How do you grow these?" people would ask. "You have such a green thumb."

I welcomed their company, their compliments, their questions.

For a long while I opened my greenhouse to the public. People streamed in to buy my daylilies, "my little experiments" as I called them. I had to wait three years to see how many bloomed, and it was a lesson in patience.

A lesson that turned out to be my saving grace, I think. *That ability to hold on to hope no matter how hopeless.*

Many of the daylilies didn't turn out the way I expected: the colors were muted, or some were too similar to others. Many didn't bloom, or I ran out of room in order to store others I was more excited about. In the beginning I'd sell those plants or seeds for two bits, then for a dollar, finally a couple of bucks.

"I feel like I'm stealing your soul," a woman once said to me, her box filled with little pots.

"They need a good home," I'd say. "Make them part of your family."

Every single time someone bought a plant from me, I would walk them out to see my roses. "These came from my great-grandfather," I'd tell them. Then I'd show them my Jonathan rose growing on my trellis. "This baby wouldn't have been possible without that rose," I'd say, showing them the peach petals. "And this child," I'd say, pulling my daughter close, "wouldn't have been possible without my Jonathan. Flowers are family."

People still send me letters, photos and emails of the lilies they bought from me, flowers that have become not only parts of their gardens but also parts of their families.

Because they tell a story. They have a history. All any of us—whether people or flowers—desire is to feel a part of something bigger, to know that our stories won't die.

I down another large swig of water and return to the earth. I am lost in my work, elbow-deep in mulch, when I hear, "Hello? Hello? Flower lady?" I stop midmotion and hold very still. "What was your name again?" A little girl's voice. "We're both named after flowers, remember? I'm Lily."

Lily. The little girl from next door.

I remain still.

"I see you," the voice says. "Iris! That's your name. I can tell by those flowers next to you. My mommy used to have some at our old house."

I pivot my body, and an eye is peering through the fence.

"What on earth?" I ask.

"What's that mean?" Lily asks.

"What do you want? I'm working."

"Oh," Lily says, her voice like a forlorn bird's song.

Neither of us speaks for a minute, but I can still see her eye at the fence. "Oh, for heaven's sake," I say. "Are you all right?"

"Yes…no…"

"Which is it?" I ask.

"No," she says, her voice sad again.

I stand with a grunt and walk toward the fence. "Go on," I say.

"I'm locked out of the house," Lily says.

"Aren't your parents at home?"

"My dad is. My mom's at work."

"Did you knock? Did he not hear you?"

Lily is quiet for a moment. "No," she starts, her voice hesitant. "He's probably asleep."

I look at my watch. "It's eleven a.m.," I say.

"Passed out," she whispers.

My heart jumps. "It's eleven a.m.," I repeat.

"I was playing on the beach," she says. "It's an off day from my camp. I think I locked myself out." Lily hesitates. "Can I come in for a while?"

This time my heart leaps into my throat, and I have to steady myself against the fence. My mouth goes dry, and I reach for my water.

"Hello?" Lily asks. "Are you still there?"

"I'm here," I manage to say. "I don't like unannounced visitors."

"I don't want to wake my dad up," she says. "I don't want to make him mad."

What is going on over there? I wonder. *What do I do?*

I hear cars whiz by on the road, and I think of that little girl, alone and scared, just out there with no one watching her. My long-hibernated maternal instincts take over, and I find myself unlocking my gate. A little girl—pretty as a picture in blond pigtails, her legs covered in sand—stands before me.

"Yes?" I ask.

She stares at me. "Can I come in?" she finally asks with a shrug of her shoulders.

I take a deep breath. *Yes, no?* It suddenly feels like the biggest decision of my life.

"Come on in," I say, ushering her inside with a wave of my hand before quickly closing the gate.

"Thank you," she says in a mannered tone.

Lily stands on the second flagstone of the curving pathway, hands grasped in front of her. She sways slightly as if there is a song in her head. Some long-dead part of my soul swells, and I can hear my Mary singing songs like she used to when I'd garden. The little girl peers around my yard, her face beaming. My initial anger begins to dissipate at her interruption.

"I like your hair," Lily says.

"I did it myself," I say. She doesn't get my sarcasm.

"It's real silver," Lily says, "like a new car."

I try not to smile. "Truer words have never been spoken," I say. I look at her. "Actually, it's more like a new paint job on an old car."

She looks at me for a minute and then laughs. "Good one," Lily says.

"I like your hair, too," I say.

"Thank you," she says. "I did it myself, too."

From out of nowhere, a laugh explodes out of me.

I stoop and extend my hand. "It's nice to officially meet you, Lily," I say. "I'm Iris."

She shakes my hand. "I'm officially Lily," she says. "Nice to meet you, too."

Lily has the bluest eyes I've ever seen. They're not really blue but more the color of a cerulean-blue narcissus. She is wearing gray sweatpants pushed up to her knees, a pink tulle skirt pulled over the sweats. And her shirt! It's a pink T-shirt featuring a rainbow-maned unicorn that reads: I'm a Unicorn Trapped in a Human Body!

I think she and I might be a lot alike, I realize, unable to stop a smile.

I now notice that Lily's mouth is agape, and she is staring around my gardens again. "Woooowww!" she finally says. "This is like that growtanical garden my mom took me to see in Chicago."

"It's botanical," I say. "Not growtanical. Although you're technically right."

Lily scrunches her face.

"I'm a botanist," I say. "I specialize in botanical gardens and nurseries, just like the one your mom took you to see."

"Wooowww!" Lily says again. "You're super smart, like my mom."

"What does she do?"

"She's an engineer," Lily says. "But it's pretty engineering."

"Oh," I say. I have no idea what this means, but I am impressed her mother is an engineer.

Lily is tottering on the flagstone step, as if unsure it's okay to step into the yard. "Want to see my flowers?" I ask.

Lily nods, her neck a virtual Slinky. I reach out and take her hand and lead her to my iris.

"These are iris," I say.

"Just like you!" Lily says.

I smile.

I kneel on my gardening pad and pull a chocolate iris toward the little girl. "These are what are called bearded iris," I say. "They have a beard, see? Just like me, too!"

Lily feels the petals and falls of the bearded iris and, without warning, raises her hand to feel my chin. "You're not as fuzzy as the flower," she says, before bursting into giggles.

The iris are taller than Lily. The sun shines on both of them, illuminating their simple beauty and new growth in this world.

"Want to know something about the iris?" I ask.

Lily nods.

"They take their name from the Greek word for rainbow, just like your shirt," I say. "Iris was the Greek goddess of the rainbow."

"Why are they named that?"

"Because they come in so many colors and varieties, just like people," I say. "Just look at my garden. I have iris of white, black, chocolate, purple, yellow."

"And beards!" Lily adds.

"Yes, and bearded iris, too," I say with a smile.

Lily pulls a chocolate iris close to her face and studies it closely. She leans into the flower and whispers into its petals, "My mommy tells me people lose their rainbows all the time. She tells me never to lose my rainbow. Don't lose your rainbow, okay?"

Her words lift my heart, and I look over at the girl.

Such innocence and purity, I think. *A miracle, like my flowers.* I stop. *Like my Mary.*

"Want to see my greenhouse?" I ask.

"Yeah!" Lily yells.

I begin to stand when Lily holds out her hand to help me up.

"Thank you," I say.

"You're welcome."

That's when I notice how cold her little hand is. It may feel warm to me—fully dressed—in the sunshine, but this tiny sprite has been playing barefoot on the beach, and it's barely sixty degrees.

"Aren't you cold?"

"No," she says, although I can see goose bumps on her arms. Lily hesitates. "Yes," she admits.

I take a deep breath to gather nerve for the offer I'm about to make.

How long has it been since I've had a guest in my home?

"Come in," I finally say. "I'll make you some tea."

"I don't know," Lily says. "My parents told me not to go into strangers' cars or houses."

I smile inside. *She's as filled with trepidation as I am. Perhaps we are kindred spirits…er, kindred unicorns.*

"That's wonderful advice," I say, a bit relieved. "Do you want me to call your father instead while you wait here? I can bring you a jacket."

Lily stops and looks me over carefully. "No, I trust you."

"Thank you," I say. "I trust you, too. This way," I say, taking her around back of the house and then onto the screened porch. When she walks into it, she utters another, "Wow!" and stops, looking outside.

"You have better views than we do," Lily says.

"I built this porch to be elevated," I say.

"That's my house, right?" Lily points.

"Technically, that's my house," I say. "My grandmother's house, actually. You rent it from me."

"But I live there," she says. "It's my house."

"You're right."

She scans beyond the screens for the longest time.

"Can I ask you a question?"

I nod.

"Why is your fence so tall? It's kinda scary. You can see out, but no one can see in."

I nod again but do not answer. "Follow me," I say instead.

I turn to ensure she is behind me and see that her mouth is agape as she tries to take in everything about my old cottage: the paintings, the furniture, the memorabilia. She stops at my desk and picks up one of my cutoff hosiery filled with seeds.

"Gross," she says. "What's this?"

"None of your business," I say. "Didn't your parents teach you not to touch others' belongings?"

I cringe at my reaction. I'm used to being alone. It's hard for me to be hospitable when I feel put upon, especially after only having myself as company.

"One of my grandmas lets me touch anything I want in her house," Lily says, her voice filled with pride.

"I'm not your grandmother," I say.

I turn and can see Lily's face wilt. *Me and my mouth. My problem is that I'm too much like Ouiser in* Steel Magnolias*: prickly on the surface like a cactus but tender as a tomato on the inside. What was it that Ouiser said? Oh, yes! "I'm not crazy… I've just been in a very bad mood for forty years."*

I lead Lily into the kitchen and pull up a stool. I fill the kettle with water and put it on the stove. I grab two bags of rooibos tea, which is naturally sweet with honey and vanilla undertones. It's also packed with antioxidants, which I think Lily could benefit from after a morning in the Michigan lake air. I open a curtain on my cupboard: I have open shelves in my kitchen, which I have covered in my mom and grandma's vintage hand towels—Michigan cherries and blueberries. I eye my mugs and search for one in particular, one I know that will make her—and especially me—feel better after acting like an inhospitable child myself. The kettle whistles, and I fill our two cups with steaming water. I plunge the tea bags into the bottom of the mugs, and tie the strings around the handle.

"I picked this mug out just for you," I say, handing the tea to her.

Lily reads the side of the cup. "In a field of roses, she is a wildflower." She smiles and looks at me. "Am I a wildflower?"

"I think you might be," I say. "And that's a very good thing. Wildflowers are tough, resilient and beautiful."

Lily beams. "Thank you, Iris," she says. "People say I'm a tomboy. But I'm just being myself."

"That's the best thing you can be in this world," I say. "Yourself." I stop. "Be careful, tea's still hot."

Lily lifts the mug to her lips and takes a sip. "Yuck," she says. "It tastes like dirt."

"It's an acquired taste," I say. "You'll learn to love it. Drink it." Lily stares at me. "Drink it. It's good for you."

Lily takes another sip, makes a face, but then takes another. "It's getting a little better," she says.

"Told you."

Lily looks around and then looks at me closely.

"Can I ask you another question?" she asks.

"Depends."

"How old are you?"

"How old do you think I am?"

She twists her face. "That's a trick question," she says.

"I'm as old as the hills and twice as dusty," I say.

"What's that mean?" Lily asks with a giggle.

"Old saying. Older than me, even. Let's just say I've lived a long time."

"Do you have a family?" Lily asks.

My heart stops. I see her eyes searching the kitchen and around the house, scanning my photos of Jonathan and Mary.

"I did," I say.

"Where are they?" I do not answer. "Heaven," Lily says for me. She looks at me closely. "I'm really sorry," Lily continues, staring at me. "My mom and dad say that's a nice place, though."

I will tears from filling my eyes. "I sure hope so," I say.

"I bet it's filled with flowers," Lily says, her voice high and hopeful. She looks at her mug. "Roses and wildflowers!"

I can't stop it. One tear trails down my cheek, and I turn my head. "I think you're probably right."

Lily is wriggling in her seat. After a few more sips of tea, she is bouncing nervously.

"Do you need to use the bathroom?" I ask.

Lily nods her head, her eyes wide.

"There's one down the hall and to your left."

Lily hops off the stool. "Thank you," she says, jogging toward the bathroom.

For a moment I sit in my kitchen. It's oddly comforting and yet oh so uncomfortable to have a guest in my home. Every question Lily asks makes me feel like a hardboiled egg being tapped by a knife. I do not want to crack. I cannot crack. Not after this long of hardening my shell.

I take a sip of my tea when I hear a voice calling outside.

"Lily? Where are you? Lily?"

It's a man's voice, deep, booming and yet tinged in panic.

"Lily?"

I set my tea down and race out the front door. I steady myself and open the gate. "She's in here!"

A tall man with broad shoulders turns. Relief is etched on his red face. His blue eyes are tired and bloodshot. He races past me and into my yard.

"Where is she? Is she okay?"

"Yes, yes, she's fine," I say. "She knocked on my gate a while ago. She said she was locked out of the house. I made her some tea. She's using the bathroom right now. She'll be out in a second."

The man's entire body deflates. He leans toward the ground and grabs his knees. For a second I think he is sobbing, but then he straightens up and looks at me.

"Thank you," he says. "I'm Cory. Lily's father."

"I'm Iris," I say. "You're welcome."

He looks at me for the longest time and says, "Don't tell my wife."

I stare at him. I have survived long enough to know that when people keep secrets, lives are being damaged. I don't say a word.

"Did you hear me?"

"I did," I say. "I don't know you or your wife. All I know is that you rent your home from me, and your daughter was locked out of her house and wandering the beach and the street in the cold all by herself. Anything could have happened."

"But nothing did," he says. Cory's words are a bit slurred.

"Are you drunk?" I ask.

His eyes narrow. "I had a beer."

I look at my watch. "It's not even noon," I say.

"You're not my mother." Cory's voice is now trembling with anger.

I see white. "Why don't you try acting like her father," I say. "You're lucky I haven't called social services. Or your wife."

"This is none of your business."

"It is when a little girl is in danger and asks for my help," I say. "It is when I could evict you from your home this very moment."

Cory takes a step toward me. He clenches his fists. "I fought for this country," he says. "I can have a beer anytime I damn well want."

I take a step toward Cory. "My husband fought for this country, too," I say. "He never came home. And, no, you can't have a beer when you want if you're looking after a little girl."

"Lily!" Cory suddenly yells. "Let's go. Lily!"

When she doesn't answer, Cory rushes into my home. "Stop!" I say.

"Lily!" he yells from my living room.

"Hi, Daddy!" Lily yells. "I'm upstairs."

My heart drops. Cory rushes up the staircase.

"Stop!" I yell again.

When I reach the top of the steps, knees aching and out of breath, I gasp.

"What are you doing?" I manage to say. "Get out of there."

"I got lost," Lily says. She turns, an awestruck gaze on her face as she scans the bedroom door she has opened. "It's so pretty. It's like I'm standing in a field of flowers. Wildflowers!"

My knees nearly buckle. I grab the wall for support.

Lily is standing in Mary's room. I keep the door to her bedroom closed at all times. It remains untouched. It has remained untouched for decades. Handmade paper flowers—roses, crepe-paper peonies, colorful wildflowers—now yellowed, still hang from the ceiling and sprout from vases.

Lily turns. "I bet heaven looks like this," she says.

"Get out!" I scream. "Get out of her room!"

Cory turns to me, his eyes wide. Lily turns, her cheeks trembling.

"Get out of my house! *Now!*"

Cory grabs Lily's hand and pulls her out of the room. "Come on, Lily," he says. "Let's go."

I slam the door to Mary's room as they head down the stairs.

"I'm sorry, Iris," Lily yells, her words garbled as she begins to cry. "I didn't mean to spy."

I look down the staircase just as Cory pulls Lily out of the house. She looks up at me, tears streaming down her face.

"Don't be mad. I'm so, so sorry. We're rainbows! We're wildflowers!" Lily begins to wail. "Say something. Please!"

I hear her voice trail off as they leave.

"She's just a crazy, old woman," I hear Cory say.

"No, she's not!" Lily yells.

As soon as they are gone, I lock my gate, kneel on my gardener's pad, bow my head and water my iris with my own tears.

PART FIVE

PEONY

"Had I but four square feet of ground at my disposal,
I would plant a peony in the corner and proceed to worship."

—Alice Harding

IRIS

MAY 2003

The doorbell rings.

I've had more people in my house today than I have in decades.

I look at the pill I have sitting on the kitchen counter, hesitate, take a step and then return, downing it without so much as a drink of water.

Reinforcement.

"I'm Abby Peterson. It's nice to finally meet you in person. Thank you for agreeing to see me. I just didn't think a conversation over the phone was adequate after your call." She stops. "And from what I've learned already."

My eyes widen at her admission.

Abby looks different than I had imagined, especially up

close. She's young, so very young, but has a professorial look that belies her current babbling. She is wearing a tan suit and a periwinkle blouse, and very little makeup. She extends her hand. When I simply nod and usher her in with a flourish of my own hand, she nervously pushes her oversize eyeglass frames up the bridge of her nose.

"I hope you had a nice May," she says. "Has been a bit rainy, unfortunately."

Her skin is fresh. It does not resemble mine, which looks like crepe paper. How do I respond to her question? *Oh, yes, it was lovely. I made a birthday cake for my dead daughter and tossed a rose onto the lake in honor of my dead husband*? Not exactly a conversation starter.

When I do not answer, she says, "Your home is beautiful." She is nervous. To be honest, I quite enjoy making others nervous. It gives one the upper hand. But there's something genuine about Abby, something innately sweet, something I see too little of in today's world.

"It's old," I say. "Just like me." I walk toward the kitchen. "I was going to make us some tea." I turn. Abby is eyeing up the place. "Do you like tea?"

"Yes! Oh, yes!" she says, with too much enthusiasm.

I fill the kettle with water and set it on the stove.

"Earl Grey?" I ask.

It's a test.

Abby hesitates. "I prefer that in the morning," she says. "If at all. Not one of my favorites. I'm sorry."

She passed.

"Me, either," I say. "Usually, people don't know the difference. Have you been to England?"

"Yes," she says. "Twice. For work. Amazing history. Makes our country look like a newborn."

"We are," I say. "And we're still learning to walk."

She cocks her head at me. "Especially now, it seems."

This Abby is filled with surprises. I lower my guard, just ever so.

"I served your daughter some Rooibos, and she seemed to quite like it."

"Lily?" Abby says, her face lifting in surprise. "That's quite a stretch from chocolate milk."

The kettle screams, and I turn off the stove. I pluck two mugs from the cupboard, fill them with water and insert the tea bags. "Let's go to my porch," I say. "It's a lovely day."

"This is stunning!" Abby says, and I can tell that she means it. She walks directly up to the screen and stares out. "This view! These gardens!" She turns. "This porch!"

"Thank you," I say. "I had it built a long time ago. All of the things out here mean a great deal to me." I stop. "Just like my privacy."

Abby lurches as if my words were a car that has just struck her. A bit of tea sloshes over the side of her mug. She takes a few tenuous steps and grabs the wood table for support with her free hand.

"Have a seat," I say. "Please."

I scooch a coaster toward her, and Abby nods. She sits down, and I pull up a chair across from her.

"I'm sorry to be so abrupt, but I like to be direct," I say.

Abby sits more upright, as if steeling herself. "Please," she says. "I do not believe in hiding anything."

"This is the second time I've come across your daughter unattended," I say.

"Second time?" Abby jerks forward, bumping the table. The color bleeds from her cheeks.

"The first was a few weeks ago. Lily was at the fence. It seems your husband had forgotten to pick her up, and she walked all the way home from camp." I look at Abby. "She was locked out of the house, just like today."

Abby lifts a hand and covers her mouth. "He didn't tell me all of that today."

"So you spoke with him?"

"Yes." She stops. "I actually am quite angry with him. We're not supposed to have secrets from one another, and it seems he's filled with them."

I lift an eyebrow, and Abby's face falls. Her eyes tear up.

"I also think he was inebriated today."

"Inebriated?"

"Drunk."

"Yes," Abby says. "I know what *inebriated* means." She stops and studies a knot on the wooden table. "I know he drinks too much on occasion. I just didn't think he did it when Lily was there." Her tone belies her words.

"He was very short with me," I say. "And I invited your daughter into my home to ensure her safety, and I caught her snooping."

"I'm so sorry, Mrs. Maynard," Abby says.

"I like my privacy. I thought that was clear when you signed the lease to rent my family home."

"It was…it is…" Abby sputters. "It won't happen again. I promise."

Abby nervously sips her tea. There is a long pause, filled only by the songs of birds and the squeaks and barks of busy squirrels. In the distance—perhaps in the woods—the echo of a gunshot silences nature.

"Guns," Abby mutters. "War. It ruins everything."

She looks at me closely, too closely, and, for once, I am uncomfortable in this power struggle. "My husband just returned from Iraq," she continues. "He's not the same man he was. He's a ghost."

My heart leaps. I feel as if I am speaking to Shirley again.

"I can't say that to anyone," Abby says, pushing her glasses up, "but I have a feeling we might not speak again, so I just need to get this off my chest, maybe so you won't hate my family as much."

"Go on," I say.

"Cory is a wonderful man…was a wonderful man," Abby says. "Great husband and father, hard worker, full of life… all of that has faded. He's like a hologram of his former self. I know you won't understand, but, well, war may not have taken my husband, but it killed his soul."

"My husband was killed in World War II."

Abby's eyes widen, and she lifts a trembling hand to her mouth. "I'm so, so sorry."

"And my best friend, Shirley, experienced exactly what you're going through with your husband," I say. "I know all about war, Mrs. Peterson. I know that, for some reason, too many of us must have something or someone to hate. And I know that it never ends and will never end. Korea, Vietnam, 9/11. It goes on and on and on, and we rarely give pause to its horrors. Fear does monstrous things to people and country." I stop. "What was it Herbert Hoover said? 'Older men declare war. But it is the youth that must fight and die.'"

Abby is staring at me, mouth open, nodding, tears plopping onto the table. "I've begged him to get help. He told me he was. I don't know what to do anymore." She stares off into the distance, and I can see her mind is far away from here. I am not a fidgeter, but her sadness and openness makes me twist my teacup in my hands. Finally, she shakes her head to break the trance and studies the McCoy vase filled with iris that I have placed in the middle of the table.

"Such a beautiful flower," Abby says. "Such a beautiful name." She looks at me, closely, as if seeing me for the first time as a real person. "Your mother must have known what a regal creation you were from the moment she saw you."

My face flushes instantly, almost as if I'm stoking a fire. To have someone in my home talking about my mother is almost too overwhelming. I try to steady my tea with a shaking hand and concentrate on bringing it to my lips.

"Thank you," I finally say. "She and my grandmother loved to garden. They loved iris." I stop. "The flower. And me, I assume."

Abby emits a tiny laugh, and I smile at my joke.

"Did you know that Van Gogh voluntarily entered an asylum in southern France at the end of his life?"

Abby tilts her head at me, confused by the question, before shaking her head.

"He considered the asylum to be a monastery and art studio all in one," I continue. "He sought isolation and removal from everyday reality so he could focus solely on his art. Between attacks, Van Gogh was incredibly productive and felt that his painting would be what saved him. He called his work 'the lightning conductor for my illness' and believed he was not 'mad' when he was painting."

I reach out and touch my majestic iris and continue. "His paintings of iris were believed to be the first works he did in the asylum. They were growing in a garden in an outdoor area Van Gogh was allowed to visit. His first painting was simply titled 'Irises' and depicted a garden of violet iris growing wildly from red soil with bright orange marigolds in the background. One lone bloom is white in his painting, and I always believed that single iris represented Van Gogh—isolated from the rest of the world because it was just too harsh of a place to survive without immersing yourself in beauty."

There is a long pause. The breeze kicks in off the lake and undulates the screens on the porch, making it look as if the house is alive and breathing. The wind carries the scent of my peonies.

"Is that why you garden?" Abby asks.

Her question shocks me, and the directness of it forces me to sit more upright.

I fake a smile. "I minored in art history in college," I say. "It was a nice complement to my botany major."

Abby nods. "That's wonderful." She hesitates. "But you didn't answer my question."

My heart shudders in my chest, and I am again thankful I took my medication or I might just pass out on the floor.

"Monet once said of Van Gogh, 'How did a man who loved flowers so well manage to be so unhappy?'" I look directly into Abby's eyes. "I often ask myself that same question. But life, Mrs. Peterson, as you are learning, can be crushing in its relentless cruelty. I've learned that I can protect my gardens from much of the harm in the world, and they reward me with their beauty. I've learned that you can wall out pain."

"But you can't wall out hope or love," Abby says. "You can't wall out memories." She stops. "And your gardens can't tell you they love you. They can't call and talk to you when you're sad."

"Oh, but they can, Mrs. Peterson," I say. "They can, and they do." I stop. "Why are you an engineer?"

"My turn now, is it?" Abby says with a small smile. "Because of my mother. Let's say I didn't have the same childhood you might have had. My mother lives in a fantasy world. She refuses to acknowledge anything that is going on in real life. Engineering was logical and fact-based. I had a need to make sense of life somehow."

"We're a lot alike, Mrs. Peterson," I say.

"Abby," she says.

"Abby," I say with a nod. "I'm Iris."

"Hello, Iris," Abby says, extending a hand across the table. "It's nice to meet you."

Her nose twitches, and I smile. “Are those peonies?” she asks. “They’re my favorite flower in the world.”

“I thought you preferred lilacs,” I say without an ounce of sarcasm in my voice.

Abby looks at me and nervously pushes her glasses up her nose. She suddenly turns, stands and scans the yard. “Did you…?” she asks. “You did see me trying to smell your lilacs.”

“Would you like to see my gardens?” I ask. “Smell the peonies?” I stop and smile. “This time without the need of a chair or a fence in the way?”

ABBY

MAY 2003

Iris's gardens are more beautiful than I could ever have imagined. I have visited many botanical gardens and arboretums, but walking in her garden is like the time I visited Monet's gardens in Giverny during my college study abroad in Paris.

"Funny you just mentioned Monet," I say, telling Iris about my time abroad. "His gardens were truly magical. You probably already know this, but he had stunning cottage gardens surrounding his home, and a Japanese-inspired water garden beyond that." I stop and look around Iris's gardens. "It was like stepping into one of his paintings."

I turn, and Iris is watching me. "Go on," she prompts. "I've always dreamed of visiting Giverny. I've only been able to do it in my mind."

"It was the first time I not only understood the magic of flowers but also impressionism," I say. "Walking through his gardens, you can see exactly what he saw—the way that light affects color as morning passes to evening, the beauty of a simple reflection in the water..." I pause, searching for the right words. "I've never seen the world around me as literal, as black or white, right or wrong. I feel the beauty and pain in the world, and that's what Monet saw, too. He didn't paint what he saw. He painted what he felt."

I look at Iris, and a wry smile slowly envelops her face. "Are you sure you're an engineer?" she asks with a little laugh. "Not a poet?"

I tell her of my job, and she nods. "I was a botanist, so I understand completely. There was an exact science to what I did—and what I still do—but there was also an artistry to it, as well." Iris shuts her eyes. "Paris," she says. "I've always dreamed of visiting Paris." She opens her eyes. "Was it everything you dreamed?" Her voice sounds like that of a young girl, filled with all the hope of springtime.

"Yes," I say. "And more." I smile. "Audrey Hepburn said, 'Paris is always a good idea.'"

"Smart woman, that Audrey," Iris says.

I look at her. "You should go."

Iris averts her eyes and nods robotically. Her eyes veer from me to the fence and then back to her gardens.

"Yes," Iris responds, her voice sans emotion. She begins to move forward but stops abruptly. "Speaking of smart women, do you have difficulty at work?" She stops. "Being a woman?"

I think of my recent meeting. "I do," I say. "I always have. College. Career. Working mother." Iris is nodding. "I can only imagine what you had to endure."

She turns, and her eyes are like lasers. "I was treated very poorly," she says, not mincing words, her voice showing zero remorse. "Men don't like smart women," she continues. "We're a threat. To their egos. Their comfort. Their very existence. We're expected to be small, act small, be window dressing." She looks away and shakes her head as if to stop herself. "But that's a conversation for another day." She turns back. "And with a stronger drink than tea."

She moves forward with a determined tilt to her aging body, which resembles a parenthesis, as if to say, *Follow me*, and I do.

Iris's front and side gardens border the house and fence, hugging a lush green lawn. But as we head into the backyard, I again am reminded of Giverny. There is no backyard, just a monstrous cottage garden with various pathways—mulch, gravel, stepping stones—meandering throughout. On one side is a potting shed and on the other a greenhouse—actually more dollhouse than greenhouse—both of which are the most adorable I've ever seen. The greenhouse is comprised of huge glass windows outlined with crisp white frames, but the structure is shingled along the bottom and in the pitches below the glass roof. Iris turns and catches me staring.

"My gardens are not quite peak yet," she says. "I must apologize."

I cannot contain my laughter. "Are you kidding me?" I ask. "It's stunning."

"Thank you."

"Do you mind if I ask what's in your greenhouse? It's so charming."

"Ah," she says with a big smile. "My babies are in the greenhouse."

I cock my head. *Her babies?*

She leads me into her greenhouse, which is surrounded by—*no, hugged by*—forest ferns and hostas. I glance down, and hidden among the dense green are a family of gnomes. The entire family is waving while sporting red caps, curled at the ends, happy smiles and pointy ears. The father is holding a shovel in one hand, the mother has a basket filled with flowers, and the boy is wearing blue overalls and the girl a red jumper. A redbud tree, as aged and bent as Iris but resplendent in its own body, sits at the edge of the greenhouse. In a knothole in the crook of its base sits the gnomes' home.

"These are my babies," Iris says, interrupting me from my thoughts and leading me inside.

The entire greenhouse is impeccably clean and quite warm. A potting bench holds a variety of garden tools, and potting soil is stacked deep in one corner. But nearly every inch of the floor and the tables are covered with pots and writing tablets like the ones my mom used in school. I look closer, narrowing my eyes and pushing my glasses up the bridge of my nose.

What is that? Oh, my God!

Hosiery hangs from nails off the tables.

"Yes, those are my hose," Iris says, noticing my expression. "Ever since the war, I still can't waste a thing." She stops. I still can't say a word. "I hybridize my own daylilies," she continues. "That's sort of my calling card. I tie nylons around the daylily stalks, tag them, break the stalks after they've bloomed and count the seeds. I plant them in here and then count how many grow." She walks over and touches a pot. "I have to wait three years to see how many bloom. I have to wait to see if the colors are right, if they match the dream I have in my own head."

"You're just like Monet," I finally say. "You bring to life what you feel."

Iris smiles. "That might be the nicest compliment I've received in years." Her eyes fill with the light penetrating the greenhouse. "It's getting warm in here," she says, pulling off a sweatshirt to reveal a body—now in a T-shirt—that is lithe and obviously still strong underneath her wrinkled skin, her forearms as thick and strong as tree roots. "You wanted to see my peonies."

I follow Iris outside and over to the far side of her garden, which is slightly elevated on a berm and filled with light. “This gets the most sunshine and less water,” she says. “My peonies love it.”

Her peonies are works of art, all as beautiful as paintings in a gallery. Some sport huge, puffy blooms as thick and billowy as cotton candy, each flower filled with endless rows of petals. Some are all white, some white tinged with pink or flicks of red, while some are light pink and others fuchsia. Others are more delicate: crinkled white with yellow centers, and some resemble beautiful bowls, cups of pink petals surrounding creamy centers.

I can smell them before I even reach them. The entire yard—the entire world, it suddenly seems—is perfumed with their sweet scent. I can’t help myself: I race toward the flowers and grab a bloom, pulling it toward my nose. I inhale.

I again think of Paris, of walking into the famed French perfumery Guerlain. The beautiful shop was filled with intoxicating scents in ornate glass bottles. I couldn’t afford to buy a thing as a poor, young college student, but I spent an hour in the shop smelling every perfume, with my favorites being the ones that evoked the scent of fresh flowers. I sniff again, and this time I am transported to my grandmother’s backyard.

“These peonies started in my grandma’s gardens, where you now live,” she says. “They came from her mom’s house. They’re heirlooms. They’ve been a part of my family history longer than I have.”

I turn and looks at Iris, whose face is abloom, just like her gardens.

“I’m sorry about your yard,” Iris says suddenly. “There were too many memories next door. I brought every plant over here.”

I stand and nod. “I wish I had taken starts of my grandma’s peonies,” I say. “Oh, the memories these bring back. My grandma had peonies with blooms as big as baseballs, and they would just flop over on the ground during the summer heat like her old dog used to do. She had a laundry line over her peonies, just so they would scent her sheets when she hung them out to dry." I stop and shut my eyes. "When I would stay with her in the summer, my sheets smelled like peonies. Like heaven."

"Why didn't you take any starts?" Iris asks.

"My mom," I say, my voice dropping. "She's not much of a gardener. She's not one for making memories." I turn to Iris. "She has cut down every tree in her yard."

"My heavens," Iris gasps. "Why?"

"Fear," I say. "Fear rules her world. A tree might fall and damage the house. A branch might hurt the roof. Peonies attract ants. Flowers attract bees. Everything is scary."

"What about your father?"

"She rules him, too," I say. "And now he just stays quiet."

For a long beat the two of us match the last word floating in the air. And then Iris looks at me and asks, "Would you like a bouquet of peonies?" She stops. "No, better yet, would you like a start of my peonies?"

Iris heads to her greenhouse and returns with a shovel and a pot. She stands over her peonies and regards them, before doing the same with me. "I think I know which you prefer," she says, before thrusting her shovel under a huge bush of peonies filled with white blooms tinged with pink. My nose twitches with excitement. Iris puts a clump of peonies—roots and all—into the bucket and adds some dirt around them.

"Plant these immediately and be sure to water them in, you hear me?" she says, her voice stern. "If they wilt, water them some more. They're hearty, so they should root." She leans down and, without warning, breaks off a few more. "For your dining room table," she adds. "In memory of your grandma."

"I don't know what to say."

"We started as adversaries," Iris says. "You let down your walls."

"So did you," I say. My eyes dart toward her fence.

"Just a little," she says, her voice thick with sarcasm.

"Thank you," I say.

Iris walks me to the front gate and opens it. As I'm about to leave, she says, "Abby, we all go crazy, but we can still create beauty out of all the horror." She stops. "Don't give up on your husband. He's alive. So is your daughter. Those are all the blessings you need in this world. That's all that matters in this world. You have your family."

I watch her as she talks, moved but unsure as to what to say. She is wringing her gloved hands, almost as if she's forcing herself to keep from saying anything further.

Like, *Don't grow to be old and alone like me. Don't wall yourself off from the world.*

My heart quickens, and I open my mouth to ask about her daughter, about what happened.

"Goodbye, Abby," Iris says. "And good luck."

"Goodbye," I say with a nod.

I walk onto the sidewalk, and she shuts the gate behind me. I can hear it lock. I stop on the other side for a moment, and I can see the outline of Iris's body through the slats, pressed against the fence, as if she wants to leave with me. The fragrance of the peonies fills the air, and I lift them to my nose. When I turn back, Iris is gone.

I look at my house. I stop, unable to go inside quite yet, hoping that it's not too late, that Cory is not already gone, or that I have not already left, either. I recall what Iris just said to me.

Such a fine line between goodbye and good luck, I think.

I take a deep breath and finally open the front door, praying for the latter.

PART SIX

DAYLILIES

"Remember that the most beautiful things in the world are the most useless; peacocks and lilies for instance."

—John Ruskin

IRIS

JUNE 2003

"Lily? Lily!"

What is all the commotion?

I am standing in my garden considering which of my babies, my daylilies, to cross on a beautiful still morning.

So much for still, I think.

"Lily?"

I stand and tilt my head like an old dog trying to home in on the exact spot of the sound. I angrily toss my gloves onto the ground and hold very still.

"Lily?"

I head toward the screened porch very quietly for a better view of what's going on. I open the door and place my face near the screen. A figure stumbles into the backyard next door.

The derelict father.

I sigh and shake my head. His voice sounds slightly slurred yet again, tinged with sleep and who knows what else.

I'm done! I think. *I will not allow that girl to be in danger any longer.* I grab my phone from my kangaroo pouch and begin to dial 911.

That's when I hear him call again.

"Where are you? Lily? *Lily!*"

There is now panic in his voice, the panic only a parent can understand when a child goes missing, even if only for a split second, the panic that screams, *No, not my child. God, let my child be okay.*

His voice is also filled with guilt, the guilt only a parent can understand when they've not been there for their child, even if only for a split second.

"Lily? Lily! Lily!"

I edge back toward the door.

"I'm on the beach, Daddy!"

My heart melts when I hear the little girl's voice drifting on the breeze.

"Come play with me in the sand!"

Silence. I place my face against the screen.

"I can't come get you, baby," he finally yells. "Come back, okay?"

"Why, Daddy? It's fun."

I watch the father take a step, open the gate and then stop. He buries his face into his hands and then bumps his head against the gate. I can see through the opening of their backyard and straight down to Lake Michigan. Lily is alone, the waves crashing into the shore. She wades into the water and fills a bucket. A wave knocks her down and carries her back into the lake. She struggles but manages to return to shore, her bucket full.

"Lily!" he screams, his voice ragged, trying to stay calm but filled with fright. "Please come back now. I can't come down there."

What is happening? I wonder. *Go get your daughter. Now.* I hover my finger over the green call button.

"Come make a sandcastle with me," Lily calls.

Cory lifts his head toward the sky and screams, his mouth open, a gaping maw, although no sound is released. He tries to step outside the gate and then toward the dune, but as soon as his feet touch the sand, he stops as though an electric fence surrounds the property.

"Sand," he says quietly. "No. No. No. No sand."

I look at the shadow box on the wall. I see Jonathan's medal of honor, and my heart races.

He is just like me, I finally realize. *Both traumatized by war, walls, life, boundaries real and imaginary. A grown man afraid of sand. A grown woman afraid of others.*

"Come back, baby," he calls. "Please."

My heart breaks, and my hand trembles. I place my phone in my pouch again. I know what I must do. I take a step, open the screen door and walk to my fence. I lean against it for support, my body moving slat by slat until I am to my back gate. I open it, my entire body quaking. "Please, Jonathan and Mary, give me strength."

I am outside the gate. My knees buckle. I peer beyond the dune grass. I can see the little girl playing in the waves. A red flag flaps in the breeze. *Rip currents.* I peer left and right. There is no one else on the beach. I take another step. The world is spinning now, the sky the earth, the grass the heavens, the sun atop me.

I find myself crawling, hand over hand, my face barely above the ground, grass scratching my cheeks, tears filling my eyes. I make it to the top of the dune and begin to crawl down it.

"Lily! Now!"

I hear a girlish scream—*Squeeeeee!*—and then the *whoosh, whoosh* of footsteps in the sand running past me. I fall into the tall grass, my heart pounding in my ears.

"Don't ever scare me like that again!" he says.

"I'm sorry, Daddy. But I was bored, and you were asleep." She stops. "Again."

Footsteps grow quieter. The back door slams.

I lie on the ground, staring at the sky until my heart calms.

I finally stand, itchy from the grass.

"Thank you."

I yelp. I look up, and Cory is standing at his fence.

"Are you okay?" he asks.

"Are *you*?"

He shakes his head and begins to weep.

"You need help," I say.

"I know."

"You realize you are risking your daughter's life and your relationship with your wife if you don't get help, don't you?"

Cory is heaving, just like Lake Michigan, huge waves crashing forth.

"Do you want me to call for you?" I ask. "Someone?"

He looks at me, this big man all little boy, and nods. "Can you?" he asks. "I can't. I just can't."

I nod.

Cory rushes inside and returns with a ream of papers. "The military gave me some names. I don't know who to call, or how to start."

I shuffle through the papers. Only one of the names is that of a woman. I call her immediately.

After Cory heads back inside, I return to my yard, picking up the crosses I'd set down moments ago. I hold them as if they were people, not flowers, or ghosts.

We are all just like these daylilies, crosses of life's traumas and tribulations, the world's good and bad.

I think of the family next door. *But we are all still beautiful, aren't we? Worthy of care and attention, just like these daylilies?*

I begin to cry softly.

Yes, I begin to realize, *the father I do not like—and the family that has trampled on my privacy—are exactly like me.*

ABBY

JUNE 2003

"Hi, I'm Dr. Trafman. You must be Mr. and Mrs. Peterson." She extends her hand.

"Cory," my husband says.

I don't know what I was expecting, but I certainly was not expecting to be here with my husband today or ever. I don't know what changed, but I am thankful something did, and I am guardedly optimistic. I also wasn't expecting an attractive, soft-spoken woman to be our counselor. Dr. Trafman resembles a working mother I might meet at a PTA meeting: soft bob and sweeping bangs, sweater over her shoulders, modern glasses. I stand motionless for too long before finally extending my hand.

"Hi," I say. "Hi."

My facial expression says everything. "I'm sorry," I say. "It's just that…"

"No need to apologize, Mrs. Peterson," she says. "I get it all the time."

I look at her, this time squarely in the eyes, and nod. "So do I," I say. "I'm an engineer."

Dr. Trafman smiles.

"And, please, call me Abby."

"Call me Kim," she says. "Follow me."

I also didn't expect to be meeting in Kim's home, a white, columned two-story house in a brand-new subdivision on the lake. Her yard is filled with daylilies, a flower I loved growing because it thrived in nearly any type of soil and always seemed so carefree.

I look at my husband in the afternoon light filtering into her home. He looks so big and yet so small. A meeting with our therapist is now our "afternoon delight" while Lily is at camp. My, how we've changed. My, how my husband has changed. I stare at him. *Can he grow again in any type of soil? Can he learn to be carefree again?*

Kim ushers us into her office, which is more of a library. The ceiling is vaulted and lined with dark beams, and the walls are filled with shelves crammed with books, awards, certificates, framed photos, art and knickknacks. French doors lead to a pergola-covered patio, with views of the lake in the distance.

"Beautiful," I say.

"Thank you," Kim says.

She does not lead us to the two chairs behind her desk in the corner of the room but rather to two high-back leather chairs by a stone fireplace.

"Please," she says, motioning to the chairs as she takes a seat on a small floral couch.

We make small talk for a few minutes—about our children, Grand Haven, my job, summer—before Kim looks at us very intently.

"My father served in Vietnam," Kim says quietly. "That's a large reason I became a counselor, and one who focuses on our returning soldiers. First, I want to thank you for taking this big first step, Cory. My father never did, and it devastated our family." She stops and leans forward. "And I want you to know that you are not alone. It's already estimated that nearly 20 percent of those returning from the wars in Iraq and Afghanistan are reporting symptoms of post-traumatic stress disorder or major depression. That's nearly 300,000 men and women, Cory. And only half seek any treatment. It's hard for our returning servicemen and women. They not only fear reduced pay or slashed retirement, or that it will place a stigma on future employment if they seek treatment, but they also just want to get back to normal." Kim stops again and leans even farther forward. "But there is no normal any longer. You must seek a new normal now."

I look over at Cory. He nods, but his eyes are wide, his jaw clenched, his hands like fists. He is sweating through his polo shirt. My heart begins to race.

"I'm not going to ask you to talk about what happened today, Cory," Kim says. "About what brought you to me. Instead, I'm going to ask you to try and reset your brain." Kim looks at me. "You, too, Abby."

Cory sighs. His shoulders slump with relief.

"I don't believe in having you relive the trauma, especially at the beginning of our work," she says. "You already deal with it every day. At some point we will talk about it. But right now you need to find a way to deal with what you've been experiencing since then, and that's extreme anxiety and fear." Kim looks at me again and repeats, "You, too, Abby."

"I don't want to take medication," Cory says, his voice oddly high, like Lily's is when she is scared.

"I don't want that, either," Kim says. "I want you to deal with this in a healthy way. And I do think that's possible."

She continues, "So we're going to start with a therapy called TARGET, or Trauma Affect Regulation: Guide for Education and Therapy."

I look at her. "Say what again?"

"I know," she says with a laugh. "Counselors and their therapy names, right? In short, what I want you both to understand, especially you, Cory, is that you are in a constant fight-flight response. It's how you were able to survive a threat on your life. Your brain has shifted into a perpetual alarm state in order to survive traumatic danger. I want to help you use your mind's capacity to focus in order to reset that alarm system in the brain. This is necessary in order to stop what is a healthy survival reaction from turning toxic. Right now your brain is being hijacked into a constant state of PTSD."

"How do I stop that?" Cory asks.

"I want to help teach you some very simple tools that will help you. TARGET calls the focusing steps SOS," Kim says. "I want both of you to close your eyes and listen."

Cory and I shut our eyes. I feel him reach for my hand to hold it.

"First, sweep your mind clear of all thoughts," Kim says. "Second, focus on one thought that is the most important thing in your life at this moment."

Cory squeezes my hand.

"Next, begin to rate your stress level and your level of control over that stress, from one to ten, with one meaning no stress and ten worst stress, and one equating out of control to ten being completely in control. Think of a recent example of a stressful situation."

My mind whirs to Iris and Cory. Cory squeezes my hand even harder.

What is he thinking about? I wonder.

"Now, sweep your mind clear of the stressful thoughts and focus on what's most important."

Kim lets us have a moment of quiet.

"What I've learned about PTSD in soldiers just like you, Cory, is that your family members are experiencing the same stress reactions as a result of not knowing if you would come home safely," Kim says. "That continues because you remain in a constant state of PTSD. Focusing as a family helps you all understand each other's stress reactions and triggers and helps you join together to heal from the trauma rather than go it alone."

Cory and I open our eyes. For a while we just talk again, about life, about our schedules, about what normal now means.

"I think that's enough for today," Kim finally says. "Any questions before we schedule another time to talk?"

"What about Lily?" I ask.

"I do have an exercise that I think you might want to try with her at home," Kim says. "It focuses on art, so it's less frightening."

"What is it?" Cory asks.

"You make masks to show how you're feeling," Kim says. "It's a way to bring our emotions to the surface. Don't be surprised if Lily's mask is sad, even though she may seem outwardly happy. Just be honest. And talk. You'll know when the moment is right to do this."

I think of my parents.

"Yes," I say. "Of course."

"And Cory?" Kim continues. "Another important aspect is for you to stay healthy. Exercise. Run. Do you do yoga?"

Cory laughs. "No," he says.

"You need to do something that keeps your body in shape because that keeps your mind focused and attuned. Everything works together. Is there an activity you like?"

Cory and I look at each other.

"I think I know something that just might be perfect," he says.

IRIS

People in Michigan talk about the sunsets, but they tend to overlook the sunrises. I am a morning person. My soul is filled with a million sunrises.

I love the beach and lake in the morning. I stand on my porch, the waves speaking only to me in the quiet. They lull, as if they, too, are just waking up. And the horizon! Oh, the horizon! At dawn it is rimmed in sapphires as if dusk and dawn had a baby of midnight blue, and I have been chosen to see the newborn at first light.

It is as beautiful as you were as a baby, Mary.

There are few things that get me through this life, but my sunrises and my flowers do because they offer hope. They demonstrate that beauty can grow out of the harshest of winters or lack of light. I hold on to these signs of beauty. I hold on to this elusive hope mostly because I'm scared. Scared to die. Scared of the unknown. Scared that I might not see my daughter or husband ever again. Scared that I will be forever alone in the next life as I am in this one.

We all must hold on to or for something or someone, or there is no reason to wake, no reason to hope, no reason to live, I think.

June in Michigan is a captivating month. After the temperature tantrums of moody May, June can feel a lot like *The Wizard of Oz*: you go from black-and-white to Technicolor. I watch the sunrise in these quiet moments, when no one has yet risen, when the world is mine and mine alone, and then get to work.

Sunny June mornings mean only one thing in my world: my daylilies.

My babies!

I can smell them even before I reach them, a sweet scent that is hard to describe even after so many years of having their fragrance fill my nostrils.

They are perfume-y, yes, but not musky, I think. *More lemony perhaps, more sugary.* I lift my head and sniff the air, the light warming my face.

They smell like sunshine, I conclude. *Like summer.*

Nearly the entire side of the fence on the far side of my house is devoted to my hybridized daylilies. Not only do they make a wonderful border garden with their impressive color and lush greenery, but they also bloom in shocking colors.

You are reborn to show your stunning beauty, I think. *And my hard work.*

I have my daylilies organized almost like a Pantone color wheel: yellows to yellow-orange, orange to red-orange, red to red-violet, purple and so on. Of course, my babies are often nestled close to their parents, their lineage on display in the subtle differences in their plumes and throats. But my daylily gardens are also lab works in progress. I scan the colorful rows, the breeze making the tags on their stems flutter, the hose wrapped around many of their stems resembling cobwebs in the first light.

It is early in the morning, the best time to hybridize, I believe. The weather is cool and not too hot. If it gets too warm, or too windy, the pollen dries up, or blows away. And it cannot rain, or the pollen will be washed away.

Daylilies thrive in full sun and partial shade, and my garden is situated so that it gets full morning sun and filtered afternoon light. Daylilies are somewhat drought tolerant, but they produce more blossoms when watered regularly.

"Don't we all, my dears," I say to my flowers. I check the soil. It is damp from the sprinklers, but I know this too-sandy soil will dry by day's end, so I walk over and turn on the outdoor faucet. I pull and unwind my hose, the kink-free kind that still manages to kink, and give it a yank to straighten, until the water finally shoots forth. I water only at the ground level, as overhead watering will leave unsightly spots on the flowers and foliage.

I talk to each daylily as I water, holding each flower as if holding a child's face, caressing each blossom, knowing it will be the only chance I get. That is the ironic life of my babies. Daylilies are accurately named, as each blossom survives only one day, opening in the morning. By the end of the day, its life is over.

"Hi, Princess," I say to my aptly named Purple Princess with a yellow throat.

"How's my beautiful boy?" I coo to Midnight, a magical daylily I named after my grandmother's beloved mutt, whose throat is as golden as Midnight's eyes were. Technically, the flower is the darkest purple I could create, but in the light, it truly looks as silky black as Midnight's coat.

I move through my daylilies, addressing each one. I call them all by name, as happily and personally as you would greet your friends. Each is as glorious and colorful as a Michigan sunrise. When I finish, I can feel it getting warmer. I shuck my sweatshirt, take a healthy gulp of water straight from the hose, lower the broken brim on my Detroit Tigers ball cap and start on my real work.

I consider my gardens and then my greenhouse. I turn and scan the horizon over the lake. My heart leaps.

Oh, Iris, you old fool! How could you have never thought of this! Shame on you! Shame!

I turn toward my daylilies, my adrenaline causing my hands to tremble in excitement.

Which ones? Which ones? I think, considering my babies. *What would make the perfect cross?*

And there, sparkling in the sun, actually calling to me as if their colorful throats can speak—*Iris! Iris! Me! Me! Right here! We'd make perfect parents!*—are the two ideal daylilies for my vision: Blue-throated Hummingbird and Summer Sapphire.

I smile, thinking of Elsie Spalding, a famous hybridizer and one of my mentors, who was famed for the full forms and pastel colors of her diploid daylilies. When someone asked how she decided which daylilies to hybridize, she simply smiled and said, "I just put pretty on pretty."

It was an awakening to the creative side of my botanist's mind. At one point in my life and career, I was a serious hybridizer whose single mission was to emphasize certain characteristics. I wanted every cross to be technically perfect: ruffles to be more ruffled, laces to be lacier, throats to be longer, taller scape heights. But over time I realized I may have accomplished a feat that was scientifically interesting, but it didn't tell a story.

Like family, I think.

So while many of my early daylilies were fascinating specimens, they weren't particularly pretty flowers. And that's what gardening is supposed to be, I finally realized: bringing beauty into this world.

So I focused on *pretty on pretty.*

And yet, there is an exact science to hybridizing daylilies, one I used to teach to aspiring gardeners for decades when I taught classes and opened my own business.

The seemingly easiest—but most difficult part—comes first: selecting which flowers you want to cross. I pick ones that I think will not only, hopefully, create the prettiest flowers but also unique crosses, ones that nobody else in the world has yet to create. But you *must* cross a diploid daylily with a diploid or a tetraploid with a tetraploid. All plants have a basic set of chromosomes; diploids have two identical sets in each cell, while a tetraploid has only one of a whole series of polyploids.

I smile, remembering how people's eyes would begin to gloss over when I began to get "too science-y." It's difficult to differentiate between the two; even I still have trouble when simply glancing at a flower. A gardener must know the ploidy of the parents before attempting a cross of the two. Fortunately, that is recorded for each registered daylily, and I know the histories of each of my crosses, so I know not to make any mistakes.

I study my two crosses. *Or do I?*

I have, quite literally, a library of notebooks devoted to my crosses. I organize them by year as well as color-cross. I shake my head to clear the cobwebs, and I kick the yard in anger when I can't easily recall whether my Blue-throated Hummingbird and Summer Sapphire are dips or tets. I finally go to the screened porch and search the stacks, before finding the right notebook.

Dips. These are dips. I knew it.

There is always a great debate among daylily devotees on whether "dips" or "tets" make better crosses. Dips tend to be easier to hybridize overall, and I think they are hardier, while tets can have more color saturation.

But the actual hybridizing process is highly orderly and routine. First, decide which flowers you want to cross and then which flowers you want to be the mom and the dad. The center of each daylily holds six stamens and one pistil. You simply pinch off one of the six filaments about halfway down and then carry that over to the other, touching the end of the filament to the end of the filament, dabbing the pollen—the "powdery stuff" I used to say—onto the end of it.

That deposited pollen will rest in place and be moistened by a clear fluid called "stigmatic fluid." Then a tiny door, called a "stoma," in the shell of the pollen grain opens up, and from within the grain a single cell of germ plasm will begin to grow its way down inside the style until it reaches the ovary, in which unfertilized seeds are attached. The cell from within the pollen bears the "flower daddy's" genetic material. And if the journey has been successful, the "mommy flower's" egg will be fertilized, and both the pod and pollen parents' genetic material will be recombined to produce a viable seed. Those seeds will grow and swell, and the small green pod will gradually enlarge on the flower scape.

Harvesting those seeds takes about two months as they must mature. It's easy to see when it's time to harvest as the seed pods begin to split open. Seeds harvested too early will likely not germinate, and many times the pod opens before it's time to harvest, which is why I devised my hosiery trick. I take my old nylons and cut them into squares, then secure them over the pod with a rubber band or twist tie. This allows air and light to filter in but keeps the seeds from falling out.

I smile looking at my daylilies. Shirley used to say, "Honey, it looks like you've put your nylons out on the clothesline to dry, and no one needs to see that."

"Shirley," I'd reply, "the end result is worth it."

When they are ready, I remove the seeds and let them dry overnight. I put mine in small plastic bags and refrigerate for another month or so, as I've found they tend to germinate better after refrigerating.

Living in Michigan means I can't plant my seeds in September, as we Northerners don't have three months of decent weather for germination considering the first hard frost comes in October. So into flats in my greenhouse they go, where they grow under lights and in warmth until spring, when I can *finally* plant them. And then the waiting begins: three years until I know if my original idea is successful. Those days before the first buds open is like Christmas morning, over and over and over again, all summer long. I usually cannot sleep, and I wake at dawn so I can spend every single minute with my babies.

I finish and then write in my tablet, a big smile crossing my face:

2003—Blue Crosses
Summer Sunrise in Michigan =
Blue-throated Hummingbird x Summer Sapphire
(TBD seeds/TBD planted)

I close my eyes, and in my mind I can already see the final version: a daylily as unique as a summer dawn in Michigan, blooms rimmed in sapphires as if dusk and dawn had a baby of midnight blue.

I open them and smile even wider, my heart racing. I had

yet to notice a few of my other babies being born. I race back inside and grab a notebook from 2000.

"Comerica Park!" I yell, remembering. I race back outside and admire the bloom I named after the Detroit Tigers' new stadium, which they moved into in 2000. The leaves are even greener than any I've crossed. I wanted them to be as green as the new grass in the stadium, a representation of baseball and summer. The color of the bloom represents the Tigers: orange lily with a navy center. "Go, Tigers!" I yell, before leaning in to give the flower a little kiss. "You're a real beauty," I whisper. "And a lot prettier than the Tigers."

My Tigers are abysmal this year, I think. *I wonder if they'll even win twenty games by the All-Star break.*

A plane flies over the lake, the boom of its engines filling the silence and echoing off the water. I look up and admire the contrail in the blue, blue sky. Contrail in a humidity-free summer sky reminds me of a streaking baseball leaving the stadium, just like the ones Jonathan used to hit. I watch the plane become smaller and smaller, the contrail fade, and as I lower my eyes back to the world, another plane comes into view.

A paper airplane flits and floats toward me, catching the current of the breeze, before finally settling atop some of my hydrangea bushes that have yet to bloom.

What in the world? I think.

I walk over and pluck the airplane from the bush. When I open it, a flower—a little pink construction paper rose—falls out. I pick it up and written inside each cut and curled paper petal are the words, "I'm sorry!" My heart jumps, and I turn toward the fence. A blue eye is pressed against a slat, watching my every move.

I don't move.

"Iris? Mrs. Maynard? Can you hear me?"

The father!

I don't respond.

"I can hear her breathing, Daddy," Lily says. "I can see her standing there."

"I'm sorry, too," Cory says. "For everything."

Silence. I try not to breathe. I remain a real-life still life.

"Are you a Tigers fan?" Cory asks. "I heard you yell. I have the game on…they stink this year."

I remain silent. And then, carried on the breeze, is the sound of the pregame on the radio. I think of my husband and my father, who always had the game playing on the radio, the announcers' voices, crack of the bat, cheer of the crowd, merging with the buzz of bees and flutter of hummingbirds.

"Hello?" Lily asks.

A little girl's voice.

The sounds of summer.

"Hello," I finally say. "Yes, I love the Tigers. Though I don't think they'll win over fifty games this year."

Cory laughs. It's more of a sigh of relief. "I'd bet you, but I think you might be right."

I chuckle.

"I didn't mean to lose my temper at your home the other day, ma'am," Cory continues. "I'm deeply ashamed, and can never apologize enough. I haven't been myself for a while." He stops. "I'm trying to be again. And Lily didn't mean to snoop. I know how important your home and privacy are to you. I'm the same way. I promise we won't bother you again." Silence. "And don't blame Lily for the airplane. It was my idea. I can never thank you enough for trying to help Lily the other day and for making that call for me." He stops. "The rose was her idea, though."

My heart is racing. I am still unable to move. I turn, and I can see my daylilies wave in the breeze, their pretty faces tilted toward the sun.

You only have one day to live, I think. *Don't think it, Iris, you sentimental sap.* And yet I think of Lily by herself the other day, and the paralyzed father unable to go to the beach, and I can't stop the thought from forming in my head. *What if this were my last day?*

"Gate's open," I say. "But only if you'd like to come over and help me with my daylilies."

I hear scrambling and mumbling.

"Be right over," Cory says through the fence.

A few seconds later the duo appears, hand in hand. Cory is wearing a Tigers T-shirt and sweatpants with an army logo, and Lily is wearing a pair of little girl overalls with a sparkly pink tee underneath. Lily ducks her head when she first sees me, in that way children do when they've done something wrong, gotten caught and just want it to go way. Her blond hair covers her face like a mask of shame.

She actually looks more like her father than her mother, I surmise, *although she has her mother's inquisitive nature.*

There are a few seconds of uncomfortable silence, no one knowing where to start. "These are my daylilies," I finally say. "These are my babies."

The two eye me suspiciously.

"They truly are," I continue. "I created nearly every single one of these cultivars myself."

"Cul-tuh-what?" Lily asks, pulling her hair out of her face.

"Cultivar," I say. "Just means cultivated variety." I lean down and look at Lily. "They're just like you. You're a cultivated variety, too. Your mommy and daddy created you, and there's not another flower like you in the whole world."

Lily blinks, once, twice, in slow motion.

"And I'm not mad at you anymore," I say. "I'm just disappointed in you." I touch her nose gently and stand, before looking at Cory. "You, too," I mouth.

Cory nods, his eyes just as wide as his daughter's. "Now, do you want to learn how to create your own daylily?"

"Yes!" Lily yells.

"Cool," Cory says.

"What do we do?" Lily asks.

"It's easy," I say. "I want you to pick out a flower you think is pretty, and I want your father to do the same. Then we'll cross them. I'll walk you through every single step, but the most important step is picking flowers you think will make the most unique baby, one that will be all yours."

A smile engulfs Lily's face, which looks as big as the sun over her head. "My own flower baby?" she asks.

"Do you want to know why I love daylilies so much?"

Lily nods.

"I love daylilies because they are like people. Every flower not only looks different but also each one has a unique personality. Some are morning people, like me, and some are night people."

Lily moves toward my daylilies and walks the entire garden. Then she heads back to where she started and promptly takes a seat.

"What are you doing, Lily?" Cory asks.

"I need to study their faces," she says, her tone very serious. "They're lilies. I'm named after them." She looks toward us. "I have to make the right choice because this flower will live forever. Even longer than you, Daddy."

I shake my head at her wisdom.

"What about you?" I ask Cory.

"Oh, I already know." He looks at Lily and then at me, before pointing toward the daylilies. "Comerica Park, right?"

I wink as Lily continues to stare at the flowers.

"You know," I say to Cory, "the name *daylily* is accurate because each blossom survives only one day. It opens in the morning but by the end of the day its life will be over." I stop. "The scientific name for daylily is *Hemerocallis*, which comes from the Greek words meaning *beauty* and *day*—literally beauty for a day—since each flower lasts only a single day. To make up for this, there are many flower buds on each daylily flower stalk, and many stalks in each clump of plants."

I walk over to a daylily and gesture for Cory to come closer. "See? Look."

I grab a ruffled daylily, whose frilly edges are nearly lime green and its petals purple.

"Many flowers can bloom on a single scape but each bloom only remains open for a short time." I stop and look at Cory. "Only one. This bloom will be gone by day's end. But another will take its place."

"But that one bloom is gone forever?" Cory asks, his voice raw and deep. "Never to be replaced?"

I stand and walk toward Cory. "Yes," I say. "And that is the beauty and tragedy of this world, isn't it? The whole world—life, people, flowers—are constantly in motion, coming alive, dying, usually all at the same time. We can choose which we want to be. Are we the bloom that is emerging, or the one that is dying?" I stop but cannot stop the words leaving my mouth. "Which do you want to be, young man?"

Cory's shoulders clench, and he looks at me. When I meet his eyes, he diverts them. He looks at Lily touching a daylily, and his chin quivers.

Such a young man, I think. *Such an old soul.*

Cory doesn't answer. Instead, he finally turns, lasering his eyes on mine. "What about you, Iris? Which have you chosen?"

He glances at my fence and then back at me.

Now it's my turn to divert my eyes. I look at my greenhouse. "I've chosen to be kept in a controlled environment," I say.

"Me, too," Cory says.

I turn and look at Cory again. I lower my voice. "I can never understand what you saw or what you go through every single day to survive, but I have experienced the horrors of war and the horrors of loss. My husband never came home from World War II. My daughter died of polio. I lost my entire family while I was still a young woman. And yet I continued. You have a daughter, young man. You cannot allow your grief and anger to overwhelm your love and obligation to her. It will end up consuming your entire family."

Cory's eyes widen, and his body begins to tremble.

"I know, ma'am. I know. You're right."

"Did you go to see the counselor I called?"

He nods. "Abby went with me. I like her. She's helping me reset my mind to deal with my anxiety. I've seen her a few times already." He stops. "I'm finally getting some help, thanks to you." He looks up at me, eyes wide, lips now trembling. "But I think I need a lot more help." His face is racked with pain.

And then, out of the blue, he reaches over and touches my arm. "Help me."

I stand in shock, unable to do a thing. *I risk everything—my privacy, my shell, my heart, my wall of security—if I do anything.* I look into the sky, searching for an answer. In my head I hear a voice that sounds like my daughter's say, *You need help, too, Mommy.*

"Can I ask you a question?" Cory asks, making me jump. I do not respond, but he asks anyway. "What about you? Did you ask for help? How did you choose to live?" This big man tries to regain his composure, but his voice is still shaky. "I've already learned there's a big difference between being alive and living."

His words give me goose bumps. I start to answer, but Lily yells.

"I have my flower! This one!"

I look over and see the one she is holding. My heart leaps into my throat.

"That daylily," I start, my voice wavy with emotion, "that one…is called My Mary."

Finally, I turn to Cory. "This," I say quietly, gesturing around my garden. "This saved my life. This kept me alive." I stop. "This keeps me alive."

"I used to garden," he says. "I need to again. I think it might be the thing that keeps me alive, too," Cory says. "Please."

I stare at him. The world is spinning.

Lily runs over and hugs her father's legs. "My Mary!" she says.

"You picked a beauty, my dear," I say.

And then I surprise myself: I simply reach out and touch Cory's arm and place my hand atop Lily's head.

ABBY

I brake nearly too late. I scream, and the water bottle sitting in the drink holder beside me springs loose and rolls loudly on the floor mat beneath me.

I look over, and an elderly couple in a sedan with an Illinois license plate is sitting in shock as their car sits sideways in the street. The husband is draped in French fries. He looks over and mouths, *Sorry*.

I'd been warned about summer tourists in Michigan. In town, locals call tourists "Fudgies" for their penchant to walk the streets as slowly as zombies while shopping and chomping on fudge. The term for out-of-state drivers—especially from our neighboring state of Illinois—who sightsee, daydream and house-hunt all while behind the wheels of their cars is much less flattering.

"FIPs," I mutter to myself, using the rather filthy acronym for—well, let's say—Frickin' Illinois People.

This particular Illinois person pulled right in front of me, while eating his fries and gawking at an old cottage for sale a few blocks from the beach.

He rolls down his window. My passenger window is already wide-open.

"Are you okay?" he asks in a warbly voice.

"I'm okay," I say. "No damage."

"Easy for you to say." His wife, resplendent in a hair color somewhere between blue and purple, leans forward. An ice-cream cone is stuck upside down in her ample bosom.

I smile and nod, stifling a laugh. I look in the mirror and a line of cars is waiting. I motion for the man to continue driving, and he does, pulling fries from his shoulders and popping them into his mouth.

I follow his car as he drives, keeping a safe distance now. I discovered this shortcut home a few weeks ago, although the term *shortcut* is generous. It's actually a long-cut, a secret, guilty pleasure. This path cuts through some of Grand Haven's cutest neighborhoods and then juts by Lake Michigan. Now that the weather has warmed, I roll down my windows on my way home and enjoy the exquisite Michigan summer air. It's my only few moments of calm, my only few minutes of downtime, between the pressures of work and home.

I turn on my blinker to go right, and the elderly couple heads left. He gives me an apologetic wave out his window as the car pulls away.

It was his fault, wasn't it? I suddenly think.

My mind, to be perfectly honest, was certainly not on driving when I slammed on my brakes. I was worried about what I would return home to this evening, while simultaneously being consumed with work. I had received an email just before five from Mr. Whitmore stating that my new metal flake paint collection was being turned over to a new team.

Of men, I think. *All men.*

I wanted to storm into his office and demand an explanation. But women can't be "stormers" in a corporate environment. So I called his assistant and asked if we could talk before we left for the day.

"Please sit, sit, Abby," Mr. Whitmore said as if all was hunky-dory.

"I'm just confused by your email, sir," I said, my voice calm. "Why is *my* project being reassigned?"

"Abby," he said, his voice filled with a tsk-tsk. "I thought you would understand, better than anyone, the culture here. It's *family*. It's *our* project. It's never an individual's. There is no *i* in 'team.'"

I despise motivational sayings and posters. I hate companies that drape their hallways with pictures of cats stuck in trees that read, "Hang in there!"

"I understand completely, sir," I had said.

"Good, good."

"But..."

"But what?"

"But it appears as though I will have absolutely no involvement going forward on a project that I not only created but also one that was largely the reason you hired me. It doesn't make sense that I wouldn't be involved in some manner."

Mr. Whitmore—the man I respected, the man I believed would be a different kind of boss—then looked at me and said, "I need that pretty little head of yours on a new project. Now, anything else? I have a golf game and beer waiting for me."

"No, sir."

"Good, good."

Golf. Beer. Pretty little head.

"When does it end?" I was saying to myself in the car, my voice escalating in anger, drowning out the relaxation station I'd put on the radio to calm my nerves. "Women do the work but men get the credit. Women do the work but men get the money. Women have a career and a family. We work all day and then work all night at home. Men golf, go to the club, work out, meet for happy hour, go to a game, and it's deemed healthy, male bonding. Women want a few weeks of paid maternity leave, and we don't get it."

When will it ever change? Will it ever change?

I walk into my house, and it is quiet.

My heart jumps. *Cory is passed out, and Lily is alone.*

"Hello?" I call, my voice sounding just as angry as it did in the car. "Hello?"

"We're back here."

Cory and Lily are sitting on the porch on this beautiful evening, the sky still bright. Lily is reading a picture book about Lake Michigan for camp, while Cory is on the laptop. Sitting beside him—and I do a hammy double take just to make sure—is a sparkling water. Lily picks from a bowl of blueberries.

"Hi, Mommy!" Lily says, her teeth blue.

"Is everything okay?" I ask. My eyes are wide, my voice panicked.

Cory looks up at me and manages a small smile, though his face looks crestfallen. "I deserve that."

I didn't mean to say this out loud. It was supposed to be a thought bubble, one that stays within my own head, like in a cartoon.

But I'm so unaccustomed to seeing things so…normal.

"I didn't mean it. I'm sorry," I say. I walk over and give him a kiss.

"No, it's okay. It's about time I pull my weight around here."

I kiss the top of his head and then walk over and do the same to Lily.

"What are you working on?" I ask.

"Reading," Lily says, looking up, her eyes quickly darting back to her book.

"And you?" I ask Cory.

"Reading," he says, before motioning his head a few times toward the right. "About Iris," he says. "The landlady. Not the flower. You won't believe what I've found out about her."

"You're a regular Hardy Boy," I say.

"Which one am I?"

"Shaun Cassidy," I say.

"Of course," he says with a laugh. "Didn't you have a crush on him?"

"I was born in the wrong era," I say.

"You were," he says. "How was your day?"

I think of telling him, but I don't want to spoil this moment. "Fine," I say. "Tell me about Iris. Did you two get into a fight again? I just made peace with her."

"I deserve that, too," Cory says.

"Sorry," I say again.

"We actually made peace, too," he says. "I apologized to her, and she invited me and Lily into her garden today. She taught us how to cross daylilies. We created our own cultivar, didn't we, Lily?"

"We did!" Lily says, looking up. "A flower baby!"

I smile and take a seat by Cory. "And?"

"She's a fascinating, strong woman." He stops. "She seemed to actually want to help me." I take his hand. "Iris reminded me of my drill sergeant, but in a more spiritual sort of way. She actually got in my head. It's like she was directly challenging me."

"To do what?" I ask.

"To rise up to the occasion. To do better." He stops again. "To be a better person."

Cory looks at me, and I swear his eyes are misty. He grasps

my hand even tighter. "I think she did, Abby. It's like she could see inside me."

I shake my head. *Is this my husband? Where has he been?*

"Look at what I found," he says, nodding at his computer. "She was known as the First Lady of Daylilies. Iris was known for making hybridization of daylilies that are still popular around America. She used to open her garden and greenhouse up to local gardeners every year and offer starts of her flowers. She then opened her own nursery right here, right out of her backyard. And she was even more famous."

"How so?"

"Where do you want me to start?" Cory asks. "Iris was one of the first female botanists in Michigan. She is credited with helping to shift production of poinsettias from field to greenhouse. She produced a heartier tomato via atomic gardening. She also made Michigan flowers as famous as its beaches." Cory looks at me, his face filled with expectation.

"And?" I ask.

"She started Grand Haven's Victory Garden during World War II, but her husband died in battle." Cory stops. "Her daughter, Mary, died of polio. She withdrew from the public decades ago, but the reasons why are a bit mysterious."

"What a life," I say. "What piqued all this interest?"

Cory looks at me for the longest time. "I don't know, I don't know," he says. "Something in my gut says we were meant to move here. She was like a therapist, too…but with flowers. Anyway, I already made hamburgers. I can start the grill whenever you're ready to eat."

"I'm impressed," I say.

"I made hamburgers," Cory says, his voice a deadpan. "I didn't pass out. I didn't lock our daughter out of the house. It's not that impressive." He stops. "I'm taking it one day at a time. New normal." And then he says, "I have something to tell you," and my heart drops like a falling elevator.

I take a deep breath, and Cory tells me about Lily's disappearance on the beach, his panic attack, Iris's bravery, her calling Dr. Trafman. My heart races, but I simply listen to him, reciting SOS, the steps Kim taught us.

"Thank you for being honest," I finally say. "I've missed you."

"I've missed me, too," he says.

I look up, and Lily is watching us, a smile on her face. The sun over the lake is glorious behind her.

"I didn't mean to go to the beach alone," Lily says suddenly, her smile turning into a frown. "I just got bored. I'm sorry."

"You shouldn't be sorry," Cory says. "I should have been with you. I will be with you. I just need time to learn again that—" he stops "—sand is grand."

Lily giggles. "You're silly, Daddy."

"I'm trying to be," he says with a small grin.

"I have an idea," I say. "Why don't we save the hamburgers for tomorrow and go for a walk. Let's check out that corndog place, Pronto Pup, everyone in town raves about."

"Yeah!" Lily yells.

"It's such a beautiful evening," I continue.

"Okay," Cory says.

"Let me change."

I run upstairs and throw on some shorts and a sweatshirt. "Ready," I call as I come down the stairs.

We head out the front door, me grabbing a jacket for Lily at the last minute as she sings a song she learned in camp about remembering the names of the Great Lakes.

Sailor Jack sailed on Lake Superior,
But its size made him feel inferior.
So sailor Jack, he came back,
High diddle diddle dum day.

I laugh, vaguely remembering singing the same song when I was young.

What is it about a happy childhood memory that can lessen the weight of a hard day? Did we know something then that made us happier? I wonder. *Or did we know nothing then, which made us happier?*

Lily scampers down the steps, still singing, and as we head down our sidewalk, I turn toward Iris's fence.

"Aaabbbyyy…"

Cory is using the same tone of voice my father used when he knew I was considering a bad idea.

"Do you think she ever eats?" I ask.

Cory shakes his head. "She's strong for a woman her age," he says. "But I'm sure it's no fun to cook for one and eat alone all the time."

I nod, thinking of our visit, her body so strong and yet her back resembling a peony stem buckling underneath the weight of its own bloom. I look at Cory and then at the fence again.

"Aaabbbyyy…"

"Doesn't hurt to ask," I say. "Iris?" I call, heading toward the fence. "Iris?"

I head toward her front gate. "Iris? Are you there? It's Abby!"

I cock my head, but it is silent.

"She must be in for the evening," I say. "I tried, at least."

Cory nods and puts his arm around me. We begin to head down the giant hill that leads toward Lake Michigan and Harbor Drive, where Pronto Pup is located. But then Cory stops.

"Coorrryyy…" I say with a laugh.

"She's not in for the evening," he says. "She's on the far side of her house, in her daylily garden."

"How do you know?"

"I just know," he says.

I grab Lily's hand, and we follow Cory to the other side of Iris's cottage. Cory peers through a crack in the fence and then puts his mouth up to a slat. "Iris!" he yells. "Iris!"

Silence.

"Iris, it's Cory," he finally says. "I can see you. I'm sorry to bug you. We have a question."

There is more silence, long enough for Lily to grow antsy and start tugging on my hand to leave, but then we hear, "Good evening."

Cory looks at me. His eyes are large.

"Evening, Iris," I say. "It's Abby."

"Yes, I know."

"It's such a beautiful evening, and we decided we would walk to Pronto Pup for dinner. We've never been and have heard such wonderful things. Would you like to join us?"

Radio silence. I look at Cory, who shrugs.

"Pronto Pup," Iris finally says, her voice suddenly light and airy like a child's. "I haven't been there in a month of Sundays."

"Well, come on, then," Cory says.

"I can't," Iris says.

"Why not?" Cory asks. "Do you need me to help you finish anything?"

"No, no, no," Iris says. "I just…can't."

"Are you sure?" I ask.

"Yes," Iris says, though her voice sounds none too sure.

"Okay, then," Cory says. "Next time."

We begin to walk away when we hear Iris saying, "Pronto Pup, Mary. Remember?"

Cory stops and looks at me. Now my eyes are wide. Cory turns and calls, "Hey, Iris! Would you like us to bring you a corndog from Pronto Pup?"

"Oh, my!" Iris says, her voice bright. "Would you mind? Maybe two? Let me run in and get you some money."

"No, no, Iris. It's our treat," Cory says. "We'll be back in a few." We begin to walk but again Cory stops. "But next time promise you'll join us. Nothing to be scared of out here."

I see Iris's silhouette at the fence. "Isn't there?" she finally whispers, as if to herself, in a tone that gives me chills.

We walk down the hill and past the historic, eclectic homes that comprise Highland Park: log cabins and storybook cottages with wide porches. Many of the cottages are literally perched atop a dune, and dizzying staircases rise straight up as if they head toward heaven. Some of the cottages have installed mini-funiculars alongside the staircases.

"Can you imagine getting your groceries into one of those?" I ask.

"Practical Mommy," Lily says.

"One day you'll understand, young lady," I say, messing her hair.

The hill leads down to Harbor Drive, the main strip of action in the summer for Grand Haven. Here, bars, restaurants, shops and cottages hug the sandy beaches overlooking Lake Michigan and the Grand River leading to the big lake.

"It's bustling," Cory says.

Indeed, Grand Haven is alive on a perfect June night: kids run on the beach, families walk the pier, people fill the restaurants and—in the distance—we see a snaking line.

"That can't be it, can it?" I ask.

A yellow-and-white stand sits along the roadway fronting the water. It is really nothing more than a pop-up shop, one you might find at a county fair.

"This is it?" I ask again. Driving by, it had seemed bigger from a distance.

An OPEN! flag flaps in the wind off the lake, and I find

it hard to believe one person could work in such a tiny stand much less churn out any food. And yet there must be at least fifty people waiting in line.

"It's gotta be good," Cory says.

"Open since 1947," says a woman in front of us. She looks like a hardy soul, a true Michigander. She is standing in wet shorts and a wet top.

"Did you get in the water?" I ask.

"Warm," she says. "Nearly sixty-two."

I'd be hypothermic, I think.

"I want fries!" Lily says.

"Only corndogs," the woman says. "It's all they do. Traditional fried-and-battered hotdog on a stick. Recipe's a guarded secret. Plain, ketchup, mustard or both for a buck seventy-five. Best corndogs in the world. Best bargain in Michigan. I'm here first day they open in April, even if it's snowing." She looks at Lily. "Don't worry, honey. You won't be disappointed. This means summer!"

For some reason my heart begins to race as we approach the glass window. I feel like a kid. A woman is taking orders, while a man is frying the corndogs.

"What can I get for you?"

"We've never been here," I blurt.

The woman leans in to whisper so Lily can't hear. "Virgins," she says. "Our favorites."

I laugh.

"Two ketchup, two ketchup and mustard, two plain..." Cory says. He looks at me. "We didn't ask Iris what she liked?"

"What do you think Mrs. Maynard would like?" I ask Lily.

"Iris? Iris Maynard?" The woman taking our order looks at me and tilts her head. "No. Sorry. It couldn't be. Anything else?"

"You know her?" I ask, my eyes growing bigger. "Iris Maynard?"

"My mother used to get daylilies from her. My grandmother, Shirley, was good friends with her a long time ago. Grandma's been gone awhile now. *Everyone* knew Iris. She was the Queen of Grand Haven gardening. She was considered sort of like an Amelia Earhart around here. Smart, independent, headstrong, but tragic life." The woman stops. "I actually thought Iris was dead."

"She's very much alive," I say. "She's just…" I stop, searching for the right words. I feel, for some reason, protective of her, as if I can't say a bad word against her. "…hungry," I finish.

"Well, if I remember correctly, she liked mustard," the woman says. "And I believe her late daughter liked ketchup."

I look at Lily, and pull her tightly against me.

"Let's make it one of each, just to be sure," I say.

Our corndogs come out of the fryer piping hot, and I remember ordering these—along with funnel cakes—from the traveling circus that used to visit Detroit when I was little. We haul them over to a bench by the water, and I take my first bite.

"Oh, my gosh," I say. "So good. I feel like a kid again."

Cory downs his in record time, and I hand him one of mine. "I couldn't," he says, reaching for it.

"Growing boy," I say with a laugh, before looking at Lily, whose face is drenched in ketchup.

"More," she says.

"How about an ice-cream cone on the way home?"

"Yeah!" Lily says.

"I'm such a good mother," I say to Cory. "Corndogs. Ice cream."

"You are," he says, his voice filled with sincerity. "You

are." I lean over and kiss him, and for a moment I feel like a college girl again, a boy kissing me on the beach, the waves our soundtrack.

"You taste like corndog," we say at the same time, before bursting into laughter.

Lily races onto the beach, and Cory hesitates.

"Lily!" I yell.

"No," Cory says. "I have to do this." He takes a deep breath. "SOS time," he says to me, shutting his eyes. He takes a step onto the sand and then another. I look over, and his eyes are still shut.

"Cory," I start.

"Not the same sand," he whispers before opening his eyes.

He puts his arm around me and leans into me, the weight of his body knocking me off-kilter. I steady myself and hold my husband, and for the first time in ages, we walk the beach together.

Lily shucks her shoes and runs in and out of the tide, pretending to be a piping plover, a cute little bird that scampers along the edge of the surf, its animated antics just like that of a child's. We stop and get twist cones at the little ice-cream store, and eat them as we walk the big hill leading home. There is a serenity to our little neighborhood this evening—porch lights pop on in cottages, log lamps are illuminated, the smell of grills fills the air—that makes the day's difficulties fade along with the sun.

"Magical night," Cory says. "Little steps, big hills, but we can make it if we do it together, right?"

I nod and hold him even tighter.

We head to Iris's house and call over the gate. When she opens it, Cory holds out the bag. Iris claps, her eyes as big as moon pies.

"Thank you, thank you, thank you," Iris repeats.

"We met a woman working there whose family knew you," I say. "Her grandmother's name was Shirley."

"Shirley?" Iris says, her eyes growing even bigger.

"Yes, Shirley was this woman's grandmother," I say. "You knew a Shirley, right? In fact, I think I recall you telling me when we talked that I reminded you of her."

Iris cocks her head at me. "Thank you for dinner," she says. "Truly. I can't thank you enough."

Why didn't she answer my question?

"Got you one of each," Cory says, nodding at the bag. "A corndog with mustard and one with ketchup. This woman said your daughter loved ketchup. Is that right?"

Iris's face dims, and she starts to shut the door, repeating, "Thank you. Good night. Thank you. Good night," until the gate is closed. I hear the lock slide shut.

"Do you want some company, Iris?" I ask. "We'd love to sit with you."

"I have company," she says, her voice fading as she moves away from the gate. "Thank you anyway."

Cory shrugs and takes Lily by the hand. They walk a few steps and when they reach our sidewalk, Cory realizes I'm not behind them. He turns. "Go on," I mouth.

"Abbbyyyy," Cory mouths.

I give him a dramatic wave of my hand and wait for them to go inside. When the front door shuts, I sneak to the far side of the fence and look through it.

Nothing.

I eye Iris's neighbor's cottage. I can see the glimmer of a TV set behind closed curtains. I take a deep breath and then sneak into their yard like a cat burglar. The neighbors have grown a long, tall row of arborvitae to try and hide Iris's fence. I crawl along it, stopping periodically to pull the branches apart to look through the fence.

What am I doing? I think. *I've lost my mind. Go home, Abby. Go home.*

But I don't. I can't.

And then I hear Iris's voice.

Who is she talking to?

I meander farther into the neighbor's yard, until I am near their screened porch. I hunker down and paw through the arborvitae until I am wedged between two of the dark green trees. A branch scrapes my face as I peer through a slat in the fence.

Iris is sitting on the ground, facing her daylilies. She opens the bag and takes out a corndog. Her eyes close as she takes the first bite.

"Tastes just the same, Mary," Iris says. She finishes a corndog and pulls the second from the bag. "And they got one for you, too. Ketchup. Your favorite. Shirley's granddaughter remembered. Can you believe it? After all these years."

Iris holds the corndog out to a beautiful daylily that is open at night, its bloom as bright as the rising moon.

"Just to think that we were there the first day Pronto Pup opened," Iris says. "How many decades ago was it, my angel? Six?"

Iris holds the corndog in front of the daylily once again as if the flower is going to eat it, and then she polishes it off before leaning forward onto her knees. "Good night, My Mary," Iris says, giving the daylily a gentle kiss. "Until next year."

My heart leaps, and I throw a hand over my mouth to contain a gasp of emotion. I watch Iris head inside.

"Hello? Is someone out here?"

I nearly faint when I hear a man's voice yell. My heart races, the branches tickling my face.

"Hello?"

Through the open door, I can hear the TV blaring, a reporter talking about the number of American soldiers who have died since President Bush declared "Mission Accomplished" in May. I hold my breath. When the door closes, I race back home and pull Lily into my lap, holding her until she says, "Mommy, I can't breathe."

"I'm taking a shower," I finally say.

I stand in the shower and sob, thinking about the innocence of childhood and the reality of adulthood, Iris's life, Cory's battles and my day. I shut my eyes, the water pouring over my head. I can clearly hear Iris's voice after Cory told her there was nothing to be scared of in the world.

"Isn't there?" I ask, my voice echoing in the shower. "Isn't there?"

PART SEVEN

HOLLYHOCKS

"As for marigold, poppies, hollyhocks and valorous sunflowers, we shall never have a garden without them, both for their own sake, and for the sake of old-fashioned folks, who used to love them."

—Henry Ward Beecher

IRIS

JULY 2003

"Thank you for your healing powers and your strength," I whisper to my tea. I look up. "And thank you for your beauty and memories."

I am seated on a blanket facing my beloved hollyhocks. The sun is on my face, and I am sipping hollyhock tea and eating lunch.

This is my Fourth of July ritual, and it has been for as long as I can remember, as long as there have been fireworks and barbecues and summer vacations.

This was my mother's and my grandmother's ritual, too.

"An old woman's garden should have white picket fences, shade trees and lots of hollyhocks," my grandma used to say. "You'll see one day."

I never saw my grandmother as old. She was a perennial. Her beauty was in her history. She would bloom forever.

Or so I thought.

"There is just something about hollyhocks," my grandma would continue. "It's like they're standing as tall as they can so they can see the fireworks, too."

While my grandfather and all the menfolk would spend the day setting up our family's fireworks on the beach—which was always titled by my grampa, who had more than a little P.T. Barnum in him, "The Greatest Fireworks Spectacular on Earth!"—the women would spend the day in the garden. It wasn't sexist: we were each truly doing what we loved most.

"The men love a boom, we love a bloom," my mom would say as we deadheaded the garden. And it was true.

There was just something about three generations being together in the place we loved most in the world: my grandma's cottage garden. I felt safer than I ever did, tucked along the lakeshore by her flowers, which had been started in her mother's and grandmother's gardens. Each flower seemed to tell a story, none more so than the hollyhock.

"Put your ear next to the bell," my grandma would say. "It's just like a seashell. It can tell you the story of its life." I would shut my eyes and shut out the world: the boom of the bottle rockets echoing off the lake, the buzz of the bees, the breeze gently rustling the leaves of the pretty sugar maples.

I am strong and proud, the hollyhocks would whisper into my ear.

"Did you listen?" my grandma would ask.

I would nod.

"The hollyhocks remind us to stand tall in this world," she said. "Never forget that."

On those perfect holidays along the lakeshore—clear skies, little wind, temperatures in the low eighties—when the boys were on the beach, my grandma would spread a blanket out in front of her hollyhocks, and we would have lunch. Nothing fancy. My grandma was not a fancy woman. She would make sandwiches with nothing more than warm, fresh tomatoes she plucked from her garden, white bread, mayonnaise and a lot of cracked pepper. We'd have cucumbers and onions, and my grandma's iced hollyhock-blossom tea.

Firecrackers boom and knock me from this memory. I take a sip of tea—a sip of summer—and smile.

My grandma taught me to make the tea when I was just a girl. Nothing more than picking four of the freshest hollyhock flowers, removing their petals and putting them into a Mason jar with a cup of boiled water. Put on the lid and allow to steep for 15 minutes or so. I like mine iced in the summer with a touch of local honey.

I take a bite of my lunch. It's still quite simple, although my bread of choice has changed over the years—I prefer a crusty seedy salt I have delivered from a local bakery—and I use an olive oil–based mayonnaise. But the tomatoes are straight from my vegetable garden, as are the cucumbers and onions. I grow strawberries, asparagus, cherries and peppers, too, as well as a lot of herbs.

I may eat a corndog once every few decades, I think with a chuckle, *but most of my sustenance comes from what I can grow or what the earth can provide naturally.*

I take another sip and stare at my hollyhocks.

I partially credit this tea, illogically I'm sure, for my longevity. I credit the hollyhocks, with complete conviction, for my strength.

Just look at them!

Many of my hollyhocks tower over me. They rise to nearly eight or nine feet tall. They are truly a natural symbol of the power and pride each of us can possess, no matter how rough the terrain.

I engage my aging spine and aching lower back to mimic my friends and sit just a little bit taller.

And their faces! Oh, their faces! Purple, pink, white and yellow. Even ones that resemble old-fashioned peppermint candies.

What is it about a hollyhock, I wonder, *that has captured my imagination ever since I was a little girl?*

I sip my tea and stare up and into their wide faces.

I smile and nod to myself. I think it's that—like me, like all women—there's more than meets the eye.

Hollyhocks are part of the expansive and diverse mallow family, which includes okra, cotton, hibiscus and marshmallow, now known as the delicious end to every Fourth of July bonfire. The plants were supposedly used by Crusaders to make a salve that was placed on the hind legs—hocks—of injured horses. "Holly" comes from holy, also from the Crusaders. Hollyhock was used to treat a variety of ailments, from inflammation of mucous membranes to cuts and bruises, as well as sunburns, cramps and kidney problems.

If our ancestors believed in your healing powers, I think, *then I believe you can heal a soul.*

I've always thought of a hollyhock as a perfect friend. They are lovely but quiet. They always stand by your side. They poke their heads over fences, and they lean into windows to say hello.

A bottle rocket squeals overhead and I yelp, sloshing tea into my lap. I laugh at my overreaction, and then think of my family on the Fourth, so long ago, the men on the beach and us in the garden eating lunch.

I hear Lily scream as another bottle rocket screeches past, her shock turning quickly into a girlish giggle, and suddenly I think of Mary.

I think of summer.

I think of hollyhocks.

JULY 1948

I am not in my body. I am hovering over my garden watching a woman who looks very much like me ripping apart my gardens. She has a sickle and is whacking down flowers—daylilies, bee balm, hollyhocks, daisies, lavender—in wide swaths, like a tornado. I watch her fall to the ground and dig her bare hands into the earth, ripping out heirlooms by their roots. She stands, her hair and eyes wild, and picks up a pretty blue-tinted lake stone from her garden border and throws it at her tiny greenhouse. The shattering of glass echoes along the lakeshore. The woman raises her head and screams, before falling to her knees once again.

"Iris! Iris, stop! Stop it! Someone, help me! Grab her and hold her down!"

I come back into my body. I am being held down by Shirley's husband and a neighbor boy. Somebody takes the scythe away. I can taste dirt in my mouth. My eyes are nearly swollen shut.

"She's dying, Shirley! She's dying! And there's nothing I can do!"

The neighbor boy's expression is stricken. He looks at me, his face red, his body strong and healthy.

"Get off me! Get off me! I just want to die!"

I push them off me and struggle to my feet. I lock eyes with the young boy. He should not be seeing these things at such a tender age.

I feel a weight behind me, and Shirley is pulling me back to the ground again, holding me as I thrash, as I weep, as I come back into the reality that my daughter is dying.

"I know, I know, I know," Shirley whispers. She is sobbing, too. "No one deserves this, especially you. But don't harm your flowers, Iris. They're the—"

Shirley stops.

"They're the only thing I have left in this world," I finish for her.

Shirley grabs me even tighter.

I stare into the sky. It is joyfully, ridiculously blue, and its beauty mocks me.

How can there be a heaven up there?

Out of nowhere, a bottle rocket shoots across the cerulean backdrop, and I suddenly remember: it is the Fourth of July.

I had forgotten what day it was. I only know that this is the day my life—along with my daughter's—will likely end.

Just a few days ago Mary was playing at the county's Fourth of July fair. She was riding the carousel and the Ferris wheel, jumping off the diving board into the county pool, eating funnel cakes and lighting Black Cat black snakes on sidewalks. The next day she told me she didn't feel well, and I thought it was all of the junk food she had consumed. Mary felt good enough to go out and play on the beach, but a few days later she began to feel dizzy, and I watched her walk around the house as if she were drunk. That's when I knew. I rushed her to the hospital.

"Polio," the doctor said. It was the word every parent feared these days, especially in the summer. But it only got worse. "Paralytic polio," the doctor continued. "Rare. Extremely rare. Very little hope."

"What about an iron lung?"

He walked me out of Mary's room. "Iris," he started. I only heard fragments.

An iron lung costs as much as a house.

It won't do any good for Mary.

The hospital administration suggests Mary return home, for the safety of the other patients.

The doctor draped hot packs of wet wool onto Mary's limbs to keep them from going into spasms. I sat by her bed praying for a miracle, praying for Mary to recover, to stand, to sprint to the beach and shoot bottle rockets into the sky.

"Go play," I say to the neighbor boy still standing over me. "Have fun. Shoot your fireworks. Be a child." He stares at me. "Go. Go!"

The shadows of those gathered to witness this spectacle extend over our bodies, but slowly, they retreat, and—shard by shard—the summer sun returns. Shirley is still holding me tightly, unrelenting in her grip.

"It's not fair," I sob. "What have I done to deserve God's wrath? My husband, my daughter... I have nothing left to live for."

Shirley doesn't say a word. She just holds me and holds me, until my sobbing subsides and my breathing calms. My cheek is pressed against the earth, and in front of my eyes lie three stately stalks of hollyhocks: crimson, yellow and white.

I shut my eyes and focus on Shirley's breathing. As I do, I can again hear the waves crashing into the shore, the buzz of the bees in my gardens and the echo of fireworks along the shore. In those sounds I can also hear my grandmother's voice. She is the one holding me now, whispering in my ear, "Just look around, Iris. The daisies remind you to be happy. The hydrangeas remind you to be colorful. The lilacs remind us to breathe deeply. The pansies reflect our own images back at us. The hollyhocks remind us to stand tall in this world. And the roses—oh, the roses!—they remind us that beauty is always present even amongst the thorns."

I jerk upright, forcing myself out of Shirley's arms.

"Iris," she says, her voice on high alert. She sits up and grabs me again. "Don't."

I reach out and grab a stalk of crimson hollyhock. "I used to make hollyhock dolls with Mary," I say. I study the flower and smile. "She loved them."

I form a skirt from the flower, a body from a bud and a head from a seedpod, and then reach over to grab a yellow hollyhock to make a hat. I pinch the parts together with my fingers since I don't have a toothpick and make the doll dance on my lap. For one short moment I am happy again. But slowly, the doll disintegrates as I play with it, the hat and head falling off, followed by the body and ruffles of the skirt. I watch it die in front of my eyes, just like my daughter. I lift my head and roar in grief. Shirley embraces me until my sobbing slows and then she picks up a white hollyhock and holds it before me. "Let's fill Mary's room with flowers," Shirley says. "Since she can't come outside to play on a beautiful summer day, let's bring the outdoors inside."

Shirley stands and looks around. She heads to my shattered greenhouse and returns with a few buckets. She begins to fill them with all the flowers I've hacked down or ripped out of my gardens.

"Stop," I say.

"No, you stop!" Shirley suddenly shouts. "I cannot imagine what you are going through, but you need to be with your daughter right now, no matter how hard it is." She holds up a daylily, as violet as Mary's eyes. "You created this for her," she says, her voice lower but still filled with strength. "These flowers will be her legacy. And every single time you give someone a start from your garden or your own daylilies, you can tell them about your daughter. And when a stranger asks that stranger about the flower, she will recount the story you told her. That will go on forever, and Mary's memory will never die as long as flowers are blooming on this earth."

Shirley is crying, her nose running. I feel my knees weaken, but my friend catches me before I fall.

"For Mary," Shirley whispers.

"For Mary," I repeat.

We gather as many blooms and vases as we can carry and fill Mary's bedroom with flowers. Her room resembles a floral shop by the time we are finished. I take a seat by Mary's bed and hold her hand. As she begins to wake, her nose twitches before her eyes open. "Smells like summer," Mary says. Her eyes flutter and then open, barely. She sees me and smiles.

"We brought summer to you," I say. "Happy Fourth of July."

Her little body is having trouble breathing. The muscles in her chest needed for breathing and swallowing are becoming paralyzed.

"Thank you, Mommy," she says. Mary tries to look around, but her head won't cooperate. I look at Shirley. She walks over and pulls a hollyhock from a vase and hands it to me. "Remember?" I ask Mary, beginning to make a doll.

A tiny smile etches her face and when I finish, she is asleep again. I bend my head to pray, but instead I ask in anger, "Why, God? Why Mary? Why me?"

The windows are cracked, and the warmth and sounds of summer fill her pink bedroom. My eyes are shut, my head is numb, my heart aches so badly I feel as if my body has been cleaved in two. In the distance I can hear a group of happy, healthy children squealing "Wheeee!" as they jump into Lake Michigan. But in my ear, I can plainly hear God ask, "Why? Whhhyyyyy, Iris? Why not you?"

My heart quickens, and my head jerks upright. I look around the room to see if someone is talking to me, tricking me. But Mary is still asleep, and Shirley has passed out in a little rocking chair in the corner, one of Mary's cloth dolls in her lap.

I stand, wanting to scream, to break all the vases in the room, but instead my body feels as if it's being moved by another force, compelled to complete a task. I leave and when I return, I wake Shirley.

"What?" she asks with a start. Her eyes widen when she sees what I have gathered: scissors, tape, string, colored construction and crepe paper that Mary used to draw on and play with. "What's going on?"

"Mary can't see the flowers," I explain. "So we have to hang them from the ceiling so she can when she wakes up. Like fireworks up in the night sky, so she can see them."

"Oh, Iris," Shirley says. She tries to stand but the little rocker stays attached to her ample behind. She pulls it free, and—for the first time in ages—I smile. "Why?" she asks. "Why are you doing this?"

"Why not?" I ask.

As Mary sleeps, we make paper flowers of all varieties and colors, and tie and tape them from the ceiling and to the walls. We work all afternoon and evening, unsure when—or if—Mary will wake.

"Mommy?" I am sitting in the chair by Mary's bed. Fireworks are going off all over the lakeshore. The night sky is illuminated through her bedroom window as if it's morning.

"Oh, sweetheart!" I say. "You're awake."

Her eyes open into a slit. "I see it now…the flowers," she says. "Summer flowers."

"Yes," I say. "All for you. Your own garden."

"And I see the fireworks, too."

We watch them for a few moments as if everything is right in the world. And then I look at Mary.

Her hair is matted, her face ashen, but there is a peaceful look on her face. "It looks like heaven, inside and outside," Mary finally says. She drifts for a second and then says, "I'm going from garden to garden."

I cock my head. *She is hallucinating*, I think.

"Your garden to heaven's garden," she says. "I'm going to see Daddy. And on the Fourth, of all days."

I put a hand over my mouth to contain my sob. "I need a gift to bring him," she says. "What should I take Daddy?"

I shake my head, holding back my tears. She cannot see me cry.

And then it comes to me.

I stand and retrieve a hollyhock from a nearby vase and begin to make a doll. When I finish, I place it on the blanket on her stomach, and she smiles.

"A doll for a doll," I say. "So you can play with it forever."

"Thank you," Mary says, her voice barely audible. "I miss Daddy. And I'm going to miss you, Mommy."

"I'm not going anywhere, Mary," I say. "I'm right here with you."

Mary nods and shuts her eyes. And then with one last ounce of strength, she closes her hands around the hollyhock doll.

ABBY

JULY 2003

There is nothing like a small-town parade.

I am tapping my feet and waving a little American flag as high school bands march by playing "The Star Spangled Banner" and "Stars and Stripes Forever." Lily is stuffing the pocket of her shorts—and mouth—with candy that firefighters toss from trucks and store owners throw from red, white and blue floats that they built on the beds of pickup trucks.

Latecomers jostle us as we stand on the edge of the sidewalk, and some older boys move in front of Lily.

"Hey!" she says.

In one swoop, Cory lifts her onto his shoulders so she can again see the parade.

"Smile!" I say.

Lily loops her hands around her dad's neck, her mouth filled with candy, and they turn toward me for a picture, the sky that blue that only warm, humidity-free Michigan summer days on the lakeshore can produce.

"Want a Tootsie Roll?" Lily asks. Cory nods his head and Lily hands him a piece of candy.

"What about me?" I ask.

"What do you think?" Lily asks her father with a giggle.

"I think she's earned it," he says.

"Here!"

Lily reaches into her pocket and hands me a pulverized peppermint that has already been crushed by someone's foot.

"Gee, thanks," I say. "Looks like a horse didn't want it, either."

A group of veterans of every age representing a variety of wars and military branches marches by. Many vets are in wheelchairs but proudly wearing crisp uniforms. One contingent holds up a sign that reads, IRAQ WAR VETS.

"You should've marched with them," I say.

Cory shakes his head. "Not my thing."

Cory doesn't seek attention. He prefers to be part of a team: sports, military, family.

Instead, Cory salutes and applauds, just one of the crowd.

Booooo! Boooo!

Every head in the parade turns as one. A group of young adults, mostly in their twenties, is loudly booing, their thumbs pointed down. I see Cory swivel, his eyes narrow, Lily still on his shoulders. A candy flies from her hand, her father's quick turn surprising her. One of the young men, hipster beard and sipping a coffee, looks at Cory and stops booing. His eyes move from Cory's face down to his arm. Cory is wearing a T-shirt, and the scroll tattoo on his arm is prominently displayed.

I will always place the mission first.
I will never accept defeat.

I will never quit.
I will never leave a fallen comrade.

The names of Cory's fallen friends are written underneath.

"Sorry, man," the guy says. "I'm not booing vets. I'm booing the Iraq War. It's such a mistake. We shouldn't be there."

"I served in Iraq."

The guy holds up a hand as if a peace offering. "I feel for you," he says. "So many American lives taken. And for what? Our government lied. We all fell for it."

Cory's face turns redder than the American flag I'm holding.

"For what? For *what*?" Cory is seething. "These guys—my friends—died for you. They died to protect this country. And we come home to this? Is this their thank-you? Is it?" Cory takes a step forward, and the guy drops his coffee.

"Daddy," Lily says. Her voice is quivering. She is scared and about to cry.

"It's okay, sweetheart," he says, putting her back on the ground. I put my arms around her protectively.

We are about to leave, but people begin to clap. Men reach out to shake Cory's hand. Women touch my back. "Thank you," they say. "Thank you for your service."

Another high school band marches by, playing John Philip Sousa, and I break down. Cory walks over and puts his arm around me.

"I'm sorry," he whispers. "I didn't mean to lose my temper."

I look at him, wiping my face. "Don't you ever say you're sorry. You did nothing wrong. You did what you thought was right."

Cory pulls me into his arms and kisses my head.

"Are you okay, Mommy?" Lily asks.

I nod. We ride home in silence, the windows down, the booms of firecrackers and happy screams of kids filling the air.

"Gonna turn on the game," Cory says when we get home. He grabs the remote and flicks on the TV. Instead of the game, a news station appears, live coverage of President Bush speaking in Ohio.

"And on this Fourth of July, we also remember the brave Americans we have lost. We honor each one for their courage and for their sacrifice. We think of the families who miss them so much. And we are thankful that this nation produces such fine men and women who are willing to defend us all. May God rest their souls."

I walk over to Cory and slide one arm around his back. I place the other around his arm where his tattoo is.

Bush continues: "Our nation is still at war. The enemies of America plot against us. And many of our fellow citizens are still serving and sacrificing and facing danger in distant places. Many military families are separated. Our people in uniform do not have easy duty, and much depends on their success. Without America's active involvement in the world, the ambitions of tyrants would go unopposed, and millions would live at the mercy of terrorists. With Americans' active involvement in the world, tyrants learn to fear, and terrorists are on the run."

A panel cuts in on the president's remarks and immediately begins to dissect the war, the government's continued use of discredited intelligence and the growing evidence that Iraq has no WMDs nor plans to develop nuclear weapons.

"We didn't know any of this," Cory says.

"I know, I know," I say in a hushed voice. "None of us knew. All we know is that you sacrificed your life for this country."

"You knew this, Abby. I could tell you never believed the reasons behind us going to war."

"I didn't know," I say. "But I had my suspicions. I just don't like war. Who does? Good men and women die. And I just think there should be definitive answers if we are putting the lives of our children, husbands and fathers at risk." I stop. "We knew what we were up against in World War II. Things are murkier these days." I stop again. "But you only need to know you gave your all for this country and this nation. And I am beyond blessed this Fourth of July to have you home and safe. You are my hero, Cory." I touch his tattoo. "You didn't leave your comrades. I will never leave you, either."

We stand, neither moving, for the longest time. I am paralyzed, in fact, by all that has occurred this morning. A wonderful day shot to hell.

Will this be his trigger? Will he run for a beer? Will he try to blot out the pain?

"I think it's time we make masks," Cory says out of the blue. "What do you think?"

My eyes grow wide. I nod, trying to keep my emotions intact. "Yes," I manage to say.

We gather construction paper, scissors, crayons and markers, and sit down at the dining room table with Lily.

"I want you to make a mask about how you've been feeling this summer," I start.

"Feeling since I came home again," Cory adds. "And Lily, just be honest about how you've been feeling, okay? We'll do the same."

Lily nods. We begin to cut and color. Lily keeps her forearm squarely in front of her mask to keep us from seeing.

"Ready?" she asks.

We nod.

"Let's all do it at the same time, okay? One, two, three!"

We hold up our masks, our eyes peering through the holes we've cut, seeing everyone's emotions and feelings fully on the surface, no longer hidden.

"They're all almost the same!" Lily exclaims.

I scan my eyes. She's right. Masks that look outwardly happy on the outside, big smiles, but tears trailing from the eyes, words coming from the mouths reading, *Lonely. Sad. Tired. Anxious.* But on every mask is a heart, a symbol of our love for one another.

"I'm glad we did this," Cory says. "Thank you."

"Thank you," I say.

"My mask is hungry," Lily says. She takes her fingers and sticks them through the opening where her mouth is. She sticks her tongue out.

I laugh. "My idea next! Let's barbecue. A big old-fashioned Fourth of July barbecue."

"Okay," Cory says, kissing me. "But don't you need to call your parents first?"

"Don't you need to call *your* parents first?"

We grin at each other. Our relationships with our families are not what you might call "storybook." My mom drives me insane, to put it mildly, and Cory's family doesn't care for "my educated ways." But all of them act as if nothing can ever be wrong in our lives. The world, yes, our lives, no. They love to see Lily, and she loves to see her grandparents, but we often use her as an excuse.

Oh, my goodness, we can't come because Lily is so busy in school.

Oh, dear, Lily is already booked with summer camps.

I wish we could, but Lily isn't feeling well.

Lily has friends staying this weekend.

Do I like that I feel this way? No. It makes me feel like crap. But have I come to grips with it for the sake of my own sanity? Yes. My mother has never understood or demonstrated unconditional love. Her love is all strings attached. *I love you, Abby,* if *you'd* only *do this, or wouldn't act like that, or don't say that.*

"Let's get it over with," I say.

Cory and I yank out our phones. We call our parents, holding the phones at a distance from our ears.

"Hi, honey!" we can hear both mothers scream simultaneously. Cory rolls his eyes. Both of our Michigan moms act as if their smartphones are childhood tin can telephones and that they have to scream to ensure their voices will travel.

"Hi, Mom," we say, walking to separate rooms.

"Happy Fourth!" my mom says. "Your father and I are so disappointed you didn't come to visit."

Well-played, Mother, I think. *Guilt, strike one.*

"I know. I'm sorry, too, but Lily only gets today off camp, and I only get today off work."

I'm lying.

"Lily is so busy," she says. My mom pauses. I already know she won't ask me about my new job or how busy I am or Cory, because she can't deal with the real world in which I exist. "How is Lily? My precious pumpkin?"

"She's good," I say. I think of putting Lily on the phone, so I can be done, but again, guilt comes to call. "She loves her camps. She loves Grand Haven and living on the beach. She's meeting lots of new friends who will be in her class next year. Oh! And she's making friends with our elderly neighbor who rents us this cottage."

No! I shouldn't have said that. I already wish I could take it back.

"Do you know this woman? Do you leave Lily alone with her? Why would she be friends with an old woman?"

"She's friends with you."

Damn! I shouldn't have said that, either. I already wish I could take it back.

"Just joking," I say.

"Oh," my mother says.

Change the subject, Abby. Change the subject.

"What are you and Dad doing to celebrate the Fourth? Are you watching Detroit's fireworks?"

I already know the answer.

"Oh, Abby, we don't go out of the house on the Fourth. It's too dangerous," she says. I can hear her starting a load of laundry in the background. She does about ten loads of laundry a day for two people who never leave the house: one towel, one T-shirt, one pair of socks at a time. *You don't want to overload the washer or it will break*, she always says. "Kids are lighting firecrackers outside. And I hear bottle rockets, too! I rush outside every half hour or so to check our roof. What if one landed on it? Our house would burn down. And what if one of those fireworks went the wrong way at the show? It could blind your father. And all those people? Pandemonium. Your father is happy watching baseball, and I'm doing some laundry and making some of those red, white and blue parfaits you love so much, the ones with the blueberries, strawberries and whipping cream."

I shake my head, hard, to process all that I've heard. I remove my glasses, set them on the kitchen counter and rub my eyes. "Wow, Mom," I say. "Sounds like a perfect day. Want to talk to Lily?"

"Yes!"

"Lily," I call. "Your grandma's on the phone."

Lily rushes in and sweeps the phone from my hand. "Hi, Grandma! We had the best day already. We went to the parade, and I got lots of candy..."

Lily heads back to the porch, chattering away on the phone.

When did she get to be such a big girl? I wonder.

As Lily and Cory have their conversations, I begin to prep all the family's Fourth favorites: peaches-and-cream corn on the cob, fresh salad, cucumbers and onions, all of which we bought at an adorable farmer's market on the way home from the parade. I start some baked beans by frying some bacon and onion, and I begin to peel potatoes and boil water for my mom's potato salad.

She's a wonderful cook, I think. *I'll give her that.*

Cory appears as I'm hunched over the trash can, peeling, skins flying everywhere.

"How'd that go?" I ask.

"As well as you're doing peeling potatoes, it seems," he says with a laugh. "I told her you were in the kitchen cooking, and she said, 'Finally where she should be.'"

I hold the peeler to my throat, and Cory laughs. He heads to the fridge and plucks out some ground beef and starts to make hamburgers, pulling myriad grilling spices from the cabinet.

"Hey," I say, trying to straighten my back when I finish. "Where's that old ice-cream maker of your dad's?"

"The wooden one?"

"Yeah," I say. "I've got whipping cream in the fridge. Fresh strawberries. Ice. Even rock salt. We can make homemade ice cream. Wouldn't that be fun?"

"For whom?" Cory asks. "Your back's already out, and all you did is peel some potatoes. You know they're electric now."

"Ha-ha," I say.

"Why don't I just go buy some ice cream?"

"I like doing it the old-fashioned way. Reminds me of my grandparents. Reminds me of being at their cottage in the summer."

Suddenly, I sing "Summer Wind" as we dice strawberries and boil potatoes. Lily skips into the kitchen and hands me my phone. "Did you enjoy talking to Grandma?" I ask.

"I did," she says. "Oh! I invited Iris to dinner."

My head jerks upright, and Cory and I stare at each other.

"What?" I ask.

"Grandma said I shouldn't be friends with her because she's a stranger," Lily says. "And I said, 'She's not a stranger. She's lonely. She seems like she needs a friend, and isn't that what friends do? Make you feel not so lonely?'" Lily shrugs her shoulders, exhales and rolls her eyes as if adults make the world much too complicated.

"You're right," I say. "You demonstrated exactly what a true friend is. You're a wonderful young lady."

"I know," Lily says.

Cory and I laugh. "I doubt she will come, though," Cory says. "You know how hard it is for her to leave her house."

"Hello?"

We hear someone calling. We crane our necks and listen.

"Hello?"

We head to the back porch and go outside. Iris is knocking on the fence. "Do you mind opening your back gate?" she asks. Her voice sounds strange. "I would prefer to avoid the front sidewalk."

Cory and I again look at each other, our eyes wider than ever. "Of course," he calls. "Hold on, Iris." He unlocks the gate, and Iris enters, holding an armful of fresh tomatoes, a clump of basil clutched in her teeth. "I thought you might like some fresh tomatoes," she mumbles, "for your burgers or a caprese salad."

Cory and I are standing there, staring at her.

"Yes, I understand what a big deal this is," she mumbles. "So don't make a bigger deal out of it than it already is, or I'll turn around right now."

"Okay, okay," I say.

Lily giggles at the way Iris is talking. "Let me help you, friend," Lily says, grabbing two tomatoes from her arms. Iris halts in our yard as if Lily's words have stopped her cold.

"Thank you," I say. "The tomatoes are beautiful. We're so glad you could make it."

Iris looks at me and then around the yard. "Me, too," she says. "I'm glad Lily asked. I was—" she looks around the yard again and then at the cottage "—missing family today."

"Happy Fourth of July!" Lily yells. "Follow me."

We unload Iris's arms and lead her into the cottage. She stops once more, her eyes sweeping through the house, growing misty. "My grandma's cottage," she whispers. "So many memories. So many memories." Iris shakes her head. "Now, what can I help you with?"

"You're a guest," I say. "Would you like something to drink? Iced tea? Water?"

Iris looks at me. "Iced tea sounds lovely. It is the Fourth of July after all."

"I'll join you," I say.

"I'll grab the tea," Cory says. "Lily, why don't you take Iris in the backyard?"

Cory and I finish making the sides. As Cory fires up the grill, I take my tea and join Iris and Lily outside. The two are sitting on a beach towel on the grass, huddled over something, talking quietly to one another.

"What are you two up to?" I ask.

They move apart, and I see a hollyhock between them. "I'm showing Lily how to make a doll."

Lily looks up at me, a pained look on her face.

"Oh," I say, trying to sound light. "We don't really play with dolls."

"Told you," Lily says.

"I'm sorry," Iris says. "I just thought..."

"They just send a bad message to girls," I explain. "You wouldn't believe how much Barbie affected my self-image growing up." I gesture at myself. "I wanted to look like her, and I'm, well, *so* not Barbie."

"I understand," Iris says. "But dolls are not just about beauty, or being pretty. They're about using our imaginations." Iris pats the beach towel, inviting me to take a seat. "Do you know what I pretended my doll was growing up? A suffragette."

"What's that?" Lily asks.

"A woman seeking the right to vote," Iris says. "My mom and grandma fought for the right for women to vote." Iris looks at Lily. "Did you know women couldn't vote until 1920?"

"That's awful," Lily says.

"Do you have any idea what it meant for my mom and grandma to vote for the first time?" Iris looks at me. "It was as if women finally had a voice in this country. That they mattered. So I pretended my dolls were suffragettes, or I pretended they were me walking into a voting booth. My dolls were strong. That doesn't mean they were GI Joes because women could be women and still be strong." Iris stops and looks around our yard. "I made hollyhock dolls with my mom and grandma right here. My grandma always said hollyhocks remind us to stand tall in this world. Women should always stand tall in this world."

I take a slug of my tea. "I stand fully corrected," I say. Iris holds up her glass, and I clink it with mine. "Show us how to make a doll."

"You know hollyhocks are magical, right?" Iris asks, seemingly more to me than Lily. We both shake our heads.

"Faeries use them as skirts," Iris says, "and they used to help heal horses."

"Wow!" Lily says.

"I cut this one from my garden," Iris says, holding up a stunning magenta hollyhock.

I watch as Iris takes a fully opened blossom and turns it upside down.

"A skirt!" Lily says.

"Now, just pinch these out," Iris says, using her fingers to remove the pistil and stamens, "and stick a toothpick through the flower with the blunt edge at the bottom."

"You came prepared," I say with a laugh.

"Always," Iris says, smiling. "Might be my last trip outside for a few more decades." She chuckles to herself and continues, "Now you can thread on as many blossoms as you wish for a billowy skirt. What I like to do is use another flower bud for the doll's body, and then a seedpod for her head. Like this. Help me."

Lily helps Iris attach the body and the head. "You can use any colored flower to create a very fashionable hat. Hold on." Iris stands and walks to the far end of our fence. She squeezes a finger through a slat and pulls a white hollyhock through the fence.

"Voila!" she says, returning. "I think white would be quite fetching as a finishing touch. Here," she says to Lily. "You do the honors."

Lily adds the hat and smiles from ear to ear.

"What should we name her?" Iris asks.

"Holly, of course," Lily says.

"And what is her story?" Iris asks.

Lily contorts her face, thinking. She looks at the doll. "She's in college studying to be an engineer, and she's going to vote. Holly will be the first woman to vote and the first woman to make a rocket that is filled with flowers to be planted on Mars!"

Iris's face explodes. "I think I love Holly!" she says.

Lily stands with her hollyhock doll and runs to show her father.

"I'm glad you could make it today," I say.

"Your daughter has a very big heart," Iris says. "This is a tough day for me." Iris stops. "Lots of memories."

"I bet," I say.

"It's a day that requires a show of strength," Iris says with a definitive nod. "I thought I'd surprise myself for once. Go on a vacation." She laughs, and I do, too.

"It's a tough day for my husband, as well. A lot of emotions on a day like this." I look at Iris and take a sip of tea. She nods. "Stronger together," I say, clinking her glass.

"Dinner's almost ready," Cory calls.

We eat on the back porch, gorging on hot dogs, hamburgers, baked beans, potato salad, lettuce, corn on the cob, caprese salad. While everyone finishes, I start in on the ice cream.

"Oh, my goodness," Iris says as I crank the old machine. "Now that brings back a lot of memories, too. We had an old hand-crank machine growing up. My grampa loved homemade ice cream. It was his specialty. He grilled and made ice cream. That's all he did." Iris points at the back of the house. "There was a dinner bell on the back of this cottage that my grandma rang to get everyone to come in for dinner off the beach. Well, my dad would ring it when he was making ice cream and his shoulder got tired, and we'd all have to take our turns."

"Ding-a-ling-a-ling!" I yell.

Iris laughs. "I'll give it a shot." Cory begins to protest. "I'm stronger than you think, young man."

Cory lifts his hands. "Go for it," he says.

Iris cranks for a good, long while as the sun begins to fade.

"Daylight seems to last forever on the Fourth of July," Iris says, not at all out of breath yet. "That's why I love Michigan. And that's why our fireworks never start until it's so late. Takes a long time to get dark."

When the ice cream is ready, we head back outside with big bowls and take seats on the porch facing the lake. The first fireworks light the sky as soon as the lake darkens. I look over at the silhouettes of my family and Iris. Everyone's heads are raised to the night sky, eyes wide and unblinking, spoons lifting to mouths, returning to bowls and then back again. Every few seconds the light in the sky illuminates everyone's faces, and I see three generations bonded by the familiar. I smile, remembering a similar moment from my own childhood. Every few seconds someone murmurs, "Ooooh!" or "Aaaahh!" but the world again grows silent save for the boom of the fireworks, the lap of the lake on the shoreline and the hum of cicadas. As the crescendo and noise of the fireworks picks up, I notice Cory fidget. His leg thumps the ground, and he begins to tap his spoon in his bowl. He looks at me and mouths, "SOS." I nod, and he stands up and departs.

Iris looks over at me. I can see a mix of concern and confusion highlighted on her face.

"The noise bothers him," I say. "It can be traumatic."

Iris nods and turns to the sky again. But a few moments later she turns to me and asks, "Do you mind if I use your bathroom?" She looks at me. "It's the tea," she whispers.

"No, not at all," I say with a smile. "It's through the porch and just off the kitchen." I stop. "Sorry. You already know that."

Iris stands.

"Hurry," I say. "I'd hate for you to miss the finale."

I scooch down next to Lily, who is so transfixed by the light show that she doesn't notice me. I watch the fireworks through my daughter's eyes for a few minutes—the colors reflecting in her eyes—but grow more distracted when no one returns. "Wait here," I whisper to Lily. "Don't move, okay?"

She nods as if in a trance.

I move toward the back porch. I take a step up the stairs and pause as I hear voices talking quietly.

"We were driving. Headed… I don't even remember where or why…but we were all in Cougars. My best friend, Todd, was in a Cougar in front of ours. We were laughing, and we were all singing Elvis for some reason. All of a sudden there's a huge explosion. An IED on the side of the road. Our vehicle was rocked, but after the smoke cleared, we saw Todd's was on its side. I mean, these are the safest infantry vehicles. They're structured to be resistant to land mines and IEDs. But this one was huge. When I got to Todd…"

I hear Cory stop. I edge up the porch stairs and peek through the door. Iris is holding him. Cory is weeping.

"He didn't have any legs. I wanted to move him, but I knew… I knew, Iris…"

"It's okay," Iris says. "It's okay."

"I screamed for help. It was total chaos. So I just held him. Sitting in the sand. The sand just soaking up his blood. And we said a prayer. I told him to think of his wife and his daughter. They'd just had a baby before he was deployed. I asked Todd, 'Can you see them?' 'Yes,' he said. He said he could see flowers. 'Flowers?' I asked. Todd said, 'We wallpapered her nursery in flowers. It was the prettiest place in the world.'"

Cory is weeping so hard, I can barely understand him.

"That's when I remembered," Cory says.

"Remembered what?" Iris asks when Cory doesn't continue.

"I had a pressed rose that I carried with me in my wallet," Cory says. "Abby gave it to me when we were married. It was white, and it looked perfect with my tux." Cory stops. "We used to grow roses, you know."

"I didn't," Iris says.

"I never told Abby I took it into combat with me, but I needed something more than a picture of my wife and daughter with me. I needed something real, something tangible. Does that make sense?"

Iris nods.

"I placed that flower in Todd's hands and said, 'Your wife and baby are with you right now, buddy.' He looked at me and said, 'I can see them, man. I can see them.' We buried him with that flower. He was only twenty-two. I watched him die. My best friend. He was just a kid. I watched him die, and there was nothing I could do."

Iris holds Cory as he bawls like a baby.

I lower my head and cry, too, my heart shattering for my husband. My own heart hurts, too.

Why has he never trusted me enough to tell me this?

"I don't know why I'm telling you all this," Cory says. "I haven't even told my therapist yet. I haven't even told Abby."

"Because I'm a stranger," Iris says. "You don't have to pretend to be strong to protect your wife and your daughter."

"I don't want them to live this," he says, his voice as small as a child's. "I don't want to relive this."

I begin to cry even harder. Iris is right. That's why. *He's being strong for us. He doesn't want us to suffer like he is.*

Iris continues. "And you're telling me because I'm not a stranger. We're the same, really. My husband died in the war. He was just a kid, too. And I watched my daughter die in front of me. We're the same. Bound by tragedy." She stops. "But bound by hope, too. You never forget that, young man. Somewhere deep inside all of our scars is resilience, and somewhere deep inside our shattered souls is faith. I believed for a very long time that God didn't exist. How could He? All He showed me was relentless cruelty. But when my daughter died, I realized I was no more special than anyone else. Life is filled with overwhelming tragedy, but it's also filled with incomparable beauty. I read somewhere that God doesn't come to us in the happy times. He comes to us through our scars and wounds." Iris stops again. She puts a hand under Cory's chin and lifts his head until he's looking her directly in the eyes. "You're a glorious scar!"

For a moment there is silence, and then *Boom! Boom! Boom!*

I turn back to the yard. It's the finale of the fireworks. I weep as I watch America celebrate its birthday.

When it ends I can hear people clapping in the distance, boat horns honking. And then I hear Iris say, "You need something to ground you moving forward in your life. You have a beautiful family, but you also need something that allows you to find your center and renew your spirit every single day. You asked me for help so let me help you in my own way. Let me show you my faith. My therapy. My hope. Garden with me tomorrow. Say seven?"

"Okay," Cory says. "Yes."

"It will set your intention for the day." Iris is still holding Cory's face. "You're a good man, Cory."

"You're a good woman, Iris."

She strokes him on the head and stands.

I stumble down the steps, nearly knocking over a flowerpot, trying to act normal.

"Thank you for dinner," Iris says as she walks out.

"Thank you for joining us," I say.

"You're off tomorrow, right?"

I think of the lie I told my mom.

"Yes," I say.

"Well, then, I'll see you tomorrow, too," she says.

"See me where?" I ask.

"Nice try, Colombo," she says with a big smile. "I know you heard every word."

I shake my head. "How did you know?"

"Let's just say you're not light on your feet," Iris says. "I take it you're not a dancer."

"I'm a tripper."

"Good night, Abby," she says.

"Good night, Iris," I say as she disappears into the yard, stopping for a moment to watch Lily sleep in her chair, cradling her hollyhock doll.

Cory appears. "You heard everything, didn't you?"

I nod. "You still should have told me. I can't replay my parents' marriage. I won't."

He nods in the dark. "I know. And you're right. I should have."

"But I understand. I'm so sorry for everything you went through. My heart breaks for you. You will come through this, but you need to tell Kim, too. Let her help you. Let Iris help you. But mostly, let *me* help you." I stop. "You're my husband. I am here for you, for better or worse."

"I want better," he says.

"Then no going back to the way it was." I stop again. "No more masks, okay?"

"You're right," Cory says. He kisses me, and we sway in the night air. Finally, he whispers, "Colombo."

PART EIGHT

LADY'S MANTLE

"A crown is merely a hat that lets the rain in."

—Frederick the Great

IRIS

JULY 2003

Michigan weather is a fickle dame.

Oftentimes—no matter the time of year and solely dependent upon the direction of the wind—our weather exhibits a split personality. It can be gloriously sunny one moment, the lake flat, the clouds pressed inland. An hour later it can be downright bone-chilling, lake-effect rain showers falling as the cold wind crosses the warmer waters of Lake Michigan.

Today can't seem to make up its mind, I think.

I look up, putting my face into the brisk wind, and half expect to see the Wicked Witch pedaling by in the sky on her bike.

The Fourth had been glorious. The fifth is ominous.

I started gardening at 6:00 a.m. in jeans, a sweater and a

rain jacket but have now stripped down to a long-sleeved T-shirt. I know that could soon change again. The clouds and rain are looming; they sweep over the lake like fighter planes, low, close and ominous. Right now, however, the sun is shining brightly, the skies are clear over my head, the temperatures moderating.

"Are we still on?"

I hear Cory's voice over the fence. It is thick with sleep.

"Of course," I call.

"Looks like it's going to rain," he says hopefully.

"Everything needs watering," I say. "Gate's open."

"Let me gather the troops," Cory says.

I continue with my work. I kneel on my pad and begin to dig up the grass and weeds that have grown through the lake stones that comprise most of my gardens' borders. I cannot tolerate anything popping through my borders: it's like a dusty frame around a piece of art. All you notice is the dust.

I love being lost in my garden at dawn, before the day intrudes. The flowers literally wake before your eyes, stretching to meet the sun, sipping their morning cup of dew. And Mother Nature wakes, too: a flutter here of a sleepy butterfly, a buzz there of an awakening bee. My hands dig into the still cool, damp dirt, and I can feel my soul settle into the earth, becoming one with nature. I am not apart from this earth; I am a part of it.

"Hello?"

I look up and Cory, Abby and Lily walk in slow motion like zombies into the yard. Cory and Abby are holding gigantic mugs of steaming coffee, while Lily is still in her pajamas, rubbing her eyes.

"Good morning!" I say.

They mumble at me.

"What are you doing?" Cory asks.

"Weeding," I say. "The most important and disliked part of gardening. But I love it."

"Why?" Lily asks.

"Because it makes everything prettier," I say. I stand with a grunt and turn to look at the trio. "I once read that gardening is a lot like life. You have to get a little dirt under your nails for the best results."

Lily yawns, looking none too enthused.

As if on cue, the sun emerges. The world glimmers. All of the garden's glorious colors are spotlighted as if they are wearing sequined dresses and dancing on Broadway. The light seems to wake everyone up.

Lily suddenly skips to the other side of my cottage garden and looks at the bee balm, balloon flower and the purple coneflower. "These are so pretty!" she says.

"You have so much color in your gardens," Abby says. "My eye doesn't even know where to begin. It's like a kaleidoscope come to life."

"I love color," I say. "Summer gardens are like Christmas trees. They should be filled with happy, bright colors."

"What's this?"

I turn to where Lily is standing. "Hardy hibiscus," I say.

"Hearty?" Lily asks, touching her heart.

I laugh. "Hardy," I say, making a muscle with my arm. "Strong."

"Oh," she says. Lily grabs a stem and pulls a bloom—as big as a dinner plate—toward her face. "So pretty," she says to it.

"A world of color, even just in that flower," I say. "Look. White, pink, red, bicolors."

In the distance, a rumble of thunder—eerily beautiful, like the sound of a timpani drum slowly filling an auditorium—echoes over the lake. "We better get busy," I say. "Now, who wants to help me weed and who wants to deadhead flowers?"

"Oh, I'll deadhead, if you don't mind," Abby says. "I used to help my grandmother do that."

"Sounds bad," Lily says.

"Oh, no, honey," Abby says. "It's just a saying." Abby walks over to a balloon flower, leans down and pinches a spent bloom. "This helps the rest of the plant have energy. Like when you drink your milk in the morning."

I smile.

"You can start there," I say to them. "Cory, looks like you're stuck with me."

Which is exactly what I wanted.

"What do I do?" Cory asks. "How do I know if I'm pulling the right thing?"

"Follow my lead," I say, starting to pull grass from between rocks and clumps of weeds that are encroaching upon my flowers. "You'll be able to tell what's a flower and what's a weed soon enough."

We work in silence for a long while, and when I look up and see everyone in my gardens working together, the scene tilts in front of me, and I have to steady myself from becoming dizzy.

People. In my yard. Working with me.

Cory sees me off balance. "How are you doing?" he asks.

"How are *you* doing?" I return.

Cory sits back on his haunches and looks at me. "Sounds like a loaded question." He stops. "With this?" he asks. "Or life?"

I wink.

"One day at a time," he says. "You know, men aren't raised to share their emotions. We just bottle everything up inside. So all of this—talking to a therapist, being so open with Abby, letting her help me—" he stops, searching for the right words "—is all new. I realized I have anger issues. And when it starts to overwhelm me, I try to bury it rather than cope with it. That's why I drank and slept and lashed out."

Cory looks at me, and I ask him, "What were you thinking about just now while you were weeding?"

"What do you mean?" Cory shrugs. "I wasn't thinking about anything."

"Exactly," I say. "The ground grounds us. Our fingers in the soil, our knees on the earth, our bodies in the sun. This..." I stop and pick up a clump of dirt and let it trickle through my fingers. "This earth is the only thing that connects us all. It is the only thing that will outlive us all. Whether we're here in Michigan, or a soldier fighting in Iraq, this earth is our common denominator."

Cory is silent. "Do you miss your family?"

"Every second of every day," I say.

"I miss my friend," he says. "I think about Todd every single day." Cory stops. "It's hard to go on sometimes with the simplest things knowing how bad the world can be." He stops again. "How could you?" he asks.

"How could I not?" I say. "I used to believe I was a coward for not having the strength to just end it all. And maybe I was and still am, but I have to tell you something, young man. Though I may not be a believer in organized religion or organized war, I am a believer in those who fight for justice. You and my husband fought for the right things." I stop, bend over and pull a hydrangea bloom, as blue as Cory's eyes. "And the world—despite its many horrors—is much too complex, intricate and beautiful for all of this to be happenstance. Just look."

Cory studies the bloom.

"And look," I say, pointing at Lily, who has tucked a stunning pink hibiscus with a peppermint center behind her ear.

"I've come to believe that God lays out many paths for us. They're not predetermined. The choices are ours. And each choice we make has a ripple effect on our lives and others' lives."

"But your daughter didn't have a choice to get polio. My friend didn't have a choice to avoid that land mine."

"You're focusing, like I did, on the most tragic part of life. The end." I sit back and look at this strapping young man. His face is searching mine for an answer. "But I had a daughter, the greatest joy of my life. Your friend had a baby, the greatest joy of his life. Their legacies continue to impact both of us. I try to choose a path that my daughter would be proud of." I look around and continue. "And I know she wouldn't be proud of how I've walled myself off from life." I stop. "You know, many of these plants began with my grandmother and great-grandmother, and were passed along to my mom and then me. I gathered many of these starts from friends. Each one tells a story. Each one holds a memory. That's the beauty of a garden. That's what reminds me to get up and do my best every day. Because my family still surrounds me."

JUNE 1958

"Atomic gardens? Radiation? Atoms for Peace?"

The voice of my boss, Mr. Garnant, is rising, higher even than the humidity of the greenhouse. I do not perspire—I am a true Michigander whose body has gotten used to adapting to nearly any temperature considering the weather can change forty degrees during any given day—but a bead of sweat snakes down my forehead and stings my eye. I am not used to my boss yelling at me, especially in public. Housewives in pretty pantsuits turn to stare.

"Atomic gardening is the newest thing, sir," I say in a hushed voice. "And I know just how to make it work."

Mr. Garnant's mustache twitches. It only does this if something excites him terribly—like when he talks about his wife's deviled eggs or his love for Swanson's TV dinners—or angers him intensely.

Like me. Right now.

"It's a *fad*!"

The housewives take off their gloves, fold them and place them in their pocketbooks, eyes darting to and fro. They pretend to examine the flowers and seed packets but continue to look our way.

"It's not a fad, sir," I continue, my voice still low. "It's just a way to find more peaceful uses for atomic energy. Botanists have been experimenting in labs all over the world for years. All I'm asking is for a small investment. If we can just expose—let's say, tomatoes—to radiation, then we can generate mutations that are bigger, or more resistant to cold weather or disease. Did you know that they've already irradiated hundreds of thousands of peppermint stems, making them more resistant to fungal disease? Usage of peppermint, in gum and toothpaste, has exploded. We have the ability to be on the cutting edge here, sir."

"We're a nursery, Iris, not a lab."

Mr. Garnant begins to walk away, and I reach for him, accidentally grabbing him by the tie on the back of the Garnant Greenhouses aprons we wear. He is jolted backward as if we were playing football, and I horse-collar tackled him.

"Iris!" he yells.

"I didn't mean to do that," I say.

He turns, his face beet red, mustache thrashing. "I strongly suggest you get back to work before it's too late."

"Sir," I continue despite the warning. "I've spent the past few years working night and day on our poinsettia production. My genetic testing allowed us to be among the first to segregate desirable characteristics like stiffer stems, new colors, longevity. The controlled breeding program has allowed us to go from buying field-grown stock to creating our own greenhouse production. Poinsettias are now our biggest seller."

"And your work has been admirable, Iris."

"Then why did you turn it over to a team of men?" I ask. "*My* work?"

"Iris," Mr. Garnant says. "You know our motto here. It's *our* work, not my work. There's no *i* in 'team.' We need you out front. Women buy from women."

"I'm a botanist, sir, not a clerk."

"You're a..." Mr. Garnant stops. His mustache droops. My anger swells as I finish his thought.

"Woman? Right?"

"Atomic gardening is a fad. It will go away just like your Victory Gardens did. Garnant's is the largest nursery in the Midwest. We need to sell. People today have TV and movies, new ovens and fancy cars. People don't spend as much time outdoors. We must fight for every dollar. And..." He stares at me as if I'm an inanimate object, an ottoman perhaps. "And women buy from women."

"I'm begging you, sir," I say. "I need to keep my brain busy. I need the importance of important work. Did you know many of the things we already eat have a long history of genetic modification, sir? We just don't talk about it. At least this way, we can use radiation for good."

"Cut the gas, Iris!" he shouts. "Cut it right now! You're going to have the House Un-American Activities Committee investigating us if you keep up that kind of talk." Mr. Garnant lifts his arms and twirls around like a helicopter, his voice booming. "Look around, Iris! Look around! We all have our families to worry about. We can't just have them eat radiation. You don't have to worry about those things."

I will myself not to cry as my eyes fill with tears.

"That was uncalled for, sir."

"I didn't mean it," he says, looking chagrined.

"No, you did," I say, my jaw clenched, my heart in my throat. "And you're right. I don't. You've made it all very clear for me today." I stop and try to take a breath, but it's too late: I cannot stop what is coming from my mouth. "I don't need you, or this job, because I only have myself to protect, myself to watch out for. Women are more than sales clerks. We are the future of this world. I may have lost my family, but I haven't lost my mind, or my faith, or my ambition, or my intelligence. I quit."

"You're making a huge mistake, Iris," Mr. Garnant warns. "You need me."

"No," I say. "I don't need anyone. I only need my flowers."

Mr. Garnant looks at me, almost as if he sees me for the first time and hates the new Iris. "You will come back here begging me to hire you back, and I won't, Iris. Do you hear me? I won't."

"You won't have to, because I'm going to drive you out of business."

He laughs.

I take off my apron and throw it on the ground. "I'll be opening my gardens up in a few weeks, ladies," I say to the women as I pass. "And I grow everything there myself."

On the bus ride home, I am inconsolable, crying—more from anger than sadness—so loudly that riders stay at least three rows away from me. I run into my house and directly into Mary's room and collapse on her bed.

"I need your help, Mary," I say. "Help me."

I shut my eyes on my daughter's bed, pull a blanket over my body and fall into a deep sleep. When I awake, just before dawn, I see the flowers Shirley and I hung for Mary so long ago dancing in front of my eyes. I sit straight up in bed. I understand what I must do.

I rush downstairs and grab an urn off the fireplace mantel. I stumble out into my yard barefoot, the moonlight illuminating my gardens in an otherworldly glow. I head directly to my daylilies, directly to my newest creations.

"You are just like a daylily, Mary," I begin to cry, falling to my knees. "A beauty for a day. You bloomed for only a short time but, this way, you will live forever, help your new friends thrive and be my constant garden companion."

I turn the urn upside down and scatter my baby's ashes over my children.

But just then, dawn breaks. I rise and watch the sun creep over the horizon. As it does, the world comes to life: a monarch butterfly appears from nowhere and lands on one of my daylilies. It is joined by a hummingbird. And then a bevy of bees.

I think of the prayer Shirley gave when Mary's empty coffin was lowered into the ground.

"We lay you down into the warm earth,
Ashes to ashes, dust to dust,
And in this place, we will remember you,
Here in the summertime with the flowers in full bloom."

"Live with me forever," I whisper to my flowers, before lifting my head toward the heavens. "Live with me forever here in my garden."

"This is the daylily you created for your daughter, right? Iris? Iris?"

I blink, finally returning to the present as Cory's question knocks me from my thoughts.

"Yes," I say. "That's it."

"And what flower reminds you of your husband?" Cory asks.

"The rose," I say. "My Jonathan roses. Those peach roses growing on the arbor in the front yard? I created them just for him. They are still as peach as his cheeks."

There is quiet for a long, few seconds. When I turn, Cory's jaw is clenched. "Where is he buried?" Cory asks. "I'd be honored to pay tribute to his grave."

"He never made it home."

Cory looks at me. "What?"

"His body is still buried in France," I say. "Or Germany. I still don't know, to be honest. The government told me his body was 'nonrecoverable.' I couldn't get him home." I stop. "Any of him. I wrote them over and over, but after a while, I gave up. I had to give up. I just had to move on, for my daughter, for myself." I stop again. "So many of our men are still deemed nonrecoverable." I shut my eyes and place my hands into the earth. "My gardens are the place that I spend time with him. My daughter's ashes are here. And so are their memories."

"I'm so, so sorry," Cory says, his voice barely audible. "Thank you for sharing that with me."

I look at this man—as big and sturdy as one of Lake Michigan's dunes—but still as vulnerable as a child who tries to climb one. I reach out my hand, and Cory grasps it. When we release our grip, clumps of dirt return to the earth.

Out of nowhere, thunder claps, and it begins to pour.

Lily yells, and Abby covers her head.

"Time to go!" Abby yells.

I stand. "Why?"

"It's raining!" she says.

"Why do we worry about getting wet in the rain? We don't when we jump in the lake, we don't when we swim, we don't when we shower. Remember how we used to jump in puddles as kids?"

I move into the middle of my yard and begin to twirl, letting the rain soak my head. "It's raining!" I say.

Lily giggles and then runs to join me. "It's raining!" she yells, spinning in her pajamas.

Together we sing:

"It's raining, it's pouring, the old man is snoring..."

Cory laughs, and Abby joins him. He grabs his wife, and the two begin to dance. They spin, water flying off their bodies. And when he dips her, she giggles—sounding even more girlish than her daughter just did—and water falls from the crown of her head.

And then, just as suddenly as it started, the rain stops, the sun emerges and the world shimmers in glistening light.

"I haven't done that since I was a kid," Abby gasps.

"How did it feel?" I ask.

She looks at me and then at Cory. "Exhilarating!"

"Daddy, I didn't know you could dance," Lily says, rushing over. "You look like a princess, Mommy."

"A soggy princess," Abby says, her face falling from excitement to embarrassment. She removes her glasses and tries to dry them with a damp shirt. "No one looks good wet, especially me."

"Don't do that," I say.

"Do what?"

"Don't put yourself down. You're beautiful."

Abby looks at me, her face now etched in surprise.

"Thank you," she says, her cheeks blushing.

"Come here," I say, gesturing for everyone to follow. I lead them over to my greenhouse where I grab some towels I always have at the ready. I hand them out. Then I take them over to a lush green border in my garden. "Not many people ever notice this plant, but look at it now."

Mounds of velvety soft olive green foliage sparkles in the sunlight.

"Those look like they're holding diamonds!" Lily says.

"They do," I say. "Good eye."

"What is this, Iris?"

"It's a perennial called *alchemilla mollis,*" I say. "Lady's Mantle."

"I've never heard of that," Abby says.

"It's a wonderful border plant," I say. "They truly frame all the other flowers.

"But this plant is very special because it's just like most people," I say as I kneel down. "It's the showy folks—the flashiest, the prettiest, the ones with the most color—that garner all the attention in this world, but it's the ones who constantly reveal their beauty when no one is looking who are truly the most stunning.

"Just look," I continue. I take a leaf of Lady's Mantle and hold it to the sun. "See how the leaves look like shallow little pleated cups?"

"Yes," everyone says as one.

"They hold droplets of water after a rain, which glisten like diamonds against their skin, and they gather the morning dew and hold it in their leaves all day. They're crafty creatures, but also quite elegant. I love how they bloom happy sprays of dainty yellow flowers that just shoot up and spill over like champagne."

I continue. "Alchemilla comes from the word *alchemy.* In medieval times, alchemists believed that the water droplets that formed on the Lady's Mantle leaves could turn base metals to gold. They also believed that these drops had magical powers to regain youth."

"Let me at it!" Abby says with a laugh.

"Actually," I start, "and I know this sounds crazy, but I sometimes drink water from its leaves."

"Ewww," Lily says, scrunching her face as she dries her hair. "It's dirty water."

"No," I say. "It's magical. Lady's Mantle is known to bring peace to your heart."

"How?" Abby asks.

I smile. "Always the engineer. I understand. I was once always the botanist. But there is a healing power to our flowers and plants, medicinally and spiritually. Do you believe that? Science is more than science?"

Abby nods. "I do."

"I use the essence of Lady's Mantle when I feel anxious, or helpless in this world," I say. "Lady's Mantle is a balm if you have difficulty loving yourself or loving others because you are wounded and hurt."

Cory jerks his head upright and looks at me.

I pluck a leaf of Lady's Mantle, tilt the soft, velvety leaf toward my mouth and sip its healing waters.

"Any takers?" I ask, holding up the leaf.

"Me," Cory says.

I hand it to him, and he lifts the leaf. Golden drops of water fall into his mouth.

"You're drinking diamonds, Daddy," Lily says.

I smile as the sun shines directly on this man—this husband, father, soldier, child—and, indeed, he is lit in a golden light, as if illuminated from within.

"Back to work, Iris?" Cory asks.

"Back to work," I say.

ABBY

JULY 2003

"Hello?" I call. "Where is everyone?"

"Out here!"

"Sorry I'm late," I say, following the voices of Cory and Lily. I head toward the backyard, my work shoes clomping loudly down the wooden stairs. "Meeting went late."

I take two steps into the backyard, and my heels sink into the wet earth. I step out of them, abandoning them there like a truck that is stuck in the mud.

Cory laughs.

"Long day?"

I walk over to him and pretend to step on the shovel sitting next to him. "Even that wouldn't compare to the pain I've endured."

Cory stands and hugs me.

"Thank you," I say. "I needed that.

"What are you two doing?" I ask, turning my attention to Lily.

Lily has yet to turn around to greet me. She resembles one of those concrete statuaries my grandmother used to have in her front yard, a woman bent over in her garden, rear pointing straight up in the air. She has a small spade in her hands, and dirt is flying straight back from her body, like a dog happily digging a hole.

"We're gardening, Mommy," Lily says. "Just like Iris taught us."

"I can see," I say with a chuckle.

"Look at what she gave us, Mommy," Lily says, still not bothering to turn around.

That's when I finally see what is literally right in front of me: endless starts of plants—in pots, trays, wet clumps in paper towels, root balls with bushes attached.

"Iris?" I ask.

"Iris," Cory says. "And look what else she gave us."

Cory bends down and pulls an envelope from one of the cardboard boxes containing plants. "It's a photo of what her grandmother's garden used to look like."

"That's *our* house?" I ask, my voice rising enough for Lily to finally turn around and look at me. I look at the picture for a long time and then around our moribund yard.

"Doesn't even look like the same place, does it?"

I shake my head.

"Iris gave us starts from her garden that actually started here, in her grandma's garden," Cory continues. "I'm going to try and plant each one in the exact same spot as the original. Everything's coming full circle."

"That's a lot of work," I say. "I knew you enjoyed gardening back in the day, but what spurred all this enthusiasm?"

Cory looks at the photo again and then at me. His gaze is so intense that it makes me shift my feet.

"Gardening makes me feel—" Cory stops, searching for the right word "—better." He puts the photo back in the envelope, sets it in the cardboard box and stands again, holding a clump of Lady's Mantle. He stares at the plant as he continues. "Better husband, better father, better person, better man..." He looks at me. "Better.

"Remember when Dr. Trafman asked if there was something I could do to keep my mind and body sharp?" he continues. "This is immediately what came to me. As if I already knew. I am feeling better, Abby."

Without warning, my heart rises into my throat. "I can see that," I say. "And that makes all of us better."

"Lady's Mantle," Cory says as if to himself, looking at the clump he's holding. "Men are outwardly strong. We speak loudly. We pound our chests. We feel we are the warriors of the world. But women are truly the strong ones." He looks at me. "The ones who stand in the rain and never complain."

"Cory," I start.

"Women are just like this plant," he says. "Look at the leaves still holding the dew they collected in the morning."

"When did you become such a poet?" I ask.

"Always have been," he says. "I just never showed it. Didn't think I was supposed to. But that's why you fell in love with me, isn't it? You always knew it was there."

This time tears well in my eyes. "I did," I say. "And it always has been. It just got hidden for a while."

"Women have reserves of strength," Cory says, tipping the Lady's Mantle so the drops of water fall into the center of its leaves. "They hold on to them until they're needed." He looks at the plant again. "Such a perfect name. Lady's Mantle." He looks at me. "Women are queens. They deserve to wear the mantle."

Cory leans in and kisses me, so intensely that I can feel my legs tremble.

"I love you so much, Abby," he says. "Thank you for holding this family together without me."

"I held this family together *for* you," I say.

Cory smiles.

"I have something to tell you," he says.

"I knew it," I say. "You set me up for the big reveal."

"No," Cory says. "It's nothing like that. It's just…well…it's just that I followed Iris today."

"You what?" I ask.

"After she gave me all these plants at dawn, right after you left for work this morning, I didn't hear her gate close. I peeked out and saw that she was walking along the edge of her fence, almost like a cat burglar. I grabbed Lily and told her we were going on a secret spy mission. We followed Iris all the way down to a little plot of land at the end of the association. It's surrounded by a fence. We looked through the slats, and it was just this overgrown mess."

"Mess," Lily says, still digging in the garden.

"We were about to leave," Cory continues, "and then we heard Iris talking."

"To whom?"

"No one," Cory says. "Well, someone. Her husband and daughter."

"What?"

"I think that must have been a place of importance in her life, and still is," Cory says. "And…"

"Oh, no," I say. "What next?"

"She told me when we were with her yesterday that her husband's body was never recovered," he says. "His body is still in France…or Germany…somewhere. It was never recovered. I reached out to a friend I know in the military, and he said this was more common than imagined. Bodies were deemed nonrecoverable, and many families just wanted to move on, so the bodies remained buried overseas. But," Cory continues, his voice rising, "they have new technology now. If we can send DNA of her husband, or anything else, then the military will keep it on file. They have a database of every soldier who never came home. Every so often, they still find bones from gravesites or from places where there was conflict."

"Cory—" I start.

"I know, I know," he rushes. "This sounds like a long shot or a movie, but..." Cory stops, and his eyes are filled with emotion. "She needs closure, Abby. She's an old woman. She deserves to know what happened." Cory looks at the Lady's Mantle and at Lily digging in the dirt. "She's helping me have a little closure, and I feel I need to help her have a little. I couldn't save Todd..."

"You can't save her, either, Cory."

"I know. I don't think she needs saving. I just want her family to be with her. Like mine is with me."

My hulk of a husband dissolves into tears, and I hold him.

"You're a good man, Cory."

"You're a good woman, Abby."

"This is starting to sound like an episode of *The Waltons*," I laugh.

Cory laughs, too, his body shaking mine as he does. "You are an old soul, Abby Peterson."

I take the plant from my husband's hands and look at it. As I do, one of his tears falls directly into the cupped leaf of the Lady's Mantle. It looks like a magical crystal.

"So are you," I say. "So are you."

PART NINE

SURPRISE LILIES

"In search of my mother's garden, I found my own."

—Alice Walker

IRIS

AUGUST 2003

"Hold on, hold on. Just be patient."

Hummingbirds dive around me like fighter pilots. I dangle a feeder off a shepherd's hook hanging from a gable on my screened porch, and then return with another, which I hang from my redbud tree. I watch the glorious creatures zip and zoom around the feeders, most waiting patiently for each other, although one iridescent green creature hides in the branches and chases off the others as they approach. I turn to the feeder on the screened porch and watch as the tiny birds hover around the feeder and insert their long beaks deep into the faux flowers that encircle it.

"My father's recipe," I tell them. "Enjoy."

I was—*how old*?—when my dad taught me to whisk together a half cup of sugar with two cups of warm water. So simple yet so magical.

"Drink up," I say. "You'll need the energy today."

It is hot today, the temperature supposed to reach ninety degrees. The sun doesn't really shine on days like this; it blares in the sky like a searchlight, its rays seeming to melt into the hazy sky like a cracked egg.

The dog days of summer, my grandma always called August days like this, when Midnight would crawl under the front porch or sneak deep into the hydrangeas and dig a cool hole in the earth.

I return to the kitchen and head back outside again, this time holding a jar of jelly and a halved orange. I've been getting orioles of late—*Oh, and what a sight to see with their flaming orange bellies!*—and I want them to remember me for next year. I scoop some grape jelly into my jelly feeders and push orange halves into nails over the sweet jelly.

"Everyone likes sugar," I say.

Despite the heat, the world smells sweet, and I lift my nose and sniff the air just like Midnight used to do. I cannot discern if it's the jelly and oranges I'm smelling or if a neighbor is baking a sweet treat for summer guests this morning, but it's a familiar, comforting scent.

I turn and yelp with excitement when I finally realize what's scattered before me.

"Surprise!" I cry.

Surprise lilies have sprung up overnight, as they always do, without any warning. Six to eight blush-pink funnels of flowers spring from the ends of completely naked green stems that rise two feet from the earth. In my very orderly gardens and tidy greenhouse, my surprise lilies are true surprises.

Mother Nature's version of a whoopee cushion.

They spring up randomly throughout my yard and gardens,

and I forget every single year about them and their whereabouts until they jump from the earth in late summer to yell "Surprise!" like hidden guests at a birthday party.

Gardeners have a lot of names for surprise lilies, all of which seem perfectly well suited: magic lily, pink flamingo flower, resurrection lily and Shirley's favorite, "nekkid" lady. "Looks just like me when I get out of the shower," she used to say. "An unsightly body holding up quite a pretty face."

Surprise lilies are, indeed, odd creatures. Their leaves appear in fall, live throughout the winter, die in early summer when everything else has come alive before flowering—surprise!—in August.

My grandma compared the annual growth of surprise lilies to cantankerous relatives at the holidays who would show up at different times to avoid one another. And they lived that way, too, almost refusing to be anywhere near the other.

Most gardeners move their surprise lilies to their gardens so they grow together in prettier clumps rather than sporadic blooms scattered randomly throughout their yard, but I refuse to move mine.

Too many memories.

I walk over to a surprise lily growing in the middle of my yard.

"Hi, Blanche," I say.

Blanche was my great-aunt—my grandma's sister—and she was as bright and unpredictable as these lilies. She painted bright red rouge on her cheeks, dyed her hair chestnut brown, wore bright scarves and palazzo pants and was once a showgirl in Las Vegas. She would breeze into town every August—to escape the Vegas summers—with stories about Frank Sinatra and Dean Martin that would send shivers down my spine. She would drink Manhattans and watch my grandma garden, and every time she was in town, the surprise lilies would bloom overnight as if they were waiting for her arrival.

"Be just like these lilies," she would tell me. "Be different, unexpected, a surprise to folks."

I walk to another surprise lily. "Hi, Cousin Doris," I say.

Doris hybridized her own surprise lilies—she was the first person to teach me that you could cross flowers—and we would plant them all over our yards, much to my mom and grandma's chagrin. They still remind me of her generosity.

I walk to the front yard and am suddenly overwhelmed by emotion at the surprise lilies popping up like moles in various spots throughout the grass.

"Hi, Daddy," I say.

My dad did not garden. In fact, if he had his preference, the yard would have been only grass so he could easily push the mower back and forth in straight lines, rather than zigzagging around trees and flowers, and trimming around endless borders.

But he loved surprise lilies, even though they took even more effort to mow around. My dad's parents were farmers in Illinois. Long after they passed, he took us on a summer vacation to Chicago, first driving into central Illinois to visit the old homestead where he grew up. When he pulled up, there was no longer a barn, a farmhouse or cornfield. Everything had been demolished, and a gas station with a restaurant attached to it had been built in its place. He was devastated.

"Let's go, Bill," my mom said.

He was about to get back in the sedan, when he stopped to look one last time as if to set a memory in his head.

"Look," he said. "They're still here."

My father rarely got emotional, but his voice sounded like that of a little boy's.

"What is it, Bill?" my mom asked.

He pointed to a field adjoining that gas station. Surprise lilies popped up everywhere.

The sight of those lilies caused my father to bend over and sob. "My mom's resurrection lilies," he said. "Still standing. Still pointing to heaven."

That day in Illinois, we dug up as many surprise lilies from that field as we could, plopped them in big cups we got from the restaurant and kept them alive until we got home, where my dad planted them in various spots around the yard. They survived storms and construction.

I kneel down and touch a surprise lily that my father planted, which came from his homestead. I hold it to my nose. A flower filled with history.

I actually hated surprise lilies as a girl as they were the first tangible sign that summer was ending and school would soon be starting.

A hummingbird zips over my head, reminding me in a not-so-subtle way that I have yet to fill the feeders in the front yard. I stand, grab two more feeders and head around to the screened porch. As the door bangs shut, the bell tinkling, I stop and turn.

I wonder, I think.

I look into Abby and Cory's yard from my porch, which is angled so I can see a slice of their lawn over my fence and shrubs.

"Surprise!" I yell, tickled that the lilies are still there, my voice so high and excited that it, too, surprises me.

I turn toward the kitchen when I hear, "How did you know?"

What in the world?

"How did you know today was Lily's birthday?" Abby yells. "Are you a mind reader?"

For a moment I am too stunned to speak. And then I realize I just yelled, "Surprise!" *It's a sign, Iris, you old fool.*

At that moment a hummingbird—a male with a ruby-red throat—zips in front of the porch and stops. The bird is perfectly still, save for its wings, which are moving at the speed of light. The hummingbird looks me directly in the eye. I tilt my head. It tilts its head. I know it does not want food because the feeders are full. I know why my visitor is here.

It's another sign.

"Hi, Dad," I whisper.

Cardinals are a symbol of my mother, and she appears when I need her the most, during the holidays when my soul aches like barren tree branches in the north wind and my heart is frozen like the lake, landing on a snow-covered holly bush to wish me Merry Christmas. Hummingbirds are a symbol of my father. He loved them as much as his surprise lilies. They appear to remind me of summer, of my roots.

"Hello?" Abby calls. "Iris? Are you okay?"

"I just knew," I finally call back. "Instinct!"

"Would you like to join us for a piece of birthday cake later?"

I knew I smelled something, I think.

"I'm filling my feeders and filthy from gardening," I say.

"Come over when you can, okay? We'll wait."

"Okay," I call. "Thank you." I stop. "Oh, and I have a little gift for Lily."

"You do?" Abby asks, her voice rising in disbelief.

"I do," I say. "But it's a surprise."

ABBY

AUGUST 2003

"But how did you know it was my birthday?"

Lily's face is covered in icing—literally covered, from ear to ear and nose to chin—and my heart feels like it is going to burst with happiness.

What greater joy is there than seeing your daughter happy, healthy and growing up to be a smart, independent, unique little girl right in front of your very eyes?

"It only makes sense that a beautiful girl named Lily would be born the day the surprise lilies are born," Iris says.

My eyes dart to Iris. My heart breaks.

Would I be able to live if Lily were to die? What if Cory had been killed in battle? How would I? How could I? Where does Iris derive her strength and sense of purpose?

We are seated in the living room—Iris in a chair, the three of us on a couch—the air conditioner working overtime to keep the poorly insulated old cottage somewhat cool. Sunlight blares through a stained glass window in the living room and prisms of blue, red and green splay across Iris's face. She resembles a Picasso painting from my vantage point, her features divided into colorful angles—blue nose, green cheeks, red forehead.

I shut my eyes and open them again.

Iris looks magical if not downright beautiful.

She is watching Lily eat her cake with such rapt attention, and yet I cannot unearth the emotions lurking beneath her face. The light illuminates Iris, but it also shows every line of her aged face, deep crevices like the ones she digs to plant seeds. And yet I don't see her age, I see her beauty.

During a college trip, I attended an exhibit hosted by the Detroit Institute of Arts featuring a group of artists—painters, woodcutters, textile artists—who had studied in Mexico. Whereas most artists focused on flowers in bloom, their collective work celebrated the beauty and delicacy of dying flowers: their diminishing color, sagging blooms, withering petals.

Most of my classmates didn't like the work.

"It's not pretty," many said.

One of the artists overheard their remarks and walked over. She was a woman around Iris's age. "It's the same flower," she said, her silver hair glowing. "It's not less pretty. It's actually more beautiful because it's lived long enough to understand that beauty doesn't last forever and that people just toss out the old."

My classmates didn't understand the depth of what she was conveying, but I nodded.

"What do you see in my work?" she asked.

"My grandma in her garden," I said, a response that elicited a hug from the artist.

I watch Iris watch Lily.

Did her own daughter celebrate a birthday in this very living room with her grandmother? Did she feel the same emotions I do right now?

"Do you want to see the presents I got?"

Lily's voice knocks me from my thoughts. Iris nods, and Lily jumps off the couch. She races into the back of the cottage. A few seconds later the jingling of a bike bell echoes throughout the house, and Lily rides into the living room on her little pink bicycle.

"Lily!" Cory says. "Don't ride your bike in the house!"

Cory looks at me, his eyes wide, before glancing nervously at Iris. His words—and the panic in his voice—literally scream, "Lily, don't ride your bike in the house in front of the woman we're renting it from!"

"That's okay," Iris says, a trill in her voice. "My daughter used to ride her bike in the house, too."

Lily shoots me a prideful glance, and I suddenly picture her as a difficult teenager.

"And look at all the cool stuff on my bike," Lily says, riding up to Iris. "A basket and streamers off both handles and a glitter bike seat..." Lily is so excited and talking so quickly that she is running out of breath and has to take big gulps of air to keep going. "And this!" She rings the bell again. "Wanna try?"

Iris reaches out and squeezes the bell. Both giggle.

"I have a gift for you, too," Iris says.

"Oh, Iris," Cory says. "That's not necessary."

"It isn't?" Lily asks, her face scrunched in confusion.

Iris laughs. "It is, isn't it, Lily?"

Lily nods.

Iris stands. "Follow me, then. It's outside."

Cory and I look at one another, and Lily jumps off her bike, leaning it against a wall, and trails Iris, who heads toward the back porch. I follow and arrive just in time to see Lily race down the stairs and into the yard.

"It looks just like Easter!" Lily yells.

Indeed, a couple of colorful packages dot the yard like Easter eggs, perched directly under flowers that are blooming randomly all across the backyard. Cory and I walk over to join Iris and Lily.

"All of these surprise lilies came from my father's homestead in Illinois," Iris says. "He dug them up, and we replanted them here. They are a reminder that—when you least expect it—you are surrounded by hope, love and family." Iris turns to Lily, kneels and places her hands on her shoulders. "You, my birthday girl, are very lucky. You are surrounded by all three." She nods at the box. "Go ahead. You can open it up now."

Lily takes a seat on the grass and pulls the lid off a box that is as purple as a Harlequin's pants. Lily looks up, confused. Iris leans down and pulls a muddy bulb from the box. "It's a surprise lily from my yard," Iris says. "These are ones that remind me of someone special." Iris takes a seat next to Lily. "I had a great-aunt named Blanche who was quite a character. She lived in Las Vegas and dressed however she wanted and lived a grand life." Iris holds up the bulb. "She used to tell me, 'Be just like these lilies. Be different, unexpected, a surprise to folks.'" Iris looks at Lily. "That is my wish for you. Now, where should we plant this?"

Lily grabs the bulb and races around the yard, considering. She stops, out of breath, before a big smile crosses her face. She races around the house, and we follow her into the front yard.

"Right here," Lily says with total confidence. "I want to plant this right here."

"That's right in the middle of the yard, sweetie," Cory says. "Why there?"

"Because this is where me and mommy first fell in love with this house," Lily says. "And this is the spot where we knew Daddy would finally be happy again."

Cory is silent for the longest time. He walks over and picks Lily up, holding her tightly in his arms. "I can't breathe, Daddy," Lily finally says.

Iris produces a spade, and I laugh. "Always ready," she says with a wink. "You do the honors," she says, handing the spade to Lily, who begins digging a hole in the middle of the front yard. She plants the bulb, and I unwind a hose to give it a big drink.

"Next!" Lily says, racing toward the backyard.

We all head to the backyard once again, and Lily takes a seat next to a prettily wrapped package with a velvet bow. Lily looks at Iris, who nods, and Lily wipes her hands on her shorts before ripping open the gift.

"It's sooo pretty," she says. "Look, Mom."

I walk over and Lily is holding up a beautiful brooch of flowers. I take the tiny pin from her little hand and gasp. Two gem-encrusted hyacinth—one white, one blue—rise from a sparkling stalk and sit on opposite sides of green enamel leaves.

"Oh, Iris. No," I say. "This must hold special meaning to you. It looks vintage."

Iris smiles. "*I'm* vintage."

"What's the story behind it?" Cory asks.

"My husband gave it to me our first Christmas. He said it summed me up perfectly." She takes the pin from me. "I love hyacinth. Their sweet, lingering fragrance, their colorful flowers, the way you can force them to grow indoors for the winter. They always reminded me of hope and of spring." Iris stops and looks toward the lake. "When he went to war, I gave it to him and told him, 'You didn't know this about the pin when you bought it for me, but white hyacinth represents prayers and protection for someone while blue hyacinth represents eternal love.' Jonathan told me he kept this in his pocket at all times, but it was returned to me by one of his friends. He said he found it wrapped in one of Jonathan's T-shirts in the barracks." Iris turns and looks at the pin again. "I kept it wrapped in that T-shirt, and I put a little piece in the box, just so..."

"Just so what?" Cory prompts.

"Just so you can know the whole story," she says, her voice low. "When you told me the story of what you gave to your friend, I knew this would be the perfect gift for Lily." Iris stops again. "For you. For your whole family."

"It's too personal, Iris," I protest. "We just can't take something this precious."

"You have to," Iris says, grabbing my hand and forcing the brooch back into it. "I have no one. There needs to be a legacy. There needs to be someone to tell my stories. You can. Cory can. Lily can." I shake my head. "It's important to me. Please."

I nod. Lily stands, and I hand the brooch back to Iris. "You do the honors."

She secures the pretty pin to Lily's birthday blouse, and her face beams. "You make it look even more beautiful," she says.

"Thank you, Iris," Lily says, reaching up to kiss Iris on the cheek.

For the longest time Iris doesn't move. She simply holds her hand to her cheek. Her face glows in the sun—like it did earlier in the living room. Finally, she stands—slowly, stiffly—almost as if she has been frozen forever, and Lily's kiss has warmed her body and brought her back to life.

Iris clears her throat. "I best be getting back home," she says. "My gardens need watering." She looks at Lily. "Happy birthday, beautiful Lily."

"Thank you, beautiful Iris," Lily says, which causes Iris to release a sudden whoop of laughter.

"Lilies and iris," Iris says as she heads toward the back gate. "What a perfect combination, don't you think?"

We see her body move along the fence and then into her yard. It is quiet for a while before we hear her turn on her hose and hum as she begins to water.

"Isn't my pin pretty?" Lily asks.

We walk over and admire its delicate beauty.

"It's old," Cory says. He wiggles the brooch on Lily's blouse. "I think the clasp may be loose."

"What?" Lily asks, her face etched in concern.

"I would hate for you to lose this. Want me to fix it for you?"

Lily nods, and Cory unclasps the brooch. "Why don't you go get your bike ready, and we'll go for a little ride around the block. How's that sound?"

"Yippee!" Lily yells, her shoes kicking up grass as she high-tails it for the house.

I look at Cory. Cory looks at me. A big smile comes over his face.

"I take it you'll need the T-shirt that's in the box, too," I say.

PART TEN

CONEFLOWERS

"Happiness is a butterfly, which when pursued, is always just beyond your grasp, but which, if you will sit down quietly, may alight upon you."

—Nathaniel Hawthorne

IRIS

AUGUST 2003

"Turn it off, Iris!"

My heart is beating so rapidly in my chest that I feel as if I might pass out. It matches the sounds of the gunfire and bombing I see on TV.

Boom! Boom! Boom!

The war drags on, no end in sight, and our politicians stand before us offering excuses as our men and women continue to die. I cannot control this. I—we, none of us—have that power. We can only control our own actions, and hope—*Hope! Oh, that much too infrequently used word and action*—that those intentions ripple outward.

I set the remote down, and my eyes settle on a tiny plaque of *The Serenity Prayer* I have sitting on a pile of books. Shirley gave it to me long ago. The plaque is decorated with pretty butterflies.

God grant me the serenity
To accept the things I cannot change;
Courage to change the things I can;
And wisdom to know the difference.

My eyes flit to the towering fence just outside the window.

Despite the wisdom of this prayer, I remain an addict. I am addicted to my own isolation. I am addicted to my own loneliness. I am addicted to my own pain.

"You should have died long ago, Iris," I say to myself, my own voice startling me in the silence of my cottage.

Why haven't I? What has kept me going? Hope? Fear? Plain, old stubbornness?

A towering stand of purple coneflowers dances in the breeze, butterflies and bees flocking to their pretty petals and sturdy centers. I stand at the window, and—over the fence—I see Cory working to dig a bed alongside my grandma's house, while Lily runs through a sprinkler in the yard, squealing as only a child can. Lily is wearing a bright pink swimsuit and—for some reason—floaties around her arms, which makes me laugh. She has a white daisy tucked behind one ear, and a soaked ponytail that smacks her back like a racehorse when she runs. Lily runs through the sprinkler again, absolutely shrieking in delight. When she emerges, she twirls in a circle, her hair cascading a ring of golden water that covers a surprised Cory. The sun hits the water shooting from the sprinkler and flying from Lily's hair just so, and—all of a sudden—the world is filled with mini-rainbows, colorful splays of light dancing across the grass.

Maybe, I think, *I've held on for so long because—despite what the world sees when they look at an old, lonely woman like me—I still see the wonder in things others cannot.*

Lily looks toward my window, and—without thinking—I

wave. She doesn't see me. Instead, she shoots her arms straight out and runs through the sprinkler again as if she's an airplane.

Maybe, just maybe, I've held on because I believed others might need me again one day.

I turn back to the plaque and the photos of my past that surround it. Our lives are all defined by wars—internal, external, real and imagined. Too many of us do not survive our wars, but many do, walking the earth as though we are alive although we really died long ago.

My eyes drift to the window and the tall fence beyond. A heavy sigh fills the silence.

A monarch butterfly flits and flutters about before taking a seat on the fence. The butterfly flaps its wings slowly as if trying them out for the first time. Its colorful expanse is a jarring juxtaposition to the warped gray fence. The butterfly takes flight, and I follow it, window to window, until I'm on my back porch and then racing down my steps, the bell tinkling on the closing door.

The butterfly drifts on the currents of the hot summer breeze, cooled only slightly today by the lake. Finally, it stops atop my purple coneflower.

But of course, I think. *The perfect resting spot.*

One of my favorite spots is my butterfly garden. It runs along the fence by Abby and Cory's house, past the potting shed, extending into the corner, where I have a bubbling fountain. The butterfly garden is comprised of purple coneflower, Black-eyed Susan, butterfly bush, phlox, milkweed, monarda—or bee balm, as I prefer to call it—lots of plants with luscious nectar that caterpillars love to eat and adult butterflies love to feed upon. I also have ornamental grasses scattered throughout to provide shade and places to hide. But butterflies and bees seem to love my purple coneflower more than anything. They are attracted by its color and stay for its nectar. As if on cue, another butterfly, a monarch, rests atop a coneflower. It flaps its glorious wings, golden panels outlined in black, matching stained glass windows brought to life.

"You know my coneflower's secrets, don't you?" I ask the butterfly. It seems to cock its tiny head as though it is listening to me. "You do, don't you?"

Native Americans used echinacea as a general cure and herbal supplement to boost the immune system for hundreds of years, and it remains widely popular today. I use it regularly and credit it as a main reason I never get a cold.

The butterfly takes flight, and a bee quickly replaces it, nestling deep into the middle of the coneflower.

"You know, too," I say.

Echinacea comes from the Greek word *chinos*, which means hedgehog, an apt description for the prickly center cone left behind by spent flowers.

I spend inordinate amounts of time right here in front of my butterfly garden. No place more in this world calms me. I shut my eyes and listen. A butterfly flaps. Bees buzz. Birds flutter. A mourning dove coos. The flowers speak, urging me to meditate, to relax, to be one with nature. These days we go to yoga, we go on vacation, we go to therapy, and yet the answer lies directly before us.

Peace is within our reach if only we choose it.

SUMMER 1967

Young men and women in flare-legged jeans and T-shirts with peace symbols line the sidewalk, daisy chains around their necks, crowns of flowers over their long hair.

On the other side of the street, protesters chant. "Go home, hippies! Go home, hippies!"

In my small town I have become a symbol of resistance, a symbol of the opposition movement to the Vietnam War. And it started so innocently, with a symbol of love.

It has been nearly twenty years since Mary died, and yet on her birthday weeks ago, I was awoken by the sad call of mourning doves, who had built a nest high in the Norway maple I had planted in the front yard, the one that blooms in bright red. The doves had started a family there, and they had yet to leave. They had moved in next door to me, a happy, chattering young family. When they woke me today, I had been dreaming of my daughter. I had padded to the kitchen, made some tea and watched the doves tend to their featherless squabs. I took a seat in my rocker on the front porch and listened to their mournful trill, a sound that seemed to emanate from the depths of their souls, a sound that seemed to mirror the sad echo of my heart, a call to those who were also sad in the world as if to say, "I hear you. I'm here with you."

I shut my eyes, and their call soothed me. I thought of Mary, who would have been twenty-nine this year. *Twenty-nine! Would she be a mother? Would I be a grandmother? Would her family live next to me?*

The doves trill again, and my mind turns to my grandma, who believed that the call of a mourning dove in the morning portended rain. I open my eyes and smile. Beyond the nest and the maple, dark clouds scoot across the sky. A dove takes flight from the nest, flits down to the railing on the front porch and stares right at me.

Oooh-wooo-do-oooo-who-who!

"Mary?" I ask, before changing my tone. "Mary!"

I understand what I must do. I rush into my backyard where my garden center is located, barefoot and in my pajamas, and gather as much sweet alyssum—white as snow—as I can. I return to the front yard and with the birds as my inspiration begin to create a white dove whose wings and body start on one side of the sidewalk and whose head and beak extend into the yard on the other side of the sidewalk. As soon as I finish, it begins to rain.

"There's a TV station here, Iris!"

I am knocked from this memory by the panicked yells of Sandy, one of my part-time workers. "NBC! They want to talk to you."

"For heaven's sake," I say, wiping my muddy hands on my apron. "This is just crazy."

And it is. In every way. When I left my job at Garnant's and made good on my threat to open my own nursery, I made only a few dollars here and there my first season. I sold some of my daylilies, I helped some neighbors design new gardens, I arranged flowers for some women's club luncheons. But I was a good saver. I had no one but me. I had my husband's insurance, and I was a grand penny-pincher, continuing to make World War II casseroles and one-egg cakes even as the world was changing. But funny thing is, it never changes that much.

And despite Mr. Garnant's prediction that TV, movies, cars and airplane travel would distract people from gardening, Americans were buying homes again, settling down, having families. They wanted to garden, grow their own flowers and vegetables, grill in the backyard with their families. They wanted the American dream. Eventually, they needed me. And my little business grew by word of mouth, until I had lines of Michiganders waiting to buy seeds from my greenhouse and plants I propagated. They wanted Iris's iris, my delightful daylilies, my Jonathan roses.

And the sadly ironic thing, too, is that war never goes away. It just simmers on the back of the stove, until we all forget and it boils over yet again, setting the house on fire.

I head to the front yard and down my sidewalk, directly between my white dove and out the front gate. The hippies began to chant, "Iris! Iris! Iris!" The protesters boo.

I look up and see my neighbors, their faces twisted in anger and hate.

"Iris Maynard? Jack Jackson from Eyewitness Two News."

Jack Jackson is all shoe polish, black hair and white teeth. A heavy foundation rings his face, giving him the look of a sunburned pumpkin.

"Ready?" he asks.

I don't even have time to take a breath before the lights and camera go on, and there is a microphone in my face.

"Jack Jackson here, *live*, with Eyewitness Two News!" He holds two fingers in front of the camera. "I'm here with Iris Maynard, owner of Flower Power, a popular, local garden center run out of her home. Iris, can you tell me how these protests started?"

"Very innocently," I begin, before Jack cuts me off.

"Did you intentionally choose the name Flower Power to protest the war?"

"I've been in business for a long time, sir. Longer than this war. So no, I chose that name because it was catchy, before it had any symbolism whatsoever."

"Iris, you do realize that the term *Flower Power* originated in Berkeley, California, as a symbolic action of protest against the Vietnam War?"

Is this a question? I wonder. *It's not posed as such.* I blink twice. The camera lights blind me.

Jack continues: "And that the poet Allen Ginsberg coined the phrase as a means to transform war protests into peaceful affirmative spectacles?"

"I don't watch much TV," I say.

Iris, you sound like an idiot, I think.

"And the peace dove in your yard?" Jack pushes. "Another passive symbol of protest?"

"No," I start, my voice rising. "I designed that for my late daughter. There were mourning doves in my tree—"

The reporter cuts me off again. "Your husband died fighting for America in World War II. What do you think he'd think of your protest?"

Why is this happening? How did this happen?

The world spins. I am back in my Victory Garden. I am

being told Jonathan is dead. I look into the air and can see dandelion floaties bouncing in the air.

What is my wish? No, what is my path?

I remember something I just read in the newspaper, something Abbie Hoffman wrote after his nonviolent flower brigade, wrapped in daisy chains, was attacked by bystanders even though they were marching in support of soldiers.

"The cry of 'Flower Power' echoes through the land," I manage to say, staring directly into the camera. "We shall not wilt."

The hippies cheer. My neighbors begin to storm my yard.

By dusk, my greenhouse is shattered, my garden in tatters, my flowers decimated, my white dove trampled. The next morning when I awake, the mourning doves are gone. I go through the phone book until I find a crew of workers who will actually come to my home.

"Build a fence around my entire property," I tell them.

When I see the fence going up, I come out. "Higher," I say.

"How high?"

"Higher."

They stack two sections of fence atop one another.

"Higher."

"How high, ma'am?"

"Until my husband and daughter in heaven are the only people who will ever set eyes on me again."

Two monarchs—wings fully expanded—sit atop a purple coneflower facing one another. Their collective weight causes the colorful dome to droop slightly, and it tilts toward me.

Are they friends? I ponder. *Enemies? How do we know who is on our side*? My mind turns to Abby and Cory. *Are they my friends? Are they on my side? Or are they just using me temporarily?*

I smile at the monarchs. The two simply sit across from one another like old men sharing stories and sipping coffee at the local diner.

"Old men like to shoot the shit, and old women like to garden," my grandma used to joke. I once believed it was a terrible stereotype, but—the older I get—I understand the wisdom of her words.

We do what we want to do when we finally have the time, I think.

I sigh, heavily, which causes the butterflies to flit to my phlox, which drop some of its flowers from their movement.

So delicate, I think, looking at the phlox. *So tough*, I surmise, looking at the coneflower.

I am both. And that is a necessary balance.

Peace is such an interesting word. We say we seek it, but too few of us mean it. We seem to relish distraction, engage in disruption, enjoy anger, our peace in pieces.

Peace. Piece. I glance from my coneflower to my phlox. *So close. So far apart.*

Without warning, my sprinkler comes on. Water rains softly on my head and on my butterfly garden. I do not move. Instead, I sit and get soaked. The wetter I get, the giddier, until I yelp like a happy child.

"Iris? Are you okay?"

I hear Cory call from beyond the fence.

The sprinkler stops, and—right before my eyes—my coneflower and phlox begin to stiffen, stand even more upright, the water whetting their whistle.

We shall not wilt, I think. *I shall not wilt.*

"I'm fine," I call. "Just got caught in my sprinklers."

"You and Lily," Cory says with a chuckle. "Hey, when you get a chance, would you mind coming over and suggesting some flowers for this border I'm putting in by your cottage? I should have gotten your okay first anyway."

"You're following the photo I gave you, aren't you?" I call.

"Yes," he says. "After I plant this, I thought I might help you get that moss off the shingles on your roof and maybe start scraping and painting the side of your house that gets all the weather."

The two butterflies return, sitting aside one another.

Are you my friend? I think. *You just might be.* I think of Shirley. *It's been a long, long time since I had one.*

"I'll be over in a bit," I say. "Back gate open?"

"Yes," he says. "Front gate open, too."

He's trying, I think. *He's pushing me.*

Peace. Piece.

"Okay," I say as another set of sprinklers spring to life. I stand and walk toward the fence. "By the way, have you ever gone to the Grand Haven Musical Fountain?"

"No," Cory says. "What's that?"

I listen to Lily shriek as she continues to run through her sprinkler.

"Magic," I say.

ABBY

AUGUST 2003

I race out of the office, late yet again, and listen to a voice mail from Cory on my way to the car.

"Hi, honey! I have a surprise planned for tonight," he says, his voice chipper. "Well, I guess it's not a surprise-surprise anymore." Cory laughs. "It's just that it's getting late, and I was kind of hoping you wouldn't be late another night. Can you be home by seven? Okay. Bye. Love you."

I hit End and look at my phone: it's 6:37 p.m.

"Dammit," I say. I open my car door and angrily toss my phone into the passenger seat. I get in and start the car when I hear, "Hello? Hello? Abby?"

I look over. I have somehow managed to accidentally call my mother.

"Dammit," I say.

"Abby," she says. "I hear you cursing."

I take a deep breath and grab the phone. "Hi, Mom," I say, my voice not nearly as chipper as Cory's just sounded.

"Are you okay? I don't like you cursing. Did anyone hear you?"

I bite the inside of my cheek, so hard in fact, that I draw blood. The fact that my mom would first worry about whether anyone actually heard me say a bad word and whether that could somehow miraculously be traced back to her—an anonymous woman in her sixties who wears dickies and a shower cap to bed to protect her perm—and, thus, cast dispersions upon her mothering techniques completely outweighs whether her daughter might be upset or in danger perfectly sums her up.

"No, Mom. No one heard me say *dammit*."

"That's good," she says before adding, "You just said it again."

"I'm so glad you called," she said, still ignoring the fact that I might actually not be okay. "Your father got on that Amazon and bought a pair of slippers that *do not* have a gripper sole on them. I'm worried that he might slip and fall, aren't you?"

I slump over and drop my head on top of the steering wheel. "Your entire house is carpeted."

"I want to return the slippers," she continues, "but I'm worried that will just make our address more known."

"To whom, Mother?" I ask.

"Everyone!" she says, her voice high. "Terrorists. Scammers." She stops and lowers her voice. "Even that Schwan's man."

I tap my head against the steering wheel. "What Schwan's man?"

"The one who used to deliver food to us!" she says, alarm dripping from every word. "I still see him in our neighborhood sometimes, even though I canceled our account."

"Maybe he's delivering to your neighbors?" I propose.

"I don't trust him," she says. "He has that mustache."

I lift my head and look at my office building. Suddenly, I feel as trapped as my mother does.

"Listen, let me call you back later this week," I say. "Cory called and says he has a surprise planned for tonight, and I'm already late."

There is silence on the other end. "It's nearly seven, Abby," my mom says, her trademark *tsk-tsk* serving as punctuation.

"I'm well aware of that, Mother," I say.

I keep saying Mother *instead of* Mom. *Not good. That's my tipping point.* Mother *is my "unsafe" word. Don't lose it tonight, Abby.*

"Cory needs his wife. Lily needs her mom."

The world around me turns white. I can feel my temples pulse.

"And our family needs a paycheck, Mother," I say. "I'm the breadwinner."

"But Cory's service..." my mother starts.

"Doesn't mean Lily will be able to go to college, or that we'll be able to retire comfortably," I say. I take a deep breath and suddenly think of Iris, who has demonstrated so much trust in us recently, so much ability to grow. *Maybe I'm reacting too negatively and selling my mother short.* I shift gears. "You know, Mom, I actually did want your opinion on something."

"Oh!" I can't tell if she sounds thrilled or concerned. "Okay."

"I'm not happy in my job, Mom."

"But it's only been a few months," she interrupts.

"I know, I know, but I feel as if I'm taken for granted as a woman," I say. "I am the one driving a large part of our business, and yet all of my ideas are taken from me and given to the men."

"But it's not your company, Abby."

"I know that. And that's what I was going to ask you. What if I started my own engineering consulting company? I could consult with a wide range of boat builders and manufacturers, big to small."

"Oh, honey, that's just too much of a risk, don't you think, considering all your family has been through?" she asks.

"I know, I know," I say.

"You know, you've always wanted more than other people," my mom says with a big sigh. "Maybe you should just be content with what you have. Maybe being a wife and a mother should be enough for you."

Her words hit me like a boxer's uppercut. *I am fulfilled being a wife and mother. Those are my greatest joys in life. And yet...it's not enough to complete me as a woman, as a person, as a soul. Is that wrong? Why should that be wrong? Why does my own mother make me feel even worse?*

"I was thinking about our neighbor, Iris, recently," I start.

My mom cuts me off. "I looked up that woman you live next to. Nasty history. War protester."

"What?"

"It's all true," she says. "You should keep Lily far away from a woman like that. And wait until I tell Cory about all of that. He will be none too pleased."

"Don't you dare, Mother!" I yell into the phone. "I adore Iris."

"Is she the one who got you thinking about quitting your job?" my mom asks. "Rabble-rouser."

"Bye, Mother!" I say. Against my better judgment, I race back to my office, open my laptop and begin to search *Alice Maynard War Protester.* A number of links to old newspaper articles pop up on what happened to her nursery. I scan them, my heart racing. I shake my head the more I read.

"She was a woman ahead of her time," I say to myself. "A woman who was totally misunderstood."

Then I click on a link to an old clip from a news station. I stare into the face of a woman not much older than I am now, a woman who had lost everything—her husband, daughter, business—but not her dignity.

"We shall not wilt!" Iris says, looking into my eyes.

I rush back to my car, lower my head onto my steering wheel and weep.

"What a lovely surprise," I say. "I'm so sorry for being late."

Cory leans over and kisses me on the lips as Lily opens the picnic basket underneath us.

"Enough smooching," she says. "I'm hungry."

It is just after eight, and we are seated in Grand Haven's Waterfront Stadium, which has a spectacular view of the Grand River and Dewey Hill, which sits on the other side of the water and where the Grand Haven Musical Fountain—the reason behind Cory's surprise—will take place.

"How did you find out about this?" I ask.

"Iris," Cory says.

"Of course," we say in unison.

I fill Cory in on my conversation with my mother and what she had discovered about Iris. He nods his head.

"Does this change your opinion of her?" I ask him.

"Nah," he says immediately, before stopping, seeking just the right words, "she doesn't need any more judgment. Look, you know how I feel about my service. I still believe it was the right thing to do to protect our country and my family. But it doesn't mean I'm pro-war. Or conservative. Or anti-liberal. It means I believe in doing what's right. And so does Iris. She created something out of love for her daughter that was completely taken out of context. That same stuff still happens today. We judge first and think later. We think we change, we think we grow more tolerant, but we really haven't that much."

I look at my husband with awe. I'm speechless at how introspective he's become.

"Did you know the first female American soldier was a woman who enlisted as a Continental Army soldier under the name of a man? Served three years in the Revolutionary War and even removed a musket ball from her own leg so no one would discover she was a woman. Now it's estimated some 200,000 women are fighting in the Iraq and Afghanistan wars." He stops. "Women are judged more harshly than men, be it in the military or business because they threaten the standard norm. If nothing changes, most people feel safe," he says. "Look at your mom. But women who are smart, independent, speak their minds, try to change the world, well, they're threats against men. You and Iris may be decades apart but you're really much the same."

I lean over and kiss my husband, knocking him back with my passion.

"Ugh," Lily says. "Get a room."

"Lily!" I say. "Where in the world do you hear such things?"

"Dawson's Creek," she says.

Cory and I shake our heads and begin to unpack the beautiful picnic dinner he has assembled: sandwiches on seedy salt bread from a local baker, fresh tomatoes, a variety of cheeses, olives, chips, hummus, grapes, strawberries and champagne.

"And a juice box for me!" Lily says, fishing through the basket. "I don't like cheap champagne."

"Don't tell me," I say, before Cory joins me to say in deadpan unison, "*Dawson's Creek*."

"No, silly," Lily says, before shoving a straw into her box. *"The OC."*

It is a quintessential summer night in Michigan, the perfect picture postcard kind that we wait all winter for, where the air is warm, the cicadas sing as the water strums, and the evening is still as bright as day. We are seated in the back of the stadium, which is equal parts amphitheater and public park. Cory has a blanket laid atop the grass, and we have ample room to spread out, despite the throng of people still arriving.

"What are we seeing exactly?" I ask. I dip a pita chip into the hummus and look across the river to a rolling hillside. There is a flag flapping on top, and I can make out the outline of an anchor and giant letters across the hillside that read COAST GUARD CITY USA.

"From what I've gathered, it's a synchronized water and light show set to music," Cory says, his mouth full of sandwich. "It runs at dusk all summer long."

"Why are there so many people here?" Lily asks.

"It's supposed to be quite spectacular," Cory says. He grabs a scrunched-up brochure from his pocket. "Hold on." He unfolds it. "Oh, here. Listen to this. It was built in 1962 and is the world's largest fountain of its kind. In fact, it was the world's largest fountain until 1988 when the one at the Bellagio in Las Vegas opened."

"Leave it to Vegas to go bigger," I say.

"What happens in Vegas stays in Vegas," Lily says.

On any other night, this might elicit a time-out for Lily, but Cory and I break into laughter at the same time. "By the way, you can no longer watch *The OC*," I say.

"Okay, I'll start watching *The Bachelorette*, then," she says.

"Champagne?" Cory asks. "You might as well feel a little OC, too, whatever that means."

"Thank you, sire," I say with a laugh. Cory fills my champagne flute, and I take a sip. "This is good."

"It's Korbel," he says. "Don't get too excited."

I take another sip. "I need this after the day I've had."

"I'm sorry," Cory says.

"It's soul-sucking," I say. "They just don't treat me equally. It's that simple."

"Quit," Cory says.

"But..."

"Don't listen to your mom, or to anyone else," Cory says. "Listen to your heart." He reaches over and grabs my hand. "We've been to hell and back, Abby. But you're a great engineer." He stops. "And a great mom and wife to boot. You'd be a great entrepreneur, I've no doubt."

"Thank you," I say.

"Maybe I could even help you with your start-up when you get to that point," he says. "Invoicing, billing, follow-up. You did it all for me when I was overseas. We were a team. I'm used to being part of a team. It could be a new adventure." He looks at me with great intensity. "I need to fight for something. It's important to me."

"I thought you had Iris," I say.

"I'm not joking, Abby."

I shake my head at my husband, feeling a mix of emotions, all of which have likely been heightened by the champagne.

Here's a man who lost his friends and nearly lost his own life, but he chose to fight for his country—for *all* of us—those with whom he agrees and those he does not because he is more than a label, even more than a patriot: he is simply a good man who believes in doing the right thing. For once, I can clearly see his side of things, that his decision to enlist *was* black-and-white, one based in strength and honor, not fear. A decision based simply on the fact that it was the right thing to do.

I think of Iris.

Perhaps my view is shaded because my husband returned home safely to me and Lily. Perhaps I would not feel this way if I had been forced to bury him, or if he had left and I'd never seen him again, had a chance to kiss him again, feel him again, or say goodbye.

I sip my champagne and study the faces of my husband and

daughter. I turn and look at the diverse group of faces that surrounds me.

What are their stories? What led them to be here, right now?

I shake my head. I know the decision I must make, if only I can be as strong as my husband was. It will not be easy. But it will be a hell of a lot easier than my husband's decision and journey, a hell of a lot easier than Iris's life.

I turn toward the hillside and think of how crazy this decision must have sounded: *why, yes, Grand Haven, I think it's a totally sane idea to build a musical fountain on the lakeshore! Of course people will flock to see it! And I want to do it across the river on that hillside!*

"You know, this is really a feat of engineering," I suddenly say. "I can only guess what we're about to see, but to be built in 1962 and only be outdone by the Bellagio…that's pretty amazing. I can only imagine what went into its creation."

An older couple sitting just in front of us turns at the same time. Both have curly white hair, BluBlocker sunglasses and are drinking a summer ale. They look almost like twins.

"I couldn't help but overhear you," the woman says. "I'm Mabel, and this is my husband, Ted."

"It's nice to meet you," Cory says, extending his hand to shake Ted's.

"We've lived in Grand Haven for over sixty years," Ted says.

"Wow," I say. "That's amazing."

"Special place," Ted says.

"This musical fountain was the brainchild of a friend of ours, a longtime resident, who was a dentist and former mayor of Grand Haven," Mabel says. "He really was a visionary, who wanted to beautify the waterfront. This fountain was modeled after a musical fountain show that he saw in Germany while providing dentistry for the US Navy after World War II. As you just said, it was the largest musical fountain in the world when it was built. And all right here in little, old Grand Haven!"

Mabel is beaming. I lift a champagne glass, and Mabel clinks her beer to my flute.

"A lot of people made fun of him," Ted says. "They thought it was a crazy idea. Some folks thought he was desecrating Dewey Hill." Ted stops. "But that's what having a vision is all about, isn't it?"

I feel as if Ted is speaking directly to me, and his words give me goose bumps.

"Is he still practicing?" Cory asks. "Your friend?"

I jerk my head to look at Cory as if he's crazy. He tilts his head and gives me a "Stay with me on this!" look.

"Oh, goodness, no," says Mabel. "But I think his son took over his practice. They did everybody's teeth in Grand Haven." Mable smiles like the Cheshire cat. "Even mine!"

"Good work," Cory says. "It was nice to meet you."

We eat our dinner in silence for a few moments. When enough time has passed, I look over at Cory and mouth, "Is he still practicing? Are you nuts?"

He moves the spread of food and scoots toward me. "My friend in the military who has connections at the Defense POW/MIA Accounting Agency lab says the pin and T-shirt samples we sent them aren't enough. He says they need a dental impression to go along with any DNA they might find. What if that dentist did Iris's husband's dental work? What if he could help us?"

"Really, Matlock," I whisper. "How far are you going to take this?"

"Until I bring him home," he says. "That's what having a vision is all about, isn't it?"

I want to shake my husband, but instead I grab his face and kiss him, hard, which elicits a few "oohs" and "aahs" and claps from the crowd.

"I can't," Lily says, covering her face.

All of a sudden, the sun slips behind the lake, the sky darkens and the fountains erupt in color. A voice bellows, "Tonight we celebrate the music from *Finding Nemo*," a declaration that makes Lily howl in delight.

"My favorite movie!"

Colorful water dances in sync to the music, almost as if the lake itself has come to life and choreographed a ballet. The colors fade, strobe and twinkle as the fountains sweep left and right, oscillates at various positions and moves in perfect beat to the selected songs. At times the fountains shoot higher and higher, hundreds of feet into the air. It is more breathtaking than I ever could have imagined, made even more stunning by the rainbow reflected in the river, a current of colors that makes the water seem as if it's on fire, as if Iris herself, the rainbow goddess, has returned to earth.

I turn to look again at my family, their faces lit in color, enraptured by the beauty. I am blessed to see a world of color.

The fountains explode in purple, and then dance left to right and back again. I see Iris's butterfly garden waving in the summer breeze. The waters stop, the show is over and everyone is applauding. My eyes remain on the hillside across the water.

I sit up straight. I look at Cory, my heart racing.

"I have a vision," I say to Cory.

He pretends to lean forward and reach for Ted and Mabel's BluBlocker sunglasses sitting on a quilt beside them.

"Should I stop it?" he asks.

I laugh and fill up my glass of champagne. "Not yet," I say. "But maybe after this glass."

PART ELEVEN

HYDRANGEAS

"If you plant a hydrangea, you're sure to find a love that lasts. Loyalty, that's what they mean to me."

—Julie Cantrell, *Perennials*

IRIS

AUGUST 2003

I am dreaming that I am in battle, fighting alongside Cory and Jonathan, rushing toward an unseen enemy. It is dark, and every few seconds gunfire and explosions light the world around us. I can feel their footsteps pounding beside me, and then, nothing. Gunfire illuminates the scene around me. They are gone. I am fighting alone.

I wake with a start.

Out my bedroom window, heat lightning flashes over the lake.

"Summer humidity," I say with relief. I feel my brow and then the sheets underneath me. They are soaked. "When is this heat going to break?"

I have my windows open, but the predawn breeze is warm

and sticky, the temperature not much different from the time I went to bed. I do not like air-conditioning. I grew up without it and, ironically, never became conditioned to air-conditioning. I feel cooped up when it runs. My nose dries out. I spend all winter with the windows shut and the heat running, so I go downright loony every second my windows are shut in the spring and summer.

I cock my head. Through my windows a whip-poor-will calls. I can see the last of the lightning bugs blink. These images and sounds make me feel like a young girl again. In the dark, unable to see my body or what's around me, much like in my dream, I still feel like a girl. I think of how school would be starting soon, what I would wear the first day of class, excited to see my friends again.

The summer peepers—the little frogs that populate our state—fill the world with their deafening chorus, an orchestra of sound. If I cannot hear the sounds of those summer peepers, I do not feel as if I am fully embracing summer in Michigan. I shut my eyes as they sing to me. Finally, their call calms, and I can hear the soothing lapping of the lake.

I sit up in bed.

Be a girl, Iris, I think. *A girl of summer. Not a child of war. Be a part of this world, not apart from this world.*

I literally hop out of bed and shuffle toward an ancient armoire that takes up an entire wall of my bedroom and which has more coats of paint on it than an old canoe. I open it, the cabinet squeaking loudly. *Where are you?* I think. *How long has it been?*

I shuffle through drawers, tossing aside long pants and sweaters, before moving on to shorts, T-shirts and sweatshirts. I'm about to give up when—*there!*—buried in a corner of the final drawer is my swimsuit. I pull it out and hold it in front of my face, eyeing it suspiciously, like one might a long-forgotten, frostbitten Tupperware meal found deep in the freezer.

My swimsuit is a colorfully striped one-piece that I bought decades ago, in seemingly another lifetime.

The Twiggy years. Or was it Cheryl Tiegs?

I wore it a few times when I used to go to the beach, but I caught a glimpse of myself one time in the mirror and realized I was not a supermodel posing for *Sports Illustrated*, unless the *SI* stood for *Stop It!*, so I put my swimsuits away. For good.

I head toward the bathroom, still holding the suit at arm's length like a skunk. *Here goes nothing*, I think. I wriggle and twist, and tug and yank, and when the suit is completely on, I stare at myself, wide-eyed.

"It fits," I say to my reflection. "It still fits."

I wouldn't say I look great in the suit—it's old, worn and threadbare, like me—but it fits and, at my age, that's all that pretty much matters anymore. I turn this way and that, feeling a bit like a young girl. I move toward the sink and then stop.

No need to wash my face, I think, grabbing a beach towel and padding out of the bathroom. I march toward the kitchen and stop cold.

What if there are early walkers on the beach? What if someone sees me?

You can do this, Iris, I think. *No pills. No thinking. You're a girl of summer. Go.*

I move toward the back porch, slide into some flip-flops, and head outside and toward the beach, my heart racing.

Suddenly, I stop. The world flips upside down. I crouch by the fence for support. I have been only to see Mary and clung to the fence to see Abby, Cory and Lily. Those have been my farthest trips, which can be measured in counted footsteps. *This*—I look toward the beach—*is like flying to the moon.*

"I can't, I can't, I can't," I whisper, tears suddenly filling my eyes. "You are an old fool, Iris."

I stand to head inside when I hear the waves crash into the shore. I turn to scan the beach yet again, and in the mist rising from the lake, I can picture Cory and Lily as I saw them just the other day. A little girl helping a grown man, a child helping a war hero, be brave. She had held his hand, and the two had taken baby steps until they were on the beach, and Cory was seated in the sand. He had actually fallen knees first into it, and tossed sand into the air as if it were gold. They had played in the lake, built sand castles...*acted like children.*

If he can do it, I can, too, I think. *Be brave, Iris. Be brave.*

I slip down the dune, one baby step at a time, sliding through the dune grass slowly like a cautious rabbit, my flip-flops churning sand as I go. I emerge, stopping at the edge. I look left and right. The beach is empty. My heart is racing. I again think of Cory, and I fall into the sand knees first. I am thankful to be covered in sand.

I did it!

I look up. The lake is like glass, the waves lazily lapping at the shore as if the heat has already sapped their energy. The water is blue-black at first, the clouds that line the horizon of Lake Michigan eerily dark, but as I stand at the water's edge, the sun begins to cast just enough light to change the scenery, one second at a time: the sky brightens to light blue; the horizon turns as pink as one of my hydrangeas and the clouds spring to life. The world, literally, glows. And everything seems to still at once as if it is as mesmerized by its transformation. I shut my eyes and listen to my lake.

Hello, old friend, it calls to me. *Nice to see you. It's been too long.*

I open my eyes and inhale. I move toward shore and dip a toe into the water, gingerly. The lake is shockingly warm. I toss my towel onto the sand and step into the lake up to my ankles. I remember my grandma once telling me that the only way to get into Lake Michigan is the same way you must approach life: jump in headfirst.

"Don't dally," she'd say. "Even when it's warm, it's not." Then she'd run directly into the lake like a madwoman and leap headfirst into the water.

"Here goes nothing, Grandma," I say. I begin to run into the lake, up to my thighs, then my waist, and then I'm airborne, diving into the water. Though it's warm by Lake Michigan standards—probably in the low seventies—it's still a shock to my system. I yelp as I go underwater. Submerged, I open my eyes and watch air bubbles drift from my nose and mouth. The sun is reflecting across the top of the water, and shafts of light illuminate my underwater world: the sandy striations on the bottom of the lake, the smooth, colorful stones that have tumbled toward the shore, the tiny fish surprised to see a visitor this early in the day.

I pop up out of breath, water streaming down my face. I clear my eyes of water, and my skin breaks into goose pimples as the morning's warmth hits my cool flesh. I look around, and scan the horizon: nothing has changed from this perspective since I was a little girl. The lake still resembles the ocean, the sky is just as magical, the dunes and beach still undeveloped. I look down at my body, split into halves by the lake. Underneath the water, my legs and waist look pearly and young, the skin magically fresh. Above the water, however, my skin is spotted like a bird's egg and as wrinkly as crepe paper. I squint. My eyes are old, but—right now—I feel no different than I did as a child.

For the first time in decades, I am out in the world, actually experiencing all that it has to offer, and it is terrifying and exhilarating.

And I do not want it to end.

And, for one heartbeat more, I stay in this moment, release a whoop into the morning that echoes across the water and then dive back into the lake.

I dry off and walk—barefoot this time across the quickly warming sand—and head back, completely refreshed, to my cottage.

I feel like a new woman, I think. *I feel like I've been on vacation, far away from home. Is that what actually being alive feels like?*

I make some tea and oatmeal, and eat my breakfast on the screened porch, my hair still damp. There was a time these cottages were filled with wet footprints and dusted with sand. I sip my tea and shut my eyes. There was a time these cottages were filled with family. I open my eyes and sigh. I used to run back and forth between my grandma and parents' houses. There was a worn path in the grass between the two.

Before the fence.

I finish my breakfast, put the dishes in the sink and head into the garden, ready to get to work before the world has even woken. I grab the hose and begin watering before the sun gets too high in the sky. It has been an abnormally hot and dry August by Michigan standards. That doesn't mean we haven't gotten rain, though. We've had thunderstorms due to the humidity, where the skies have opened and wept inches of rain. But we've had few gentle rains or days of lingering showers. And here, the sandy soil soaks up the rain like a sponge. I start watering my hanging baskets and then fill my fountains and birdbaths. Within seconds of fresh water, cardinals and wrens splash and dunk, chirping excitedly.

"You remind me of me this morning," I say to them. I watch them play, my hose soaking the ground, before I move to my butterfly garden and around to my daylilies. By the time I reach my hydrangeas, the sun is already blaring, and my hydrangeas are wilted.

"Sorry, Blanche DuBois," I say, picking up a sad bloom and talking to it.

My hydrangeas are very dramatic. In the summer heat the bush's tender branches cannot hold the weight of the heavy flowers, and they droop until they touch the ground. Even the beautiful blooms of blue and pink look downright discombobulated. The big blooms spread apart and the color fades, and the hydrangeas become highly temperamental, just like the Tennessee Williams character.

I soak the earth with the hose, and slowly, the hydrangeas perk up and come back to life as if I've just served them an ice-cold gin and tonic on a blistering hot summer afternoon.

"My beauties," I call to them.

I have rows of hydrangeas that hug my house. They are huge now, some that are probably fifty years old. And I have a couple, though gardeners would scoff and say my memory is as wilted as my beauties, that are older than I am and were started by my mother. There is nothing that compares to the longevity and beauty of a summer hydrangea. They are loyal companions whose simple loveliness always takes me by surprise, like a lifetime friend.

There was a candy store downtown when I was a little girl—Ye Old Fudge Factory—and the counter ran the entire length of the store. It was lined with glass globes filled with a rainbow world of candy: jelly beans, gumballs, gummy bears, sours, licorice, caramels, chocolates. The colors of my hydrangeas remind me of that candy shop. I have more than just white, pink and blue; instead, the colors of my hydrangeas are like cotton candy: iridescent blue, lilac, lime, purple and the most beautiful strawberries-and-cream panicle hydrangeas.

I also have lace cap hydrangeas, woodland hydrangeas and oak leaf hydrangeas.

"Morning."

I jump at the sound and turn the hose on myself. I yelp when the cold water douses me.

I turn, and Lily is standing behind me.

"Why are you wearing a swimsuit?"

"How did you get in here?" I ask.

"The gate was open." She looks at me. "Should I leave?"

I turn the hose back to the hydrangeas. "No, no, you're fine. You just startled me." I look at her. "Where are your parents?"

"My mom had an early morning meeting, and my dad is doing some QRX 400 workout or something on the TV. Why are you wearing a swimsuit?"

"It's hot," I say. "And I went for an early swim in the lake." I look at her. "Is it okay that I'm wearing a swimsuit?"

Lily nods. "You should," she says. "It's summer. Everyone should wear a swimsuit when they want to."

I nod at her and then notice what she's holding. "What do you have there?" I ask.

"My Powerbook," she says.

I am stunned by the boom of technology these days. It seems to be growing more quickly than weeds in a spring garden.

Lily looks up at me, her face drooping just as my hydrangeas had earlier.

"Are you okay?"

She looks at me for the longest time. "Not really."

"Do you want to tell me what's wrong?" I ask. "It's okay if you don't want to, either."

Lily sighs. "My new teacher sent a letter welcoming me to Grand Haven and her class," she says. "She wants everyone to write about their summer to share with the class. But she also wants me to tell the class about myself, too." Lily stops. "I've met a lot of my classmates in summer camp already, but..." She stops again. "But I'm nervous."

"That's natural," I say. "But you know what? I never say I'm nervous. Do you want to know what I say?" Lily nods. "I always say I'm excited. And that's what you need to remember. You're not really nervous, you're just really excited. There's a big difference between being scared and excited. That's what makes you feel all fluttery inside, like you ate a million butterflies."

"That's exactly how I feel!" she says.

I smile. Behind Lily, the surprise lilies are fading. It was my signal growing up that summer was ending, and school was just around the corner.

"I used to be excited every year to go back to school," I say.

"You were?"

"I was. In fact, I used to hide right here," I say, pointing to my hydrangeas.

"What do you mean?" Lily asks.

"I'd hide under these hydrangea bushes," I say. "It was like hiding from the world. No one knew I was there, except my grandma, who'd pretend she didn't know until she'd start to weed and tug on my leg."

"Why were you nervous?" Lily asks. "I mean, excited?"

"My family was poorer than most of the other families," I say. "My dad was a miner, my mom was a seamstress. We didn't have a lot of money. But we had a lot of imagination." I wink at Lily. "Hold on." I turn off the hose, rush inside and throw on a T-shirt and some shorts. I come back outside, look at Lily and say, "Follow me." I get on my knees and sneak into a little tunnel between my hydrangeas, crawling all the way until my back is against my stone foundation. A few seconds later Lily appears, her face animated.

"What are we doing?" she asks.

"Hiding from the world for a little while," I say.

It is dark behind the dense hydrangeas, and the wet earth

soaks my shorts. It smells like summer, and my heart races just a little, like it did when I was a girl.

"How do you feel?" I ask.

"Excited," Lily says, before adding, "Safe."

We sit there for a few moments, our breath coming out heavily, moving blue hydrangea blooms as if we were the breeze.

"I used to hide under here with my grandma's dog," I say. "Just the two of us."

"Tell me a story," Lily says.

"What kind of story?"

"Any story that has you in it," she says.

I smile in the dark. "You know, I went to the same elementary school you went to," I say.

"You did?"

"I did. It's very different now. They built a new school, and you have computers these days like the one you're holding. But everything else is still the same really. Teachers, students, subjects." I stop. "Everyone excited for that first day of school."

I shut my eyes, remembering what it was like to be a child, hidden here in the hydrangeas, school just a few days away. "I grew up in the Depression," I say.

"What's that?"

"It's a time when America was very poor, and no one had much money," I say. "We couldn't even afford to go back-to-school shopping for new clothes, so my mom and grandma made all my clothes. And do you know what they made them from?"

"No," Lily says, her eyes wide in the dark.

"Feed sacks and flour sacks."

"What's that?"

"Well, flour used to come in cotton bags, not the paper bags they come in today," I explain. "And my grandparents used to have chickens, and we'd go to the feed store to buy egg mash to feed them. The cotton sacks that flour and feed used to come in were decorated with pretty patterns, and I'd go with my mom and grandma to pick out the prettiest patterns. It always seemed like the prettiest patterns were at the very bottom of the stacks, so my dad and grampa would always have to hoist and restack endless bags to get to the patterns that my mom and I loved the most. When the flour or feed was gone, my mom and grandma would take those cotton sacks and make dresses out of them for me. They were so beautiful, and my friends would have no idea how they came to be."

"What was your favorite?" Lily asks.

"I knew you were going to ask me that," I say. "Of all the patterns, my favorite dress was made from a feed sack that had the prettiest blue and pink hydrangeas all over it, just like the ones in front of us. I always felt safe when I wore that dress."

"Do you still have it?"

I laugh. "Oh, I outgrew that dress," I say. "And I wore it until it was threadbare." I grab Lily's leg and give it a shake. "Oh, my goodness," I say. "You just made me remember something. When I outgrew my dresses, my mom would make quilts out of them. I think I still have a few of those in the attic. It's been years since I thought of those."

"Why?"

"I have an electric blanket now," I say. "And..." My voice grows quieter. "I think I wanted to forget."

"Why?"

"Because sometimes it's too hard to remember," I say.

"Like my dad," Lily says.

"Yes, sweetheart, like your dad." I stroke Lily's hair. "Sometimes, it's nice to get a different perspective on life. We see things in a new light, and that's important. Thank you for reminding me of that."

There is a sudden illumination in the dark, and I see that Lily has opened her Powerbook.

"What are you doing?" I ask.

"I'm going to write something for my teacher," she says. "About my summer. About my life."

"What are you going to write?" I ask.

I look over and see that Lily is tapping on the screen. Instead of writing she is sketching a picture.

"I'm not writing." She stops and looks at me, her beautiful face basked in light from the computer. "It's called Kid Pix. You can now draw on a computer. Pretty cool, huh?"

I nod.

"New perspective," she says, sounding very much like an adult.

"I'm very proud of you," I say. "You're just like these hydrangeas: colorful and unique."

"I'm very proud of you, too," Lily says, fully concentrating on her drawing.

"Me? Why?"

"Look."

I glance at the screen, and Lily has drawn a picture of a fence. One hand is reaching over it, holding a beautiful blue hydrangea bloom. Another hand is extended, accepting the flower.

ABBY

AUGUST 2003

"I have a lunch meeting," I say. "I'll be back in a couple of hours."

My assistant, Traci, clicks on her computer and then looks at me in that way only spouses and assistants can look at you. They smile and nod, fully aware that you're lying, but also fully aware that the smartest thing to do is not stir the hornet's nest.

"Of course," Traci says. She begins to type. "Let me just make sure I have that noted in your calendar." She looks up. "My apologies for the oversight."

Traci is as bright as the summer sun shimmering outside. She is raising a young son all on her own and going to college at night. Within a few months we know each other as well as we know anyone in the world, family included. I cover for her when she heads out early to spend time with her son or study for class, and she covers for me when I have what will officially be termed a "lunch meeting" but unofficially known as a "sanity break."

"Thank you," I say, turning to leave.

Her computer trills, and she clicks on it. "I think you may want to see this, Abby." I can hear her printer quietly come to life. Traci grabs the papers and a stapler, and then hands them to me.

"No," I say. "No. Mr. Whitmore told me this wasn't going to happen."

"Go to lunch, Abby," Traci says.

"He can't do this," I say, my voice almost a shout.

"Abby, go to lunch," Traci repeats very slowly, her voice calm.

She looks around and clears her throat. Colleagues have stopped moving, like actors in a movie who've been put under a spell. They are staring.

I pivot and walk down the hallway, my head spinning, robotically saying hello to people who greet me. Once I am outside, I run to my car, shut the door and scream. I turn on the car, crank the AC, take a deep breath and pick up the papers Traci printed for me. It's a memo from my nemesis, Pete, head of marketing, that reads in bold letters:

Proposed Name Changes to New Paint Line.

My heart is thumping so loudly that it's overpowering the sound of the car's air-conditioning, which is on full blast.

"Pete's Paints?" I read. "He's calling these 'Pete's Paints: Colors for Men'?"

I continue reading, my eyes growing wider. My Iris color has been renamed "Minnesota Vikings Purple." My Hydrangea Blue is now called "Michigan Wolverines Blue."

"They're not even the same colors!" I yell in the car. "He can't do this!"

I grab my phone and call Traci. "He can't do this! I bet he hasn't even contacted these sports teams to acquire rights to use their trademarked names, color or logos."

"You haven't left the parking lot yet, have you?" she asks.

That makes me smile.

"Listen to me, Abby," Traci whispers into the phone. "You're right." She stops. "But you're not going to win this one." She stops, and I can hear Traci breathing—almost as if she's doing yoga breathing—for the longest time. "It's a beautiful summer day. Go enjoy it for a while. See all those colors the only way they should be seen. Through your own eyes." Traci stops again. "Maybe that will bring you some clarity." I can hear her phone trill in the background. "I have to get this," she says. "Bye, Abby."

I take my scenic way home, meandering along the beach, which I realize is bustling even more than usual. Banners reading, Grand Haven Coast Guard Festival line the streets. A massive street carnival—complete with Ferris wheel—is being constructed. The colors of the carnival—combined with the colors of the lake—are nearly too much to take, and I gawk like a tourist, before a honking car knocks me from my thoughts.

I pull all the way down my driveway in an attempt to hide my car and feelings of guilt about sneaking out of the office and coming home for lunch on a pretty summer day.

Why do women feel guilty? I think.

I look at Pete's memo one more time, before wadding it up, tossing it into the back seat.

Outdated. Just like the paper it's printed on, I think.

I hop out of the car—the heat hitting me with a wallop—

and notice our back gate is open. I walk over to it and look into the backyard. "Hello?" I call.

"What a surprise," Cory says.

I walk inside the fence, and Cory is standing alongside a plethora of new pots, a hose in his hands. "I planted some herbs," he says. "Basil. Oregano. Parsley. Since we're in a nice routine now and cooking more at home."

My face droops. *Nice routine*, I think. *I can barely hang on at work.* I look at Cory. *But I can't uproot our family.*

"I know what you're thinking," he says. "We're really late in the season, but they told me these would do well through the fall." Cory laughs. "Annnnddd, I didn't really plant these. They came this way. All grown and ready to eat."

I walk over and kiss Cory. "I'm good except for the cilantro," I say. "Tastes like soap to me."

He smiles. "You don't taste like soap to me." Cory pulls me close and kisses me even harder. "To what do I owe this honor?"

"I decided to take a break," I say. "Mental health moment." I look around. "Where's Lily?"

Cory cocks his head next door. "With Iris. Been there all morning. She told me they were hiding and not to interrupt them."

I laugh. "What's that about?"

"They're friends," he says. "Friends cover for each other."

I think of Traci. "I'm going to sneak over and take a peek," I say. "I need a lot of reasons to smile today."

"And I'm not enough?" Cory asks, acting as if he's hurt.

"You are, my sexy soldier," I say.

He plucks some basil from his new pot. "Would I be sexier if I made you lunch?"

I smile and nod.

"Would I be sexier if I did this?"

Without warning, Cory turns the hose on himself, soaking his tank top. He grabs me. I nearly stop him, thinking of my work outfit and worrying about it getting wet, but instead I stop myself and fall into his arms.

"How did I get so lucky?" I ask.

"I was thinking the same thing," he says. "It's been a long road. Thank you for sticking by me."

I might be saying the same thing to you in the near future, I think.

"I love you," I say.

"Me, too."

Cory pulls off his shirt, and my heart stops. Sometimes I am still surprised that a man this good-looking would be married to me. Then I think of Iris's recent admonishment to stop downplaying myself and her compliment to me: *you are beautiful!*

I watch Cory look at me, with as much hunger as I look at him.

Why do I do this to myself? I wonder. *Why do we women do this to ourselves? I have always been so hard on myself, always deemed myself less-than. I must stop that. Now.*

"I'll make lunch," Cory says. "Why don't you relax?"

"Thank you," I say. "I'm just going to peek next door. I'm curious to see what those two are up to."

"Okay," he says. "Maybe they just didn't want a man intruding on their girl time."

He heads off, whipping himself on the back and rear with his wet T-shirt, before turning around to wink.

"I'll take a shake with my fries," I say. He stops and pops his booty before disappearing.

I head out the gate and tiptoe into Iris's yard. There is no one around. I gingerly step through the grass toward her cottage. I stop. I hear giggling.

I follow the noise, taking one cautious step after another.

Where are they?

I cock my head.

They're hiding in the hydrangeas?

I stiffen and still, just like my coworkers did earlier.

"You try now," I hear Lily say.

"I love to paint," Iris says. "But I've never drawn this way."

"Time for new things," Lily says. "Are you excited?"

"Yes," Iris says.

"Here," Lily says. "Hit this. Now use your finger like this."

There is silence.

"You're good," Lily finally says. "Really good."

"Thank you," Iris says.

I take a small step forward.

"We can see your feet."

"Lily?"

"We can see your feet, Mommy. Why are you spying on us? Why are you home?"

"I'm not spying," I say. "I just came home for lunch. I'm playing hooky."

Lily giggles. "Bad mommy," she says. I hear whispering.

"Do you want to join us?" Lily continues. "There's a password."

Silence.

"Are you going to tell me, or do I have to guess?"

More whispering.

"You have to guess," Lily says.

I look around. "Well..." I look down and think. I see Pete's memo. I look up and see pink, blue and limey-white blooms. I think of Traci. I see colors. Hydrangea Blue. My colors. Through my own eyes.

"Hydrangeas," I say.

"Wow!" Lily says. "You're like a spy. You can come in now."

I hesitate, looking at my dress clothes. But then I brush aside caution just as I did with Cory, and I lower myself to the ground and crawl through a tiny tunnel between Iris's hydrangea bushes—blooms brushing my face, branches scraping my arms—until I see legs. I tug on each one, and the duo giggles.

"Just like your grandma used to do!" Lily says to Iris.

I scooch up and turn around until I am seated by Lily.

"Fill me in," I say.

"I was telling Lily that I used to hide under here as a little girl with my grandma's dog, Midnight," Iris says. "And my grandma would pretend she didn't know I was here. I would fall asleep back here next to Midnight on days just like this, when it was so hot and still Midnight could barely catch his breath—the dog days of summer my grandma called them—and my grandma would water her gardens. Out of the blue, I'd feel her tugging my leg, as if she were pulling a weed, and it would always make me laugh."

"That's a lovely story," I say.

"She has lots of stories, Mommy," Lily says. "She wore dresses made out of flour and feed..."

"Flour and feed sacks," Iris adds.

"And before school would start she would get so excited she'd hide here," Lily continues.

"Excited?" I ask.

"I don't like to say *nervous*," Iris explains. "I prefer *excited*." She looks at me in the dark. "It puts a better spin on things, don't you think?"

Her question hits me out of the blue, and my breath hitches. It is much cooler here, hidden in the shade away from the glare of the sun and the world, and it smells like my grandma's root cellar. Suddenly, I feel protected yet powerful, just like I did when I was little and believed I could be anything I dreamed. "Yes," I say. "I do."

I grab Lily's leg, which is cool. "Is that why you're down here, Lily?" I ask.

"Yes," she says. "I'm a little…excited…to start school. But Iris told me she went to the same school, and it would all be okay."

"And it will," Iris says.

I can feel my heart pound in my ears, just as it had done earlier. "I'm excited, too," I say in the dark.

"What are you excited about?" Lily asks.

"Lots of things," I say. "New beginnings, I guess. Like you." I stop, and my voice comes out husky and raw. "Tell me it's all going to be okay. I think I need to hear that, too."

"Oh, my dear," Iris says. In the dark, I feel a hand brushing mine. It is Iris's. I clasp it tightly, and she gives it a mighty squeeze. "It's all going to be okay."

I feel Lily's hand join ours, and for a few blissful moments, we sit in silence, three generations joined as one, hidden in hydrangeas. A light penetrates the dark finally, and Lily says, "Look at what Iris drew."

I look at Lily's Powerbook. On its screen is a beautiful sketch of a hydrangea, its branches drooping under the weight of its pink and blue blooms.

"My goodness," I say. "It's as stunning as your real hydrangeas."

"Thank you," Iris says. She reaches out and pulls a branch toward our faces. "You know, these hydrangeas must be—oh, my word—at least fifty years old or so. They were my mother's." She stops, and I can hear her breathing. "They're older than the two of you combined."

"How do you get the blue so blue?" I ask. "Do you toss in rusty nails?"

"Old wives' tail," Iris says. "And I'm an old wife who hasn't gotten a tetanus shot in a very long time." I laugh. "Hydrangea color indicates the pH of the soil. Strongly acidic soil turns hydrangeas blue. In alkaline soil, they turn pink. In neutral soil, they can be both colors, even on a single bush. Adding a little sulfur makes them bluer, and adding a little lime makes them pinker."

She pinches off a pretty pink hydrangea bloom and hands it to Lily, who shakes it in the air like she's holding a pom-pom. She then pinches off a beautiful blue bloom and hands it to me.

"You can create your own world of colors, too, you know," Iris continues.

My heart pounds.

"I used to work for a large nursery," Iris says. "I quit."

"What?" I blurt, feigning ignorance about her past. "I didn't know that."

"I did. I worked for a man who was quite set in his ways. So I quit and started my own garden center, ran it right here, from these two backyards."

"I didn't know that, either."

Iris is silent for a second. "I decided to believe in myself," she says. "I decided to test my strength." Iris taps the ground. "Test my own roots, as it were."

She continues: "Women too often don't believe in themselves. We follow the path that has been established by men. But what I've learned is that we're depriving the world of our own colors." Iris touches the pink hydrangea in Lily's hand. "My business went under, Abby, due to circumstances beyond my control. But what I started still blooms, every year, in gardens everywhere. My daylilies, my roses, my hydrangeas...my heirloom flowers are my mark on this world, and those will never die. And, the ironic thing is, even though I lost that business I still make money from it."

"How?" I ask.

"Passive income. When I went out of business, I sold many

of my hybridized flowers to seed companies. They loved my new colors, stronger stems, more cold-tolerant and disease-resistant flowers. I get checks every few months to this day."

"That's amazing."

"But my best royalties are the pictures people still send me of their heirloom gardens," Iris says. "They're my connection to the outside world. I see photos of the flowers I started, right here, ones inspired by the color of my husband's cheeks or my daughter's life. I have hundreds of photos of grandmothers with their daughters and granddaughters—three generations—standing in their heirloom gardens, posing with my flowers. Oh, Abby, and the stories they share with me. The meaning behind each flower, its history, how they've passed it along to those they love. That's my legacy." Iris stops. "I may live behind a towering fence, but my soul has been planted all around the world." Iris reaches out and plucks another bloom from the hydrangea. She tucks it behind her ear as if she was posing for a back-to-school photo. "My grandma said at the end of her life that one should never die with regret."

"Do you have regrets?" I ask.

"Oh, my life is littered with tragedy, but I only have two main regrets."

Tell me, I think. *Tell me.*

"I'm working to rectify one of those now," she says, reaching over to tuck the pink bloom behind Lily's ear.

It's the fence, I think. *She's trying to reach out to us. She's trying to have a family and a life again before it's too late.*

"And the other?" I have to ask.

"There's nothing I can do about that anymore," she says.

Your husband, I think. *You never got to say goodbye to your husband.*

"What about you, Abby?" Iris asks. She doesn't wait for me to answer. "How much risk are you willing to take? Really, the question for you is, how much risk is it compared to life itself?"

I grip the hydrangea. She can see right through me. My mind whirls, spinning first to my mother, then to Iris and her husband and daughter, finally to Cory, our marriage and Lily.

What am I frightened of? What if I wake up and I'm Iris's age and I'm filled with regret for not pursuing my own dreams?

"What color is the flower you're holding?" Iris suddenly asks.

"What do you mean? Blue."

"No," Iris says. "What color do you see?"

My heart explodes again. "The color of history, the color of family, the color of longevity..." I stop and then smile in the dark. "I see Hydrangea Blue."

"Lunch!" Cory yells. "Where is everyone? Lunch is ready!"

"Bye, Iris," Lily says, scooting between the hydrangeas. She takes off in a flash.

"Thank you, Iris," I say. I crawl out of the bushes, turn and hold out a hand.

Iris takes it. When we are both in the light, Iris reaches for the bloom still in my hands and tucks it behind my ear.

"You look positively radiant in Hydrangea Blue," she says.

PART TWELVE

BLACK-EYED SUSANS

"A little girl is waiting where I found her years ago,
Something tells me that I'm welcome where the Black-eyed Susans grow."

—Al Jolson, "Where the Black-Eyed Susans Grow"

IRIS

AUGUST 2003

Thunderstorms boom outside, the sound echoing off the lake. Wild turkeys, which have taken residence in a few nearby pines to stay dry, call back to the thunder, thinking it may be a mate. I smile in the dark.

"Everyone gets lonely," I say to the turkeys.

I've been lonely for a long time, I think to myself.

It has been a rather stormy summer, and the lakeshore—like my head—has been filled with the sound of thunder. Contrasting emotions are causing internal boomers.

I am at risk here, I think. *Right now, right here, I am safe, tucked into my bed in my home behind my fence. And isn't that better than getting too close to anyone again, like I'm doing? Because if I do...*

The turkeys warble.

I could lose everyone all over again.

And I would not survive that devastation this time around.

Turkeys call yet again.

If you've never heard a turkey call, it's a sound that defies logic: a warbling gobble-scream that comes from deep within, a release of a thousand emotions via a nonsensical warble that simultaneously amuses you and makes you feel bone-achingly solitary.

I sit up in bed, slip my feet into my slippers and walk to the window. A turkey is perched awkwardly in a branch, its body too big for its current seating arrangement. I lean toward the screen, put my elbows on the sill and inhale the sweet scent of rain, fresh grass, pine and the lake. My gardens are getting a good soaking and a much-needed break from the heat. The temperature has dropped dramatically, and I actually shiver. The turkey catches me in the window, cocks its head and then jumps into the air, a true leap of faith for the ugly bird. Watching a wild turkey take flight defies gravity. I watch the bird free-fall for a brief moment before its wings kick into gear. The bird lands in my yard with a thud, struts around for a second, pecking at the ground.

And yet, I think, *if he can take such a big leap of faith and make it, maybe I can, too.*

In the nearby trees, its friends gobble, and the wild turkey begins to walk-run through my yard before spreading its wings and taking flight—barely—flapping crazily until it reaches a low branch beneath its friends. I smile. It's like watching a fighter plane try to take flight in an old movie.

I suddenly think of Jonathan, and I stand too quickly, banging my head on the window frame.

"Ouch!"

I walk to a dresser and pull out an old scrapbook. I hesitate—I'm rarely this lazy, but it's cool and rainy and I'm introspective this morning—and then kick off my slippers and slide back into bed, propping a pillow behind my back and pulling the blankets up to my waist. I reach over and click on the lamp on my bedside table. Black-eyed Susans brighten my room.

One of my most prized heirlooms—besides my flowers—is a beautiful lamp that has been passed along to me by Mom and Grandma. It's a faux Tiffany lamp—we could never afford a real one although we pretended this was—and the gorgeous glass shade is resplendent with Black-eyed Susans. The panes of glass fade from pale to dark green, and it sits atop a brass base.

I adore this lamp because it reminds me of the hours spent reading beneath its beautiful light with my mom and grandma. I also adore this lamp because I love Black-eyed Susans. I love them because, to me, they symbolize encouragement and strength. They are adaptable, having moved across America, determined to survive and bloom where planted.

And if there's one thing a gardener needs, especially in the dog days of August, it is a symbol of encouragement.

In college I learned that the genus name for Black-eyed Susans is Rudbeckia, named for the Rudbecks, a famous Swedish father and son both, ironically, named Olof. The elder Rudbeck established Sweden's first botanical garden, and his son continued his father's studies as a scientist and professor, teaching Carolus Linnaeus, who devised our system of plant nomenclature and eventually named Black-eyed Susans Rudbeckia for his mentor.

I reach over and touch the glass shade, running my fingers over the flowers.

"You're so smooth," I say, "unlike your real sisters," which feel fuzzy, almost hairy to the touch.

My mom especially loved this lamp as Susans were among her favorite flowers. She cherished it mostly because of its simple beauty. "You don't have to be showy to be beautiful," she said during that summer car trip with my father as we passed a ditch filled with Black-eyed Susans. "Look at them!

They're pretty enough to have a place of honor in my garden and yet they can proudly wave to the world growing right here alongside the highway." She turned around and looked at me in the car. I will never forget how beautiful she looked that very moment, her face flushed, her hair whipping in the wind as Bing Crosby played on the radio. "And just think of our lamp! No less a man than Tiffany himself believed that a common wildflower like the Susan was as pretty as any fancy lily or peony that he put it on one of his lamps."

I touch the lamp again.

What is common? I wonder. *What is ordinary? Women are so hard on themselves, calling their looks ordinary, holding themselves up to standards of beauty set by men. Does a Susan consider itself any less beautiful than a peony? Does a wildflower growing in a ditch think of itself as less than one growing in a garden? No! So why do we?*

I look at the scrapbook and run my fingers over the old leather cover. *Photo Album* is embossed in black on the cream-colored leather. I open the album, and the familiar, familial scent hits me—*that* smell of old photos and forgotten memories. My heart leaps. Jonathan is staring at me from a black-and-white photo that he sent me from overseas—one of the last photos I have of him.

I knew everything about you, I think, *and yet I barely had a chance to get to know you.*

He is young, so young, *too* young. He is looking into the camera—*who took this photo, I wonder?*—wearing a goofy grin, which belies the seriousness of his situation and what he is wearing: a soldier's uniform, a shiny helmet, a rifle in his arms. His teeth are white, his eyes sparkling. I trace my finger over his nose, which I don't remember being so pointed, and then his chin, which I don't remember being so strong.

"I don't remember sometimes," I say to the photo, which I notice is held in place by three black photo corners. I look, and one photo corner is trapped in the spine of the album. I give the album a little shake to free it, and turn a page to release it, but the thick paper begins to crumble in my fingers. Suddenly, a yellowed piece of paper comes free and falls into my lap.

My heart stops.

It is a letter from my husband. One I hid away a lifetime ago. One I never wanted to read again.

I start to hide the letter in the middle of the album once again, to put it away, never to retrieve it again, but then—in the distance—I hear a boom.

At first I think it's thunder, or the turkeys, but I cast my eyes toward the window, and the skies have begun to clear, the pines empty.

Boom!

Boom!

What is going on? I think. And then I remember: it's the kickoff to the annual Grand Haven Coast Guard Festival, a celebration to honor those who sacrificed their lives in service to their country.

Firecrackers and bottle rockets continue to explode.

Boom!

Jonathan and I attended one of the early coast guard festivals, long before it was the big deal it is today, where hundreds of thousands attend. Back then they held rowing competitions for the service members stationed in Grand Haven, and Jonathan and I would sit on the beach and watch their amazing strength, spirit and agility as they rowed wooden boats over the waves of Lake Michigan. Many times the winds were fierce, and the waves would swell. The men would row their boats up, up, up, to the tip-top of a wave and then suddenly disappear. I would stand, panicked, searching for them. A few seconds later, the initial wave would disappear, and there they would be rowing farther out into the lake until up, up, up they would go again.

And all in service to their country, I think, looking again at Jonathan's photo. *All to save a life.*

"I can still remember the coast guard motto," I say to Jonathan. "*Semper Paratus*. Always Ready."

In the distance a wild turkey calls, and my heart simultaneously swells with pride and then dips in anguish, just like the waves.

I look at the letter.

You're reaching out to me today, aren't you? On today of all days.

I slowly open the letter, knowing I must read it again.

My Darling Wife:

How are you? How is our Mary? You two are my flowers, the only things that keep me going.

This will be my last letter from here. We are on the move. Where, they will not tell us, and I do not know. I do know that you and Mary will be beside me wherever I am, and that gives me strength.

Are you getting my checks from the army?

Don't you worry about me, sweetheart.

I urge you to take care of yourself. You keep the home front safe, and I will do the same here. I show all the fellas your Victory Garden, and how you are helping to feed so many people. They tell me my Iris is the prettiest flower in the garden. Boy, is that ever the truth.

When I start to worry, that's what I remember, you know? You, in the garden, with your flowers. You aren't just the most beautiful flower I've ever seen, Iris, you're the strongest one, too. The smartest one.

I think about our life when I am back, and all I see are the three of us on the beach and in our garden. The three of us. Forever.

Well, it's time to eat. Tell your mom to have an apple pie waiting for me when I get home. Have Mary draw me a pic-

ture. I keep them over my bunk, with pictures of you two. My flowers. I dare not think of how long it might be until I see you again—it's too maddening.

For the moment I'll say good-night and I love you. If you need to talk to me, take a walk in your garden, smell a rose, and I'll be there.

Always Yours,

Jon

I don't realize I am crying until I see my tears plop onto the photo album, making the ink on the old paper run, a river of darkness going nowhere.

I weep, my shoulders convulsing as fireworks continue to boom over the lake. I rise from bed without thinking, the album falling into the sheets, head downstairs and zombie-walk directly into my yard in my pajamas.

There I stand, an old widow in her garden.

I gaze upon my flowers, resplendent from the rain, water dripping, colors alive.

The miraculous thing about flowers is that—although they will die—they are always reborn every spring. I may not be a believer in organized religion, but I must call myself a woman of faith or I would not be standing here today.

"I *will* see you again," I say, repeating the words Jonathan wrote.

I think of him, my parents, his parents and Mary all together, and that makes me smile. I have read—and have known—many a scientist who would say I am a ninny, that my reason for such belief has no root in science.

You are fooling yourself, Iris, they would say. *You are being simplistic, childishly wishing for something you know does not exist, like Santa Claus or the Easter Bunny. You are simply trying to make this world a bit more bearable, but study the facts.*

A good part of my life has been to study facts: What will make a plant more resistant to certain diseases? What crosses will yield the sturdiest stems? And yet so much of everything I have done—so much of life—comes down to pure faith.

I look down at the Lady's Mantle catching the water. I watch the hummingbirds dart to hover atop my pink phlox.

"Are you telling me that this is just happenstance?" I ask the universe. "Are you telling me there was not a guiding hand in creating all of this intricate beauty?

"No!" I say. "No!"

We are all parts of a garden, each playing a role, even though we may never realize it.

Finally, I see my Black-eyed Susans standing proudly, their perky faces shining.

Jonathan thought I was the most beautiful flower in the world, but I am truly as common as a Black-eyed Susan. Not in a bad way, I think, but I was never an unusual beauty, like a lily.

But what is common? I wonder again. *Isn't an ordinary life a grand one all its own, filled with great drama and tragedy, hopes, love, losses, dreams?*

What is ordinary? I think of Jonathan defending our country, of Cory and 9/11.

There are no ordinary people. There are no ordinary days.

My Black-eyed Susans smile at me.

There are no ordinary flowers.

I walk to my greenhouse, the wet grass cool on my bare feet. I grab some shears and return to my garden. I snip some Black-eyed Susans, knowing they will last in a vase for nearly two weeks, knowing they will keep standing and smiling until the first frost.

They are strong. They are fragile. They are beautiful. They are common.

They are me, I think. *They are every woman.*

I turn to head inside, but a firework booms and a turkey calls. I walk into the front yard. There bloom Jonathan's roses.

Perfect peach.

I hold a bloom to my nose and inhale, and then pull it free and stuff it into the pocket of my pajama top.

I head back inside, pull on some warm socks, grab my scrapbook, arrange the Susans in a pretty McCoy vase, make a cup of tea and light a fire in the lake-stone fireplace on my screened porch, and spend the morning with my husband, just like I used to do.

Just like I will again someday.

ABBY

AUGUST 2003

There is a clearing line over the lake, a distinct break on the horizon, and yet the other half of the sky is dark and foreboding. When the wind kicks up, rain pellets Lake Michigan.

The weather mirrors my life. I think I can see clear skies ahead, but—right now—things seem downright gloomy.

I quit my job an hour ago.

The most irrational thing rational Abby, the cautious engineer, has ever done in her life.

I barely remember quitting: I simply marched into Mr. Whitmore's office, asked him to reconsider giving my project to Pete and the name change to my paint line.

"Let's just move on, Abby," he said. "New day. Don't live in the past."

"You're right," I replied. "Don't live in the past. Time for a new future. I quit."

Logical Abby, of course, had studied every line of her contract. I had not signed a noncompete, nor had I agreed not to take any of my work moving forward. I will go it alone. I notice on one side of the lot an aged redbud—body bent, limbs cracked—sitting in the shadow of an ancient oak, yet still reaching toward the sun.

I will be the tiny redbud versus the might oak, I think. *I will be Iris.*

Sunshine breaks out and yet it is still raining.

I am in a new world, in two places, momentarily trapped but knowing that there are clearer skies ahead. I am young, I am smart, I am motivated, I have my health and my family, and I am… I stop and smile.

Excited.

"And I have a severance," I suddenly say out loud, which makes me laugh.

Two months. It was Mr. Whitmore's way of paying me off. "We've treated you well, haven't we, Abby?" he asked in the way men do when they know they haven't. "Let's just sweeten the pot so you understand how much your service has meant to us."

He stood and extended his hand. I remained seated.

"I just want to be up front and honest," I said. "I plan to take my paint line public. With *my* names. I plan to be your competitor."

Mr. Whitmore withdrew his hand. "Abby, you don't have the backing, facilities, production or research to pull that off. You know that."

"No," I say. "But I can consult with a company who believes in what I'm doing. Say, like Tiara Yacht."

Mr. Whitmore's eyes narrowed. "You will fail, Abby. Miserably. And you will come back to me one day in the not-so-distant future, when you're about to lose your house or can't afford braces for your daughter, and you will sit in this same chair and beg me to hire you back. And I won't."

My heart leaped into my throat, and I felt like a child who wanted to cry in the principal's office. But I didn't. I stood, smiled and said, "You don't know me very well. Thank you for the opportunity."

I gathered my things in a little box—including the glitter heart Lily drew for me my first day—and left.

"Funny how all the things that really matter can fit into one box when it comes down to it," I told Traci as she walked me out—despite the stares—and hugged me, whispering, "Holy shit," the whole way.

"You're an inspiration," she said once we were outside. "Remember me when you hit it big."

"You'll be my first hire," I said, hugging her tightly.

"Good luck."

"I'll need it."

"I'll call you for drinks," she says as she turned away.

"I'll need that, too," I said.

I am standing in the overgrown lot at the end of the Highland Park Association, where Cory followed Iris. I don't know why I came here, but it was the only place I could think of to come, a quiet place where no one would find me and where no one comes to visit any longer.

It's literally as if this forgotten plot called to me.

This parcel of land reminds me of the big yards that surrounded the once-grand homes in Detroit, neighborhoods empty, mansions boarded up like a ghost town. And yet the yards always told a history: flowers still grew through the rock and glass shards. *Who planted you?* I always wondered. *How did you get here?*

I turn and walk into the middle of the fenced area. A random assortment of living history still grows in this lot, right through the stone and sand, the tree roots and crabgrass. I kick my shoe around the earth, and then stoop to look more closely.

I analyze the land, and walk hunched over, studying it. Decaying stakes and posts have rotted into the ground and become covered in moss, like old tree roots. I grab a meaty stick and begin clawing around.

What is that?

A wooden block turns up, and then another, and another. They are wet and weathered, but seem as if they have been well protected by layers of sand and snow. I squint. They also look as if words have been carved into them. Suddenly, I remember the game I played as a kid, and I root around in my purse for a piece of paper and a pencil. I laugh. I have "taken" lots of paper, pens, pencils and staples from the office over the past few weeks. I lay the paper over the block and begin to rub the pencil lead over the words.

Swiss Chard.

Tomatoes.

Beets.

Peas.

This was someone's garden!

I stand upright and spin.

But where was the house? The foundation?

I walk in a circle around the lot and then do it again.

I feel like I've hit a home run and am rounding the bases, I think.

I stop, jam my trusty stick into the earth and begin to dig in earnest. My stick hits what I think at first is a stone. It is smooth and rather large. I keep digging around it, going deeper and deeper, until I have to kneel and stick both hands into the earth. I pull it free with such force that I fall onto my rear end, which immediately becomes soaked.

I look at the muddy orb I have in my hands, knocking earth from it with my stick.

No! It can't be… A baseball!

Did a family live here? I wonder. *Or did kids use this empty lot to play in back in the day?*

I stand and study the lot. In the corner, near the fence, I finally notice that Black-eyed Susans are blooming, oblivious to the rain or their circumstances. And, as if on cue, the sun comes out, its yellowy glow and happiness matching that of the Susans.

I walk over and pick a Black-eyed Susan, stare into its face and speak directly to it: "I am resilient, too. I am blessed. I am able to make the best of any situation." I tuck the flower into my bag. "Thank you for the reminder," I say. "Thank you."

Suddenly, I look around the lot. I turn and then turn again, my heart racing. It finally all makes sense. The puzzle pieces lock into place in my mind.

This was the Victory Garden! This was Grand Haven's baseball field! This is where Iris comes to visit her family, her past, her heart. This holds the key, I finally realize, *to all of our pasts and all of our futures.*

I race out of the lot and to my car. I head home, parking on the street and sneaking in through the front door, quietly, filled with guilt and panic like a teenager who missed curfew. I tiptoe into the kitchen and toward the doorway. Cory and Lily have not heard me come home. They are engrossed in their work: both are sitting on the porch, working on drawings. Lily is working on her back-to-school assignment, and Cory is sketching a detailed map of our future garden—down to exactly what plants will go where—the old photo Iris gave to him beside him, guiding his efforts.

I stand behind them, not moving, watching them. My heart

fills with joy, and the emotion makes my body twitch. A floorboard squeaks. Cory and Lily turn at the same time.

"Mommy!"

Lily comes running toward me and hugs my legs.

"Abby?" Cory asks, his eyes wide. "Home for lunch? Twice in just a few days? To what do we owe this honor?"

"Yeah, Mommy? Why are you home?"

They both look at me, faces so happy.

"Mr. Whitmore gave everyone the afternoon off," I say. "It's the Coast Guard Festival. Big deal in Grand Haven. Kind of like a holiday here."

I hate lying. I've lectured Cory about it. And I hate secrets, thanks to my parents. So I don't know why I lie, but I do. I just can't bring myself to say I quit yet for some reason. For the first time in a long time, my family is normal, and I don't want that to change just yet.

"So that's what all the fireworks were for," Cory says. "We can hear the people and boats all the way from downtown."

"Can we go?" Lily asks. "Please?"

"I think we should," Cory says. "It's why your mommy got a day off. She should put in an appearance so the boss can see her."

I can feel the blood drain from my face. I nod. "Let me change."

We walk down our hill to avoid the potential parking nightmare, and we are stunned by the crowds: hordes of tourists line the beach and streets, while ships cruise up and down the channel.

"Look! A carnival!" Lily yells, pointing to a makeshift midway complete with rides, games and the sweet, sweet smells of elephant ears and funnel cakes.

Cory buys an elephant ear and Lily and I purchase funnel cakes, and then we wait to ride a blinking Ferris wheel.

"All that sugar was *not* a good idea before doing this," I say to Cory as we rise higher, our arms around Lily, who is snuggled tightly between us.

"Look around," Cory says. "Just enjoy. How many days do we get that are gifts like this?"

His words touch me, and I extend my arm around my two favorite people.

The skies have cleared from earlier, and the sun is bright, the temperatures cooled into the seventies. As we near the top of the Ferris wheel, I literally gasp: the view is stunning. Lake Michigan is stretched out before us, and I can see a line of large ships making their way toward Grand Haven. The south pier's wooden catwalk is jammed with people, and its two historic red lighthouses stand proudly like sentinels watching over the coast.

When we hop off the Ferris wheel, we follow the crowds down toward the pier.

"Look!" Cory points.

The ships I'd seen in the distance are now lined up and entering the Grand River channel. Giant plumes of water shoot off the sides of the boat, a beautiful spectacle as they approach. A booming voice announces the ships as they arrive: "Welcome, US Coast Guard Cutter Hollyhock!"

"Hollyhock!" says Lily. "I wish Iris was here."

"I do, too, honey," I say. "I think she is, though."

Lily smiles.

"Say hello to US Coast Guard Cutter Mobile Bay, US Coast Guard Cutter Morro Bay and Canadian Coast Guard Ship Constable Carrière!"

We applaud as the massive ships pass by, and then we meander around town before we notice a crowd gathered at the park along Grand Haven's waterfront. A massive banner reads: SIXTIETH ANNIVERSARY OF THE ESCANABA.

An elderly man with a cane takes the podium, and the crowd becomes hushed. He turns to an American flag and salutes.

"Seaman First Class William Kelley." The man is wearing a uniform—dress whites, Cory calls them—thick glasses, his back is hunched, and yet his voice is strong and filled with pride. The gold buckle on his belt shimmers in the sun, and a huge spray of flowers sits alongside him. People applaud. "Today marks the sixtieth anniversary of the US Coast Guard Cutter Escanaba, which was sunk by a torpedo during World War II in the North Atlantic. That ship sailed from Grand Haven, and was filled with one hundred and three men, many of them our local boys. One hundred and one died on an ordinary morning at 5:10 on June 13, 1943. I am one of two men who survived. Today we are dedicating an area in this park—Escanaba Park, named for that ship—with the names of the individual sailors who were lost during that time, as well as the names of the two survivors. I hope you will join me in a silent prayer before we do so. Thank you."

Many in the crowd bow their heads. I lower mine but, after a few seconds, open my eyes to glance at Cory. His head is bowed, tears falling. I reach out and grab his hand. I can feel him try to control his body, which is shaking. We raise our heads and as each name is read, Cory salutes. After the names are read, two officers lift the spray, carry it to the Grand River and set it into the water. Slowly, the spray drifts into the current.

After the service, Cory waits and, when the crowd has dissipated, approaches Seaman Kelley. The two shake hands.

"It's an honor to meet you," Cory says. "I served in Iraq."

Seaman Kelley shifts his weight and leans heavily onto his cane, and then lifts his right arm and salutes Cory. Cory looks down at Lily and says, "This man is a hero."

Seaman Kelley bends down on his cane. "Your daddy's a hero."

"I know," Lily says, grabbing her father's leg.

"See that mast and that lifeboat over there?" Seaman Kelley asks. "They were recovered when the Escanaba went down and returned home. That ship was built in Michigan. It was stationed in Grand Haven. It was the center of this community. When it was torpedoed, so were the hearts and souls of Grand Haven." He stops and takes a deep breath. "And do you know what the residents of Grand Haven did? They organized a war bond drive and raised over a million dollars in three months to pay for a second Escanaba, which was commissioned in 1946. That was a lot of money back then. That ship never visited Grand Haven, but it did represent that our community could rise again." Seaman Kelley lifts his face to the sun and then his cane to the heavens. "We may never have returned home the bodies of our boys, but I'm darn certain they sailed again on the prayers and dedication of good people who never forgot—and will never forget—their sacrifice."

The man stops, and—for a moment—his life flashes before my eyes: as a boy swimming in Lake Michigan, as a young man falling in love, as a sailor who miraculously manages to survive, as a husband and father and grandfather. As an ordinary man who has done extraordinary things.

"This isn't an ordinary community," he says as if reading my mind. "It's one with a history of service. My wife was even part of a Victory Garden during World War II. Right up the hill there, at the end of Highland Park."

I can feel time stop. His mouth is moving in slow motion now.

"Victory Garden?" I manage to say.

"Yes, ma'am. They helped feed the town during lean times."

Without warning, my eyes well with tears.

"I didn't mean to upset you, ma'am," he says.

"You didn't upset me, sir," I say. "You awakened me." I stop, trying to say just the right thing to capture my emotions. "You are like the first snowdrop of spring."

Seaman Kelley smiles. "Thank you," he says. "My wife loves snowdrops. Bursting through the snow to signal spring."

"To signal hope," I add.

Seaman Kelley nods. "Sometimes that's all we have to get us through. Sometimes we survive and persist on a glimmer of hope before we even believe it's real."

I take a deep breath.

"I have an idea," I say. "A big idea. An Escanaba idea. A Grand Haven Musical Fountain idea. A Grand Haven Coast Guard Festival idea." I stop. "A grand Grand Haven idea."

Cory is staring at me openmouthed. "Are you okay?"

I nod. "But I need your help," I say to both men. "I need the community's help." I turn to Cory.

"But I have to tell you something first," I say to Cory. "I didn't mean to keep a secret from you, but…"

I take a deep breath and begin just as the spray of flowers drifts out into Lake Michigan.

PART THIRTEEN

DAHLIAS

"My heart is a garden tired with autumn,
Heaped with bending asters and dahlias heavy and dark."

—Sara Teasdale

IRIS

OCTOBER 2003

"My autumn friends! How are you this fine morning?"

The falling faces of my dahlias and asters greet me on a chilly autumn morning. There is a curtain of clouds over the lake, and fog hangs low to the ground like a weary ghost. Frost coats my garden. The dahlias and asters have been my constant companions these past few weeks telling me, "Not yet! Not yet, winter!"

But the first hard frost has taken a toll, and their fading faces now whisper, "It's time, Iris. It's time."

My fall cleanup takes as long as my garden's spring rebirth. In a way, my cleanup is akin to a closing sale at a department store: *everything must go!*

"Even you," I say to my dahlias.

Though autumn brings a sad finality to my gardens and a rather unwelcome welcome to quickly approaching winter, I do adore fall.

And there is nothing like autumn along the coast of Michigan.

I take in the view from my back gate. The sugar maples and aspens rimming the dunes above the lake literally glow, and their colorful spirit lifts my soul. The recent cold snap has made the fall color peak. It's hard to describe the colors: not just red, but flaming red. Not just yellow, but heart-stopping gold. The colors are reflected in the lake, a magical mirror that makes the leaves look even brighter. I hear what sounds like angels playing trumpets in the sky. I look up, and a group of sandhill cranes are bugling their goodbyes to Michigan as they migrate.

"Saying goodbye, too?" I ask.

I watch them fly in a *V*, bodies pointed south, their voices finally disappearing over the lake.

Shadows begin to form around me, and I cast my eyes back to the sky. The temperature has warmed just enough for the fog to dissipate and the clouds to clear.

"Get to work, Iris," I say to myself.

I return to my garden and admire my yard in its autumnal dress. Leaves, trapped by my fence, are ankle-deep. It's like walking around on midcentury shag carpet, all burnt oranges and harvest golds. My fountains are filled with leaves, and my garden gnomes are now partially hidden by them.

I inhale. It smells like only fall can, that earthy scent no autumn-scented candle can equate.

I pick up a perfect maple leaf, just like I used to do as a girl, when I would press them in a book, or take them to school as part of a science project. The leaf is as red as a fire ember, its golden skeleton outlined in the sunlight.

I admire its glory. "Thank you for your life," I say.

When leaves fall, they die, literally take their final breaths and exhale gases through stomata. Among those released is one that smells like pine, a main scent of fall. I inhale the leaf and then tuck it into my pocket.

"You'll make a lovely bookmark," I say.

This is the in-between time: just between fall and winter, just between Halloween and hibernation.

I walk around to my front yard and hear a world filled with life. Kids are bustling to school, moms and dads headed to work, everyone back in their routine. I put my face against the fence and line my eye up between the slats. Neighbors' yards are decked out for Halloween: hay bales stacked in the yard, pots of pretty mums, scary witches and goblins dangling from tree branches, carved pumpkins on porches.

No one can see my yard. No one—save Abby, Lily and Cory—has seen it for decades. I turn. My fall decor is the simple majesty of my dying garden: I love the silhouettes of the seed heads and stems, beautiful browns, deeply textured, and the autumnal glory of a hydrangea bloom—no longer colorful—but gorgeous still, dried and frozen in time.

The leaves on my Norway maple, which I planted a lifetime ago, are the exact color of the sun today, and I know that they will be forever, long after I am gone.

I watch a golden leaf leap from the tree—its last journey on earth—and despite that knowledge, it twists and tumbles as gleefully as a child on a slide before landing on my shoulder. I can hear it exhale. "It's time, Iris."

Is it? I ask.

The leaf does not respond. Instead, the wind catches it, sending it along for another happy ride.

That's how we all should go out, I reflect. *On a happy ride.*

I watch the leaf run in the wind. Suddenly, it stops, trapped by the fence.

I turn away.

The past few autumns, whenever I begin my annual fall cleanup, that question rings in my head. *Will this be it?*

I am not in bad health, but the truth is I am a fading garden, too. I am an old woman. I have survived many seasons, like my garden.

I bloom, I wither, I hibernate, I hope.

But hibernation is the longest season in Michigan, and it has been mine, as well.

I shake my head.

The cold stings my fingers but the sun warms my face. I love that juxtaposition in fall.

I head around back, grab a bucket, some tarps, my wheelbarrow and my pruners and set to work.

My fall cleanup is long and exhausting. It takes me at least two weeks on my own, if the weather cooperates. But it also gives me great pleasure. I am preparing it with as much love and care as possible for a long rest, which will make it thrive even more in the spring.

As I cut my phlox down to the ground, I place my hand on the cold earth. One of the most difficult duties on this earth has been losing my husband and watching my daughter and my parents die. And yet, one of the most humbling and life-affirming moments has been to be there to hold their hands as they pass, a goodbye I did not get with Jonathan.

"It's a great gift," my grandma once told me. "It's beautiful to be there when a baby is born, but it's just as important to be there when a soul passes."

Will anyone be there with me?

I pray that I will just go, right here, in my garden, and someone will find me tucked amongst my flowers. It only makes sense that my flowers be my witnesses as I journey from this earth.

"But can you hold my hand?" I ask my phlox.

I continue pruning and shed my jacket as the sun continues to warm the lakeshore. What is warm to a Michigander, I know, is cold to many Southern folk, a crisp day like this in the fifties. But we Michigan folk know that days like these are numbered, that soon after the first frost comes the first snow, usually around Halloween.

Warm, I've learned, is just a state of mind, like age.

I smile when I come to my dahlias, some still holding on for dear life, but the hard frost has turned their stalks black.

"It's time," I tell them in my sweetest voice.

My grandma called dahlias "the Queen of the Autumn Garden," and I wholeheartedly agree, feeling a kindred spirit with their moniker. She used to believe that dahlias—the national flower of Mexico—symbolized inner strength, creativity and dignity.

"They represent those who stand strong in their values," she said.

My dazzling dahlias embody that spirit: they stand strong even as the rest of the garden fades into oblivion. My dahlias are as diverse as our world: I have orange, red, maroon, yellow and pink, but the varieties of dahlias are what make them unique. I have dahlias whose tightly clustered lemon yellow petals make them resemble pom-poms. I have dahlias whose blooms resemble cactus, their spiky yellow petals tinged in flame red. I have stargazer dahlias with sensual, curving petals. Some dahlias look like small peonies, while others resemble water lilies.

I finish cutting back my dahlias and then take a seat on the ground. Only the tips of cut stalks remain. In two weeks I will return to this spot and prepare them for their winter burial.

I will dig up my dahlias with a garden fork and take them inside where I will lay them out to dry, dirt and mud intact, so a protective skin forms on the outer layers of the tubers. I will trim the roots, wrap them in newspaper, top side down, and put them in plastic grocery bags, which I will label—*very important at my age!*—so I know what variety is enclosed come spring. I will haul the bags to my basement and place them in a cardboard box, checking on them every month or so to remove any rot. In April I will move them to a warmer area to come back to life, and bring their eyes to the surface.

I look at the bodies of my dahlias scattered around me.

How long can I continue to bury myself, dig myself up and bloom again?

Each spring I am always surprised to find that I have more tubers than I need, since one tuber alone produces an entire bush of flowers.

And suddenly I smile, knowing that Cory will be happy to receive such a spring surprise.

There will be a dahlia blooming one day, many years from now after I am gone, that will be the Queen of the Autumn Garden.

Just like me.

ABBY

OCTOBER 2003

"Do you want to go as a character from *Finding Nemo*?"

"No."

"Do you want to go as a pirate, like Jack Sparrow?"

"No."

"Do you want to go as something scary, like a witch or a vampire?"

"No."

I stop carving my pumpkin and look at Cory, exasperated. "Help me," I mouth, giving him the look that says, "I'm about to throw a pair of glasses on her, hand her a stick for a wand and call her Harry Potter."

"We only have a few days to figure it out," Cory says.

I look at him. "We," I mouth. He smiles.

Lily is hunched over a pumpkin, elbow-deep, scooping out its guts onto newspaper covering the dining room table. She flicks seeds off her fingers and looks at us. "I have to be something special."

"Of course," Cory says, and I give him another glare.

The first two months of my new engineering consulting business have been trying. In fact, my pitch meetings with potential clients have gone just about as well as the conversation we're having right now.

But then last week I received a call from a national competitor of Mr. Whitmore's, a family-owned business now headed by two of the founders' daughters. I flew to Florida to meet with them. They not only loved my paints but they also loved the *names* of my paints.

"We wouldn't change a thing," they said, before adding, "Stop doubting yourself."

I signed my first consulting contract a few days later.

Navigating this new life is a lot like carving this pumpkin, I think as my new knife slides in the wrong direction from the outline I've drawn, and I slice off one of my pumpkin's intended teeth: *a bit treacherous and no straight lines.*

I step back and study the pumpkin's new face.

And yet, it all is managing to work, no matter how many times I slip up. It's actually more exciting, I've learned, to draw outside the lines, to carve my own way, each and every day.

"What would be special?" I ask Lily.

She wipes her hands on a dish towel and sits back on the chair, legs tucked underneath her body. She scrunches her face and then leaps off the chair and scampers away, yelling, "I have an idea."

"I bet that idea involves hours of labor and hundreds of dollars," I whisper to Cory.

Lily races back in with something hidden behind her back.

She unveils it with a big "Ta-da!" and places a large piece of paper on the table.

"That's my garden sketch," Cory says. He looks at me, his face scrunched in the same way Lily's just was.

"We don't understand, sweetheart. Help us out a little," I say.

She points at the drawing. "See, you have a flower or plant for every season."

"So something will always be blooming, no matter the season," Cory says.

"Holly in winter, tulips in spring, peonies in summer, mums in fall," Lily says.

"Yes?" I ask, still not following.

"Duh, Mom," Lily says. "What if we went as the seasons?"

"I love that, Lily," I say. "What a great idea. You could be fall, and I could glue leaves all over you..."

"No," Lily says, hand in the air, stopping me. "I was thinking we'd go as a flower to represent the seasons, like Daddy's garden." She stops and twirls her hair, leaving pumpkin gunk on the ends. "Like Iris's garden."

"That still works," Cory says. "You could be a daffodil for spring, or something like that, right?"

"Yeah!" Lily yells.

"And Daddy and I could follow you around as a—what, Cory?—help me out."

"A rose for summer and a sunflower for fall."

"Yeah!" Lily yells again. Then her face falls like a soufflé. "But we're missing a season."

She looks at us, blinking her butterfly lashes, her bottom lip stuck out. "What about Iris?"

"Oh, honey," I say. "That's so sweet of you to want to include Iris, but she's not going to go out on Halloween. We've talked about this. She just likes to stay home, remember? Like that time we asked her to go to Pronto Pup. I'm so sorry."

"Can we ask?" Lily opens her big eyes even bigger. "Pleee-assse?"

I look at Cory. He shrugs. "Sure," I say.

"And let's bring her a pumpkin," Lily says. "I think she'd like that."

"Good idea," I say. "You draw a face on yours now, and I'll—no, Daddy—will carve it, how's that sound?"

Cory laughs. "Not sure of your skills?" he asks.

I hold up my severed tooth and stick it in my upper lip. "No," I say.

The next day after school I accompany Lily to see Iris. I am carrying the pumpkin, and Lily is carrying way too much childlike hope.

"What a surprise!" Iris says when she sees us.

She opens the back gate just as we are about to knock. Iris is pulling a giant tarp filled with leaves.

"Don't tell a soul I dump my leaves back here," she says.

"We won't," Lily says. "We brought you a gift."

I hold out the pumpkin, and Iris's eyes bug, just like a kid who receives an extra-big scoop of ice cream and surprise sprinkles.

"I haven't had a carved pumpkin since…" She stops and drops the tarp.

"I'm sorry, Iris," I say.

"No, no, don't be," she says, grabbing the pumpkin and turning it so she can study its face. "Oh, this is just spectacular. I like a happy jack-o'-lantern. Perfect candy corn eyes. Goofy smile. One tooth on top and two on the bottom. Did you do this, Lily?"

Lily nods. "But Daddy carved it, and Mommy helped."

"Team effort." Iris nods. "Best pumpkins always are. Now, let's find a perfect home for it."

"I know, I know," Lily says. "Follow me."

She races into the front yard and by the time Iris and I arrive, Lily is sitting on the front steps. "Right here!"

Iris carries the pumpkin over to Lily, who moves at the last minute and helps Iris place it just so.

"All we need is a candle now," Iris says.

"Already have one in there for you," I say. "It's the kind you just have to turn on at night."

"Thank you, Abby. That's so sweet." She looks at Lily. "How's school going?"

"Exciting," Lily says with a giggle and a wink. "We had a pop quiz in math today. I got an A."

"Smart cookie," Iris says. "Just like your mom. And how's your business going?"

"Exciting," I say, which prompts a laugh from Iris.

"I bet," she says. "I'm very proud of you. It's not easy to change your life and do something you never expected you could do. It's—" Iris stops "—exciting, but I know it's scary, too. But your life will never be the same now. You were courageous enough to take that first step, and there's no looking back now."

I nod.

Lily is squirming on the steps, twisting and turning, her sneakers squeaking.

"Do you need to use the bathroom?" Iris asks.

"No," I say, "but she does have a question she wants to ask you."

"Ask away, my dear," Iris says.

"Would you be a part of my Halloween costume?" Lily blurts, the excitement too much to take any longer.

Iris cocks her head. "What do you mean, Lily?"

Without taking a breath, Lily outlines her plans about the costumes. When she is finished, Iris sits on the front steps next to the pumpkin and pats the wood. Lily scoots next to her.

"Do you know what a sweet girl you are?" Iris asks, putting her arm around Lily and drawing her close. "Such a special soul." Iris looks at me. "Have you started making the costumes?"

"No," I say, my face blushing.

"You're so busy, Abby, between your new business and your family." Iris slaps her hands together. "Why don't I do this? I'll make the costumes..."

"No." I hold my hand up to stop her. "No way. I could never ask you to do such a thing."

"You didn't ask. I offered." Iris raises an eyebrow. "I used to make all of Mary's costumes. I learned how to sew from my mom and grandma when they made my clothes from those flour sacks I told you about. And I know all about flowers." She looks at Lily. "That way I will not only be part of your Halloween costume, I'll be making them."

Lily smiles halfheartedly and then ducks her head. "But you didn't say you'd dress up and go with us."

"Let me finish my raking and then I'll get started," Iris says, her voice rising. "I already have an idea for your costume. Just send me all your measurements." She tweaks Lily's nose and then looks up at me.

"Sounds good," I say, my voice flat at Iris's nonanswer.

A few days later Lily comes racing in after school. "There's boxes on our front porch!"

I race outside, and Cory follows with a pair of scissors. He slices open the tape on the top of the box. He pulls something out of the box and when he turns, Lily shrieks, loudly enough to cause a group of squirrels collecting acorns in our front yard to scamper up a tree.

"A daffodil!" Lily screams. "For me!"

Cory holds it up in front of her, and a giant smile engulfs my face. Green tights—emblazoned with sequins—lead to a row of giant yellow petals that drape around the neck.

"There's more," I say, leaning into the box. I hold up a golden cap that looks exactly like the daffodil's trumpet-shaped center. I also pull out a bag to collect candy that is covered with spring flowers: tulips and pansies.

"What's this?" Cory asks. A note is pinned to the costume. "For Lily," he reads. "You are a spring daffodil! Remember to paint your face yellow!"

"And we have more boxes," I say.

We open them and pull out two more costumes: a poinsettia costume for me—complete with red-and-white-striped leggings, a skirt of red poinsettia flowers and green leaves, and green bodice with poinsettia wings—and a giant sunflower for Cory, complete with a black bodysuit and a hood absolutely covered with summer sunflowers.

"We have to try them on," Lily says. "Help me!"

We haul everything inside and try on our costumes.

Cory looks in the mirror. "She's amazing," he says. "Although I look absolutely ridiculous."

I bend over, laughing. "You do," I say. "Adorably ridiculous." I turn and look at myself in the mirror. "I, on the other hand, look like a crazed elf who escaped Santa's workshop."

"Winter's always been hard on you," Cory says, before bursting into laughter. He grabs the camera and begins snapping photos of me.

Lily rushes in, looking completely adorable as a daffodil. We take a family photo, but when Cory shows it to Lily, she says, "We're still missing a season. Summer."

I look at Cory. I hold my arms out and Lily comes in for

a hug. "I know, sweetheart. But look at all that Iris did for us, right?"

Lily shakes her head. "Can we go show her?"

"Let's surprise her on Halloween," Cory says. "She'll be our first stop."

Halloween night is damp and chilly but, thankfully, not raining or snowing, a definite treat for trick-or-treaters.

"Is this daffodil ready to get some serious candy?" Cory asks Lily.

Lily nods her head, her petals billowing around her.

"Is the insane poinsettia ready to scare children?" Cory asks me.

I nod my head, my red wings fluttering.

"Let's hit it, then," Cory says.

We troop out the back and over to Iris's. The back gate is open. We head to the front yard, and my heart drops. You can hear kids laughing and dashing up and down the street, yelling, "Trick or treat!" Neighbors are having parties. Everyone is connected and yet Iris is here, alone and isolated.

Lily races up the front steps and rings the doorbell. She drops her basket when Iris answers the door.

She is dressed, head to toe, in purple, just like an iris: purple rain boots, purple tights and a skirt of pretty purple petals. But the pièces de résistance are a headdress that looks just like an iris in full bloom and an iris wand, complete with a long green stalk.

"You didn't think I'd let you miss a season, did you?" Iris asks. "And I just had to go as my namesake for summer!" She taps Lily on the head with her wand and says, "Happy Halloween!" She reaches inside the door and returns with a full-size candy bar. Lily picks up her basket, and Iris drops the candy inside.

"I don't get many trick-or-treaters," Iris says in a deadpan. "I thought one candy bar would get me through the night."

I smile, and Cory laughs and then takes a photo of "his three girls."

"I can't thank you enough for making these," Cory says. "You are—" he stops, and his voice is suddenly quivery "—family."

"Thank you," she says, her voice quiet.

"Well, we best get on our way," Cory says, "before all the good candy is gone." He looks at Lily. "You don't want an apple tonight, do you? Or a penny?"

Lily shakes her head and then looks at Iris. "But you have to come with us," she begs. "You complete us. We can't go without all the seasons."

"Lily, we talked about this," I say. I look at Iris. "I'm sorry."

"You go have fun," Iris says. "And tell me all about it tomorrow." Iris takes a step inside and begins to shut the door. "Have fun!"

"No!" Lily puts her hand out and stops the door from closing.

"Lily!" Cory says. "That's not nice."

"But no one will know who you are," Lily insists. "You'll be safe. I promise! Halloween is like a game. You can do it. Please."

"I can't," Iris says, her face etched in pain.

"You can if you want," Lily says. "Pleeeassseee."

The wand is shaking in Iris's hand.

"I'm so sorry," I say. "We'll tell you all about it tomorrow. Say good-night to Iris, Lily."

"Good night," Lily says, her voice low and sad.

The door shuts. For a moment none of us moves. For some reason I sneak to her window and watch Iris, worried about her reaction to all of this. She walks through the dining room and into her kitchen. I see her pick up a bottle of pills and then put them back down. Iris walks back into the dining room and stands, a flower frozen.

"Let's go," I say.

We head down the sidewalk and begin to open the front gate.

"You two go ahead," Cory says. "I'll lock it behind you, go around back and meet you next door, okay?"

Without warning, the front door opens, and Iris appears.

"Will you hold my hand?" Iris calls to Lily.

I look at Cory, mouth wide. He looks at me. Without warning, a tear falls from his eye.

Lily races back to her.

"Of course!" she says. "The whole time!"

"I'm excited," Iris says. "*Very* excited."

"I know," Lily says.

She grabs Lily's hand, and the two of them walk toward the gate. Iris stops. Lily opens the gate. Iris takes a tentative step and then another and another until she is on the sidewalk outside her fence.

I grab Iris's other hand and squeeze it tightly. We take another step and another. I can feel Iris's pulse race in her hand.

"I'm so proud of you," I say. "Remember what you just told me?"

Iris stops and looks at me, her face filled with panic. She shakes her head.

"You told me it's not easy to change your life and do something you never expected you could do. It's—" I stop "—exciting, but I know it's scary, too. But your life will never be the same now. You were courageous enough to take that first step, and there's no looking back now."

"Thank you," Iris says.

When we reach the first house, we stop. "Go on," Cory tells Lily.

"Not without Iris," she says.

Lily continues to hold Iris's hand and leads her up to the front door. Lily knocks. "Trick or treat!" she yells when a husband and wife open the door.

"A daffodil!" the woman says. "How cute. And who's this flower with you?"

"It's a secret," Lily says, "but you might want to give me a little extra candy in my basket to share with her later. She forgot hers."

"Oh, I see," the woman says with a big laugh before dropping a handful of candy into Lily's basket. "Happy Halloween!"

I watch the daffodil and the iris walk the neighborhood, each resplendent in yellow and purple, each seeming to bloom right in front of my eyes, a child teaching an old woman how to be strong again and an old woman demonstrating unconditional love to a child.

As I watch them scale the steps to another home, Iris shouting, "Happy Halloween!" with even more glee than Lily, I have to stop and duck behind a tree so no one will see me weep.

PART FOURTEEN

CHRISTMAS CACTUS

"Every gardener knows that under the cloak of winter lies a miracle."

—Barbara Winkler

IRIS

DECEMBER 2003

The entire world is wearing a soft coat of white. I look out the door onto the screened porch, and the endless white nearly blinds me. Lake-effect snow showers move in bands across the lake, dumping snow upon the lakeshore. I squint, but there is little contrast between the world in front of me and the world in the distance.

When the temperatures fall and the lake has yet to freeze, the skies dump snow upon the coast of Michigan, squalls descending from out of nowhere to pummel us. As a child I loved the snow. It provided endless games: snowmen and snow angels, snow forts and snowball fights, snow ice cream and snowshoeing.

It rarely, however, resulted in a snow day, I think, *no matter how much snow we received or how much a child prayed.*

There's an old joke in these parts that school isn't canceled until the top of the stop signs are covered with snow.

As an adult I lamented the snow. It caused a disruption in life's routine.

The last thing I need is a disruption in my schedule, I once told Mary during a particularly bad storm.

Why? she asked. *That's just what adults need most.*

She was right. We do.

I stare into the snow.

Even my gardens need it.

They are now buried under a foot of snow. My flowers are asleep, tucked away for the winter, dreaming of the day they once again get to wake up, stretch and return to life.

Like I've done.

In my advanced years I've learned to love the snow again, to see it as a necessary interruption, a way to force me to slow down for a day.

Winter in Michigan is a long season, the longest actually. Spring may officially begin on March 20, but that's just a punch line in the Mitten State. The first day I'm comfortable that the frost is over and I can return to my garden is Mother's Day, a good six weeks after spring has sprung.

You learn to be patient in Michigan. And I am the most patient of all.

How many years did I not walk my neighborhood? I think. *Miss Halloween? Miss connecting? Miss people?*

I shut my eyes and think of the past few weeks. I am like Rip van Winkle being taught about the world again. Each day is new. I have gone to the grocery store with Abby. I have gone to a movie with Cory and Lily. I even got a chance to eat at Pronto Pup before it closed.

I look over toward Abby and Cory's. The lights are on upstairs, and smoke chugs out of the chimney.

We are to go sledding later if the weather's not too bad.

Me! Sledding! With a family!

The wind kicks up and snow forms into tiny tornadoes that scoot across the yard before crashing into the fence.

And yet I still feel… I stop myself and ask a question: *Protected or isolated? Which is it, Iris?*

The skies darken even more, and I hear thunder clap. Snow falls from the sky as if God has opened the back of a dump truck.

Thunder snow! I think. *What a rare occasion!*

I suddenly think of my mother, who believed that thunder snow was a great mystery and portended that something mythical was about to happen.

Boom!

My heart jumps, and I watch the snow pile up.

I am living in a black-and-white world now, I think.

I put my arms around my body and head into the kitchen to make some soup. When I round the corner, I smile when I see my Christmas cactus.

"Hello, Pretty Boy, hello," I coo. "Who's a pretty boy? How beautiful are you today?"

My Christmas cactus is fifty-five years old. I know, I know. Gardeners would howl and roll their eyes if I said that to them. The *Farmer's Almanac* says thirty years is the oldest most survive.

No one believes me, of course, and I understand why they think I might be mistaken, or lying, or simply an old woman who has grown forgetful. But I am not. I know the exact day and year I got Pretty Boy.

Shirley got me this cactus the first Christmas after Mary died, when I refused to leave the house.

"You need something to care for," Shirley bluntly told me. "You need something to brighten your winter days."

She had received the cactus as a white elephant work gift, but she hadn't known what to do with it.

"This is a regift," I told her. "You didn't even get it for me."

"Look at it," Shirley said. "It already looks bad." She knew just what to say to get me. Tell me a plant needed help, and I'd take it every time and nurse it back to life.

"You may have a knack for off-color jokes, but you never had much of a green thumb," I told Shirley.

"Name it," she told me. "Think of it as a dog or cat."

"Get out," I told her.

My mom and grandma had both had Christmas cacti, which had seemed to live forever, as well. Every Christmas they would bloom and brighten the house with color, just like the lights and ornaments on our Christmas tree.

I look at Pretty Boy and then out my kitchen window. I can still see my grampa trudging through the snow. My grampa was a black-and-white man. He never wore much color, save for Christmas Day when he would appear in a sweater as red as Santa's hat. My grandma loved it when he dressed up that one day a year.

"Who's a pretty boy?" she would tease him, patting his belly, pinching his cheek and planting a big smooch on his cheek. "You are!"

My grampa's face would always turn as crimson as his sweater.

"Time to hand out the gifts!" he'd call.

I named my cactus after my grampa because—at the very least—I would still have family surrounding me, even if just in memory. I would have something to decorate my house at the holidays, too, because retrieving the ornaments was just too painful.

"Happy birthday, Pretty Boy," I say. "You're old, just like

me now. We've come a long way. Both survivors. And you're going to bloom again for Christmas, aren't you, Pretty Boy?"

He has yet to bloom, which has me worried, but I believe in my soul that he will.

"You rest up, hear me? Get ready to bloom again, okay?"

I talk to my cacti, as I do all my flowers. Like people, they bloom when shown love and kindness.

For as long as I can remember, my routine with my Christmas cactus has never changed. I begin to cut back on its water in late October, allowing it just enough for its topsoil to remain moist. This forces it to go dormant, which is critical for it to bloom. I move the cactus to my hallway, where it receives some indirect light but fourteen hours or so of darkness every day, which is not difficult to achieve in winter in Michigan.

Once its buds are set, I move Pretty Boy to my kitchen counter where it receives bright, indirect sunlight and is out of any draft.

My grandma used to believe that Christmas cactus were miracles, a sign that God was present everywhere and could appear even in the most unlikely of places. Every year her cactus bloomed, my grandma would tell me, "I told you! I told you!"

Miracles were something with which I was not familiar, a fantasy my life had never been afforded, but with each passing year my cactus lives—and blooms—I become more convinced of my grandma's story.

I begin to make soup, homemade chicken noodle, which I made for Mary on days like this. I pull a chicken from my refrigerator and begin to boil it on the stove. I grab some carrots and start to chop them into chunks.

Everything has been delivered to me for years, on my rules, on my order, to my front gate: from groceries to gardening soil. It was a joy to go out and walk through a store, touching the carrots, picking a chicken that looked just right, experiencing the bustle and joy of people at Christmas.

I turn down the stove and my cottage shudders. The doors in my house rattle. I peer outside, and the wind is shaking the entire world. I set down my knife and head to the screened porch. I wrap my arms around myself and walk onto it. Snow is thick on the screens, which are undulating. Tree branches are swaying, the snow falling from them in thick chunks. Snow drifts against my fence, which bows in the wind. I can hear the earth harden its stance against the wind. Trees groan and ache and crack.

I am just about to turn and head back to the kitchen when I hear a loud snap. A branch of one of the pines outside my fence atop the dunes snaps and falls into my yard with a resounding thud. The phone in my pocket immediately vibrates. It's a text from Abby.

Are you OK?

Yes, I type. Fine. Just a pine branch.

I turn to head inside when I hear another crack, this one so loud I think the world has simply frozen and split in two.

I look, and the towering pine that had lost its branch just moments before is falling, seemingly in slow motion. The tree lands against a section of my fence, bounces and then hits it again. Both the fence and the tree fall, one right after the other. They hit the ground in an explosion of snow. For a moment I see only a cloud of white. When the snow clears, the pine and a massive chunk of the fence are on the ground.

I grab a coat, gloves and scarf, and slip on my winter boots. I trudge outside and survey the damage. The beautiful pine has cracked and split about halfway up.

The pine that held my wild turkeys and swayed in the summer breeze.

My fence, now in pieces on the ground, is bigger than I ever imagined. Actually seeing it in perspective, lying across my garden and extending well into my yard stuns me. I step over the broken branches and onto the fence. Finally, I look up.

There is now an unobstructed view to the lake from my backyard. Kids are sledding down the dune. The lake is gray and churning, playing in the snow just like the kids.

I can feel a tear trickle down my face.

A chunk of my history has fallen, and yet…and yet, I can actually see my future.

I walk over to another section of fence, the neighbor to the one that has just fallen. It is bowed, arcing at a thirty-degree angle, making an agonizing groan in the wind. I walk out the opening in my fence, stand behind the section and push with all my might. It falls with a mighty crash.

"Are you okay?"

I look up, and Abby, Cory and Lily are rushing toward me.

"What's going on?"

"Home renovation," I say, my words coming out in jagged breaths.

"We can get someone out here once the storm clears to clean this up and get the fence back together," Cory says. "You need to get back inside. It's dangerous."

"No," I say. "It's a Christmas miracle."

"What?" Abby asks.

I walk to another section of the fence, which is damaged and shaking in the wind. "Help me," I say.

I get behind the section and put my hands on it, leveraging my body against it.

Cory and Abby stare at me. Only Lily runs to help. She is wearing a sock monkey stocking cap that makes her look as if she has two faces. "Thank you," I say, before looking at Cory and Abby. "Well? Help me."

The four of us line up, grunt with all our might and—*Wham!*—another section of the fence goes down, the snow billowing as if there's been an avalanche. I stand, hands on hips, out of breath, and begin laughing like a crazy person, while Cory and Abby simply stare, their eyes wide and faces red.

"What's going on?"

I turn, and the kids who I saw sledding are standing at the top of the dune, watching us. Snow is swirling around their ruddy cheeks, and I feel as if I am in the midst of the Charlie Brown Christmas special, all of the Peanuts kids gathered around me.

"Push," I say, nodding at another section of fence.

They shout in glee, their voices echoing in the cold, and we all push another section to the ground. I am out of breath, literally seeing stars, and I stoop again to catch my breath. I hear another crash, and I jerk upright. A crowd of maybe twenty people has now gathered at the back of my yard and is toppling another section.

"Iris? I'm Barb, and this is my husband, Kirk, and our two kids, Kate and Connor. We've lived catty-corner across the street from you for over a decade." The woman extends her hand. "It's nice to finally meet you."

My eyes are watering, and I can't tell if it's the cold or my emotions until another neighbor and then another introduces themselves, and I am sobbing.

How long has it been since this many people have surrounded me? How long has it been since this many people have been in my yard? Seen my house? Seen me?

"Okay, okay," Cory says. "I think that's enough in this weather. Let's stack these sections of fence over here and start cleaning up the brush."

I look around at everyone working, strangers handing out hot chocolate, neighbors helping neighbors. A chain saw powers up, filling the air with smoke and gas, and an older man starts to cut up the large tree branches scattered around my yard. When he begins to cut up the fallen pine tree, I yell, "Stop!"

He turns off the chain saw and looks at me. "You want me to leave it like this?"

"No," I say. "I want you to help me make a Christmas tree out of it."

"It's awfully big," he says doubtfully.

Cory comes over and studies the fallen pine. "What if we just topped it?"

The crowd gathers and nods. "Yeah! It could be perfect."

A few hours later my fallen fence is stacked, the branches cleared and the tip-top of the errant pine is in a stand, my grandma's special tree skirt tucked around it. Cory, Abby and Lily are polishing off a pizza they ordered. I will finish my soup tomorrow.

I yawn.

"You must be exhausted," Abby says.

"I am bushed," I say.

"We better let you get some rest," Cory says. "What a day, huh?"

"What a day," I repeat.

"When is the rest of the fence coming down?" Lily asks. "That was fun."

"Soon," I say. "Soon."

"You're still coming over for Christmas, right?" Abby asks. "I'm roasting a turkey with all the fixings, and we're going to bake cookies."

"You're decorating," Lily says, pointing at me, "and I'm eating."

I laugh. "That's a good plan."

Everyone leaves with a big hug, and I shut the door.

As soon as they are out the front gate, I return to life. I check my watch and then rush up the stairs and head to the attic, pulling out boxes of heirloom ornaments. I blow dust off the tops of the boxes.

Handle with Care! is written in my mom's handwriting.

"You haven't seen the light of day for years," I say. "It's time."

I take box after box down to the tree, make some tea and turn on the TV just as the Charlie Brown Christmas special begins. It is the show I've watched for decades, the only thing that made me feel like I had a family again.

Until this year.

I pull out my grandma's and mom's vintage glass ornaments in bright colors and begin to hang them from the branches, watching Charlie Brown as I go.

"I never thought it was such a bad little tree," Linus is saying. "It's not so bad at all, really. Maybe it just needs a little love."

I stop and look at my tree, and my heart fills with joy. I sit on my couch, sip my tea and stare at my tree, remembering Christmases past. I think of spending Christmas Day with Abby and her family.

"It's not what's under the Christmas tree that matters, but who's around it."

"You're right, Charlie Brown," I say, staring at the TV.

I head to the kitchen and set my cup in the sink. The sky has cleared, the wind calmed and the stars are bright. I can see the moon shimmer off the lake.

I have the best water view in Michigan now, I think.

Moonlight illuminates my Christmas cactus, and I smile.

"You will finally have some company, Pretty Boy," I say.

I move the cactus underneath the tree, lie down on the couch and pull a blanket over my aching body.

I fall asleep on the couch in front of the tree, just like I did as a girl.

When I wake, hours later, I cannot believe my eyes. In fact, I blink—once, twice—rub my eyes with my fingers and then reach for my glasses.

My Christmas cactus is in full bloom, its prickly green arms weighted down with beautiful red blooms.

I jump up and do a little jig around the tree.

"You were right, Grandma! You were right!"

I lean down and touch a bloom on the cactus. "I told you!" I can hear it say in my grandma's voice. "I told you!"

ABBY

DECEMBER 2003

I haven't seen Cory this excited for Christmas, *ever.*

There is a photo his mom has of him as a little boy in her scrapbook during a famed Christmas blizzard. Cory is probably seven—around Lily's age—and is standing outside in a snowsuit, white up to his chest. It appears as if he was set down in quicksand and is disappearing. A brand-new sled he got for Christmas sits beside him, actually above him, right around his shoulders. But the most incredible element of the photo is the smile on his face, that smile only a child can have when it's a white Christmas and you just received the toy you wanted more than anything in the world.

Cory is wearing that exact same expression right now.

"You look just like Ralphie from *A Christmas Story*," I say, "and you just got your Red Ryder BB gun."

"I can't believe it," he says. "It's a miracle."

He is staring at a letter in his hands, which arrived late last night, just after he received a call from his friend at the Defense Department. His hands are shaking, and his smile morphs into a pained expression. Suddenly, my big rock of a husband dissolves into tears, shaking so hard I have to walk over and hold him.

"There, there," I whisper. "Don't cry. This *is* a miracle. You did it. You did it."

We found out only yesterday that the remains of First Lieutenant Jonathan Maynard—Iris's husband—had been positively identified.

"I'm so nervous," he says, pulling back to look at me. I run my fingers under his eyes to dry his tears. "What if she's angry I got involved? What if it's too much of a shock for her? She's come so far. What if this causes her to retreat again?"

"You found her husband," I say. I give his shoulders a shake. *"You."*

Cory begins to cry again. "I had to bring him home," he says. "I had to give Iris closure." He stops and pulls me into his arms. "I had to try and give myself closure."

I hold my husband until his crying subsides. I shut my eyes and rock him. In my head I see the picture of him in the snow. When I open my eyes, a blanket of snow covers the land. I think of Iris. I think of Jonathan. I think of me.

We all grow up, many of us much too quickly. Some of us wall ourselves off from our memories because the pain is too much. Some of us refuse to take on responsibility; some take on too much. Some of us become who we think we're supposed to be rather than who we dreamed of being as a child.

But all of us remain—somewhere inside—kids at heart:

vulnerable, joyous, scared yet unscarred by life. It's just that we keep that child hidden and protected, because we must.

Lily comes rushing into the kitchen. "Time to make cookies?" she asks.

I smile, and Cory laughs. He wipes his face, and I kiss him on the cheek.

"Yes," I say. "But we have to wait for Iris to help us decorate."

"Okay," Lily says. "But I get to lick the beaters first."

"We each get a beater," Cory says. "Deal?"

Lily hesitates. She is wearing a new red velvet dress with a matching bow in her hair that she got for Christmas. "Okay," she says with a sigh.

"Let's start grabbing ingredients," I say.

We begin making the dough when Iris knocks. "Come in!" I call. "Merry Christmas!"

"Merry Christmas," she says. "I'll tell you what, it sure smells good in here."

Cory shoots me a look. I can see actual panic registered on his face.

"We're just about to start cutting out the cookies," I say.

"It is perfect timing! Thought you might need these," Iris says.

I turn, and she is taking the lid off a Tupperware bowl filled with vintage cookie cutters.

"These were my grandma's," she says. "Older than the hills, but still work like magic. Aren't they adorable?"

"Wow!" Lily says, pulling out cutters in the shapes of Christmas trees, wreaths, bells and reindeer. "This is my favorite!" She holds up a cutout of Santa's face, hat and all.

"Mine, too," Iris says. "You can really load those up with icing."

Lily's eyes grow large.

"Cory, would you mind helping me carry a few gifts over?" Iris asks. "It's a haul in this snow. Though I don't have to worry about opening a gate any longer." She laughs.

"You didn't have to do that, Iris," Cory says.

"Yes," she says. "I did."

"I'll miss you," Cory says to the cookie dough. "Let me grab a coat."

They exit and return a few minutes later, their arms filled with boxes and bags.

"Iris!" I say. "What in the world?"

I follow them to the tree we have on the porch. Cory has a fire going, and the lake sparkles beyond. It is magical.

"Small things," she says, setting gifts beneath the tree. "With big meaning."

I nod and look at Cory.

"Same here," he says, his voice wavering a bit. He points at an envelope tucked in the branches of the tree, lights flickering upon it.

"You didn't have to," Iris says.

"We did," Cory says.

"Okay," I say. "Who's ready to cut cookies and decorate?"

"Me!" Iris and Lily say in unison.

We cut cookies, place them on a cookie sheet and set them in the oven. As they bake, Iris asks, "Where's your family?"

I look at Cory. I think of my mom, bleaching her sink and counters over and over because a raw turkey had touched it. I think of her roasting it for hours, just to be sure it's fully cooked, until it comes out so dry it's like eating sawdust. I think of my mom unable to ask questions about my new life, Lily's school, Iris, anything of importance.

"We couldn't make it back this year," Cory finally says for me.

"My family is right here," I blurt.

Iris raises her head and looks at me for the longest time, her eyes seeming to search my soul. "That means the world," she says.

I nod, my face blushing with emotion, and begin to make cream cheese frosting. I split it into thirds, adding some red food coloring to some and green to another. I spoon it into bags and cut a tip off the end. I retrieve a world of sprinkles from my cabinets, along with coconut, chocolate chips, white chocolate chips and nonpareils for decorating.

"You do it up right," Iris says.

The timer beeps, and I pull the first batch of cookies from the oven.

"Want to start with Santa?" Iris asks Lily after the cookies cool.

"Yeah!"

As they start, I put another batch in the oven.

"I like to fill Santa's hat with red icing and then use white to outline it," Iris says, showing Lily how to pipe icing along the edges of the cookie. "And wait until you see how much the coconut looks like his real beard!"

I stand back and watch Lily and Iris decorate. The two are deeply rooted—flowers of different names and histories that have grown together. Iris started as a stranger, a nemesis, a landlord but now she is…

Lily's grandmother, I think. *Lily's friend.*

Iris holds up her finished cookie.

"It looks just like Santa," Lily says.

"Now you know what we have to do, right?"

Lily shakes her head.

"Eat him!" Iris bites off Santa's head, and Lily squeals. "You get his beard!"

"Sorry, Santa," Lily says with a giggle.

I pull the next batch of cookies from the oven, then prep

the turkey and put it in the oven while the girls finish decorating. Cory and I work together to prep the sweet potatoes and stuffing. As everything bakes, we retreat to the porch.

"Time for presents?" Iris asks.

"Second Christmas!" Lily yells.

"Start with this one first," Iris says, handing Lily a large box.

Lily rips into it, wrapping paper flying left and right. She pulls out a frame and hugs it to her body.

"What is it, sweetheart?"

"It's a picture of us," Lily says.

"Can we see?"

Lily hands us the photo. It is one I'd taken of Iris and Lily on Halloween, two flowers holding hands and walking down the sidewalk of the neighborhood. Their faces are turned toward each other, petals from their costumes floating in the wind, mouths open. They were singing "Monster Mash," best friends out for a night of trick-or-treating.

It's such a simple photo that belies the magnitude of the event, I think. *An image that will stay with me forever.*

"What do you say, Lily?" Cory asks.

"Thank you," Lily says, standing up to hug Iris.

"No, thank you," Iris whispers into her ear.

She reaches over and grabs two more gifts and hands them to me and Cory.

"Iris," I start, sounding like a mom.

"Abby," she mimics. "Open, open!"

Cory and I unwrap our gifts with nearly as much enthusiasm as Lily.

"I love it," Cory says. He holds up an old, old book entitled, *A Gardener's Guide to Michigan Flowers*.

"I have a copy myself," Iris says. "There's no better guide. I thought it might come in handy this spring when you create that new garden of yours."

"We," Cory says. "When we create that new garden."

Iris ducks her head, and I finally notice how much effort she's put into getting ready today: her hair is done, she is wearing makeup and lipstick, black slacks and a red turtleneck featuring the most beautiful vintage brooch of a reindeer.

"What'd you get, Mommy?" Lily asks.

"Oh, my gosh!" I say, ripping off the rest of the shiny paper. "Iris! This is beautiful."

I hold up a watercolor of Iris's garden in full bloom: hydrangeas, iris, daylilies, peonies.

"You are so talented," Cory says. He stands. "I know the perfect place to hang it, too." He walks over to the fireplace and points above the mantel. "We finally have the perfect piece."

"One more gift," Iris says. She stands and gingerly picks up the next box before handing it to Cory. "Be careful."

Cory pops off a tall lid on the box, and a bemused look fills his face.

"A cactus?"

"A Christmas cactus," Iris says.

Cory pulls a small pot from the box and sets it on the coffee table in front of us.

"This is a start from my Christmas cactus, which is fifty-five years old. Today!"

"No," Cory says. "That's not possible."

"I know," she says. "But it is."

"A cactus that blooms?" Lily asks, leaning over to look at it closely. "How?"

"All cacti are flowering plants," Iris says, "so every kind can bloom when it matures." Iris looks at Lily. "Some cacti don't start blooming until they are more than thirty years old."

"Why?" Lily asks.

Iris smiles. "They're really just like people. They bloom depending on the type of love and care they receive."

She looks at Cory and then me. "My hope is that this will continue to bloom for decades more, long after I'm gone, and that every Christmas it will remind you of me."

"I don't want you to leave." Lily's voice is high.

"I'm not going anywhere," Iris says with a wink. "Pretty Boy isn't going anywhere, either."

"Who?" Cory asks.

Iris laughs. "That's the name of my cactus. Pretty Boy. Long story. It's named after my grandfather. What are you going to name yours?"

The three of us look at each other, our heads angled.

"How about Pretty Girl?" Lily asks. "Named after you!"

"I love it," Cory says. "And it keeps the legacy going."

"And I've been known to be a tad prickly," Iris says with a wink. "You know my grandma used to believe that Christmas cactus were miracles, a sign that God was present everywhere and could appear even in the most unlikely of places." Iris stops. "And mine bloomed again this year. More beautifully than ever. I think all of you are responsible for bringing great joy into my life."

Cory looks at me, and I look at him. My heart is racing. I nod.

"Speaking of miracles," Cory starts awkwardly. He retrieves the letter from the tree and hands it to Iris. I can see his hand shaking.

Iris opens the envelope. "It's so pretty," she jokes, before pulling out the letter. "But I can't read it. Left both sets of glasses at home."

I laugh and hand Iris mine, which she slides on the end of her nose. "Thank you."

I have to squint now to see Iris. She begins to read in silence, her head cocked and eyebrows scrunched. She throws a hand over her mouth, tears fall onto the letter and she looks up at us.

"Is this real?"

"We found him," Cory says, his voice barely audible.

"This can't be, this can't be, this can't be." Iris begins to rock, and, out of the blue, she releases a howling cry that gives me goose bumps.

Lily runs to her and begins to rub her back. "It's okay," Lily says.

After a few moments Iris regains her composure. She reads the letter again, returns my glasses and asks, "How? Why? I don't understand."

Cory takes a seat on the rug beside Iris. "I have a friend with connections to the Defense Department," he starts. "This all started as sort of a secret mission." Cory stops. "Please just know I didn't mean to interfere. I had to do this. For you. For me. For our country."

Iris nods. "I wrote the army for years. I gave up eventually. I had to."

"I know," Cory says. "But there is new technology now. There are new methods. The Defense Department now has state-of-the-art computer data and mapping programs, and DNA comparisons. We sent that pin you gave Lily because it likely still had your husband's DNA on it. We located your and your husband's old dental records. I used every connection I had."

Cory takes the letter. "Jonathan was stationed along the Rhine River along with other soldiers, strung out in foxholes to keep an eye on Germans who were on the opposite bank. Jonathan was stationed alone not far from the riverbank. He had only a helmet and a Browning automatic rifle. In the middle of the night, the enemy crossed the river. There was gunfire, and when Jonathan's unit made their way to him, he was gone. Only his helmet, with a hole in it, remained."

Iris puts a quivering hand over her heart. I stand and go to her. I put my hands on her shoulders.

Cory continues: "It turns out all the soldiers were told to remove unit patches and any sign of identification in case they were captured. This is what caused so many issues in trying to find him. The army believed his body had been thrown in the Rhine, and that's when you were notified of his death. They told you they would follow up if any new information was uncovered."

"I kept writing," Iris says. "Until I couldn't..." Her voice trails off.

"The Germans buried Jonathan in an unmarked grave on the other side of the river. Years later a soldier scouting for the American Graves Registration Command actually located his grave and had it exhumed, but, by that time, there were only remnants of clothing remaining and no ID. His body was designated with a number and reburied with thousands of other US soldiers in what is now the Lorraine American Cemetery in Saint-Avold, France.

"It turns out that a friend of mine knew a government historian who was now working for the Defense Department, and our calls, letter and evidence prompted him to reinvestigate the case," Cory says. "He researched a database of sites where unidentified bodies of World War II servicemen had been recovered and compared that to a database of known locations GIs had disappeared. He then had to convince the army to exhume the body in France. Between what we sent and what he found, it's conclusive that it's Jonathan. We just found out."

Iris is silent for the longest time.

"Please," Cory says. "Don't be angry."

"Angry," Iris says, tears streaming. "I'm honored. Exhausted. Relieved." She stops. "I'm an old woman. The only thing I ever wanted was closure. I finally have it."

"So do I," Cory says. "This is for Jonathan. This is for all the men who lost their lives and didn't come home. For all the forgotten soldiers. For every man and woman who sacrificed their lives for this country." Cory stops. "The historian says that there are still over 70,000 Americans unaccounted for from World War II. If I could, I would not stop until I brought every one home." Cory looks at Iris. "I returned home a shell of a man, husband and father." He grabs Iris's hand. "You've helped bring me back to life."

"You did the same for me," Iris says. "Now what?"

"Your husband comes home to you," Cory says.

"When?" Iris asks.

The timer in the kitchen chirps, breaking the tension.

"Not today," I say, "but soon. We have a plan. But first we eat Christmas dinner."

We stand and head to the kitchen. I pull the turkey from the oven, along with all the sides, and we carry them to the dining table. As we take our seats, Iris stops as she pulls out her chair. She surveys the table, and I can see her count the place settings.

"Are we missing someone?" she asks. "Is another couple coming? There are six settings, and only four of us."

"Check the place cards," Lily says. "I made them."

Iris looks to the two settings beside her. "Oh!" she says, her eyes brimming with tears. "Jonathan! Mary!"

"Everyone is home for Christmas this year," I say.

"May I give the blessing?" Iris asks.

"Of course," I say.

We all link hands, and Iris begins to pray. "Dear God, thank You for bringing my family back to me." She stops. "Old and new. And thank You for this Christmas miracle. Thank You for allowing an old woman to have faith again."

When she finishes, Lily jumps from her seat.

"Young lady, where are you going?" Cory asks.

She returns, holding the Christmas cactus and sets it in the middle of the table, in between all of the food.

Lily looks at Cory and then at Iris. Finally, she focuses on me. "You all bloomed again!" She points at the cactus. "Just like her!"

EPILOGUE

THE VICTORY GARDEN

"To plant a garden is to believe in tomorrow."

—Audrey Hepburn

IRIS

SUMMER 2004

A flag-draped casket is carried off the plane. Service members in white gloves stop in front of me. An officer comes to the front and salutes. I lean forward and kiss the casket.

"Welcome home, Jonathan."

The officer salutes Cory, and he and Abby put their arms around me and lead me to the hearse. I stop. Lily is standing at attention, saluting the coffin.

The story of Jonathan's return has garnered a lot of media attention, and reporters and camera crews hold out their microphones for comment.

"He's finally come home," I say. "He's back where he belongs."

I know not to say too much.

The cool air of the hearse calms me. Abby takes my hand, and I rest my head against the car's window.

It is a stunning August day, just like the day I lost you, I think. *Full circle.*

I emerge at the small cemetery in Grand Haven. An open grave sits under a tent, fresh dirt piled high.

American soil waiting for you, I think.

I walk to the gravesite and take a seat in the front row. It is a private service, and only a few people are here, including representatives from the military.

The minister speaks of Jonathan's bravery and his return home. *Ashes to ashes and dust to dust.*

When it is over, I ask for a few moments by myself. Everyone walks away.

Jonathan's grave is next to Mary's. Mine is waiting on the other side of my daughter. I kneel on the warm earth and look at my family.

"Finally," I whisper, "after sixty years, we're together again."

I lower my head and pray.

Why have I lived so long? Why have I endured? Perhaps, it was for this, I now believe. *This moment of closure.* I lift my head and look over at Abby, Cory and Lily, holding hands, waiting for me. *Perhaps it was for them, as well. This moment of new beginnings.*

Life is but a short journey, filled with such horror and beauty, that too often allows our potential and destiny to die unfulfilled or allow us to bloom in ways we never imagined. But I—all of us—really have only one joint destiny: to leave this world a better place for those who follow.

I stop and nod at Abby and Cory. They move toward the hearse and return with two pots of poppies.

"Thank you," I say. "Will you help me?"

"Of course," Abby says.

I've chosen red poppies—Flanders Fields poppies, in fact—

to plant on Jonathan and Mary's graves. These poppies grew over the graves of fallen soldiers in World War I, and the remembrance poppy has become one of the world's most recognized symbols for soldiers killed in combat.

We plant the poppies in front of Mary's old tombstone and Jonathan's new one, the red vibrant and alive on this summer day.

"They're so beautiful," Abby says.

"And so is that," Cory says. He stands and walks to the beautiful headstone on Jonathan's grave.

I had the poem "In Flanders Fields," written during World War I by Canadian physician and officer John McCrae, inscribed on it.

"May I read it?" Cory asks.

I nod.

In Flanders fields the poppies blow
Between the crosses, row on row,
That mark our place; and in the sky
The larks, still bravely singing, fly
Scarce heard amid the guns below.

We are the Dead. Short days ago
We lived, felt dawn, saw sunset glow,
Loved and were loved, and now we lie
In Flanders fields.

Take up our quarrel with the foe:
To you from failing hands we throw
The torch; be yours to hold it high.
If ye break faith with us who die
We shall not sleep, though poppies grow
In Flanders fields.

And for the first time today, I cry.

"They're not sad tears," I say to Cory and Abby, "but tears of relief." I wipe my eyes.

"Thank you both," I say. "I'm okay. I just need a second alone."

They take Lily by the hand and walk toward the car.

I stand and give Mary's headstone a kiss and then walk to Jonathan's.

"I am tired, so tired, my love," I whisper. "But it's not my time, sweetheart. Not yet. I have a few more springs and summers to spend in my garden. Get everything ready so I can be with you and Mary. Sound good?"

The poppies sway their approval.

Before I leave I pull two peach Jonathan roses from inside my purse. I place one on each grave.

When I arrive home people are flocked around my yard. They clap and yell, "Iris! We love you!" as I emerge from the car.

There is no fence any longer, and my yard is lined with flags, and balloons bounce on my porch. Inside, casseroles and pies fill my dining room table.

"It's so overwhelming," I say. My voice is ragged, my body tired.

"Let's go for a little walk, then," Abby suggests. "Clear your mind."

"Where?" I ask. "People are everywhere."

"Let's sneak out the back," Abby says. "Walk to the little plot of land you love. Always quiet there, isn't it?"

"Let me change," I say.

"No, you look lovely for a walk," Abby says.

"At least some tennis shoes," I say. "My feet are starting to ache."

"Okay," she says.

We head out the back, like cat burglars, and sneak along the hillside, until the pines and dune grass disguise our getaway. When we reach the plot of land, Abby grabs the gate and swings it open for me.

"Surprise!"

I take a big step back, and Abby and Cory catch me, hold me, strengthen me. Nearly one hundred people are jammed inside what was once my secret hiding place.

"What's going on?" I ask.

"We...the community...everyone...made this possible," Abby says.

"Abby made it possible," Cory says.

Abby looks at me. "I met William Kelley at the Coast Guard Festival this time last year," she says. "His work to commemorate the Escanaba resonated with me." She stops. "I felt like we needed a memorial for Jonathan, for Cory...and for you."

"Me?"

"So we never forget the men and women who not only sacrifice their lives during every war—and still do to this day—but also the efforts made by communities like Grand Haven. You helped establish a Victory Garden here. Your efforts helped feed neighbors." Abby stops. "You were one of the first women in Michigan to become a botanist. Your hybridized flowers are a living legacy to our state and coastline. Your garden is a living legacy to your family." Abby gestures around the park. "We've made this a war memorial park, a community garden and a teaching garden," she says. "It's also a place where people can come and just relax among the beautiful flowers."

Abby takes my hand.

"You bamboozled me but good," I say.

This was the first year I didn't come here to celebrate Mary's birthday. Instead, Abby had suggested we celebrate it somewhere different, somewhere out in the open, in my new world. So we went to Pronto Pup, we walked the beach and Lily and

Abby helped me make Mary's special cake. For once I had forgotten about my secret hiding place because, for once, I was living in the open.

The lot has been transformed.

"I heard all the commotion down the street, but I thought it was just another new house being built," I say. "You got me good."

"Good!" Abby says.

The fence, I finally realize, is new and now lined with huge, weather-protected signage narrating the history of the park, from baseball field to Victory Garden. Oversize black-and-white historical photos bring the narrative to life.

"Oh, my gosh!" I say, pointing. "Where did you find these?"

"Your scrapbooks," Abby says. "I'm sorry. We all sort of worked as a secret group of spies to make this happen."

I walk over to a photo of Jonathan playing baseball. In one, he is catching a fly ball; in another he is with his teammates, just a group of young men on a beautiful summer day, their whole lives ahead of them.

I touch his face, his cheek, and a tear trails down my own.

I turn, and Shirley greets me in another photo. We are standing together, leaning against our hoes. Shirley is laughing, and there is a rose tucked in my overalls. Behind us an army of women work the earth.

"Oh, my!" I say, finally noticing Mary playing in the background of the photo, a bouquet of dandelions in her hand.

THE HISTORY OF THE WWII VICTORY GARDEN IN GRAND HAVEN

A sign detailing Victory Gardens and their importance to the war effort sits alongside historic posters urging women and communities to start Victory Gardens: PLANT A VICTORY GARDEN!, JOIN THE WOMEN'S LAND ARMY!, DIG ON FOR VICTORY!

In front of the signage, a large swath of earth has been prepped for a garden, and it is lined with rows of vegetables, already growing: tomatoes, carrots, lettuce, beets, peas, Swiss chard and kohlrabi.

"May I demonstrate how to plant and grow your own tomatoes?" a woman asks me.

"We will have volunteers from May first to October first," Abby says. "They will not only work the garden but also teach visitors and school children about Victory Gardens and how to grow vegetables."

I can feel my legs quake, but Cory comes from nowhere to put his arm around me.

"And over here," Cory says, "is a memorial and tribute to your husband."

A life-size photo of Jonathan in uniform, the photo of him from my scrapbook, stands before me. Next to that is a photo of the two of us when I was pregnant with Mary. And next to that is the three of us.

"My family," I whisper.

"We felt it was important to teach young people about their own families, their own histories, of those whose sacrifices helped make them who they are today and our country what it is today," Cory says, his voice filled with emotion. "America today tends to have a collective memory that spans only a few minutes. We are always looking ahead. But how can we become who we're supposed to be if we don't know from where we've come? I want people to understand the sacrifice that came before them. We can and should never forget."

A history and timeline of America's war involvement lines

one entire segment of the fence, the one that used to signify the outfield when Jonathan played ball. Signs detail the lives lost in each:

World War II: American Military Deaths
416,800

World War II: Worldwide Casualties
Battle Deaths-15 million
Civilian Deaths-45 million

I fight back tears and run my fingers over the numbers. *Jonathan was but one of so many, of too many. But would I be standing here right now without his—without Cory's, without all of these men and women's—sacrifice?*

"And in Iraq and Afghanistan, nearly fifteen hundred American soldiers have died in recent months," Cory says, leading me to another plaque. "Thousands and thousands of Iraqi civilians have been killed, as well." He takes my hand. "I plan to volunteer and teach here, talking to people and children about war, its cost and what it means to serve." He turns and points toward the rest of the park, which is comprised of beautiful gardens in full bloom. "I also plan to garden here. And I hope you will help, considering..."

He gestures, and a woman pulls a tarp, revealing a large, beautiful brass plaque.

The Maynard Memorial Garden

"No, no, no," I say.

People burst into applause, and everyone starts snapping photos.

A poem underneath the plaque reads:

"A garden is a grand teacher.
It teaches patience and careful watchfulness;
it teaches industry and thrift;
above all it teaches entire trust."

—*Gertrude Jekyll*

"We're hoping you will be a big presence here, as well," Abby says. "The world needs you, Iris. Your community needs you." She stops. "*We* need you."

"I don't know what to say. I'm overwhelmed."

Abby takes my hand and leads me to the plaque. Beside it is a photo of me, in my garden, my flowers surrounding me. I have a peony lifted to my nose, and there is a slight smile on my face, pure peacefulness, the sun casting our images in a golden light.

"Who took this?" I ask. "When?"

"I did," Abby says. "Last summer."

An old photo of me hybridizing daylilies in my greenhouse—hosiery everywhere—sits alongside another photo taken of me the day I opened my own business.

My life is spread out before me, all seeming to have passed as quickly as one blink of God's eye. All seeming to have more meaning than I ever could have imagined.

Beyond those photos, a mammoth garden is in bloom. A butterfly garden sways in the breeze in one corner, bees and hummingbirds darting all around. Peonies, hollyhocks, coneflowers and hydrangeas—all marked by pretty signs—are planted in a beautiful border along the fence. A sign reading, Teaching Garden, is just beyond that, where roses, irises and daylilies bloom.

My hybrids—the Jonathan rose, my Mary daylily—greet me.

"How did you...?" I start.

"You taught us well," Cory says. "We're hoping you can pass along the knowledge of how to hybridize these flowers to a new generation of gardeners. Teach them the joy and beauty of gardening."

"While sharing the stories of your family," Abby adds. "That way, none of this will ever die."

People rush over and begin asking for my photo.

As they hug and congratulate me, I see Lily playing with friends in the back of the garden. She is running and laughing, screaming in pure joy as only children can and should.

I turn and smile for another photo when I feel someone tugging on my sleeve. I look, and Lily is standing beside me, her fist filled with dandelions.

My heart races, and I shut my eyes. I can feel Mary standing in front of me.

"Those aren't just weeds," I say, "those are perennials. They're members of the daisy family. Dandelion means lion's tooth."

Lily roars like a lion. "You know everything about flowers," she says.

"Not everything," I say, opening my eyes. "I learn something new every day in my garden."

"Well, did you know dandelions are magic?" Lily asks.

"They are?"

"Yup," she says, holding up a hand filled with dandelions that have gone to seed. "You have to pick one very carefully, the one that you know has all the magic."

I take a moment and look at all the dandelions, then around the park—taking it all in—before finally plucking one from her hand.

"Now that you have your stem, you have to think about your wish. Got one?"

She looks up at me, her eyes large.

At one time all my wishes died. I did, too.

And what does an old woman wish for anyhow? Do I wish for

history never to repeat itself? Sadly, I know that is a wish that will never come true.

Lily stares at me.

How do I convey all of this to such a little girl, so filled with light and life?

And then it comes to me.

I nod at her. "I've got it!"

"Awesome! Now, just keep thinking about your wish as you take a deep breath," Lily says, "and then shut your eyes and blow."

I take a deep breath, shut my eyes and blow.

"Okay," Lily says, her voice rising. "Open them up."

I pop my eyes open, and white floaties fill the air.

Lily grabs my hand with her free one. "Let's watch them together, until your wish floats out of sight."

The murmur of the crowd dims, and—for a second—it is me and Lily, me and Mary, holding hands in the same magical place from sixty years ago.

A lifetime ago, I think. *A moment ago.*

A breeze from the lake sweeps over the fence, and the floaties take flight. Lily giggles in glee.

"Wow," she says. "Your wish is really powerful. It must have come true."

It has, I finally realize. *My wishes—all of them—have finally come true.*

"What did you wish for?" Lily asks.

A million white puffs of dandelion fill the air, the wind carrying them toward heaven. I look at Lily.

"Hope," I say. "I wished for hope."

★ ★ ★ ★ ★

Acknowledgments

"Turkey Run," the knotty pine cottage where I live, is nestled on nearly eight acres of woods just outside the resort towns of Saugatuck-Douglas, Michigan, where *The Summer Cottage* was set, and just south of Grand Haven, where *The Heirloom Garden* takes place. Since winter is the longest season in Michigan, often lasting November through April, the remaining six months are a magical, madcap mix of spring, summer and fall, all three seasons often occurring in a single day.

Summer is most magnificent! Turkey Run is surrounded by stunning sugar maples and swaying pines, walking trails wind through the woods, neighbors' blueberry fields await picking and from my screened porch I can often hear the roar of nearby Lake Michigan. But the most beautiful part of Turkey Run is its gardens. The last decade has been spent transforming Turkey Run's acreage and filling it with jaw-dropping cottage gardens, which contain most of the flowers I write about in the novel, many of which were passed down to me by my own grandmothers and mother, as well as family and friends.

A part of nearly every nice day is spent in my gardens. And every day, I am the recipient of its beauty and bounty. Those I love have taught me what it means to be a gardener. I have learned to slow to the pace of nature when I am too manic or frazzled. I have learned how to plant, weed, mulch, deadhead, water, nurture. And that has brought me to life again.

I spend countless hours at my writing desk, but it is filled nearly every single day with flowers from my gardens. And when I look up, when I look out my window, when I stop for a cup of coffee and take the dogs outside, I am reminded how blessed I am. My years are defined by deadlines: manuscripts, essays, edits, events. My years are also defined by flowers—daffodils, tulips, peonies, roses, hydrangeas, mums and dahlias—and that allows me to inhale and exhale, remember to be at one with the season, no matter how many deadlines call. From the spectacular summers and fabulous falls in Michigan to sun-drenched winters in Palm Springs, the flowers and plants on my desks—be it crocus or cacti—reflect my life. And I am forever grateful.

My grandma Shipman was a grand gardener. She used to grow rows and rows of peonies, giant white blooms whose soft petals were tinged in pink. The blooms were so big they would exhaust the stem, causing the peony to flop on the ground like an old hound dog. Oh! And the smell! "This is what heaven smells like," she used to tell me. My grandma Shipman intentionally hung her clothesline over one long row of peonies, so that when she dried her sheets outside and made the bed, your sheets smelled like heaven. That's one of the reasons why peonies are, and remain, my favorite flower. And I still have her peonies in my garden! After my grandmother grew ill, my mom took starts of her peonies. I then took starts to my first home in St. Louis, and they then traveled with me to Michigan and Turkey Run. Now peonies pop up everywhere. Those memories are the reason I wrote *The Heirloom Garden.*

As an author, I always start my novels *not* with an heirloom in mind, or certain character, but a question. In this novel, my questions were, "What makes us isolate ourselves from the world? And what gives us hope?"

With every novel, my goal is simple: try to write the best novel I possibly can. To write a unique story that universally connects. Authors sit alone in coffee-stained robes for months and years writing. We can only hope and pray that our work resonates with readers as deeply as we intend. I have been humbled by your response to my novels. I do not write books about psychopaths, killers or adulterers. I write about bad things that too often happen to good people, and how we soldier through life with hope, faith, love, kindness and each other. I believe ordinary lives are extraordinary, and the ripple effect of our positive actions have incredible power. I would not be where I am today without the love, support and sacrifices of my elders, so I hope my stories give you pause to stop and remember your family, your stories, your heirlooms and your worth.

Every book I write is a blessing, and its journey, completion and launch into the world would not be possible without the following people.

To my literary agent, Wendy Sherman: You've been with me from day one, from Wade to Viola, from memoir to fiction, from humor to poignancy. You've been cheerleader and counselor, sounding board and ship's captain, always guiding me to a calm, loving port, no matter how powerful the creative or professional storms that surrounded me. Thank you a million times over.

To Susan Swinwood: You and Graydon House are now my port, and I could not feel more loved or appreciated. You make my work better and champion it through word and deed. I am blessed.

To the Graydon House team, Lisa Wray, publicist extraordinaire; Pam Osti, marketing guru; Gigi Lau, gifted cover artist; as well as everyone else at HarperCollins, Harlequin and Graydon House: You all do your jobs brilliantly and do them with great talent and little ego. We make a great team. Again, blessed.

To America's servicemen and women: Thank you for your service and sacrifice. I simply wanted to portray the struggles, courage, honor and hope found in your sacrifice as well as the ways America supports—and often doesn't support—you on your return. I wanted to show the honor and difficulty of being in the military. I also wanted to show how your service affects your families. I've had family and friends who have served, and I have spoken to them about their service and return. They pointed me to many outlets of information (military counseling services and therapists, and media such as *Psychology Today* and NPR). I can only hope I even got just a little of your sacrifices and journeys right; I know I only scratched the surface. You are our heroes, and we can never thank you enough. This is a small thank-you from me.

To Gary Edwards: This book is largely a tribute to you, as well. You *are* Iris, the gifted gardener who can grow anything and nurture anything back to life. I'm beyond thrilled that your beautiful illustrations are featured in this book so the world can witness your talent, beauty, gifts and love.

To gardeners everywhere: This book is for you. You understand, better than most, the grace and gifts of this world. To me, you are Mother Nature's authors. Keep blooming!

To the grand ladies of Grand Haven's Highland Park Association, especially Laurie Kelley, Patty VanLopik and Brenda Johnson: Thank you for making me part of your lives since

The Charm Bracelet! I know not all the details about Highland Park are perfect, so don't push me off a deck at our next party, but I knew I had to use your beautiful, historic setting in a novel, and I had to take a few liberties for fiction. I hope you can see the beauty of your cottages, the quirky charm of Highland Park and the lifelong friendships you and your families have created—as well as your love for Grand Haven—shimmering in the novel.

I'd also like to thank the following, whose sites and information helped inform this novel:

The story about Iris's husband was inspired by a story of a family from Missouri who struggled for decades to locate and return the remains of their father and grandfather, who fought in World War II and whose body was deemed unrecoverable. Their story moved me deeply and eventually led me to stories in the *St. Louis Post-Dispatch* and *Washington Post*. A *Washington Post* feature by Michael E. Ruane about WWII soldier Jack Cummings, whose remains were identified using state-of-the-art technology and returned to America and his family after seventy-four years, succinctly captured and stated everything much better than I could through my own notes and research. Thank you, Mike, for your powerful reporting and writing. Your incredible work helped me complete an integral part of this novel.

Much of the information regarding the care and growth of heirloom flowers in the novel was taken literally from my own backyard. I also reached out to local garden centers and experts, as well as websites specifically focused on each of the heirloom flowers I write about in the novel. I researched numerous books that detail the history of heirloom flowers as well as Michigan flowers and plants, along with their care. I tried to get everything right. I know heirloom gardeners will likely find errors. Please know I did my darndest to be as accurate as I could. Also please know this is fiction, and I hope you will wave off any mistakes like an annoying horsefly for the overall impact of the story.

Finally, thank you to my readers, who literally make me run to my writing desk every morning, excited for the journey that awaits.

xoxo!
Viola

1. Do you garden? What type of gardens do you have? Were any of your family gardeners? Do you have any heirloom flowers or plants that were passed on by family or friends?

2. Whether or not you garden, do you have a favorite flower? Is there a special memory associated with it, or is it simply the beauty of the flower you love? Do you have a favorite growing season?

3. Iris uses her garden as a way of honoring and remembering the people she has loved and lost. What do you love most about gardening? And how does it help you mentally, physically, spiritually, creatively?

4. Have you or has anyone in your family served in the military? What does your or their service mean to you? How has it impacted you and your family? How have you or they been impacted by their service? Discuss.

5. Do you think we demonstrate enough respect for our veterans and their service and sacrifices? Why or why not? How could we do better?

6. Have you ever had a boss or colleague disrespect you? If you are a woman in a career that is male-dominated, how do you manage prejudiced and antiquated attitudes? And do you think our society and corporate world has gotten better in its treatment of women in the workplace and such issues as job discrimination, equal pay, promotion, etc.? Discuss.

7. Overcoming loss is a major theme in *The Heirloom Garden*. Have you ever lost someone close to you? How has that impacted you? Do you think you handled the grief in a healthy way? Is there any one "right" way to grieve?

8. Cory is initially very resistant to seeking professional help, believing he can handle things on his own. Do you think asking for help is a sign of weakness or of strength? Have you ever sought therapy? Did you find it helpful?

9. Do you think certain family and small-town community values and traditions are being lost today—be it gardening, parades, or simply being neighborly and checking in on one another? Why or why not? Discuss.

10. One of the most important relationships in the story is the friendship between Iris and Lily, which transcends age or experience. Do you think our younger generations still respect and learn from our elders? Do you think our family stories and heirlooms are being shared or forgotten? How will this impact our country and our future generations? Discuss.